a drop of
PRETTY
POISON

USA TODAY BESTSELLING AUTHOR
KELSEY CLAYTON

Editing by Kiezha Ferrell at Librum Artis
Proofreading by Tiffany Hernandez

To my husband.
Thank you for always being my rock
and for inspiring such a perfect hero.
I love you.

CONTENT WARNING

This book deals with sensitive topics that may not be suitable for all readers. As some readers have said they find descriptive trigger warnings to be spoilers, I have provided a link to where you can find all of the trigger warnings for each of my books. Please read safely.

For trigger warnings: Please go to www.kelseyclayton.com/triggerwarnings

Laiken
CHAPTER ONE

HAVE YOU EVER HAD ONE OF THOSE MOMENTS THAT take your breath away? Not like a two-second gasp. I'm talking about the kind that literally sucks the air straight from your lungs. The kind that makes you need to grip onto something just to keep you upright.

The life-altering, feel-yourself-step-into-a-whole-new-chapter-of-your-life, never-going-to-be-the-same kind of moment.

This was mine.

The moment I hear his truck roaring down the street, I lose my focus. Standing in my driveway, in the middle of a conversation with Mr. Zimmerman, and my every thought just falls right out of my brain. All I can focus on, all I can *see*, is Hayes haphazardly throwing his truck into park and marching toward the detached garage like he's about to do something impulsive. Something dangerous.

"What are you doing?" I call out, feeling like I'm about to witness a bloodbath.

And when he doesn't answer, that feeling intensifies. It's as if I'm not even here. He keeps his eyes on his destination and his feet moving.

"Hayes!" I shout, but still nothing. "*Shit.* Hayes, stop! What are you doing?"

I try to catch up to him, try to stop him from whatever life-threatening thing he's about to do, but I can't. He walks through the doorway seconds before I slam into it—gripping the doorjamb as I watch him hand Cam his switchblade.

"You're going to need this," Hayes says with a level of confidence I've never heard.

Cam takes it from him. "What? Why?"

"Because I'm falling in love with your sister."

Hearing the words come from his mouth, I expel all the air I had in my lungs. Never did I imagine *this* is how he would tell him, while giving him the weapon to kill him with. Either this is a suicide mission, or he's trying to call Cam's bluff when he said that he would kill any of his friends for touching me.

Everything plays out in slow motion in front of my eyes.

Cam puts his tongue in his cheek, laughing dryly as he puts the blade down. For a second, I think I can breathe again. Even Hayes looks relieved, if a little confused.

"Wow," Hayes says. "I thought for sure you were going to—"

His words are cut off as Cam turns, fist clenched tightly as he slams it into the side of Hayes's face. The blow is so hard that it spins him around and knocks him into the table.

"Cam!" I scream, taking a step forward, but Hayes stops me.

"Don't!" he demands. The look in his eyes keeps my feet glued to the floor. "It's fine. I deserved that."

Cam scoffs as he shakes out his hand. "You're damn right you did! My fucking sister? Half the goddamn town wants you, and you have to have my sister?"

Hayes puts a hand on the side of his face, stretching his jaw. "You think I planned this? I tried for weeks to stay—"

"*Weeks?*" Cam roars. "How long has this shit been going on for?"

As he realizes his slip up, Hayes's eyes fall closed, and he sighs. "Cam."

"No, you know what?" Cam shoves past Hayes. "I can't do this right now."

I step out of the way, letting him leave and going over to Hayes. He leans back against the workbench as I carefully inspect the damage. There's already the start of some swelling and the cut on his cheek looks painful.

"You're insane, you know that?" I tell him.

"It's really not that bad."

Giving him a no-bullshit look, I lightly press my finger against his injury, and he hisses. "Yeah, not that bad."

He smiles and rolls his eyes. He knows better than to think I wasn't going to call him out on that. And speaking of...

"So, you're falling in love with me, huh?" I smirk, still in disbelief that he spoke those words.

His expression turns skeptical as he hums. "I mean, you're all right."

I chuckle. "Oh! Well, in that case..."

As I start to walk away, he grabs my wrist and pulls me back to him. My hands rest on his chest as he stares into my eyes, like he's been missing this all his life.

"I'm already there, but I figured you deserve to hear it first." He takes a nervous breath and tucks my hair behind my ear. "I love you, Laiken. I am *so* massively in love with you, and I'm sorry that I didn't realize it sooner."

There are no words that even begin to explain the feelings shooting through me like the finale of a fireworks show. *Three years.* Three damn years I've fantasized about him telling me those words. And hearing them now, I don't think I ever could've imagined it would feel this incredible.

My eyes fill with tears of joy as a gush of air leaves my mouth and I smile back at him. "I'm in love with you, too."

I wish someone was getting this on camera—the way we're looking at each other like there's nothing and no one that could make us happier. Sliding his hand to the back of my neck, he pulls me in and kisses me.

It feels so different, being able to be with him like this and knowing that it doesn't matter who walks by. He won't push me away or play it off like nothing was happening. It's just us, and this moment, and the love between us that demands to be felt.

As he pulls back to look at me, my mind clears a little and my eyes narrow.

"Are you fucking crazy?" I ask, smacking his chest with every word. He catches my wrists and chuckles, but I'm not done yelling at him. "What were you thinking, handing him a knife? What if he actually stabbed you?"

The grin doesn't leave his face as he shrugs. "I would've deserved it. I knew the rules. But I couldn't stand to be away from you anymore. The pain of missing you is worse than anything he could've done to me."

Sighing, I wrap my arms around him, and we hold each other close, my head on his chest. "I wasn't trying to force you into telling him, you know. I just wanted to know it could happen eventually. That you saw a future with me."

"Lai," he says, bending his neck and moving me away so he can look into my eyes. "You are the *only* future I see."

4

I kiss him again, unable to help myself. It's been too long since I've been in his arms like this. And now that I know that my feelings are reciprocated, I just want to stay here and never move.

But an old garage turned workshop isn't exactly the most sanitary place, and the things we're sure to be doing soon will only cause further injury if done in here.

Hayes grabs his switchblade and closes it, putting it back in his pocket before interlacing his fingers with mine. It honestly feels surreal to be able to walk outside holding his hand. Something so small to anyone else, but it's everything to me.

As we get closer to the house, I cringe when I realize Mr. Zimmerman is still here. It probably wasn't the smartest decision to ditch my boss and run after Hayes like a crazy person, but if I hadn't, I wouldn't have heard his confession.

So, if he fires me for being rude, at least it was worth it.

"I should probably handle this," I tell Hayes.

He nods. "Do what you need to do. I'm going to go attempt to defuse the chaos bomb I just set off."

"Be careful, please."

"I will."

Kissing the top of my head, he releases my hand and I instantly feel colder without his touch. Hayes gives Mr. Zimmerman a respectful smile and heads inside.

"I'm sorry," I tell my boss. "That was rude of me."

He waves it off, much to my relief. "Don't worry about it. Is everything okay?"

I don't think there's any way I can explain this without someone coming out of it looking like an asshole. "It's a long story, but it'll be okay."

"Are you sure?" he questions. "Your brother looked pretty pissed."

He did. And now he's inside. Alone. With Hayes.

Glancing back at the house, I wince. "Yeah, I should probably get in there before you lose your best player because his best friend slaughtered him with a broken hockey stick."

Mr. Zimmerman nods as he snickers. "I'd appreciate that. I'm looking to take home another championship title this year."

"Then I *definitely* need to get in there," I joke.

Or at least I hope I'm joking. Right now, I'm not sure I put anything past my brother. Betrayal is one thing he's never really had to deal with, and I'm sure this one cuts deep.

Mr. Z opens the car door to climb inside. "I'll brief my assistant on everything we talked about and have her reach out to you to go over anything you may need from us and vice versa."

I nod. "Thank you. I really appreciate the opportunity."

Sitting at dinner and finding out that I was officially getting to take full control of the lessons department, I thought that would be the highlight of my week. Little did I know, it wouldn't even end up being the highlight of my night.

"You earned it," he replies through the open window. "You're a talented skater. I'm excited to see you succeed at this, too."

He pulls out of the driveway as I head inside, and I'm not sure if the silence I walk into makes me feel frightened or relieved. Everything looks in place, not like there's been a struggle. Even the kitchen is completely untouched—the knife block full.

Well, that's a good sign.

I make my way up the stairs, only to find Hayes sitting on the floor outside Cam's bedroom. He's leaning back against the wall, and I frown at the defeated look on his face.

"He won't come out?"

He shakes his head, exhaling heavily. "I tried to go in, but he threw *this* at my face." As he holds up the hockey puck, my eyes widen. "Don't worry. I managed to catch it."

Ruining his friendship with my brother was never my intention, and I can see that Hayes is trying to play it off like it's not a big deal, but it is. They've been best friends for almost six years—hanging out almost every day for most of that time. It makes me sad knowing he may have given that up for me.

And to be honest, a little nervous.

I put my hand out to help him up, grateful when he takes it. "I'm sorry, H."

He doesn't let go as he trails behind me up the shorter stairs to my bedroom. "Don't be. It sucks, but I don't regret it."

"You don't?"

"Not at all." As we step into my room, he turns me around to face him. "You have no idea how much I hated being away from you."

My nose scrunches as I hum. "I think I did, but if you want to show me, I won't complain."

He doesn't need to be told twice. His hands move to grip my waist, and I jump into his arms. The kiss is frantic, desperate, as my legs wrap around him. He carries me over to my bed and lays me down.

The whole fucking time we were apart, I was a mess of heartbreak and sexual frustration. No matter what I did, what vibrator I used or what I pictured in my head, none of it was enough. It didn't feel the same. It was missing something.

His touch is magic, and I need it again like air.

"Fuck, I missed you," he groans against my mouth.

I press my head into the pillow as he starts kissing my neck. "I missed you, too."

It feels incredible, and all I can imagine is getting him

inside me again. I need to stretch around him as he fills me completely. But as I arch up against him and let out a moan when he grinds down into me, he stops.

"Don't," I beg. "I need it."

He chuckles breathlessly. "I do, too, baby. Trust me. There's nothing I need more than this right now."

"Then why aren't you fucking me right now?" I whine.

"Because Cam is right downstairs," he says. "And you tend to lack volume control. I don't regret telling him about us, but I'm also not trying to rub it in his face, either."

Everything he says is totally understandable. And that sucks because I know I can't beg him to do it anyway. I don't want to make the situation worse for them anymore than he does.

"Okay," I tell him, pouting slightly.

He smirks and presses a quick kiss to my lips then sits up. I run my fingers through my hair, but the sexual tension in the air is still so thick I could choke on it. I can clearly see the outline of his cock through his jeans, and my pussy clenches around nothing.

Silence falls over us and I'm about to suggest watching a movie, when he comes up with a better idea.

"So, you want to go for a drive?"

"Yes!" I answer without missing a beat.

The two of us jump up and start to head for the door when he stops. My brows furrow as he turns around, tossing me two pillows before he grabs my comforter and my chunky knit blanket.

"What are these for?" I ask, still confused.

He bites his lip and bounces his brows once. "You'll see."

THE MOON SHINES DOWN from the sky, reflecting off the ocean at the abandoned beach. *Our* beach, as Hayes called it. To think we were here a couple weeks ago with shattered hearts and broken dreams. It feels so surreal now. I wish I had known then that we needed to fall apart to fit back together.

Maybe then it wouldn't have hurt as much.

Eh, scratch that. It still would've sucked.

Hayes hops out of the truck and stops for a moment before nodding. "Perfect."

It isn't until he grabs the comforter from the backseat and pulls me toward the beach that I finally figure out his plan. We each take a side and spread the blanket out over the sand. As he goes back to get the pillows and the other blanket, I sit down and wait for him.

I watch the waves crash against the rocks, remembering how he saved my life. The cut may have healed, but the scar that remains will always be there—as will the memory.

"One for you," Hayes says as he hands me a pillow.

He tosses the other one down on the comforter and lies down, kicking off his shoes and covering us both with the second blanket. His arm slips underneath my neck as we lie on our sides, face to face.

The sound of the ocean fades into the background as our gazes stay locked on each other. It's like our eyes are saying all the things we've kept behind our lips, locked away out of fear.

Fear of letting the other in.

Fear of revealing too much.

But that was then, and this, being here with him, is the only thing that matters now.

"Tell me again," I say softly.

He smirks. "I think I can show you better."

With his hand on my lower back, he pulls me closer, covering my mouth with his. It starts out slow. Gentle. He licks into my mouth and hums as our tongues tangle together. I throw my leg over him, needing to be closer.

"I need you." My words come out like a desperate plea.

Hayes deepens the kiss, only stopping for a second to respond. "You have me, baby. You always have me."

This can't be real. There's no way I'm not about to get woken up by Mali jumping on me or screaming *wake up, sleepyhead* in my face. But as he bites my lip, shooting a mix of pleasure and pain right through me, I know it's real. I can feel every inch of him pressing against me, making me want him even more.

His hand slides up my leg and underneath my dress. "You need to wear dresses more often."

"Why?"

"Easier access." As he says it, he hooks his thumb around my panties and starts to pull them down.

Rolling onto my back, I let him slide the only clothing keeping him from me down my legs, discarding them to the side. He teasingly lets his fingertips graze my skin on the way back up. He's barely touching me, but it's still leaving me breathless.

"It's been too long since we've had sex for you to tease," I tell him.

He chuckles and stops his movements. "Then show me what you want, babe. I'm all yours."

Yes. He. Fucking. Is. I grab his wrist and put his hand right where I need him, damn near exploding just from the contact. He bites his lip as he slides his finger down over my clit and into my pussy.

"Look at you," he murmurs. "So wet for me and I've hardly even touched you yet."

As he switches back and forth between fingering me and rubbing my clit, he starts to move faster. My head presses into the pillow, and I moan softly. It feels incredible, like he knows exactly where to touch to make me putty in his hands, and he uses it to his advantage.

"Hayes," I beg, needing more. *Needing him.* "Please."

"Please what, Laiken?" he asks.

I try to arch into his hand, but he lets up on the pressure.

"Nuh-uh. Use your words."

"Fuck me," I breathe. "I want you to fuck me."

He slows down as he leans forward and kisses me. "Not tonight, baby. Tonight, I want to love you."

God. I swear if he was touching me just right when he said that I would've flown right over the edge. Still, it brings me closer. It's one thing when we fuck. When the only goal is for both of us to be sweaty and panting, completely sexed out and sated by the end of it. But when he holds me and slides into me for the sole purpose of being closer, like that night on the boat, it's everything.

I watch as he undresses, still stopping every few seconds to touch me in sensitive places. At one point, he even bends down to suck on my clit. My whole body trembles at the feeling, and he can't put the condom on fast enough.

I fucking need him *now*.

He lines his cock up at my entrance and laces his fingers with mine as he pushes in, and holy shit, going without it for the last few weeks was too damn long. I feel him bottom out before he pulls back. He rubs circles in my clit as he slowly slides in again, and I swear I'm not going to make it through this.

My orgasm is going to cause my heart to burst.

Hayes hovers over me, holding my hand and kissing each one of my fingers as he slips in and out of me. His movements are deliberate, and when he pulls out for a second just to rub his cock against my clit, the moan that leaves my mouth is animalistic.

"You're flawless," he tells me as he presses back in. "So fucking perfect. And beautiful. And mine."

"All yours," I confirm.

He smiles in that way he has and my insides melt. I know there isn't a thing in the world I wouldn't go through for him. All the pain and all the heartbreak—it was worth it because it got us here, where he's loving me the best way he knows how.

"I need it, Lai," he groans. "I need you to cum on my cock."

With each slow thrust, he pushes his dick into me as deep as he can, moving his hips just right to rub against my clit. I moan, and he bends down to kiss me as his motions continue.

"That's it, baby. Always so good for me. Feels so damn good."

I bite my lip as the pressure builds until finally, I'm freefalling. The pleasure that rips straight through me is nothing but pure euphoria, and it pulls Hayes right along with me. He breathes heavily as he pushes deep into me, his cock pulsing against my walls.

"Never make me go without that again," I tell him through labored breaths.

He chuckles quietly and drops a kiss on my forehead. "Never."

After a moment, he pulls out, rolling over and pulling off the condom. I watch as he stands up, stark naked and gorgeous, and walks all the way back to his truck to throw it away. I can't help but watch him the whole way back, checking him out and reveling in the fact that he's mine.

Hayes fucking Wilder is *mine*.

I don't think I'll ever tire of that.

As he gets closer and sees me staring at him, he smiles and winks. Sometimes I wonder if he has any idea what he does to me. Or how something as simple as that can make me feel like I'm floating.

I may not have ever *done* drugs, but I can't believe anything could feel better than this.

Hayes puts his boxers back on and helps slide my panties back up my legs before lying beside me. He covers us with the blanket as I rest my head on his chest, hearing the sound I've been craving for weeks.

"I love you, Laiken," he says softly, pressing a kiss into my hair.

My stomach flips in the best way. "I love you, too."

I know without a doubt that I'm always going to remember the night he threw caution to the wind and then made love to me under the stars on our special beach.

And if in the morning, we go skinny dipping just to fuck in the water again...well, that's just how it goes when you're young and in love.

Hayes
CHAPTER TWO

My mom always used to tell me that when there is a fork in the road, make your decisions wisely. Think things through, trust your gut, and act accordingly. Well, I didn't do that. I chose my friendship with Cam over my relationship with Laiken out of fear.

Fear that Cam would hate me.

Fear that I will never be good enough for her.

Fear that I was destined to be just like my father.

I chose the wrong road and lost the one girl who means more to me than anyone. So, I turned the fuck around and chose again.

Every part of me meant what I said when I told Laiken that I don't regret it. I *don't*. There have been hookups in my life, girls I flirted with, and even someone I thought that I liked at one point. But there has never been anyone like her. She's that once in a lifetime kind of person for me, and it reached a point where I knew that if I let her slip away, I'd live in constant regret.

But it still hurts as Cam hits the fuck-you button for the third time today.

"Hey, it's Cam. Leave—" His voicemail starts to play, and I hang up.

It's not like I blame him for not talking to me. If the situation were reversed and I found out he was fucking Devin, I probably would have stabbed him. Does that make me a hypocrite? Absolutely. But I can't change it now, and I wouldn't if I could.

I toss my phone on my bed and rub my hands over my face. There's no point in texting him—they just go unanswered. Well, except for the one. Though I'm not sure a single middle finger emoji really counts as a response.

Exhaling slowly, I get up and head toward the bathroom. I have to take a shower before work, and responsibilities don't stop because your best friend would rather eat glass than talk to you. At least there's hockey practice tonight. I'll try talking to him there.

EVERYTHING FEELS OFF. NOT in the way that it did when Laiken wouldn't talk to me—that was worse. But still off. Like pieces of my life aren't in the right place. I don't have someone sending me random hockey videos throughout the day or asking me which breakfast shake looks better.

Neither. They all taste like chalk.

Honestly, in all the time I've known Cam, I don't think we've ever gone this long without at least sending a text or two throughout the day. The summer before I turned sixteen, we spent every single day together. Either he was with me at my house, or I was with him at his. But I don't think we spent more than a couple hours apart. Looking back on it now, I'm surprised we didn't kill each other.

There were so many things different about that summer compared to this one—the biggest being the fact that Laiken hated my guts. It lasted a couple years, actually. See, Cam and I weren't always friends. That happened because of a girl, I guess you could say.

I was the new kid. My parents moved Devin and me here under the guise of wanting us to go to a better school and be closer to the beach. In reality, my mom was just trying to get my dad away from his drinking buddies. Devin absolutely hated it, though what girl wouldn't? She had gone to the same gymnastics studio since she was three. Grew up with all the same girls. And then she was ripped away from it all.

Me? I didn't really care so much. My only concern was finding out where the closest ice rink was and seeing what kind of team they had. The NHL was my dream, but when your dad walks out the door without even a goodbye, hopes and dreams are the first things to go. This, however, was before. When everything was still…normal.

Being the new kid in school, you always seem to get the most attention. Guys want to know what your deal is, and girls want to find out if you're datable. And one girl in particular was more interested than the rest. She invited me to be her date for her sister's Sweet Sixteen, and I had no reason to say no.

I didn't find out she had already asked Cam and then canceled to go with me instead until he came up to me out of nowhere and shoved me against my locker.

The two of us went at it, throwing punches and taking each other to the ground. No one tried to stop us; they just crowded around and watched as we beat the shit out of each other. To this day, I don't think either of us knows who won that fight. By the end of it, we were both sucking in air like we were dying and throwing punches that barely made contact, let alone did any damage.

Finally, with the most respect I've ever had for anyone, we shook hands and walked away. The girl ended up not having a date to her sister's party after I told her to fuck off. She tried going back to Cam, but he wasn't interested either. And he and I somehow became friends.

But to Laiken, I was the guy who gave her brother a fat lip, and she hated me for it. It didn't matter that we were friends, or that not even Cam's parents cared much about the fight. After all, he started it. But Laiken cared.

And while she glared at me like she wanted to set me on fire and watch me burn, all I wanted was to see her smile. She's always had such a pretty smile.

"H," Laiken says, snapping her fingers in my face.

I jump as she gets my attention. "I didn't even hear you walk in."

She leans over the counter and kisses me hello. "I'm not surprised. You were really zoned out. You okay?"

"Yeah, I was just thinking about when Cam and I had that fist fight and you hated me for it."

Her nose scrunches in disgust. "You were the worst."

I chuckle as I watch her look through the jewelry. "I'm still the same shithead. What changed for you?"

She looks back at me and smirks. "Puberty hit you like a fucking truck."

A bark of laughter emits from my mouth and she shrugs.

"You and Cam came back from hockey camp when you were seventeen, and you had grown your hair out and got muscles," she explains. "I was done for at that point."

My mind clings to each one of her words, specifically *seventeen*, and I can't believe how long this has been a thing for her. "That was three years ago."

She looks anywhere but at me as she sighs. "Yeah."

Chapter 2

Walking over, I wrap my arms around her from behind. She spins around, and I gently press my lips to hers. It's always the best feeling when she melts into me.

"I'm sorry it took me so long to come around," I tell her.

She reconnects the kiss once more and smiles. "It's okay. You fell in love with me eventually."

I pull her just a little closer. "Hard and fast."

"Mm. Just how I like it."

My head falls back as I laugh, releasing her for the sake of not giving Marc's cameras a show. Any sexual innuendo that comes out of her mouth, or any mention of sex at all, and I seem to lack all control for what I do next. And being as I'm at work, it's the wrong time and place for that.

"By the way," Laiken says. "I meant to ask you if you plan on coming to the bonfire this Friday."

Ugh. I knew this topic would come up, but I was hoping it would be through a text, where I could pretend it doesn't sting, and where she can't coerce me with her puppy eyes and pouty lip.

"I don't know, Lai." I run my fingers through my hair and put my hat on backward. "He clearly doesn't want me to come. He won't even answer the damn phone. I just don't think it's the best idea."

She takes a deep breath and comes over to sit on the counter. "I get it, but he's going to have to get over it at some point."

"Uh, have you *met* your brother?"

The only person I know that holds a stronger grudge than Cam is Laiken. They're both so stubborn that her even suggesting Cam will just *get over it* makes me laugh.

"Right, you don't have a vagina," she murmurs. "Well, still, you're his best friend. He doesn't like the other guys enough to replace you."

19

I place my hands on either side of her and lean in to kiss her. Her arms rest on my shoulders as she lightly plays with the hair sticking out under my hat.

"I'll think about it," I tell her, kissing her once more before stepping away.

And thankfully, she accepts it.

FOR SEVEN YEARS, I have played on the same hockey team with Cam. He has come to practice with the flu, hungover, still drunk, and with a sprained ankle. He even came the morning of his assault trial. But he finds out his best friend has a thing for his sister, and he's nowhere to be found.

According to the guys, he sent out a text saying he has an appointment and won't be here, but I know that's bullshit. Unless it's a certain kind of *appointment*, specifically with Mali, there's no way he wouldn't schedule it for a time he doesn't have hockey.

I've been trying not to overstep. I don't want to make him uncomfortable or give him a reason to hate me even more. But as I skate around the rink and run drills without him, I'm starting to think Laiken may have a point.

It's too easy for him to ignore me when I'm not in front of his face.

I have to go to the bonfire.

I NEVER THOUGHT THERE would be a day when I would pull into this driveway and feel uneasy. Sure, when Laiken and I weren't talking, I had a range of emotions running through me, but I still felt welcome. I guess my mind just always associates it with being Cam's place instead of Laiken's. But when Cam is the one who doesn't want me here, it feels like I shouldn't be.

A knock on the window catches my attention, and I turn my head to see Laiken standing there. She smiles sweetly at me, giving me no choice but to unlock the door. It's not like I can drive away now, not with her standing there looking at me like I'm her favorite person in the world.

I should've thought this through before I agreed to come. Realized that it was a stupid idea before it was too late. But as Laiken opens the door, I know the chances of her letting me change my mind now are slim to none.

"Come on," she tells me. "It's going to be fine."

I snort as I climb out. "You do know I can tell when you're lying, don't you?"

Her eyes roll. "Okay, then tell me this: what is the worst possible thing that could happen?"

"Do you *want* me to go back home?" I joke. "Oh, I get it.

You secretly love the way Lucas hits on you, and you don't want your boyfriend to hear it."

"Boyfriend, huh?" She smirks, raising her brows at me. "Last I checked, I was never *asked* to be anyone's anything. And you can't just skip steps, it's against the rules."

I move my hand to her back and pull her in as I snicker. "Is that right?"

"Mm-hm." She's fighting to keep a straight face, but I can see right through it.

My lips purse as I hum. "That information is going to make some women very happy."

Her jaw falls open in disbelief and she pushes me away. "Jerk."

"Hey," I chuckle playfully. "You walked right into that."

She glares back at me, but I'm more than used to that, so I kiss her anyway. No matter how much she tries to stop it, she can't keep the smile from forcing its way through. But the moment has to end eventually.

Grabbing my hand with hers, she starts tugging me toward the back yard. My head falls back as I groan, but she's not going to let me off.

"Nope," she says as she pulls me along. "I was thinking about letting you change your mind, but after that little comment you made…"

Laughter bubbles out of me. "Oh, so this is revenge."

"Don't do the crime if you can't do the time."

Her teasing has a way of making me feel better, but as we get closer to the bonfire and I watch Cam glance back at me only to scoff and shake his head, that feeling fades. There's never been a time where he looked at me like this. And the guilt that settles in my stomach is uncomfortable.

I wasn't going to drop Laiken's hand. I've done that enough to her this summer, and we have nothing to hide now. But as she lets mine go, I appreciate that she understands the last thing I want to do is rub our relationship—or non-relationship, according to her logic—in Cam's face.

"Hey, man," Owen greets me.

"Hey." He and I exchange a bro-handshake, followed by doing the same with Aiden and Lucas.

Usually, I'd go to Cam next, but by the way he won't even look at me, I don't attempt it. Better to play it safe than risk feeling the rejection of that. I'm already hanging by a thread here.

I'd normally grab one of the camping chairs and set it up beside Cam, but something about being within swinging distance of him doesn't seem like a good idea. Especially while my cheek is still sensitive to the touch. Let's just say I know firsthand why that drunk bastard from the party hit the ground as hard as he did. His punch has improved since we were fourteen.

I should sit somewhere neutral, not close to Cam but not close to Laiken, either. I know she would be understanding of it. And yet, the thought of being even five feet away from her makes up my mind for me.

Hopping up onto the picnic table, I take a seat beside her. It's a small move, but one that shows her I'm still serious about this, and she smiles down at her lap. The guys are too busy glancing between Cam and me to notice it, though.

"What's going on?" Aiden asks.

Cam tosses a wrapper into the fire. "Nothing."

I thought the tension was strong when Laiken and I were broken up, but it's nothing compared to this. That was painful. Cruel and unforgiving. This, however, is the agony of knowing the guy who has been the closest person to me for a few years short of a decade wants nothing to do with me now. It wraps around my throat and makes me choke on it.

But as I subtly put my hand on the table, letting the edge brush against Laiken's, at least my heart is back in one piece.

Again, worth it, no matter how shitty that may sound.

"You didn't even say hi to each other," Owen points out.

I roll my eyes and nod toward Cam. "'Sup, bro."

"Bro," he mocks. "That's a bit incestual, don't you think? Taking a page out of Owen's book?"

Ouch. "Better that than not going after what I want when it's right in front of me."

Okay, so maybe that wasn't the smartest thing to say, but I'm not the type to bite my tongue. I never have been. This is why I tried telling Laiken that coming here is a bad idea.

His brows raise in surprise. "Well, fuck me for having some loyalty. But I don't expect you to know anything about that."

"Oh, fuck all the way off with that shit," I throw back. "If anyone has been loyal to your ass, it's me. If this cancels all that out in your mind, then that's on you."

"Hayes," Laiken whisper-shouts.

I know she's right. I really should shut my damn mouth, but I'm not going to sit here and watch him act like I'm some piece of shit friend. And trust me, he's had his fair share of those. I'm sure as fuck not one of them.

He laughs dryly, looking down at the ground in disgust, but says nothing. Silence falls around the entire group. Everyone now feels the same tension I did since I first walked up. We couldn't even go three minutes without getting into it.

But if he had answered his phone, or any one of my fifty goddamn texts, we would have had this out in private instead of putting on a show for all our closest friends.

As my anger fades, regret starts to take its place. Laiken may have been trying to help make us better, but coming here may have only made it worse. The truth of my words doesn't make the way I said them okay. He has every right to be pissed at me. I just also have the right to defend myself when he oversteps.

And it's Cam.

Overstepping is his specialty.

"What the fuck," Aiden mutters.

Lucas minds his own business while Owen looks like he's still trying to figure it all out, but Cam and I don't even attempt to explain it. We can't even look at each other.

Laiken is clearly struggling between keeping her distance for Cam's sake and comforting me anyway. Her pinky carefully moves over my own, then more of her fingers slide until half her hand rests on mine. But she's moving so painstakingly slow that when she hesitantly puts her head on my shoulder for only a second before she picks it back up, it doesn't surprise me when Mali groans.

"My God! Stop acting like you haven't tasted each other's cum before!"

The sound of Lucas choking on his beer mixes with Cam's whine. "Mali! What the fuck?"

Her words make all the pieces fall together for everyone else and Owen gestures between Laiken and me. "Wait, you two...?"

Lai looks over at me and scrunches her nose, feigning disgust. "Psht. I'm a total saint. A future nun. He's just trying to steal my virtue."

Just like that, all my problems disappear as I laugh and she smiles. "Is that right?"

Taking her bottom lip between her teeth, she nods.

"So, if I were to mention when you—"

I don't even have a chance to finish that sentence because her eyes widen and she rushes to kiss me, effectively shutting me up. It's obviously not the first time I've kissed her, but it's the first time we're kissing in front of everyone else. Hell, it's the first time I've kissed *anyone* in front of them when I wasn't actively trying to get laid. The setting is different. The reason is different. And as my hand comes to rest on her cheek, the weight of the moment only makes me even more confident in my decision.

She breaks the kiss, and I give her a smug grin. "Now who's the one stealing virtues?"

Her shoulder shoves me away as she chuckles.

"This is bullshit!" Lucas yells, standing up and throwing his empty beer can to the ground.

Everyone else finds it funny, but Cam looks like he'd rather be anywhere else. "Sit down, Drama Queen."

He grumbles to himself as he does what he's told, but Owen's attention is solely on Cam.

"So *that's* why you've been so pissed lately?"

"How would you feel if you found out a guy you consider your brother was fucking your little sister?" he counters.

Technically, I never told him I was *fucking* her. If I had, he would've stabbed me for sure. But he's known me long enough to figure that out for himself. And I find more comfort than I should in the fact that he said *consider* instead of *considered*.

"I mean…" Mali says with her shit stirring voice. "Before you knew who it was, you were fully on board." Her finger moves to her chin as she pretends to think. "I believe the words you used were 'Good pussy is hard to find these days.'"

Cam crushes the beer can in his hand, spilling beer over the edges and down the arm of the chair. Meanwhile, I focus on the girl who will be responsible for my murder.

"You *want* him to hate me, don't you?"

She shrugs and smiles sweetly. "You took my best friend. It's only fitting I take yours."

Honestly, I'm sure Cam would love for her to do exactly

that, just in a different way. Shit, if she had, we might not be in this predicament. But I came too close to exposing his secret earlier. I won't walk that line again.

"Please," I scoff. "As if we both don't know she loves you more."

Mali smirks, opening her arms and giggling at the way Laiken goes willingly. It moves her further from me as she cuddles against her best friend. And I can't help but laugh at the way Mali winks at me because of it.

"So, what?" Aiden asks, still stuck on the topic. "You two just aren't friends anymore?"

I don't give him the chance to answer—partly because I'm afraid of what would come out of his mouth. "Nah, he just needs to punish me adequately and then he'll get over it."

Mali and Laiken whisper to each other and try to hold back their laughter, but I'm focused on the way Cam snorts.

"Are you kidding? You're dating my sister. That *is* the punishment."

I roll my eyes and glance over at Laiken. She pouts for a moment, but then glances over at Mali and it's right back to trying not to laugh.

"Okay, what the hell are you two giggling about?" I finally ask with a sigh.

Mali does everything she can to keep her composure as she answers. "Are you going to call him daddy and take your punishment like a good boy?"

And that's when Laiken loses it, throwing her head back while she breaks out into hysterical laughter.

THANKFULLY, CAM DOESN'T HATE me enough to skip any more than the one practice. Though I'm not sure if that speaks more about his grudge against me or his love of hockey. If I had to guess, I'd probably choose the latter.

Last night wasn't as bad as it could've been. We didn't say much to each other after arguing, but Laiken and I also didn't spend the whole night rubbing our relationship in his face. The kiss I all but tricked her into was only one of two for the night. But I still managed to subtly say *I love you* by writing it into the condensation of her beer bottle.

Yeah, that one may have scored me a few points.

I finish getting ready, making sure to keep my distance even though our lockers are beside each other, and head out of the locker room. I thought Laiken had left already, but as the rink comes into view, I see her gliding around the ice like it's what she was born for.

I probably look like some lovesick puppy, standing here and watching her like this. But the same way as everything else with her, I can't fucking help myself. Except now that the cat's out of the bag, I don't have to do it from a distance.

Stepping onto the ice, I have this image of catching her like something you'd see in movies. But what happens is not at all like what I pictured in my head. Instead of some romantic scene, we both go crashing to the ground. The only good thing about it is the way she lands on top of me, keeping her from getting hurt.

I chuckle as I groan. "I did not think this through."

"You think?" Laiken replies, her voice laced with her own giggle.

I don't even realize Coach is there until his voice echoes through the rink. "Smooth move, Romeo. Now get up. No banging on the ice." Cam groans from the gate and Coach winces. "Oops. Sorry, Blanchard."

Laiken stands up and puts out her hand to help me just as Isaac steps up next to Cam, placing his hand on Cam's shoulder.

"Yeah, sorry bro. I told you your sister's hot." He turns his attention to Laiken. "Sweetheart, if he doesn't make you happy…"

"Jesus!" Cam snaps, pushing his hand off him.

Isaac fakes innocence. "What? She isn't off limits anymore."

"Want to fucking bet?" I growl.

With every word he speaks, my rage intensifies. I try to move closer to him but Laiken puts her hands on my chest. Isaac smirks as he gets the exact reaction he was looking for.

Cam stares at Laiken. "Can you please go?"

She nods, knowing the last thing either of them want is for Isaac and me to go at it. With my hand on her lower back, we step off the ice and go over to the women's locker room.

"I'll see you later?" I ask, twirling her hair around my finger.

"Definitely."

Her arms wrap around my neck as she pulls me in. Our mouths meet in the middle, and we kiss like any normal couple would as they say goodbye. Except, ours may last a little bit longer.

"I love you," I tell her as I take a step back.

She smiles. "I love you, too."

I go to head back over to the rink, but halfway there, I

turn around to kiss her once more. She giggles into it, but the moment is ruined when Owen yells *get a room* loud enough for the whole rink to hear. And I don't miss the way Lucas glares at me.

Well, at least Cam has some company in the Hating Hayes department.

IT'S HALFWAY THROUGH PRACTICE when I finally get my revenge on Isaac for his comments earlier. We're separated into two groups, and we're supposed to be passing the puck to each other. It's a basic drill that we do every practice, and they always go without injury...until today.

The fact that Isaac doesn't wear a cup is no secret. Coach has been on him about it for years, but the idiot claims his dick is too big for them. Cue massive eye roll. Owen fucked a girl Isaac used to date and said she was so tight, he almost couldn't get it in. But that's beside the point.

He stands across from me, not paying as much attention as he definitely should be, and I line the puck up with my stick. The second I send it soaring through the air, I hear Owen's breath hitch. And then it hits its target dead on.

A high-pitched noise emits from Isaac's mouth as he falls to the ice and curls into a ball. Coach pinches the bridge of his nose and shakes his head, while Aiden watches Isaac thoughtfully from beside Cam.

"You better hope that never happens to Hayes, or there will be no nieces or nephews in your future," he tells him.

Cam looks like he's living in hell as he deadpans at Aiden. "Must you?"

Lucas tilts his head to the side, admiring the sight of Isaac mewling in pain. "Nice aim."

And nothing can wipe the smirk off my face.

Next time, maybe he'll think twice before hitting on my girlfriend.

Laiken
CHAPTER THREE

"Stop moving," I tell Hayes as I try to get the bleeding to stop.

Apparently, he thought it was a good idea to shoot a hockey puck at Isaac's junk. Revenge for hitting on me. *Fucking caveman.* But he should have known Isaac would retaliate, which he did—by elbowing Hayes right in the nose as they were getting off the ice.

And I'm no doctor, but this looks broken.

"Will you just hold still?" I say exasperatedly.

He turns his head away and pushes my hands down. "No. I don't care how much I'm bleeding. You are *not* sticking tampons up my nose."

I sigh. "Fine. Bleed out and let Isaac take credit for your murder. That's your choice."

His glare somehow looks more intense when it's mixed with the slowly intensifying black and blue shade under his eyes. Before he can answer, the front door opens and closes, and his mom's voice rings through the house.

"H?" she calls.

"In here," I answer for him, and the look he gives me makes my eyes roll. "She would've found out eventually. And she's a nurse. She can help you."

His mom turns the corner and freezes. "Oh my God, it looks like there was a massacre in here."

Hayes mumbles something about her being a drama

queen, but I can't say I disagree with her. Bloody tissues are all over the sink and the bottom of his shirt is a mess from his drive home. I told him he should've let Coach take care of it at the rink, but he claims he didn't realize how bad it was bleeding until he was already on his way home.

That's code for "my pride is too big to let Isaac know he caused damage."

As I step out of the way so his mom can get in front of him, she lightly places her fingers on the sides of his nose. His eyes pinch closed and he whines.

Yeah, definitely broken.

"Well, it's not out of place, but it *is* broken," she tells him, and I shoot him an *I told you so* look. "Care to tell me how this happened?"

"Just a hockey thing," he tries, but she knows him better to buy that.

"Try again."

Hayes exhales through his mouth as she works to get the bleeding to stop. "I took an elbow to the face."

"Because…" I press, earning a glare that tells me I'll probably pay for this later.

"I shot a well-aimed hockey puck into his no-no place."

I snort at his choice of words, and my laughter gradually builds when I realize that was for his mom's benefit. Around his friends? Sexy motherfucking badass. Around his mom? Angelic mama's boy.

"Take off your shirt," she instructs him. "It's garbage now."

He whines. "It's one of my favorite shirts!"

"Well, you should've thought about that before you shot a hockey puck into your teammate's lower region. Now it looks like part of a crime scene."

His mom holds up the garbage can, looking at him expectantly, and he mutters "such bullshit" under his breath as he pulls it over his head. The minute his abs come into view, I force myself to look away.

The last few days, we haven't been able to keep our hands off each other. It's like I've become some kind of sexually addicted monster who can never get enough. And being this turned on in front of Hayes's mother is not my idea of fun. But it might be Hayes's, if the way he smirks when he notices how affected I am is anything to go by.

His mom comes back with a new shirt for him, and she turns to me while he puts it on. "So, I saw your car outside. Are we not playing hide and seek with Cam anymore?"

Hayes and I share a look, and he answers for us. "Nope. She finally came to her senses."

My eyes meet his and I raise a single brow at him, warning him of what's coming next. The moment he catches on, I smile at his mom.

"You should have been there. Hayes handed Cam a knife and told him to stab him."

Her jaw drops and she backhands Hayes in the stomach. "You did what?"

He squeals at her smack then whirls around to frown at me. "Seriously?"

I shrug, smiling sweetly. "What? I can't be the only one mad about your reckless move."

"It was romantic!" he shouts.

"Oh, yes," I sass. "Your blood all over the ground and my brother getting hauled away for your murder would have really sealed it for me."

He turns to his mom. "Do you see the abuse I deal with?"

She chuckles. "I like her. Someone needs to keep your ass in line."

I fist-pump and grin. "Ha! I have your mom on my side. I win!"

As I do a happy dance just for the sake of rubbing it in his face, he groans. "There is not enough testosterone in this house."

I'M STANDING IN THE kitchen, scrolling through my phone, when I hear Cam coming down the stairs. The second he sees me, however, he turns around to go back up. I roll my eyes as my mouth opens.

"He's not here."

Without a single word, he comes down and goes straight to the fridge. I know I shouldn't get involved. It may be a battle that centers on me, but Hayes has made it clear that this isn't my fight. But there's only so long I can sit around and watch him miss his best friend, and it's already been a week.

"Do you want me to break up with him?" I ask.

His actions halt. "What?"

"Do you want me to break up with him?" I repeat. "Is that what it's going to take to get you to talk to him again?"

Cam pulls his attention from the fridge and turns around to face me. "What did he do, send you to yell at me?"

"No. Actually, if he knew I was even talking to you about this, he'd probably yell at *me*. But this is ridiculous, and you know it. He's been your best friend for years."

"Yeah, which is all the more reason for me to be pissed," he argues. "He knew you were off limits, and he didn't care. He fucked me over without a second thought."

Wow, he really is delusional. "That's bullshit. You weren't there. You didn't see how fucking hard he fought against this. He didn't want to be with me, even though we're both crazy about each other, because of *you*. For fuck's sake, he chose your friendship over me at first!"

I check the time and notice I need to leave, but as I head toward the door, I stop—glancing back at Cam.

"And for the record, you don't own me. The only person who can deem me *off limits* is me."

He says nothing as I leave the house, but I didn't expect him to. Cam is as stubborn as they come. I had no hope of getting through to him. I just wasn't going to let him think I was okay with him being a dick.

THE PARKING LOT IS empty as I pull in, and the rink looks closed. *That's strange.* I open the text thread with Hayes to make sure I came at the right time.

> Don't ask questions. Just meet me at the rink at 8 p.m. 😏

Looking at the rink again, my brows furrow. His truck isn't anywhere to be seen. My only option is to shoot him a text.

> Hey. I'm here, but it looks closed.

His response comes in seconds.

I'll be right out to get you.

Get me? Since when does he need to come get me? I've been coming to this rink longer than he has. But sure enough, he pushes open the door and waits for me.

I shut my car off and hop out, walking over to him. "Where's your truck?"

"In the back," he answers, but offers no further explanation.

All the lights are off. It's so dark, I can barely see Hayes standing beside me. And if he were anyone else, my mind would probably be going crazy with scenarios on how I'm about to die.

"What are we doing?" I ask. "Why are the lights off?"

He chuckles, pulling me closer against him with his arm around my waist. "Didn't I tell you not to ask questions?"

"I don't follow the rules. And besides, that was before you brought me into the pitch black."

"So impatient," he murmurs. "Don't worry. We're almost there."

His body moves behind me, and he circles his arms around my waist as we go a little further. I don't even know how he can see where we're going. Even as my eyes adjust to the dark, I can barely see anything at all.

"Okay," he says, stopping us.

He pulls a remote out of his pocket and presses a button, and the entire rink is cast in soft twinkly lights. They're strung over the glass and go all the way around. In the middle of the ice, there's a table, set with a tablecloth, two covered meals, one which has a rose on it, and a candle in the middle. Two chairs sit on either side.

My eyes water as I take it all in. "You did this?"

"Do you like it?" It's hard not to notice the vulnerability in his voice.

I let my eyes rake over everything once more and then turn my head to look back at him, as much as I can anyway. "I love it. You're amazing."

"*You* are amazing," he corrects me with a kiss. "I'm just trying to be somewhat worthy of your attention."

My heart melts as he takes my hand and leads me onto the rink and over to the table. He's a total gentleman, pulling out the chair for me to sit and then sliding it in. As he hands me the rose, he lifts the lids off the meals to reveal subs, and I can't help but giggle.

"I know," he says with a grin. "But we're on an ice rink, so it was either that or salad."

I shake my head with a smile. "No, it's perfect. You're perfect."

Over all the years I've had a thing for Hayes, I always knew what kind of guy he was. I never fantasized about romantic things with him because I knew that wasn't him. It was always more sexual, though there was the occasional *picture our future together* ones mixed in.

This is more than I could have ever imagined.

He lights the candle and sits down, taking a sip of his beer. "I really missed you today."

"Clearly," I joke as I look around once more. "How did you do all this?"

"I got some of the guys to help me," he confesses.

"Cam?"

He shakes his head. "No, he still hates me. But we managed without him."

A pit forms in my stomach, knowing how hurt he is about it, and I sigh. "I'm so sorry, H."

But he reaches over and puts his hand on mine. "Don't.

We're not going to talk about it tonight, okay? This night is about us."

And somehow, I melt a little more as butterflies come alive in my stomach.

AFTER WE'RE DONE EATING, Hayes suggests we take the opportunity we have to skate together. It's not often that we get the chance. My shifts usually line up either right before or right after his hockey practices, and by the end of them, we're both exhausted. Putting on skates is the last thing on our mind.

But not tonight, so we lace up our skates and hold hands as we leisurely glide around the rink.

The lights that Hayes and the guys hung make it so much more intimate in here. I can only imagine all the shit they gave him for this, too. He probably had to listen to Owen's comments for hours.

"So," Hayes starts. "Is this up to your romance standards?"

I chuckle as I nod. "Yes, definitely."

"Good, because there's something I want to ask you, and I need it to be memorable."

My mouth goes dry as he stops us and turns to face me, looking deep into my eyes. "A-are you about to propose right now?"

Jesus Christ, Lai. If he is, way to ruin the damn moment.

But it doesn't ruin it at all. He doesn't get scared at the thought of that much commitment or look at me like I'm insane. He just smiles and shakes his head.

"No," he says with a small laugh. "I'm sure that will happen eventually, but you once told me I'm not allowed to skip steps. So, Laiken..." He pauses just to drive me insane. "Will you *officially* be mine? My out-in-the-open, hold-your-hand-no-matter-who-can-see girlfriend?"

There is so much happiness in my heart, so much pure joy that it radiates out of me and I beam at him as I nod. "Yes."

He smiles just as brightly, wrapping his arms around me and picking me up. Our lips meet and he spins us around while we both smile into the kiss. He said he wanted to make it memorable, but I think he could have asked me this anywhere and I would always remember it.

Who could ever forget the moment all their dreams came true?

ONE THING ABOUT THE two of us is that we're super competitive. To be honest, it's why I don't enter figure skating competitions anymore. I was too hard on myself, and it started to take a toll on my mental health. But that part of me is still there just as much as Hayes's is. So of course, when the topic of me beating him in a race came up, he demanded his rematch.

We slide the table and chairs out of the way and then take

our places at the one goal line. I know he's determined to beat me, and after everything he did for me tonight, I should let him have it—but what's the fun in that?

"Ready?" he asks, and I nod.

He counts down from three and we both take off. It's neck and neck up until the halfway point, but with a little extra push, I take the lead. And being the showoff I am sometimes, I spin around and wink at him as I cross the goal line backward.

"How in the fuck?" he asks in disbelief.

I skate circles around him. "Just face it, babe. Figure skaters do it better."

He scoffs playfully. "Only because you don't have to focus on as much. We have to worry about our speed and our balance while controlling a small block of rubber with a wooden stick. Oh, and we have to fight off grown men at the same time."

Giving him a look, I glide away from him, and I can feel his gaze on me. I pick up speed just before I execute the trick I've been working on. The one I haven't let anyone see yet.

The fucking triple axel.

It's as if everything is in slow motion as I spin through the air, and relief floods through me as I land it. Hayes's jaw drops, and he looks even prouder than I was when I finally got it.

"When the hell did you learn to do that?"

I shrug. "You're not the only one who needed a distraction after we split."

And that's when he slips up. "Bullshit. I would have noticed that when I—"

His mouth clamps shut as he realizes what he was about to admit, so I smugly finish it for him.

"While you were watching me from the office? Yeah, I

made sure not to work on it then. I didn't need you seeing me fall on my ass."

He exhales. "You knew I was there?"

A small laugh bubbles out of me. "Contrary to what you might think, you're not exactly good at being discreet. You're good at hockey, though...for the most part."

"Damn." He clutches his heart like he's been shot. "You've been my girlfriend for all of twenty minutes and already you're insulting me."

I skate up closer to him and wrap my arms around his neck, kissing him quickly. "Don't worry. You'll get used to it."

"All right, Rochester," he says, using the nickname I haven't heard in a while. "Let's make this interesting. You get three shots. If I block all of them, I get to fuck your mouth again."

God, it was so damn hot when he did that, it hardly sounds like a punishment. "And if I score?"

He smirks in a way that would have my panties ripping themselves right off if they could. "You can sit on my face for as long as you want."

Holy fuck. That's something we haven't done yet, surprisingly, but with the way it feels when he eats me out, I'm sure it'll feel incredible. And an unlimited amount of his mouth on my pussy is more than enough incentive.

Still, I don't want to seem too eager.

"You're not a goalie," I point out.

The look he gives me shows he's at least somewhat hoping I win, and I shiver at the thought. "All the more reason to do it."

I STAND IN THE middle of the ice, holding the stick firmly in my hands while he blocks the goal. I wonder if I should tell him that I used to play against Cam when we were younger. But if he's underestimating me, that's no one's fault but his own.

He keeps his gaze laser focused on me as I take the puck and start skating toward him. I try to use his lack of pads to my advantage, but as I shoot, he blocks it with his skate.

First shot missed.

The second doesn't go much better, this time getting blocked by his stick.

"Last chance, Blanchard," he taunts.

I weigh my options between each possible outcome. If he wins, I know I won't mind him fucking my mouth again. I never imagined it, but choking on his cock and seeing the reactions it pulled out of him was nothing short of incredible. But he'll always bring up how I couldn't score a goal against him.

If I win, however, I get his mouth on my pussy for as long as I want. And getting to wipe the smug grin off his face is an added bonus.

Sorry, babe.

I move a little further away, then allow myself to gain speed before grabbing the puck on the way. Hayes's brows furrow as he watches me. It's clear he's determined to block this last one and win the bet, but as I fake right and shoot left, it goes straight into the back of the goal.

He puts his tongue in his cheek and drops his stick, while I raise my arms in the air and celebrate. But the second I hear him skating after me, I squeal. There's nothing I can do to get away from him. He grabs me, and the stick falls to the ground as he lifts me up.

When he places me back on the ice, I spin around to face him, smiling proudly. "I scored!"

His eyes move across my face, and he puts his hands on my cheeks. "So did I."

Closing the gap between us, he kisses me softly, but it doesn't take long before it turns heated. His one hand slides down my side until he grips my ass, making me arch my hips against him. I moan breathlessly against his mouth.

"You know what Coach said," I warn. "No sex on the ice."

He hums, and I can feel when he gets an idea because he smirks. "Yeah, but he said nothing about the locker rooms."

This night just keeps getting better.

Hayes
CHAPTER FOUR

LORD KNOWS I WAS NEVER THE TYPE TO WANT A relationship until Laiken went and fucked with everything that I used to think I knew. But if someone had told me they were like this, I might have reconsidered. The moment I realized I was in love with Laiken, I knew that a big part of me wanted to be with her.

Exclusively.

Officially.

Completely.

In a way, that scared the shit out of me, because I was running out of reasons not to be. She kept ticking off each one like a goddamn checklist. Looking back on it, I should've known I never stood a chance.

This was going to happen because we're meant for each other.

Now that it's happening though, you won't hear a single complaint out of me. This is fucking great. I get someone who is constantly there for me, someone to talk to about everything and nothing all at the same time, and sex on demand. Plus, she brings me lunch.

And everyone knows the way to a man's heart is through his stomach.

Or is it his dick? If it isn't, it should be. I'm just saying.

Laiken is sitting on the counter of the surf shop, picking

at her fries, when her phone rings. Her mom's picture fills the screen and she answers it.

"Hey, Mom," she says. "I'm not sure exactly. Why?"

Her mood goes from a ten to a solid four in seconds. It's times like these I really hate only hearing one side of the conversation.

"Okay, well, I know I have to go over some stuff tonight with Mr. Zimmerman. Can we have this talk tomorrow?" Another pause while she listens to her response. "Okay. Yep, love you too."

She gets off the phone and rolls her eyes but makes no move to explain. And I am not the type to just let it go without asking.

"Everything okay?"

Her chest rises as she takes a deep breath. "I guess. My parents want to talk to me about my *life choices*. It's code for they want to harp on me more about when I'm going to go to college."

The thought of her leaving puts a heavy weight on my chest. It's not a foreign concept she's springing on me. She was supposed to leave last summer. Her dorm was even assigned. But then Cam got arrested, and when her parents tried to get her to go anyway, she downright refused. And she had already turned eighteen. She was a legal adult who could make her own decisions.

There was nothing they could do.

I guess I just didn't realize it was still a possibility. Once I threw myself at Cam's mercy and admitted to being in love with her, the whole idea faded from my mind. The only thing I thought of was her and me.

"They're on your case about it?" I choke out, trying to seem unfazed.

She nods. "I mean, I get it. The agreement was that I

would go once Cam's case was settled, but what if I don't want to go to college? Is that really so bad?"

"Well, that depends," I tell her. "If it's because you were serious about making a killing with prostitution, then yes. But if you have an actual dream you want to achieve, I don't think so."

"I do," she admits. "Or I did. I don't know. I go back and forth on it."

I tilt my head to look in her eyes. "What is it?"

Her nose scrunches as she shakes her head. "I don't want to say it. You'll laugh at me."

What she doesn't know is that I could never laugh at her, not when what comes out of her mouth could determine if she stays here with me or leaves me behind.

"Please? I told you mine."

The corners of her mouth raise as she remembers our little rendezvous with the cops at the airfield. That was the day I first started realizing how deep my feelings for her actually ran. When I *really* started feeling like I was fucked.

Finally, she sighs. "I want to be a songwriter." Her eyes won't meet mine as I go quiet, imagining her writing love ballads that I'd add to my secret playlist of songs that make me think of her. "It's fine. You can laugh."

"No way," I answer. "It suits you."

She looks over at me and scoffs. "It's a pipe dream."

I can't help but smirk. "So was I, but you got me."

My words manage to pull a laugh out of her, and I can feel the way her mood lightens just slightly. "Oh, wow. That's a lot of cocky."

Tossing the rest of my lunch into the garbage can, I lean forward and kiss her quickly. "Your words, not mine."

I WISH I COULD say that the worst thing about Isaac breaking my nose was the pain. The crunch I heard when he made contact was anything but fun. But honestly, I think the guard I need to wear on my face during practice is worse. Coach almost didn't let me play at all, but that argument came with enough obscenities and threats against Isaac's life that he changed his mind.

Speaking of the prick, I look around and notice he's still not here. I figured that Coach suspended him for the incident, but he should be back by now.

"Owen," I call. "Where's Isaac?"

His brows furrow. "Cam didn't tell you?"

"Tell me what?"

Realization fills his face. "Oh yeah. He's still not talking to you. Damn, he knows how to hold a grudge."

Yeah, not about to talk shit about him. "That doesn't answer my question."

"Isaac, right," he nods. "He's gone. Cam had him kicked off the team for breaking your nose."

Out of all the answers I saw coming out of his mouth, I don't think I ever considered that one. "Seriously?"

"Yeah, man. After you left, he went into Coach's office and screamed at him that he wanted Isaac out. He said if Isaac stayed on the team, he was going to walk. And no coach is ever going to let himself lose one of his best players." He heads toward the door of the locker room. "Isaac is pretty pissed though, so I'd keep an eye out if I were you."

"I will," I say. "Thanks."

Alone in an empty locker room, I give myself an extra minute to reflect on what he just told me. Cam still isn't talking to me, and I'm honestly not sure if or when he ever will again. But while I thought he hated me, this proves otherwise.

He may be livid, but he still has my back.

I slip my phone out of my pocket and type out a quick text.

> Heard you got Isaac kicked off the team. Just wanted to say thanks.

Putting it away, I grab my bag and head out. But by the time I get to my truck, my phone dings, and a response for Cam shows on the screen.

> Didn't do it for you.

It's meant to be a slap in the face, but it only makes my grin widen because he and I both know he's completely full of shit.

I PULL INTO MY driveway and turn off my truck. The

whole ride home, I kept thinking about the way practice has been without Isaac there, now that I know it's permanent. And there really has been a shift. He's not being an asshole or putting people down. We all get along, and that's exactly what you want in a team.

Once Cam and I get back on track, we'll be fucking unstoppable.

Everything feels like it's starting to fall into place. I've got the girl of my dreams. The biggest pain in my ass is gone. And my best friend might not be talking to me right now, but this was the sign I needed. The one that tells me it'll be all right.

Maybe I can have both after all.

I'm in such a good mood that there's a pep in my step as I hop up onto the porch. But the second I open the door, I know there's something wrong. My mom is sitting in the living room with Devin, and I don't know if it's my sister's tear-stained cheeks or the grave look on my mom's face, but my stomach sinks.

"What's going on?" I ask carefully.

Mom smiles sadly, and it blasts me right back to the day she finally told us that Dad wasn't coming back. "Come sit down, H."

My brows furrow as I walk around the couch and sit next to Devin. She leans against me, the way she used to when we were kids and she needed someone she could rely on. I know whatever it is, it can't be good.

"Lawrence Gent stopped by today," Mom tells me, her voice cracking as she speaks.

That's a name I haven't heard in a while. Lawrence is my dad's best friend, or at least *was* the last I saw him. But that doesn't explain why he would be coming here. Unless...*fuck*.

"Say it," I tell her. "I need to hear the words."

She takes a deep breath, her eyes full of sympathy. "Your father is gone. He passed away."

WHEN I WAS A kid, I used to hear my parents arguing through the walls. My dad would come home drunk again, and my mom would scream at him about what a piece of shit he was being. That he was wasting all their money away on booze.

You're going to drink yourself to death and leave these kids without a father, she would say.

Never knew my mother was a psychic. Though he left us without a father long before he finally drank himself into liver failure.

I remember being so confused when he left. I think I spent weeks going over everything in my head, wondering what I did wrong or what I could've done differently to make him stay. As I got older, I realized it had nothing to do with me and everything to do with himself. He was a selfish prick who chose alcohol over his own flesh and blood. But man, as a fifteen-year-old kid, I really beat myself up over it.

Even as years passed and I accepted the fact that he wasn't coming back, there were still times where I'd think about it. I imagined what I would say if he came walking through the door, or if he called me up. I never told my mom, but I used to check the mailbox every day for the two weeks around my birthday—hoping a card from him would show up.

It never did.

And now, it never will.

I sit on the porch, a lit cigarette in my hand, as the door swings open and Devin storms out. She marches right past me and over to her car, peeling out of the driveway like a bat out of hell. I glance back at the door to see my mom standing here, a hopeless expression on her face.

"She'll be okay," I assure her to ease her nerves. "Her emotions are just running a little wild right now."

I know because mine are, too.

I don't think there's ever been a time where I was so conflicted. Not even during the push and pull with Laiken. There's a part of me that wants to be sad. It's that fifteen-year-old kid tucked away, who still wishes for his family to be whole again when he blows out his birthday candles. But I can't find it in me to be.

He doesn't *deserve* for me to be upset. Or to even care that he's gone. He was so fucking absent in my life that he's been dead for six months, and the only reason Mom found out is because his best friend came by to let her know. He said his assets are out of probate, and he needs Devin and me to come by his office and pick up our inheritance checks.

According to what Mom told us, he hit it big at some casino about a year ago and he used it to drink himself into the grave. He died before he could spend it all, though, and being his kids—at least biologically—it goes to us by default.

Joke's on him because I don't fucking want it.

Laiken pulls into the driveway and I stand up, tossing my cigarette I've been too zoned out to smoke and walking toward her car. The minute she steps out, I pull her into my arms and hold her tightly.

"Hey," she coos.

I wonder if she knows how much even the sound of her voice manages to relax me. The moment I walked out the front door, my phone was pressed to my ear. I told Laiken that I needed her, and that was it. Nothing else mattered. She just got in her car and got her ass to my house.

I mentally add that to the endless list of reasons why I will love her for the rest of my life.

She waits patiently, hugging me back and waiting for me to initiate letting go. When I finally do, she looks at me worriedly.

"What's going on?" she asks.

Nodding toward my truck, she follows me as I walk over and put down the tailgate. The two of us sit and she waits patiently for me to fill her in, until the silence becomes a little too much to bear.

"Hayes, you're scaring me a little here," she tells me.

I swallow down the lump in my throat, finally allowing myself to say the words out loud. "My, uh…my dad died."

She gasps. "Oh my God. H."

My defense mechanisms kick in and I shake my head, metaphorically waving it off. "No, it's fine. I mean, it's not fine, but the past six years have been like he was dead anyway, so it's not this massive change."

Her hand rests gently on my arm. "Yeah, but just because he wasn't around doesn't mean you can't be upset about it."

"That's the thing though. I'm not *upset*," I admit, hearing how heartless it makes me sound. "I'm just angry. While Devin and I were growing up and Mom was working her ass off to provide for us, he was out there somewhere, drinking his life away—not even trying to get his life back together. He was completely content being the same worthless lowlife that walked out on his family. And now we find out he left Devin and me an inheritance, as if money makes up for the past six years."

Pulling the folded-up piece of paper out of my pocket, I hand it to her. She carefully opens it, and her eyes widen when she sees the number.

"Wow. How does a drunk even get that much money?"

"At the casino, because while you gamble, you drink for free." I crumple it up and toss it into the bed of the truck behind me. "I don't know. I think I'll just let Dev have my share. He gets no comfort in hell from knowing that he did anything to help me."

She looks over at me with nothing but warmth and fondness in her eyes. "If that's what you want to do, I fully support you. There's no right or wrong way to heal from all the trauma he caused you and your sister. But technically, that money isn't coming from *him*. He didn't write a will or decide to give it to you out of the goodness of his heart. The money is coming from a bunch of people in an office whose only job is to figure out where shit goes when someone passes away."

I know she has a point, but it does nothing to relieve the heaviness in my chest. "It still feels dirty. Like I'm letting him buy my forgiveness from beyond the grave or something."

"No one is expecting you to forgive him, babe. Or even asking you to," she says calmly. "I don't think anyone who knows what you've been through ever would. That is something only you could decide to do. But let me ask you something."

"What?"

"What would you do if your dad hadn't left?"

My brows raise. "Well, I would've had a lot less commitment issues."

She chuckles, bumping her shoulder into mine. "I mean with the money."

For the first time since my mom broke the news, I let myself think about it, but it doesn't take long.

"I'd use the money to buy a bar," I answer.

"Then personally, I think you should do that." She hops off the truck and stands in front of me, slotting herself between my legs and staring into my eyes. "He's stolen enough of your joy. This is your chance to take some back."

My gaze stays fixated on her, and I don't think there's ever going to be a time where I'm not in awe of everything she is. She's so calm, so caring, that sometimes all I can do is admire her.

"You know, it's a little infuriating how you always tell me what I need to hear," I quip.

She smiles, giggling softly. "You'll get over it."

I wrap my arms around her shoulders and pull her in. She sighs against me as I press a kiss to the top of her head. If there's ever a time when this girl is all I have, I'll be okay, because she's all I will ever need.

I SIT INSIDE MY truck, staring at the lawyer's office like if I do it long enough, I'll wake up and this will all be some weird dream. For the rest of the day yesterday, I was okay. Laiken was there, keeping me grounded and distracting me when I needed it. She even managed to put Mom and Devin in better moods. I don't know how—it's just part of her magic. And I was able to sleep because she was there, with her head on my chest and her thumb rubbing back and forth on my stomach. But now that I'm sitting here, I can't explain what I feel.

I should've brought her with me.

It's a useless afterthought. This office is an hour away. While I'm sure she would come if I called her, I'm not about to make her drive all that way just so I have enough strength to sign a damn paper. I have no choice but to do this on my own.

Taking a deep breath, I exhale and force myself out of the truck. As I walk through the doors, a receptionist greets me from her desk.

"Can I help you?"

"I think so," I reply. "I'm looking for Lawrence Gent. I have to pick something up."

She gives me a professional smile. "Have a seat and I'll let him know you're here."

"Thanks."

As I sit and wait, I look around the room. There's decor and pictures hanging on the walls, but all the colors feel so dull. Then again, there's nothing colorful or fun about lawyers so I guess it's fitting.

"Hayes."

The call of my name has me looking up to see Lawrence walking toward me. It's been years since I've seen him, but I remember him being around a lot when I was younger. Even after my dad left, he came by a few times to help my mom with things, but it used to make Devin ask where Dad was, so they decided it was best if he didn't come by anymore. And then they just...lost touch.

"Man," he tells me as I stand up. "I don't think I expected you to look so grown."

"Yeah, well. That's life."

It may be short of me, but the last thing I want to do is small talk with a guy who still stuck around my dad after he walked out on his family. Mom always said that he felt obligated to him. That they were friends for so long, he couldn't just ditch him when he needed him the most. But why not? That's what my dad did to us.

He leads me back into a room with a conference table surrounded by chairs. There are papers laid out with tabs on where to sign, and he gestures for me to take a seat.

"Are your mom and sister coming?" he asks.

"Another day. My mom wants to come with her to read it all over, but she had to work today." I offered to wait until we could all come together, but they told me to go, knowing I just want to get it over with.

He nods. "Understandable. It will be here when they're ready."

One by one, he starts to hand me things to sign.

A paper that states my father had no will and that the money he had at the time of his passing was decided by the Probate Court of North Carolina.

A paper that states I acknowledge and agree with the court's decision to split the money equally among his children.

A paper that states I have received my portion of the money as legally required of the executor of the estate.

And finally, one stating that I have no plans or intentions of trying to sue the estate for more money, even though there won't be any after Devin and I cash our checks.

I sign my name on each of the required lines, initialing in other places. But I make sure to read them all thoroughly. It's making it so I'm spending more time here than I need to, but my mom would have my head if she knew I signed legal documents without reading them.

"You know, your dad was really proud of you," Lawrence says, breaking the silence.

I snort. "Don't really know how you can be proud of someone you have nothing to do with, but okay."

He leans back in his chair, not at all affected by my response. "I know what your feelings toward him are, and I respect that. I don't want you to think that I don't. I was friends with your father for many years. He made his mistakes, I'm not denying that, but he also had his issues."

He pauses to take one of the signed documents from me, then continues.

"You may not believe a word that comes out of my mouth, but he loved you and Devin very much, regardless of if he was there or not. He was just battling demons that he thought were best kept as far from you two as possible."

I honestly don't know what to say to that, so I don't say anything at all. My eyes skim through the rest of the documents and I sign them, ready to get the hell out of this place. And once I'm done, he hands me a check for more money than I've ever had at one time in my life.

"There's one more thing," he tells me just as I go to leave.

He gets up and walks into another office and then comes out with a leather box. My brows furrow as I look at it, until I see my father's name embossed into the top of it. *His fucking ashes.*

"Yeah, I don't want those," I tell him. "Why don't you keep them? Since you two were such close friends."

He shakes his head. "He specifically requested they be given to you."

"That's great and all, but if I'm honest, I'm just going to throw them in the trash on my way out." There's no sugarcoating it. No playing nice. *I don't want them.*

Lawrence shrugs. "If that's your choice, then so be it."

It's obvious he's not going to let me leave here without taking the damn box. But fine. If he's okay with his best friend's ashes ending up in a dump somewhere, I won't ask any more questions. I grab the box with one hand and force a smile on my face.

"It's good to see you turned out okay," he says honestly.

I nod, mumbling a small thank you, but as I go to walk out the door, I stop. "Actually, can I ask you something?"

"Sure. What's on your mind?"

"You said he wanted his ashes given to me, so he obviously knew he was dying," I start.

He nods once. "He did. Yes."

"So why tell us now?" I question. "Why wait six months after he died to even let us know that he's gone? Why didn't you get in touch when he was dying?"

The look on his face tells me he was expecting this, and his answer is simple. "Because he asked me not to. He knew he let you guys down by leaving and said you two didn't owe him a thing. Not a goodbye. Not a funeral. And certainly not your forgiveness."

His words hit a weak spot, but I force myself to numb it out. "Then why not right after?"

"Probate takes six months to a year in most cases," he explains. "I didn't think you deserved to have this hanging over your head for that long. This way, you can deal with it all at once. The grief won't come back every time there's an update on the status of his estate."

I huff, a little amused by his words. "No offense, but there is no grief. I refuse to miss someone who never missed me enough to put down the fucking bottle."

He nods in understanding but says nothing as I turn around and head for the door.

As soon as I get outside, I look for the nearest trash can. There's one right at the corner of the building, where people must take their smoke breaks. I walk over to it, completely determined to put his ashes where the trash like him belongs. But as I open the box to pour it out, I stop.

Lawrence's words play through my mind, making it so I can't. No matter how hard I try, I just can't seem to throw them away.

Giving up, I close the box and go over to my truck. I climb in and place the check *and* the box on the passenger seat, staring at it for a minute before scoffing.

"Fuck you, old man."

Laiken
CHAPTER FIVE

WORRY BUILDS INSIDE ME AS I CHECK THE CLOCK for the fifth time in seven minutes. Last I heard from Hayes, he was on his way to the lawyer's office. As much as he may *act* like he feels nothing from the news that his dad died, I don't buy it. His dad wasn't a good man by any means, but children are predisposed to love their parents. The mistakes he made and the trauma he caused don't change the fifteen years that Hayes loved his dad.

I'm just afraid he's going to break and I won't be around to catch him when he does.

Another ten minutes pass before I give in and text Devin.

> Hey, have you heard from your brother?

She doesn't respond right away. I run my fingers through my hair and tug at the strands. I can't sit still. I can't think of anything but Hayes. Finally, as I start to pace my room, I feel my phone vibrate in my hand.

> Not since he left this morning. Everything okay?

> I'm not sure. He hasn't answered me in a little while.

> He's probably just blowing off some steam.
> He's a hothead. Give him time. I'm sure he'll
> reach out.

I know she's probably right, but I still can't seem to shake myself of this feeling that something isn't right. There hasn't been a day since he told Cam about us that he hasn't responded when I text him. Not answering his phone is just not like him. Not anymore. And being as he was supposed to leave the lawyer's office with a large check—I don't think I'm wrong to be worried.

It only takes another ten minutes before I decide to call the lawyer's office, but when they tell me that the gentleman I'm looking for left about an hour ago, it doesn't help me feel much better.

"Okay," I say to myself as I sit on my bed. "He's probably just driving home, with music loud enough to not hear his phone. Don't freak out."

BY HOUR FOUR, MY pep talk goes flying right out the window. Both his mom and his sister have tried to call him, but they went unanswered. They said that this isn't unusual for Hayes. Disappearing when shit got a little chaotic is apparently his specialty. But he has never done that with me.

"I'm telling you," I say to Mali as I try to log into his Apple ID to check his location. "Something isn't right."

Invalid password.

When I go to try again, it locks me out for five minutes. My grip tightens on my phone and I move to throw it out of pure frustration, when Mali intervenes.

"Laiken, stop." She grabs my phone from me and puts it down on the counter. "You need to breathe."

"Don't you get it? I can't breathe." Tears start to well in my eyes. "What if something happened to him? What if he's out there somewhere, hurt and needing help, but no one is looking for him?"

My panic isn't getting any better, but Mali is used to this with me. She takes my hand and puts it on the center of her chest.

"You're going to breathe with me, okay?"

I nod, and she slowly starts to take deep breaths. Closing my eyes, I focus on the movement of her chest as we breathe together, until I finally feel like I'm in control again.

"Thanks," I tell her.

She hugs me and holds me close. "Just relax, babe. I'm sure everything is fine."

Cam comes down the stairs just as I'm wiping the tears from my eyes. "What's wrong with *you*?"

"I can't find Hayes," I choke out. "He won't answer his phone."

He scoffs, shaking his head with a humorous look on his face. "This is why I told him not to touch you. This shit—the *only-answers-you-when-he-wants-something* thing—it's what he does with girls."

I shake my head. "No. That's not what this is."

"Okay," he grunts. "Don't listen to me then. Suit yourself. But I don't want to hear it when he breaks your heart because he got bored."

Yeah, I am definitely *not* in the mood for his shit right now.

"Can you shut the fuck up?" I snap, not caring as my mom chastises me on my language from the other room. "You have no idea what you're talking about."

"Oh, I don't? I'm his best friend," he argues.

Crossing my arms over my chest, I level him with a look. "Are you? Because from where I've been standing for the last two weeks, you haven't been fucking acting like it. I bet you don't even know his dad died, do you? Or that today he went to pick up an inheritance check and that he was answering me all the way up until he said he was at the office and he'd call me after before he went radio silent? You claim to be his best friend, but you've been a really fucking shitty one lately, if you ask me."

"Laiken Rose!" my mother yells. "Watch. Your. Language!"

"Watch your language," I mock, fed up with all of this shit. "Fuckity fuck, fuck, fuck."

"What the hell did you just say?" my dad roars.

Mali quickly moves to cover my mouth. "Nothing! She said nothing." After a moment, she removes her hand and sighs. "You're going to get your ass grounded, and then it won't matter if you can find Hayes or not."

My attitude makes me roll my eyes, but deep down I know she's right. She's only looking out for me. And when my emotions die down, I'll thank her for it.

In the meantime, I look around and notice my brother is gone.

"Where did Cam go?" I ask.

Mali shrugs. "He grabbed his keys and stormed out the door while you were busy displaying your colorful vocabulary."

Of course he did. He always has been a fucking coward when it comes to having to face shit he doesn't want to deal with. I love him, but that doesn't mean I don't get the urge to strangle him at times. And he's being exceptionally infuriating lately.

Going back to the task at hand of getting into Hayes's Apple ID, I put in another guess.

Invalid Password.

"Son of a motherfucking bitch," I mutter under my breath, only for Mali to raise her brows at me warningly.

As if she doesn't say worse.

Hayes
CHAPTER SIX

I WATCH AS THE WAVES BREAK AGAINST THE SHORE. It's been a long time since I've come up here. This shitty old ice cream place closed down a few years ago, but its bones still remain. After my dad left, this is where I came to think. To give myself a minute of not having to pretend to be strong. I'd climb up to the roof and sit on this ledge, letting my feet hang off the edge, and just watch the ocean.

I guess old habits really do die hard.

My phone goes off, adding to the building list of notifications, but I can't bring myself to look at it. There are so many different emotions running through me. Emotions I can't seem to make sense of.

Hurt.

Anger.

Chaos.

Confusion.

It's like yesterday, only intensified.

I'm sure if I answered one of Laiken's calls, she would be able to make me feel better, but right now, I just can't. I need to feel this. It's all the things I forced myself to block out after I accepted the fact that he was never coming back. And even though I knew it then, there was still that little sliver of hope.

A part of me wonders if it would bother me less if he had

gotten his life together. If it was something about us that made him drink until he passed out every night. At least then I'd have something to blame it all on, rather than having to come to terms with the fact that he simply loved his alcohol more than anything else in his life.

I think the worst part is remembering the times he wasn't drunk. When I was little and he was an actual father. And believe it or not, he was a good one. He bought me my first hockey stick after we watched a game together on TV. God, he was so fucking proud when he came to my first game.

My parents always looked so happy together. Dad would come home every payday with a bouquet of flowers just to show Mom he loved her. And when Devin got jealous, he would pull one of them out and hand it to her. But she was only seven when he started drinking.

They kept up appearances, making us look like this loving family, but inside those four walls, it was hell. My mom never told us what led to his drinking. She always said it wasn't our burden to bear. All I remember is him coming home one day, stumbling through the front door, drunk off his ass. And it only got worse from there.

The fighting was the hardest part. All of the screaming that would come through the walls, no matter how much Mom tried to keep her voice down. I sheltered Devin from it as much as I could. She thought I was just being a cool big brother who wanted to listen to music with her while dancing around the room or jumping on the bed. I don't think she ever realized I was just trying to keep her from hearing it.

Then the time came where he left, and the sound of the door slamming shut haunted me for months.

Mom was an emotional basket case—crying every night after spending the day being strong for us. The house that was once so loving and warm was now a *Groundhog Day* nightmare that never seemed to end. Devin couldn't understand that he wasn't coming back, and I was left to be the man of the house.

Let me tell you, fifteen is too young to be given that kind of responsibility. I was still trying to figure out who the hell I was when the world I knew was ripped out from under me. All the lies I told myself—that it would get better eventually —they were shot to hell with everything else I thought I knew.

But if he was such a shit person, why do I feel like I lost something?

The sound of someone climbing up the side of the building barely registers as I keep my eyes on the ocean, but I don't turn around to see who it is. There's only one person who knows about this place. And when Cam sits down next to me with a six pack of beer, he pops one open and hands it to me.

"Thanks," I say quietly.

We sit there in silence, letting the cold beer battle against the heat as it slides down our throats. It's a little ironic— drinking to get over the loss of my alcoholic father—but Devin has made sure to drill into my head that I am nothing like him. The thing is, I want to be.

Not the version of him that walked out on his family. I'm talking about the dad that would play hockey with me in the street and taught me how to lace up my skates. The one that danced with my mom in the middle of the living room just because he knew it made her smile.

That's the one I want to be like.

That's the one I'm grieving.

My phone goes off again, cutting through the silence like a knife, but I don't make a move to look at it.

"They're worried about you, you know," Cam tells me.

I take another sip of my beer. "No reason to be. I'm fine."

He snorts. "Oh, yeah. Because going off the grid and not answering your phone for hours really shows that you're just peachy."

Leave it to him to force a smile out of me. "You're such a dick."

As I finish the one and turn to replace it with another, we fall quiet again. But I can't seem to make sense of everything running through my head. It's like I'm being torn completely in half.

"I don't even know why I care right now," I admit. "I mean, the guy didn't give a shit about me, why should I give a shit about him?"

"Because you're human, and you care, even if you think you shouldn't," Cam answers. "That doesn't make you a bad person or naive for giving a shit. It just goes to show that you're better than he was."

"Is it wrong that I didn't want him to die? That I'm actually pissed he's not stumbling around drunk somewhere?"

He shakes his head. "Nah. You're feeling the same loss you did six years ago, but this time is more permanent. It's understandable, at least to me anyway."

I nod slowly and then shrug. "I think it's just that I can't come to grips with hating him as much as I did a few days ago. Before I knew he was gone."

"Because you don't hate him anymore." The way he says it is like it's the most obvious thing in the world to everyone but me. "You did. I know you did. And I'm sure there are parts of you that still do. But the drunk that you hated died, and all that's left is what you choose to remember. The alcoholic is the one who walked out on you, but the dad that you still have some memories of, he died, too. It doesn't make you less of a person for feeling the pain of that."

I let his words set in as I watch the ships on the horizon,

and every last thing he said hits home. The more I think about it, the more it registers. I might not understand all of what I'm feeling, but what Cam said definitely helps put me in a better place. One where I'm not about to self-destruct out of chaotic rage.

"Thanks, man," I say genuinely.

"No problem," he answers, and the text message tone goes off again. "But for the love of God, answer my sister before she has a stroke."

Cringing, I take out my phone and see the endless string of notifications. I open Laiken's and type out a text—I'll read everything she sent later.

> I'm okay. I love you.

I send a quick message to the group chat with my mom and Devin, too, and then slip my phone back into my pocket.

"So, are we good?" I question, because if when we leave here, he's going to go back to hating me, I think I'd choose to stay for a bit.

He rolls his eyes. "I mean, I can't say I like it. The idea of you and Laiken together makes me want to wash my brain in acid."

I can't help but laugh because I get it. I'd feel the same way if I found out he was hooking up with Devin. But after a minute, we both turn serious again as it goes quiet.

"Do I have to worry about you hurting her?" he asks after a moment.

I shake my head without hesitation. "I'm crazy about her."

He nods slowly, turning his head straight and taking another sip. "Then I guess I'm going to have to learn to deal with it."

Relief floods through me, numbing out all the feelings I

was struggling with before. I love Laiken. I really do. And if she was all I had, I know that I would be okay. But if I have her *and* my best friend, nothing can ever bring me down.

"Hey," I nudge him. "She can't get mad at you if you go for Mali now."

Cam snorts, raising a brow at me. "Is that your silver lining?"

"It's all I've got," I say with a shrug, and he shakes his head humorously.

We get up and go over to the maintenance ladder, climbing down. But as we start to walk back to our cars, an idea comes to mind.

"You have any interest in owning a bar with me?"

He looks over at me. "You serious?"

I nod. "Yeah. There was a decent bit of money left in his account when he died, and I want to open a bar with my half of it. But I don't think I could handle it on my own."

His expression turns thoughtful as he considers it. "I think that's something I could get on board with."

I may not know where my future is going, but I have a feeling it's going to be great. Laiken was right—taking back some of the joy he stole does feel good.

Laiken
CHAPTER SEVEN

Leaning against the counter, I stare at the five words he sent. I've been reading it over and over. Right before he answered, I was seconds away from getting all of our friends together to form a search party. Overdramatic? Maybe. But I was worried. And honestly, I still am. The text helped, but what I need right now is to be in his arms.

The muffled sound of two voices outside grab both mine and Mali's attention. We share a confused look just as the door opens and in walks Cam, with Hayes right behind him.

"Why not?" Hayes groans.

Cam rolls his eyes, going straight to the fridge. "Because The Salted Rim is a stupid name."

"Oh, because it's so much worse than Island Reef?"

"It is!"

Hayes stares at him like he's lost his mind. "Dude, we live in North Carolina. Where the fuck do you see any islands?"

"The outer banks," he points out.

"We don't live there!"

Cam scoffs. "Whatever. The Salted Rim sounds like a chick bar. It'll be filled with people asking for appletinis and watermelon margaritas."

A smirk spreads across Hayes's face. "Oh, so you'll fit right in then."

My brother laughs. "You're such a prick. Let's just settle this over a game of Center Ice. Winner names the bar."

"You're on."

All Mali and I can do is watch with wide eyes as they banter like the last two weeks never happened. But seeing Hayes, perfectly fine and ten times happier than he was this morning, makes my heart swell with joy.

Cam goes to head upstairs when he stops and glances back at Hayes.

"I'll meet you up there," he tells him.

My brother glances between the two of us before sighing. "I wonder if bleach would work."

Hayes chuckles and then turns to me. With a hand on the back of my neck, he pulls me in and wraps his arms around me, holding me close. I breathe in the smell of him and feel as my blood pressure returns to normal again.

When he backs away slightly, he rubs his thumb against my cheek and stares into my eyes. "I'm sorry I disappeared. I just needed to get my head on straight, and I didn't want to drag you down with me."

"You don't need to apologize for needing some space," I tell him, shaking my head. "But I want to make sure you know that you're *always* able to come to me."

"I do. I know that," he confirms.

Eliminating the space between us, he kisses me, and I melt right into it. This, right here, is exactly what I needed. The feeling I get when I'm around him. The way he makes me feel safe and loved.

He breaks the kiss and smiles. "You're so important to me."

"Stop macking with my sister and get up here so I can kick your ass!" Cam yells from upstairs.

Both of us chuckle, and I can't help but love how carefree he looks right now. It's the look I've been craving to see back on his face.

"Go," I tell him softly, nodding toward the stairs.

His brows furrow. "Are you sure?"

"Definitely. I know you've been waiting for him to stop icing you out."

Hayes beams back at me, kissing me once more and then almost running up to join Cam. Meanwhile, I can't seem to wipe the smile off my face or get the butterflies in my stomach to calm.

I look over at Mali, only to see her smirk and shake her head. "You're so lovesick, it's disgusting."

Laughter bubbles out of me as I flip her off, but there's no point in denying it. She's right.

I'm so fucking gone for him.

I always have been.

GROWING UP WITH CAM, the only thing I was ever jealous of was his curfew. Our parents were basically the king and queen of double standards. Cam could do no wrong, while I was grounded if I walked in the door two minutes late. It didn't matter that I was in the driveway on time. I was late.

As we got older, it got a little better. Not completely—he's still their favorite despite the fact that he has a criminal record and I don't—but I stopped being jealous of him and grew to appreciate our bond more.

Until he started hogging my boyfriend.

Okay, maybe that's a little dramatic. He's not exactly

hogging him, but he *is* getting to spend all Hayes's free time with him. And I'm just a teeny tiny bit cranky about it. Turns out Hayes isn't the only one who must have failed sharing in kindergarten.

They've spent the last week and a half looking for a location to open their new bar. Every possible hour they have, they've been going around with a realtor, and they've seen a decent number of buildings. But each one has either been too expensive, was in a shitty area, or wasn't big enough. So, the search continues, and I stay missing my boyfriend.

Granted, I get nights with him. Either I lie to my parents and tell them I'm sleeping at Mali's, or my parents assume Hayes is here for Cam, and he climbs through my skylight. But by the end of the day, he's so exhausted that within a few minutes of wrapping his arms around me, he passes out cold.

He does his best to make it up to me, though—sending me super sweet texts and having flowers delivered to the rink when I'm working. I could've done without the kids cooing about the fact that Miss Laiken has a boyfriend, but the gesture was adorable.

And messing with him when I have the chance has been fun, too.

My phone vibrates in my lap as I figure out where to put my little prodigy. She's ready to move up to the twelve-thirteen class, but both of them are full. I know her parents can't afford private lessons, so I'm trying to see if there is a way that I can add another time slot for that age group. If she's the only one in it for now, well, I won't exactly complain.

Giving myself a break, I open my phone to see a picture from Hayes. They're at another potential location that's for sale and I can't help but cringe.

> Is that a blood stain on the floor?

> Realtor claims it's rust.

I chuckle as I type out my response.

> I think you need a new realtor.

Another picture comes through, and this time, it's of a massive bar in the middle of the room. The kind where the bartender stands in the center. It's a good size, but I don't really think it's what he's looking for.

> Sorry, babe. I'm not seeing this place having the right vibe. But sex on that bar could be fun.

> 😩 What'd you have to say that for? Now I have to buy it.

> You are not buying the murder bar. Know your audience.

> We're going to have an audience? I didn't know you were into voyeurism, baby.

> Still got that one-track mind, I see.

> Can you blame me? It's been too long. This search is going to cause me to die from lack of sex.

Snorting, I'm not at all surprised that he's losing his mind from this. I practically am, too. But I know this is what makes him happy, which makes it worth it for me.

> Tell my brother that. Let me know how it goes.

Okay, hold on.

My eyes widen as I rush to text him back.

No!

I was kidding.

Don't do that.

When he doesn't answer, I know he's only fucking with me. It's only fair that he has to take what he gives.

Well, at least the floor already has one blood stain. One more won't make much of a difference.

The response I get is in the form of a picture of his face, looking offended. I open my camera and switch it to video, recording myself winking and blowing a kiss at him, only to laugh as I press stop. Shooting him the short video, I try to go back to what I was working on when my phone vibrates four times in a row.

Three things...

1. You're gorgeous.

2. I'm the luckiest man alive.

and 3. Thank fuck that live wallpaper is a thing.

My cheeks start to ache as my smile won't fade. This is why all of the distance right now and all the lonely days I've spent whining to Mali about missing him, they're all worth it. Because of this. Because he still manages to make sure I know that I'm one of the most important people in the world to him.

THE SURF SHOP IS dead, which is a little strange for this time of day, but it is approaching the end of summer. Who really wants to buy a surfboard they can only use for a few more weeks?

Hayes is scrolling through more listings that his realtor emailed him while I sit on his lap. If a customer comes in, I'll move, but for now, I just want to be close to him.

"Ugh," he groans. "This is not even remotely fun. I'm starting to wonder if trying to make this happen was a bad move."

I press a kiss to his cheek. "It wasn't. You just have to keep your eyes on the end game. You have a vision for it, and I'm sure you'll find the right place eventually."

He turns to look at me, and I laugh at the way I can read his mind—like how he's currently thinking that I'm a pain in the ass when I'm right. With a quick kiss, he goes back to looking at his computer and switches to the next listing.

"This one might have some potential."

It's a few minutes later when Marc walks in. Hayes's eyes move to the door for a second then back to the computer. I've only seen him a few times at events, but we've never actually spoken, and here I am sitting on his employee's lap while he's supposed to be working.

I move to get up, but Hayes's arm tightens around my waist as he holds me in place.

"Hey, Marc," he greets him.

Marc looks amused by how close we are. "Hey? That's it? You're not going to introduce me to your friend?"

Hayes doesn't look away from the computer as he scrolls through more pictures. "Boss man, girlfriend. Girlfriend, boss man."

There's something about the way he says it so naturally that makes my stomach flip while Marc chuckles.

"Oh wow. She really hit the jackpot with you," he teases Hayes.

I smile sweetly at him. "I'm Laiken."

Realization crosses his face, and he snaps before pointing at me. "That's right. You're Cam's sister." I nod in confirmation. "I knew you looked familiar. What are you doing with this idiot?"

Hayes rolls his eyes, making me giggle, and he answers for me. "I'm her pipe dream."

I whine playfully. "Oh my God, let it go."

"Absolutely not," Hayes tells me. "That knowledge does wonderful things for my ego."

"I'm sure it does, but your ego is big enough. It really doesn't need anything else."

Marc chuckles as he watches us, then leans over the counter as Hayes goes back to what he was doing. "What are you looking at that shithole for?"

Hayes's head drops and he groans. "Well, that rules out that place."

Closing out of that tab, it only takes a glance at the next one to rule out that one also. There is nothing about boarded up windows with graffiti and a cemetery in the background that screams *buy me.*

"Care to fill me in?" Marc presses.

Hayes leans back in his seat. "Did my mom tell you that the drunk bastard kicked the bucket?"

Marc's eyes widen for a moment, but he shakes it off as he snorts. "She told me he passed away, yes."

"Well, I got some money out of it. Turns out, his gambling ended up being good for something after all," he tells him. "Cam and I are going to open a bar with it."

"A bar?" Marc looks intrigued. "What kind of bar? A biker bar? A speakeasy? What are we talking about here?"

Hayes shakes his head. "No, nothing like that. I can't fully explain it, but I've had this picture in my head since I was younger, of this bar. Just a laidback beach bar. Nothing crazy, but a good place to go after a day of surfing or fishing."

Marc nods as he follows along, but then his expression turns concerned. "Do you know what is entailed in all of that?"

"What do you mean?"

"I *mean* you can't just buy a place and open up a bar," he explains. "There are things you need to do. Steps you need to take. Have you been looking at places where opening a bar is allowed? Making sure it's a decent distance away from any already existing bars and restaurants?"

Hayes's brows furrow. "Yes? The realtor is briefed on all that. She's taking care of it."

"And what about zoning and planning? Permits? You're not twenty-one yet. How would you secure a liquor license?"

Suddenly, it's starting to feel like I'm in the middle of a firing zone. And judging by the way Hayes's shoulders tense, he's feeling it too.

"My birthday is like a month away," he answers. "We wouldn't be ready to open before that anyway. But why are you giving me the third degree?"

"Because if I'm going to help you with this, I want to be sure you know what you're getting into," Marc says. He turns to glance around the surf shop. "This place up to your standards, princess?"

Hayes isn't even bothered by the nickname. "The surf shop?"

Marc's head whips over to us. "You mean this isn't a Chuck-E-Cheese? Yes, the surf shop, dipshit."

As Hayes taps my leg, we both get up. He walks around to the other side of the counter and leans back against it, crossing his arms over his chest.

"It's definitely big enough," he acknowledges. "And the location couldn't be better. But are you sure you want to close the shop?"

Marc pats Hayes on the shoulder. "Son, I've been playing with the idea of closing this one ever since we opened the new one over a year ago. The only reason I left it open was because of you."

I've always heard about the bond these two have, and how Marc stepped up when Hayes's dad walked out. There were rumors at one point that he was hooking up with Hayes's mom, but nothing ever became of that. Standing here, though, and seeing how supportive he is of Hayes firsthand, it makes me glad that Hayes has someone like Marc in his life.

"How about this," Marc says. "You think about it. Talk it over with Cam. Do whatever you have to do. And the three of us will get together Wednesday afternoon to discuss the details."

Hayes nods. "All right. Yeah, that sounds good. Thanks, Marc."

"I'll see you then," he tells him, then turns to me. "It was nice meeting you."

"You too," I reply.

His eyes land on Hayes again and he nods toward me. "Close up early and take her out to dinner."

Chuckling, Hayes nods. "You got it, boss."

Marc walks out the door and Hayes goes back to looking

around the surf shop—no doubt picturing it all in his head. I come closer and slide my arm around his waist. My head rests against his chest and he mindlessly presses a kiss into my hair.

Thank God for Marc and finally getting my boyfriend back.

Hayes
CHAPTER EIGHT

THERE'S SOMETHING CALMING ABOUT DRIVING down the street with Laiken's feet up on the dash as she sings along to the radio. Most of the time, she's even better than whoever the song belongs to. I wonder if she would be opposed to replacing every song in my music library with her singing it.

I pull into her driveway, and she hops out of the truck, coming around to the driver's side while I shoot a text to Cam. Today is our meeting with Marc. We spent the last two days going over all the possibilities, and it'll take more work than we originally thought, but it's definitely an opportunity we don't want to pass up.

"I'm so tired," Laiken says as she leans against the door. "Seriously, I'm feeling the lack of sleep today."

I chuckle, remembering everything from last night. My mom was at work, and I may or may not have bribed Devin into sleeping elsewhere. It had been too long since we were able to get lost in each other. And I don't think there is a single surface in my room that we didn't take complete advantage of.

"Regretting it?" I ask.

She rolls her eyes. "You know I don't. But I *am* going to take a nap while you and Cam are at your meeting."

The thought of lying next to her and getting some more rest is so tempting. I certainly didn't get any more sleep than she did. I shut off each one of the five alarms I had set, but when Laiken took matters into her own hands—*and mouth*—I was up in both mind and body.

My head falls back against the seat. "Mmm, can I join you?"

"I wish," she replies. "But *you* have a deal to make. And besides, with you in my bed, I don't think we'd get any sleep."

I unbuckle my seatbelt. "Yep. I'm not going. I'll tell Marc I'm sick."

Her whole face lights up as she laughs, just in time for Cam to come out. He walks around to the passenger side and climbs in. We had discussed him meeting me there, but this way, we can go over everything on the way there.

"What's up?" he greets me then frowns. "Why do you look like shit?"

Laiken covers her mouth with her fist while I pinch my lips together. "Yeah, you don't want me to answer that."

His face falls, and that bleach idea is probably looking real good to him right now. "Oh, for fuck's sake."

Turning to Laiken, I give her a tired smile. "All right, we should get going."

"Good luck," she tells me, and then she arches up to kiss me through the window, only for Cam to whimper. She breaks the kiss and stares blankly at him. "You do know you're an actual child, right? *Yuck, cooties.*"

"All girls *do* have cooties," he jokes, then immediately whips his head over to me. "Say a single word and I'll fuck you up, Wilder."

My mouth slams shut as he stops the words before they come out. Laiken goes for one more kiss and I throw my hand over Cam's eyes while my lips meet hers.

"Love you," I murmur.

She smiles. "Love you, too."

As she heads inside, Cam starts looking through the glove box and then over to the center console. I watch him for a second until it dawns on me that this isn't his car.

"The fuck are you doing?" I question.

He keeps searching around. "There has to be something I can shove into my eye sockets around here somewhere."

I snort, shaking my head as I put the truck into reverse and pull out of the driveway.

IF YOU SAW MARC on an average day, you would think he's just some surf bum who has never held a steady job. His long hair is pushed out of his face and he is constantly wearing a pair of shorts and a half buttoned shirt. But pulling up to his house, I'm reminded of just how rich he is.

See, he doesn't just own Wax and Waves, which has four different locations from here to the top of the state, mind you. Believe it or not, Wax and Waves was his passion project. Something he did to feel closer to the ocean again, since he grew up surfing. His main income earner is a string of coastal cuisine restaurants that stretches all the way up the coast.

"Goddamn," Cam says with a whistle. "This place is massive."

I hum as I put the truck in park and turn it off. "This is his vacation house."

"Can he adopt me?" he jokes.

We both climb out and climb the ten concrete steps to the front door. As we press the doorbell, the tune of "Somewhere Over the Rainbow" by Israel Kamakawiwo'ole fills the house. Seriously, I don't think he does anything small.

"Hey, guys," Marc says as he opens the door. "Come on in."

He leads us through the house and into the backyard, where his own personal oasis looks like a tropical vacation. Cam may be onto something. I wonder if he would adopt *me*.

"Have a seat." He gestures toward the two seats with contracts in front of them. "Did you get a chance to talk it over?"

I nod. "We did, and we agreed that the surf shop is the perfect place for the bar we want to open, if you're still offering it."

"I am, but I'm also offering something else." He folds his hands on his lap. "Being in the hospitality industry, I have knowledge and expertise that could be invaluable to you. There's a lot that goes into something like this, and if you don't know what you're doing, it's easy to end up in over your head."

"We'd definitely appreciate the guidance," Cam confirms, and I nod in agreement.

Marc smiles. "I'm prepared to offer you one better. Hayes, you have come a long way since the troubled kid I first met. And over the years, you've become a cherished member of my family. I hope you know that."

"I do," I tell him. "And I'm grateful for everything you've done for me and my family."

The underlying meaning is only received by him, and he smiles as he realizes that I know. It's a secret he and my mom would never let get out, but when my dad first left, my mom almost lost the house. I remember seeing the foreclosure notices come in the mail. And then one day, they just stopped, and everything was fine. I thought she had just managed to catch up on things with some extra overtime. It wasn't until I was older that I learned it was Marc.

He paid off my mother's mortgage, making sure we kept a roof over our heads. And he did so while asking for nothing in return. Because of that, the man sitting in front of me will always have the utmost respect from me.

"Anytime," he says, then gets back to business. "I made a few calls and did my due diligence, and this is what I'm willing to do. I will *give* you the surf shop—my gift for you taking such good care of it over the years. But I'd like you to consider taking me on as a silent partner while you two get this started.

"The legalities of this sort of thing can be overwhelming, and I'm afraid your age will make people try to take advantage or dick you guys around. I already have most of the right pieces in place, and I'm willing to take the brunt of the setup costs. You two will be responsible for the renovations. This is *your* vision, after all. But if you do end up running short, let me know and we will reevaluate terms."

I'm not seeing a single flaw in the deal. Ever since he drilled me with questions the other day, I've been doing more research on it, and the legalities involved look like a pain in the ass. You wouldn't hear a single complaint out of me about not needing to deal with it.

"Why do I feel like we're on an episode of *Shark Tank*?" Cam quips. "What's the catch?"

Marc chuckles and shrugs. "No catch. I had to work my way to where I am today, and while I think it taught me a lot, there's something to be said about giving a couple young men the support they deserve."

"So, what? We'd each own a third of the bar?" I ask.

"No, I don't want to be that involved," he answers. "The

only thing I'd like in return is ten percent of the profits for the first year. After that year, I will sign the bar over to the both of you. I just want to be able to keep an eye on things for the first year. But this is your business. Your venture. I'm just the helping hand."

I turn to my left to look at Cam, and he grins back at me.

"I think you have yourself a deal," I tell Marc.

He looks happy with our answer. "Great. I really believe in you both. In front of you are the contracts just stating the terms, so we can get things moving. Read them over. If you feel you want to have a lawyer look at them, please do so."

I snicker as I pick up the small packet. "I don't think that'll be necessary."

Everything is cut and dry anyway. It's not filled with a bunch of complex words I've never heard before. It basically just states everything he explained to us. And when I sign my name on the line, I take a picture and send it to Laiken.

"I'm looking forward to this," Marc tells me as I hand him the signed contract. "I think you're really going to thrive, and it'll be a sight to see."

"Thank you," I reply. "Seriously. I really appreciate you."

He tears up as he nods. "You're a great guy, Hayes. You were just dealt a couple shitty cards."

"Can't argue with you there," I chuckle.

Cam gets done reading everything over and signs his copy before handing it to Marc. They shake hands as Cam thanks him as well.

"We're all set," Marc says. "Put a sign on the door of the surf shop stating that the location is closed with the address for the nearest Wax and Waves. And I'll send a crew over there tomorrow to get the merchandise out of there so you guys can get started."

We both nod, thanking him again. He's given us an amazing opportunity, and we're both grateful for it.

After we say goodbye, Cam and I walk out of Marc's house with smiles on our faces. I know the whole ride home is going to be spent going over all the different ideas, but as I see Laiken's text telling me how happy she is for us, last night plays through my mind once more, and I come up with an idea of my own.

THE EXCITEMENT RUNNING THROUGH my veins is better than adrenaline. I've spent most of my life just trying to get through to the next day, but for the first time, I feel like I have something to look forward to. And it's only going to get better from here.

Cam and I walk into his house, and as we enter the kitchen, my eyes land on Laiken. She has her hair pulled back and she's dressed in an oversized t-shirt and a pair of loose shorts. It's such a casual, don't-give-a-fuck look, but she still manages to take my breath away.

She takes a step toward me, but her eyes stay on her brother. "I'm going to kiss him, so if you're going to whine about it, I suggest you look away."

He mocks her and flips her off before giving me an up nod. "I'll catch you later."

The second he goes up a few steps and turns the corner, Laiken jumps into my arms, pressing her lips to mine in a bruising kiss. "I am so fucking proud of you."

"I couldn't have done it without you," I tell her honestly.

She hums. "Totally not true, but I'll take it."

Kissing her once more, I put her down. "I can't stick around. I have to go down to the shop and put a sign on the door. But I was wondering if you have any plans tomorrow."

She squints and looks up toward the ceiling. "I don't think so. Why?"

"I want to take you somewhere. Can you be ready by nine?"

Surprise takes over her features. "Nine? In the morning? Do I get to know what's getting you out of bed that early?"

I shake my head. "Nope."

She pouts but I lean forward and press a quick kiss to her lips. I turn around and go to leave, when something dawns on me, and I glance back at her.

"Do you want to go for a ride?"

Her grin widens as she bites on the tip of her thumb. "In your truck or on you?"

And that's all I need to hear before I walk over and pick her up, throwing her over my shoulder as she squeals.

SURPRISES HAVE NEVER REALLY been my thing. I'm not good at coming up with them, and even when I do, I manage to let something about it slip before it happens. But this time I got lucky. Only needing to keep the secret for less than a day is manageable.

I had planned on picking Laiken up in the morning, but being as she slept at my place again, I had to bring her back to hers to change instead. I offered to take her out to breakfast, but when we noticed no one was home, I opted to eat her instead.

The diner's choices just don't compare.

Now we're in my truck, and as my phone tells me we're getting close, I'm starting to get nervous. What if this was a stupid idea? What if she doesn't want anything to do with this? What if she thinks I'm insane for bringing her along?

I see the sign outside of the house, and the realtor's car parked in front. I pull up behind her as Laiken looks around.

"H?" she asks. "What are we doing here?"

An anxious smile stretches across my face. "Well, with the deal Marc made us, I have a decent amount of extra money, and I was thinking about buying my own place with it."

She bites her lip as she thinks about the exact same thing I did when I got the idea. "Do that. You should definitely do that."

My nerves settle in an instant. "I'd really love to have your input."

Her head turns to look at the house and then back to me. "This is going to be fun."

We get out of the car and I introduce Ramona, my realtor, to Laiken. Ramona begins briefing us on the property as she leads us to the front door, only for Laiken to add her two cents.

"Did he make sure to tell you that a dishwasher is a requirement?"

I stick my tongue in my cheek as I roll my eyes. And as

Ramona walks through the door, I put my arm around Laiken's waist and tickle her side.

Leave it to her to keep me humbled.

TURNS OUT HOUSE SHOPPING is even harder than bar shopping. The first one we saw was way too big. It was pretty, don't get me wrong, but the moment Laiken mentioned that someone could sneak in and live on the other side of the house and I'd probably never know about it, I ruled it out.

At the second, I didn't even want to go inside. There was no yard, front or back, and the house was placed way too close to the busy road we were parked on. I would never be able to sleep if I had to listen to cars whizzing by all night.

With each house we see, I take a mental note of Laiken's reaction. The look on her face when we pull up, and again when we walk through the front door. Every single thing she says gets tucked away like there's going to be a test on it later.

The third house shows promise. It's located in a nice neighborhood, and it's within walking distance to a few bars and restaurants. We step inside as Ramona opens the door, and the inside is probably the nicest we've seen. The living room has a fireplace, and the kitchen is right off it.

"This would make the *perfect* bachelor pad," Ramona tells me.

The moment the words leave her mouth, I know I'm going to get shit for them. Sure enough, Laiken spins around and raises her brows at me.

"Do you *need* a bachelor pad?"

I chuckle at the jealousy in her tone. "Oh, definitely. With a stripper pole and everything."

I'm expecting her to flip me off or roll her eyes, but nothing prepares me for the way she purses her lips as if that's actually not a bad idea.

Such a fucking temptress.

THE FOURTH HOUSE TAKES the cake for the worst of it. Hands down. From the moment we walked in, something felt strange. The walls were painted black, and the carpet was all ripped up, leaving the subflooring exposed. But we looked around anyway for the fuck of it. And that's when we found *the door*.

You know in horror movies, when they're walking around the abandoned house, and they see something that looks like it could be a door but it's not supposed to be? Yeah, it was one of those. Maybe we should have considered the fact that Ramona decided to stay in the living room while we looked around, but the moment a cold chill ran over us both as we stared at the door, we booked it out of there.

I PULL UP TO the final house of the day, and Laiken gasps as she sees it. The large porch is similar to the one she has at home, and the cedar shakes give it that homey look. I can already tell this is going to be her favorite.

"This one is a little higher than the price range you sent me, but it's too beautiful not to show," Ramona says.

The moment we walk through the door, I feel at home. It's two stories, with the living room being right inside the front door. There's a fireplace with a mantel that Laiken falls in love with, rubbing her fingers along it as she admires its beauty. The kitchen is a good size and features a large island in the center.

"Look!" Laiken says. "It has one of those racks to hang your pots and pans."

I smile at her excitement. "There's just one problem. You can't reach that."

Her eyes narrow as she glares at me, only to hoist herself onto the island and touch it just for the sake of proving me wrong.

There's a bathroom downstairs, along with one of the bedrooms, but the main suite and two more bedrooms are upstairs. Laiken looks around, talking about how much potential this place has and all the things I could do with it, while I stare out the window at the large yard.

I'm not sure this house has any flaws, other than the price. It's close enough to everything and big enough for us to have a family in one day. We may not be buying this house together, but that doesn't mean we can't end up spending our lives here. Besides, if she's going to be over all the time, she needs to like it.

But the *bachelor pad* is also still an option, and it's within the price range that I wanted to pay. I'm sure if Ramona hadn't made that comment, Laiken would have loved it. She seemed interested when we first walked in, anyway.

All I know is I have a lot to consider.

AFTER A DAY FULL of looking at house after house, we're famished. There's a place that Laiken has wanted to try but hasn't because it's a little off the grid, but we're only twenty minutes away from there so we decide to go. And I won't lie; the food is great, but that's not what has my attention.

As I sit across from Laiken, listening to her talk and getting lost in the sound of her voice, I can't help but think about our relationship. We've come so far in such a short amount of time. From games of cat and mouse, to sneaking around, to hitting rock bottom. It was all worth it because it got us here—where I can reach across the table and hold her hand just for the fuck of it.

There's a glint in her eyes as she tells me about the song she's been working on. That's one of the things I love about her. She's so passionate about the things she cares about. The kind of person where if you're lucky enough to have her attention, you hold onto it with everything you've got. I'm just glad that I realized the mistake I was making before it was too late.

I'd never be able to forgive myself if I lost her forever.

I've always heard that age-old saying, the one that says *when you know, you know*. Honestly, I used to think it was just bullshit that people said to buy into the whole idea of love. But sitting here, looking at her now, I realize they're right. You just fucking know.

And I know without a fraction of a doubt that I will spend the rest of my life loving the woman sitting across from me.

As she excuses herself to go to the bathroom, I take out my phone and send a text to my realtor.

> Put in an offer on the last house. Take 15k off asking.

Her response shows she was waiting for my message.

> To be honest, you could offer lower than that and they would probably take it, but there is another offer on the table.

Yeah, that's not going to work for me.

> I don't want to risk losing it. 10k off asking and tell them I'll pay cash.

> Okay, but that's still higher than you originally wanted to spend. Even higher with the closing costs.

Chapter 8

I picture the look on Laiken's face as we pulled up, and the way she was in awe of the inside. I can see it all. The two of us sharing the same space, raising a family and growing old together in the house Laiken fell in love with from the moment she saw it. And I want it all.

I don't care. Do it anyway.

Laiken
CHAPTER NINE

HAVE YOU EVER FELT LIKE YOU'RE ON TOP OF THE world? Like everything is going exactly the way you want it to and you're loving it, but in the back of your head you're waiting for the other shoe to drop? I mean, things can't possibly be *this* good, can they?

I walk out of the restaurant with Hayes's hand in mine, and honestly, I couldn't be happier. Buying his own house has the ability to change things for us. Make it so we don't have to find a place to be alone or bribe his sister to leave the house for the night. All day today, as we looked at different houses, I couldn't stop picturing cooking breakfast together in the kitchen and watching movies in the living room, curled up on the couch. And it made me realize how perfect everything really is right now.

Hayes walks around to the passenger side of his truck and opens the door for me. It's such an antiquated gesture, but it still makes me smile.

I hum teasingly. "Maybe chivalry isn't dead, after all."

Wrapping my arms around his neck, I pull him down for a kiss. My tongue dances with his. I can still taste the beer on his tongue—courtesy of his fake ID. As I lace my fingers into his hair and tug just slightly, he pins me to the side of the truck. And the moan that leaves my mouth when he grinds against me reveals just how much I want him.

He groans and breaks the kiss. "There's nothing chivalrous about what's going through my mind right now."

"Ugh, same." But then I get an idea, and I look up at the night sky. "I wonder how pretty the stars look from our beach right now."

For a second, he looks up, until the underlying meaning dawns on him and he smirks. "Get in the truck before I fuck you right here in the parking lot."

"I mean, that's an option, too." Less wait.

He chuckles, grabbing me by the waist and lifting me up to put me in the truck. "You know, I was kidding at the time, but I'm really starting to wonder if you have a voyeurism kink."

I pretend to think about it for a moment, then scrunch my nose. "I'm far too possessive to let any other woman see you like that."

"That's my girl."

He kisses me once more, and I spin to put my feet in the truck before he closes the door.

Hayes drives in the direction of our beach while I let my hand hang out the open window. The breeze blows my hair out of my face as I rest my head on my arm. I can feel him glancing over at me every now and then, and I know that this is true happiness.

I'm so damn blessed.

My phone vibrates in my pocket. Then again. And again. Confusion overtakes me as it doesn't stop and I pull it out expecting a phone call, but instead, I'm faced with an onslaught of incoming texts and voicemails.

"That's weird," I murmur. "I must not have had any reception in that restaurant."

Hayes looks concerned. "Is everything okay?"

"I'm not sure yet."

The texts are from a mix of both Mali and Cam. I open Mali's first.

> Hey. Any chance you're back from your surprise date?
>
> Guess not. Let me know when you get this.
>
> Lai, I really need you to come pick me up if you can.
>
> Would it be weird if I call your brother? It would, right?
>
> I need you.

She left a voicemail in between the third and fourth text, which means whatever's going on, it's not good. Mali is rarely the type to ever ask for help. She says it'll damage her badass reputation.

I switch to the texts from Cam.

> Where are you?
>
> I'm on my way to get Mali, but why the fuck aren't you and Hayes answering your phones?
>
> JFC. You have your phone glued to you at all times and this is the time I can't reach you?
>
> WHEN YOU SEE THIS, GET TO THE FUCKING HOUSE. NOW.

Dread flows through me as I read his messages getting progressively more urgent. And when I switch to the voicemails, it only gets worse.

"Hey Lai. I don't really know where you are, but if you see this, I need you to come pick me up. I'm at a party at Heather's and I just

really don't want to be here anymore. I'll fill you in more when I talk
to you, but yeah. Just call me back."

There aren't many times I've heard Mali sound nervous.
She's normally a headstrong, scared-of-nothing firecracker.
But something in her voice sounds off to me.

The only two left are from Cam, and he never leaves
voicemails—or calls me for that matter. He's more of the text
or nothing type.

"Dude, I swear to God, now is not the time to go missing. When
you get this, fucking call me. Better yet, tell H to call me."

I get to the last one and goosebumps spread across my
skin as I hear Mali crying in the background.

"Shit. Where the fuck are you guys? You need to answer your
goddamn phones! No one has sex for this fucking long!"

The message cuts out, and in any other circumstance, I'd
probably find the sex comment funny, but not in this one. I
look over at Hayes with nothing but fear in my eyes.

"Your seatbelt is buckled, right?" he asks, and I nod.
"Good. Hold on."

My back gets pressed into the seat as he sinks the gas
pedal into the floor. The roar of the engine is louder than I've
ever heard it, but all I can focus on is the fear in my brother's
voice and the sound of Mali crying in the background.

THE TRUCK HARDLY COMES to a complete stop
before I'm jumping out and running inside. Hayes is right

behind me as we burst through the front door. I check each room as I run through the living room and the kitchen, but there's no one there. Cam's Jeep was in the driveway when we got here, so that can only mean one thing.

I take the stairs two at a time and barge into my brother's room, finding him and Mali sitting on his bed. My best friend is curled into a ball with tear-stained cheeks. She lunges and wraps her arms around me tightly.

"I'm sorry," she sobs. "I'm so fucking sorry."

My brows furrow and my eyes meet Hayes's as he stands in the doorway. Neither one of us have any idea what she's apologizing about. But I'm guessing the angry look on Cam's face has something to do with it.

"Wait. What the fuck happened to your hand?" Hayes snaps.

Huh? Mali cries harder as my attention turns to Cam's right hand, and the icepack sitting on top of it. It's then that I notice the blood on his shirt.

"Cam!" Hayes yells when he doesn't answer.

But he doesn't respond then either. He just keeps his eyes trained on Mali, like Hayes and I aren't even here.

"Okay," I say softly, not trying to make an already tense situation worse. "Mal, baby. I need you to breathe, okay?"

I feel as she shakes her head against me. "C-can't. You're going to hate me."

"I could never hate you. Not ever. But I need to know what's going on, and I can't until you calm down, so you have to breathe."

Hayes and I share a nervous look, and I run my hand through Mali's hair. It takes a few minutes, but she finally manages to control her breathing—with the exception of a few hiccups. I sit her on the bed and bend down in front of her, wiping the tears and the makeup from under her eyes.

"What happened?" I ask.

She looks over at Cam and then back to me. "I, uh...I went to a party. Heather was throwing a small one for her boyfriend's birthday, and it sounded like a good idea. And it was, at first. Everyone was drinking and having a good time, but then they started playing beer pong and I didn't have a partner, so Isaac offered to join me."

The moment his name comes out of her mouth, I have a better idea where this is going, and I can't say I like it. But I need to know what would make Cam snap the way he must have to need an icepack on his hand.

"He was fine in the beginning," she continues. "A little flirty, but that's how he is. It was obvious he was hoping to hook up. He kept trying to put his arm around me and hold my hand. But I figured he was just drunk and gently shrugged him off or pretended like I needed my hand for something else."

Cam's knee starts to bounce as he listens to her. Whatever he did to Isaac didn't get even half his rage out. And as Mali opens her mouth to keep going, Hayes stops her.

"Hang on a second," he says, pulling his air pods and his phone out of his pocket, then handing them to Cam. "Put these in."

Cam shakes his head. "No, I'm okay."

"I wasn't asking," he shoots back.

It's obvious that Cam doesn't want to. He wants to hear every word she says, down to every last detail of what happened. But his probation makes this a more fragile situation than it would usually be.

"Cam," Mali says, and I watch my brother's eyes soften as he looks at her. "It's okay. Put in the earbuds."

That manages to get through to him, and I could chalk it up to him being just as protective of her as he is of me, but I don't think I'm naive enough to believe that. Still, that's a topic for another time. Right now, my best friend needs me.

Hayes gives me the go-ahead once he presses play and Cam's ears fill with music.

"Okay," I tell Mali. "So, he kept trying and you were rejecting him as gently as you could…"

She nods. "It got to the point where it was uncomfortable, and I told him I was feeling a little lightheaded. That I needed to go sit down. I walked away from him and sat on the couch in her back room for a minute, and that's when I tried calling and texting you, but then he came over with a drink and handed it to me. He said that he was worried about me and said I just need to relax."

The further she gets into the story, the more upset she gets. Tears begin flowing down her cheeks, and her bottom lip quivers. It breaks my heart seeing the strongest person I know be brought down to this.

"I wouldn't drink from the cup he gave me," she confesses, and I feel slightly relieved. "I'm smarter than that. I mean, everyone has always taught us that you don't take a drink from *anyone* at a party. And the more he kept pushing me to drink it, the more convinced I was he had put something in it. I don't know what, but there was definitely some type of drug in it."

Hayes's jaw clenches. "I'm going to fucking kill him."

"*You* are going to stay right where you are," I demand and then turn my attention to Cam, who has his eyes closed but his knee is still bouncing. "Besides, we're not even sure Cam didn't do that himself."

Mali cries harder. "I'm sorry. If I had known that Cam was going to go after him, I never would have—"

"Hey, hey," I tell her, shaking my head. "No. You have nothing to apologize for here. You hear me? Not a single thing."

"But if he gets caught, he'll go to prison," she argues.

"He'll get arrested for violating his probation, and it's all my fault."

I'm not going to sit here and let her take the blame for this. "No, Mal. This was Isaac's fault. He should have gotten the hint the moment you first pushed him away. And if I had gotten your call and wasn't close enough to get to you fast enough, I would've sent Cam myself anyway. Okay? You did nothing wrong." She swallows harshly as she nods. "He didn't…"

I can't even manage to get the words to come out of my mouth. They're too much. Too heartbreaking. And if she tells me he did, Cam is the last person any of us will have to worry about because I'll be on trial for murdering everyone at the party for not stopping it.

Defendant: Laiken Blanchard.

Crime: Mass Homicide.

Plea: Guilty and not at all sorry.

But thankfully, Mali shakes her head. "He didn't get that far, but he kept trying. I had pretended to take a sip so he would stop harping on me to drink, and I guess he thought it was only a matter of time before it kicked in." She pauses to take a deep breath, exhaling shakily. "H-he started kissing my neck and I tried to push him away, but he's so much bigger than I am. I couldn't get him to move. And when I said no—that I didn't want to do anything with him—he told me I just needed to calm down. That he'd make me feel good. And his hand kept sliding up my leg. I pressed my thighs together, but that didn't stop him.

"I finally managed to shove him off me and called for Heather. He wasn't very happy about that. He put his hand over my mouth and told me to shut the fuck up. And then he grabbed my boob, and he squeezed it as hard as he could."

My eyes move down to her chest. Her tank top isn't super

low cut, but I can see the hint of finger shaped bruises starting to form.

"I knew if I didn't get out of there, he was going to do it. He was going to rape me and there wasn't a damn person around that would stop him. He started telling me that he knows I've always secretly wanted him, and that trying to tell him I don't makes me a tease. He didn't care that I was crying at this point, or that I was constantly trying to fight him off. There was no talking sense into him. So, I did the only thing I could.

"I reached back and grabbed the lamp behind me, and I slammed it as hard as I could into his head. I don't know if it cut him. There was no sticking around to find out. I could just hear him shouting and calling me a bitch as I ran as fast as I could out of the house."

It's definitely a relief that he didn't manage to get any further, but that doesn't mean she's not broken. Sexual assault doesn't have to be rape for it to cause trauma.

"The second I got outside, I threw up. But I had no way to leave. I'd been drinking, and I was way too emotional to drive, so I called Cam. He was right down the street and said he would be there in a second. I was so fucking relieved when he pulled up, but when he saw me, his eyes went dark. That's when I realized how disheveled I looked. My tank top was pulled down on one side, and I was crying.

"He asked me what happened, and I wasn't going to tell him. I said that I just wanted to go home. But then Isaac stumbled out of the house and took one look at both of us and laughed. He mumbled something about us being a match made in hell and that Cam should be careful because I'm scrappy. And that's when Cam followed him back into the house."

From what I've heard so far, there's not a single part of me that is mad at my brother. He did what any half-decent guy would. And even if there are consequences from it, I wouldn't expect even a hint of an apology out of him.

"Mali," I say as she cries. "I need a yes or no answer here, okay? Is Isaac still alive?"

She stares back at me, absolutely terrified. "I don't know."

And that's when the flood gates open.

Every part of her that was trying to stay strong, shatters in that moment. She falls forward, hitting the ground and crumbling into my lap as she cries. I have no choice but to watch helplessly as she scratches at her skin in an attempt to scrub herself of his touch.

I don't even notice Cam has moved until he's by my side and on his knees—the air pods long forgotten on the bed. He looks just as powerless as I feel as his hands hover over her. He doesn't want to touch her, in case she doesn't want that, but he needs to do something.

"Cam." Hayes gets his attention. "Did you kill him?"

My brother looks over at me and then back to his best friend. "No."

Hayes and I exhale in unison. So, we're not looking at murder charges here. If Isaac presses charges, Cam is looking at jail time—for both the original assault *and* this one. But at least he's not potentially facing spending the rest of his life behind bars.

His gaze lands on Mali, and I swear I see a part of him break. "But I should have."

MALI FINALLY MANAGES TO fall asleep in my bed. I helped her take a shower and gave her pajamas to wear, ones that are light enough not to hurt after she scrubbed her skin raw. She's definitely not okay, but how could she be?

I drape a blanket over her and turn around to see Hayes leaning in my doorway. He was responsible for keeping an eye on Cam while I took care of Mali. I needed him to find out exactly what happened when Cam went in that house.

"She okay?" he asks.

Glancing back at my best friend, I can feel her sadness like it's my own. "No, but I'm hoping she will be. In time." I force my eyes away from her and run my fingers through my hair. "How's Cam?"

"Homicidal," he answers, and I know it's not even an exaggeration. "He said that he was unconscious when he left and beaten pretty badly, but they got out of there before the cops came. Apparently, no one at the party even tried to keep Cam from killing him. He probably would have if Mali hadn't come in and begged him to stop."

The weight of everything rests on my chest as I exhale. "Does it make me fucked up that I wish she hadn't?"

"No. I was thinking the exact same thing."

Hayes must be able to see when I need him because not even a single tear falls before he's pulling me into his arms. Mali is the greatest person I know. My absolute best friend. And as I watched her break down, she took a part of me with her.

My head rests against Hayes's chest as I cry, and he just lets me—pressing light kisses into my hair and rubbing his hand up and down my back. He knows I just need to get it out. That there's nothing we can do to help the closest people to us, and that sucks.

I force myself to calm down and pull away from him to dry my face. "Thanks."

He smiles sadly, leaning forward and kissing my forehead. "You staying in here?"

I nod. "Yeah. She needs me, and I think right now, I need her, too."

"Hey, you don't have to explain anything to me. I get it," he tells me. "I'll be in Cam's room. Wake me up if you need me."

"I will," I promise. "I love you."

"I love you, too."

As he heads down the stairs, I turn around and crawl into my bed, cuddling close to Mali. She panics for a second but then relaxes when she sees it's only me. Her eyes just start to fall closed again, as she murmurs softly.

"Don't let him hurt me."

I drape my arm over her. "Never. I promise."

SMASH ROOMS NEVER USED to make sense to me. The idea of going somewhere just to break a bunch of old shit felt pointless. Not to mention exhausting. But while the guys were going to start the renovations next week, Hayes decided Cam and Mali could use the outlet.

We stand in what used to be the surf shop, but now it's an empty building. Racks are still on the walls, and the counter is still there, but everything else is gone. Marc had all the merchandise moved to another location.

Now the renovation can begin.

Chapter 9

"I never realized how big it is," I say as I look around.

"That's what she said," Mali replies, and while it lacks the same enthusiasm that would normally come with it, it still shocks the hell out of all three of us.

We all turn to look at her. She's seemed somewhat okay today, but I don't know if that's real, or if she's pretending. Mali is the last person to let herself be the victim, so the latter would not surprise me.

"What?" she asks.

"Nothing," Cam and Hayes say in unison, but nope.

Not me. I'm not doing it.

"Are you good? Because you don't have to put on a brave face here. Not with us."

She hums, walking over and picking up the hammer off the counter. "Hayes brought me here to break shit. Trust me, I'm great right now. Though I won't be able to say the same for this counter in a minute."

We all watch as she swings the hammer right through the wood, the sound of it breaking echoing through the empty room. Then she does it again, as the counter splits into pieces she looks like she can breathe a little better.

I lean closer to Hayes. "That counter *was* going, right?"

He snorts. "If it wasn't, it is now."

There's a lot to be done, and no possible way to do it all in a short time. Not only is there the demolition—which includes breaking down part of a wall that was used to hang more boards and tearing up the floors to put down new ones—but there's also building the backroom he mentioned. This project is going to take weeks. But with the four of us, plus the occasional help of our friends, we should have this place ready to go by the end of fall.

"I'm going to go make sure they didn't leave anything upstairs," Hayes tells us.

My brows furrow. "Wait, what? There's an upstairs?"

"Yeah," he answers simply. "We've been using it as a storage room."

I look back at Cam and Mali, seeing them smashing away like it's their own personal playground, and my lips purse. "I'm coming with you."

It's no surprise I never knew there was a whole second level to this place. The stairs are tucked away toward the back and hidden behind a door. Honestly, I always just assumed it was a storage closet. But as we climb the stairs, I realize how much space is actually up here. It spans across half the building and even has its own bathroom.

"Damn," I say as I admire the empty space. "You could rent this thing out as an apartment if you wanted to."

Hayes hums skeptically. "As a studio, maybe. But that would require putting in a kitchen or letting them use the bar as one. And besides, I would *not* make a good landlord."

Okay, he has a point. "Fair enough."

We step into the bathroom to make sure everything has been cleared out, and right before we head back down, I stop and turn to Hayes.

"Do you think she's okay?" I ask him. "Like, *genuinely* okay?"

"Mali?" he replies, and I nod. "I mean, she looks like it to me, but you know her better than anyone."

"I know I do, and I can't shake this feeling in my gut like I should be worried about her. I *am* worried about her. Last night was...intense."

He exhales slowly, pulling me in for a hug. "You're allowed to be worried. She's your best friend, and she went through something that has the power to change her. But Mali is one of the strongest people I know. I don't see her letting herself be a victim."

That's definitely all true, but I still feel uneasy about it. "I just want her to be all right."

"She will be," he promises. "And in the meantime, we'll keep an eye on her. Though personally, if I were Isaac, I'd be afraid of running into her while she's sober. That girl is ruthless."

I chuckle because he's right.

But there will be no sympathy from me for anything that happens to him.

ONE OF THE BEST parts of not having to hide anymore is being able to enjoy these bonfires while sitting on Hayes's lap. Sure, Cam had some complaints about it at first, whining like the child he is, but he got over it. Everyone else, however, keeps looking at us like we're some kind of circus act. And feeling like we're in a fishbowl isn't exactly pleasant.

"I still can't believe you two are together," Owen says.

Lucas obviously isn't too happy about it as he grumbles *fucking bullshit* under his breath.

"I'm still trying to figure out how long it was going on. How the hell did this even happen?" Aiden questions.

My lips press together in a thin line as Cam sarcastically looks at Hayes. "Yes, H. Tell me. How *did* you end up corrupting my innocent little sister?"

"Innocent?" Hayes scoffs. "She's practically corrupted *me* at this point."

Mali snorts, knowing everything that's gone on in the last couple months, but something tells me Cam isn't looking for the dirty details. He's only looking to find out when it started so he can bitch again about how long we hid it from him.

Cam cringes. "Gross. I did not need to know that."

"You started it," Hayes quips. "But it was when I kissed her in front of Craig that shit changed a little. It didn't become a thing until I got kicked out of that hockey game, though."

"I fucking knew it!" Aiden shouts, putting his hand out to Owen. "Pay up, motherfucker."

"A bet? Really?" I deadpan.

Owen rolls his eyes as he passes Aiden a twenty and Aiden's grin widens. "I called that shit. Hayes doesn't give his jersey to *anyone*. I don't give a shit who you are."

Cam doesn't look impressed, or even slightly amused, but I think with the shock of it wearing off, he's becoming more accepting of it. At least, I hope he is.

"So, when you came over to talk about Laiken a month ago…" he starts.

Hayes finishes it for him with a nod. "I was trying to tell you."

My head whips toward him. "That's news to me."

If I had known that he was even considering telling Cam about us, I don't think I ever would have turned him down when he tried to get me back. There are no words to explain how badly I wanted to just fall right back into his arms. But I knew the pain I felt when he left all too well at that point, and I couldn't risk going through that again.

Instead of responding, he smiles sadly and half-shrugs. I know him well enough to know what's going through his mind right now. He's thinking about how he *didn't* tell Cam and how he left me instead. But none of that matters now because we got here eventually.

I put my hand over his and tap my thumb three times.

I. Love. You.

He smiles as he exhales and does four back on my leg.

I. Love. You. Too.

There are parts of our relationship we'll let others see, but there are some things we just want to keep to ourselves. To keep hidden and protected from everyone else. It's ours, and it's sacred.

I keep my eyes on Mali, watching closely as she seems to guard herself a bit. No one else is paying enough attention to see it, but there are little things she does that show me that while she's okay for the most part, she's still affected—like how it took her twice as long to decide to crack open a beer. Or how she gravitated toward Cam once the guys showed up.

But Hayes was right when he said she's strong, because if that were me, I'd probably still be curled up in my bed right now. Not Mali, though. She's a spitfire, and while I'll continue to keep an eye on her, I know she's going to be fine.

Owen's phone rings and he pulls it out of his pocket. "Hello?"

Everyone else goes back to normal conversation, but I notice the way he becomes concerned and looks toward the front of the house. It isn't until I see the two police cars pull in that I put it all together, and my heart sinks.

"Cam," I breathe.

We all stare as two cruisers come closer and the officers get out. There's a small, naive part of me that hopes it's a misunderstanding. That this isn't happening. But as they walk toward us, with one clutching a piece of paper in his hand, I know that's not the case.

"No," Mali pleads.

"Dude, you're a fucking dick for this," Owen says into the phone, but I'm too focused on the officers approaching.

"Cameron Blanchard?" one asks.

Cam sighs. "What can I do for you?"

He walks over to my brother. "For starters, you can stand

up and put your hands behind your back. We have a warrant."

Hayes's grip on me tightens as Cam stands up. Finding out he was arrested before was hard, but seeing it firsthand is one of my worst nightmares come to life. And judging by the look on Mali's face, she feels the exact same way.

The sound of the handcuffs breaks through the silence. "You're under arrest for the assault of Isaac Morrison."

He reads him his Miranda rights as my heart breaks inside my chest. Cam keeps his mouth shut, his eyes only meeting mine for a second as they start to take him away. He only says four simple words.

"I want a lawyer."

I can't do this. The further they get, the more I start to panic. I fight against Hayes's hold, finally managing to free myself, but before I can cross the yard, he catches me.

"He can't—" I shout. "They can't—"

Mali jumps in front of me as I struggle to get to Cam. "Laiken!"

"He's going to go to prison," I cry.

Tears build in her eyes, too. "I know. We're going to do everything we can to help him. But there is *nothing* you can do right now. Okay? We have to do this right, or we'll all end up in jail."

I feel like I'm breaking. Like my entire world is crashing down around me and all I can do is watch it fall. But her words manage to get through to me enough for me to stop fighting against Hayes's hold.

"I know what he did," Owen argues, still on the phone. "But this is a new kind of fucking low."

Hayes's body tenses up against me. "Is that Isaac?"

Owen doesn't even get a chance to respond before Hayes rips the phone right out of his hand, but the call ends immediately. The coward hung up. Hayes tosses it back to Owen and grabs one of the camping chairs—sending it flying.

"I'm going to kill that little bitch!" he growls, then turns to Owen. "I know he's your boy, but I swear to God, when I get my hands on him—"

"He's not," Owen corrects him. "Not after this. I can't believe he stooped that low."

"What the fuck are we going to do?" Lucas questions.

I wrap my arms around myself and lean into Mali. "You three are going to go home. Hayes will update you when he knows something. I have to call my parents and get to the police station."

"I'm coming with you," Hayes tells me as he lights up a cigarette.

"Me, too," Mali adds.

And I know there's nothing I could say that would change their minds.

Not a damn thing.

THE WAIT IS EXCRUCIATING. My parents were pissed, insisting that we stay outside while they go deal with this. Somehow, standing outside the police department and knowing Cam is in there is worse than waiting around at home. Every time the door opens, I find myself hoping he'll come walking out, but it never happens. And when my parents come back out with a lawyer, and without him, my stomach drops.

"What's going on?" I ask in a rush. "Is he okay? Is he coming home?"

My mom shakes her head sadly. "Not tonight, sweetie."

What? "Why not? We bailed him out last time."

"This time it's a little more complicated," the lawyer answers. "He violated probation, which means a judge isn't going to set a bail tonight. He will have a bail hearing within the next ten days, but until then, he has to stay in custody."

Hayes throws his head back, trying to take a deep breath but needing to walk away for a second to calm himself down. Meanwhile, Mali holds my hand tightly.

"How bad is it?"

The three of them share a look, like they don't want to answer, but my dad gives him approval to tell me anyway.

"Honestly, it's not good," the lawyer says. "This is his second assault in a short period of time, while he's still on probation for the first incident. It's going to be hard to prove to a judge that he's not the violent person this makes him look like he is."

"But it's his word against Isaac's, right?" Mali asks.

The lawyer frowns. "Afraid not. The police said there's a video the victim's brother took of Cam committing the assault. The case is airtight."

I swear to God, if I ever get ahold of Craig's phone, I'm going to shove it so far up his ass he'll have to hiccup to make a call.

Mali shakes her head rapidly. "But he was only doing it to defend me. Isaac...he..."

She can't seem to get the words out, no matter how badly she may want to, but they don't matter anyway.

"Trust me, I know what kind of people the Morrisons are," he says. "But unfortunately, there's no excuse for assaulting someone, as infuriating as that may be sometimes."

He goes on to tell us that we need to just sit tight and wait, but I don't see how that's possible. One of my favorite people in the world is sitting in a jail cell right now. Patience isn't exactly my strong suit on a normal day, let alone now.

I FEEL NUMB INSIDE. It's as if I'm watching my life play out, watching everything go wrong, but I can't move. I can't stop it from happening. The only thing I can do is watch and wait for a broken system to save my brother.

A system that nearly failed him the last time.

When we left my house, the three of us piled into Mali's car. I was shaken up, and Hayes was far too pissed to drive. But as Mali slams on her brakes in the middle of Main Street, I'm starting to wonder if we should have taken an Uber.

"Oh, hell no," she says, unbuckling her seatbelt and throwing the door open.

I don't even see what she's talking about at first. It isn't until I see her storming across the street that I see him. Isaac has definitely had better days. His face is covered in angry bruises and swollen so much I didn't even recognize him. But honestly, I think he's lucky that's all he got.

"Shit," I murmur.

Cars behind us honk as Hayes and I rush out onto the street. We don't even shut the doors as we rush to catch up to Mali. But we can't get there in time before she shoves him with all the strength she has.

"What the fuck is wrong with you?" she screams. "You know exactly what happened that night! You know that you deserve every fucking bit of what you got! But you just had to get him arrested, didn't you?"

Isaac snickers, and I have to grab Hayes's wrist to hold him back. As much as we love Cam, and as pissed as we are, this isn't our battle. It's hers. And she needs to do this.

"He did this shit to himself," Isaac argues.

Mali scoffs. "That's bullshit. I was drunk and you took advantage!"

He rolls his eyes. "Such a typical girl. Hook up with a guy and then regret it later so you cry sexual assault."

"Oh, fuck off!" she sneers. "You knew damn well I wanted nothing to do with you. But your ego just couldn't handle that, could it? Just like it couldn't handle getting kicked off the hockey team."

That strikes a nerve, and I watch as Isaac's jaw locks. "That was *my* fucking team, and he stole it from me. He deserved a little payback."

"So, you try to rape me to get it?" she roars.

"Keep your goddamn voice down," he snarls as he steps closer. "It wasn't even about you. Sure, you're hot, but you're way too much of a handful for me. I just wanted to fuck you so Cam could hear all about it. Rumor is he's had a thing for you for a while now, and I knew he would just *love* to know all about how I watched you come apart on my cock. Not nearly enough justice, but it would've pissed him off. But him spending the next few years in prison? That's so much better."

I can't see Mali's face, but when I see her fist clench at her side, I know exactly what's coming next. She rears back and punches him in the face, right on top of the bruises that intensify the pain of it.

Isaac stumbles back for a moment, then his eyes pin Mali with a vicious glare. "You're going to regret that."

She steps toward him. "What are you going to do? Press charges on me and have me arrested, too? Do it! I fucking dare you!"

But something tells me that isn't what he has in mind, and as he moves, so does Hayes. He steps in front of Mali and pushes her back before getting in Isaac's face. While Mali is much shorter, Hayes is his height as they square up against each other.

"Here's what's going to happen," Hayes growls. "You're going to get the fuck out of here. And I don't mean out of my face. I mean out of fucking town. You're going to take your little trust fund and you're going to leave because this is the only out you're going to get. If I see your face around here again, I'll slit your throat with the bottom of my skate and make it look like a goddamn accident."

Isaac stares back at him, but no matter how hard he tries to hide it, his fear is evident. He didn't stand a chance against Cam. Hayes could do more damage on a normal day, but when he's defending someone he cares about, I can't be sure that he's bluffing. And neither can Isaac as he steps back and walks away.

Hayes watches him leave for a moment and then turns around to march past us. "Let's go."

Mali and I start to follow him back to the car when she leans closer into me. "You're going to jump his bones tonight, aren't you?"

"Abso-fucking-lutely."

Hayes
CHAPTER TEN

THERE'S A SORT OF HELPLESSNESS THAT YOU FEEL when someone so close to you is hurt or in trouble. I felt it every night I listened to my mom cry after my dad left. I felt it when Devin finally broke down after realizing he was never coming back. And I feel it now, while Cam sits in prison and Laiken looks like she's aged ten years in the last few hours.

Her hair is piled on top of her head, and she looks like she wants to sleep, but she can't. None of us can. Instead of going back to her house, we got my truck and came to mine. It's the only place where we can figure out how to help Cam without worrying about someone hearing us.

"I'll press my own charges," Mali says.

Laiken shakes her head. "You couldn't even say what he did out loud tonight. You would have to relive that in front of an entire courtroom."

"I don't care," she spits back. "This is my fault."

"Mali," I warn, but it's too late.

Laiken glares at her best friend. "Say it's your fault one more time and I'm going to duct tape your mouth shut. You. Did. Not. Ask. To. Be. Assaulted."

"No, but I'm the one that called Cam."

"To get out of a dangerous situation!" Laiken snaps. "Stop beating yourself up for this! It's not doing anyone any good."

Chapter 10

Mali drops her head, and I can tell Laiken feels bad for yelling at her, but I've been watching her patience thin every time Mali says something self-degrading for the last few hours.

"Besides," I add. "Even if Isaac went to jail, it wouldn't get Cam out."

It's well past one in the morning when my phone vibrates, showing a text from Owen.

> What's going on? Any updates?

The girls toss a few more ideas back and forth as I type out my reply.

> He's stuck in jail until his bail hearing. Should be within the next week or so. It doesn't look good tho.

> Damn. That fucking blows. Is there anything we can do? You know we all have his back.

> Always, but I don't think so. We're trying to brainstorm now.

> Okay. Let me know if that changes. In the meantime, I'll let Coach know tomorrow that you and Cam won't be at practice.

"The lawyer said that Craig took a video, right?" Mali asks. "So, what if you pretend to be into him again? That way you could get his phone and erase the video."

That grabs my attention and I look up from my phone to glare at Mali. "If that motherfucker comes anywhere near her, *I'll* be in jail next to Cam."

Mali pouts. "Come on, you can't shut your inner caveman off for a second to help save your best friend?"

I chuckle humorlessly as I put my phone down. "Do you really think *Cam* would be on board for pimping his sister out to her sleazy ex?"

She grimaces, realizing she's got nothing. "Okay, I'll count that as a veto."

I go back to texting Owen, letting him know I appreciate it, when Mali curses under her breath. My brows raise as I watch her and Laiken gaze at each other as if they're having a silent conversation, and I am not in the loop.

"We can't," Laiken tells her.

Mali smiles sadly. "I can't think of any other option, can you?"

Running her hands over her face, Laiken groans. "No. Fuck!"

"Uh, one of you want to fill me in?"

They both look at me and then each other. I didn't know it was possible to feel so much like a third wheel while in a room with my own girlfriend. Whatever it is, they already know I'm not going to like it.

Mali holds her hands up. "You have to be the one to tell him. I got his best friend thrown in jail. I'm not his favorite person right now."

Laiken's head drops as she sighs, and when she turns it to the side to look at me, I realize I won't just *not like it*—I'm going to fucking hate it.

WE STAND IN THE very public park, with kids running around and moms bitching about other moms. Someone should really record this shit, then put them all in a room with a big screen and press play. They could sell tickets and popcorn. It could break the world record for the biggest catfight.

I lean against the picnic table, my arms crossed in front of my chest. If it were possible to trade places with Cam right now, I'd do it. Then again, depending how this goes, I may end up in there with him.

"H," Laiken says, resting her hand on my arm, but I can't look at her right now.

It's not that she did anything wrong. I know this is the only option we have that even has a chance at working. But that's what I hate most about it. It's not *her* I'm angry at—it's myself.

"He could have stayed home," Mali tells her.

I scoff. "And let her around him alone? Not a fucking chance."

"She's *not* alone. She has me," she argues.

"You're biased."

"Stop bickering," Laiken chastises us both. "I think that's him."

Turning my head, I see the one person I dislike more than Isaac coming toward us. The one person I never wanted to see walk back into our lives.

Montgomery fucking Rollins.

"Hey," Mali greets him with a hug.

"Hey, Mal," he replies.

When he goes to say hi to Laiken, he stops, and his eyes meet mine. I wait to see if he's going to try hugging her too, but he must have some sense of self-preservation because he nods his hello.

Moneybags put his thinking cap on today.

"Sorry for making you come out here," Monty says as he looks around. "I had to be sure this wasn't a setup so Hayes could jump me."

I snort, because if we weren't about to discuss my best friend's freedom, that's exactly what I would be doing. Laiken turns around and gives me a look, silently telling me to knock it off, and I roll my eyes.

"It's fine," she tells him. "I'm just grateful you're willing to help my brother."

"It's no problem. I'm happy to do what I can." He slides his hands into his pockets. "So, tell me what's going on."

"Cam was on probation for an assault case he should've never been charged for," Laiken explains. "He was just defending his satanic girlfriend at the time, and the guy was drunk. He got hurt, pressed charges against Cam, and Cam almost went to jail for it. Since being put on probation, he's done really well at staying out of trouble.

"But a guy Cam got kicked off the hockey team had a vendetta. He came onto Mali at a party a little…aggressively, and because of it, Cam beat the shit out of him. So, the cops showed up last night and arrested him for it."

"Ouch," Monty cringes and looks at Mali. "Are you okay?"

She hums. "I'd be better if Cam wasn't behind bars."

He nods. "Understandable."

"We thought it would just be his word against the other guy's, but apparently his prick of a brother recorded the whole thing," Laiken adds.

Mali scoffs. "What kind of person records his brother getting his ass kicked instead of helping him, anyway?"

"The kind who knew Cam was playing right into Isaac's hand," I answer. "They're both scumbags. They knew exactly what they were doing."

"That's what it sounds like," Monty agrees with me. "Well, for starters, from what I know about the legal system, our first goal is getting Cam out on bail. How is his representation?"

Laiken shrugs. "It's okay, but it's not great. My parents can only afford so much, and they're still paying off the legal fees from his previous case."

"Okay, well..." Monty pulls his phone out of his pocket. "First things first, I'm going to have my dad's lawyer take him on. I'll make sure his retainer is paid for, so you don't have to worry about it. He should be able to make sure Cam is granted bail, but are you going to need money for that also?"

"No," I answer before Laiken can. "I'll take care of paying his bail."

The realtor let me know last night that the owners of that house accepted my offer, but there are inspections and things that need to be done before I actually have to pay for it. Hopefully, that's enough time to get this shit dealt with. And if it's not, there will be other houses.

"Okay," he says. "I'll get on this and keep you updated. I know it's hard, but just keep your heads down and try not to get in any other trouble. I'll make sure he comes home soon."

Laiken sighs in relief. "Thank you, Monty. Really. You have no idea how much I appreciate it."

He smiles at her in a way that makes me want to knock him out. "It's the least I could do. I'm glad to see you two worked it out."

"I'm sure you are," I mutter under my breath, and Laiken smacks me lightly.

"Thanks again," Mali tells him. "I'll walk with you to your car."

As the two of them leave, Laiken turns to me, and she does *not* look happy.

"What?" I ask indignantly. "I hate that guy."

"I know you do, but do you really have to be such an ass?" she sasses. "He might be our only hope at keeping Cam out of prison for the next few years."

I stay quiet, not because I don't agree with her, but because I *do*. There is nothing I hate more than the fact that we had to turn to Monty for help with this. That there was nothing I could do, and everything he could. She needed a hero, and I couldn't be that for her. She has to get *Monty* to save her.

And for that, I hate him a little more.

I PULL UP IN front of the rink, and when she realizes I'm not parking in a spot, her brows furrow.

"You're not coming in?" she asks worriedly.

I shake my head. "Nah. I just have a couple things I need to take care of. But I'll see you after."

Her eyes bore into mine, like she's trying to figure me out. "Okay. I love you."

"I love you, too."

She gives me a quick kiss and then hops out of the truck to go to work. I watch her until she's out of sight, hating how I feel so useless right now. Once she's gone, I spin the truck around and pull out of the parking lot.

And later, as I spend four hours of her eight-hour shift

smashing shit at the old surf shop, I think about how I'll never forgive myself for failing her.

If he steals the only girl I've ever loved away from me, there's no telling what I might do.

Laiken
CHAPTER ELEVEN

No matter how hard I try, I can't seem to sit still. How can anyone stay calm when they're in a courtroom? The environment alone is enough to have you on edge. But with today being Cam's bail hearing, I don't stand a chance. Either I'm making excuses to have to walk around —like excusing myself to the bathroom so much it looks like I have a bladder infection—or I'm fidgeting while I sit.

"Someone should have brought a goddamn pop-it for her," Mali says.

Hayes reaches over and puts his hand on my knee. "You okay, babe?"

"I feel like I might throw up," I tell him. "Like projectile vomit all over everything."

He smirks. "You are so sexy right now. Keep talking dirty like that."

For the first time all morning, I laugh. It's soft, and it doesn't last long, but it's there. And Hayes smiles proudly, knowing he caused it.

"I hate you," I lie, and he winks at me.

But as he interlaces our fingers, it manages to calm me down a little. He has been my rock the last few days. He's always checking on me and making sure I've had something to eat or drink recently—because stress always manages to destroy my appetite. And the one night I came close to having a breakdown, he laid with me and watched Gilmore Girls for hours while running his fingers through my hair.

Honestly, I wonder if he knows how amazing he truly is.

"He's here," Mali tells me, and I turn around to see Monty walking in with Cam's new lawyer.

The man is middle-aged and looks professional in a suit that probably costs more than my car. He stops to talk to my parents while Monty comes over to us.

"Hey. How are you guys holding up?" he asks.

"Been better," I answer. There's no point in sugar coating shit.

He nods sadly. "Well, Brent is very good at his job. If all goes well, Cam should be home by this afternoon."

God, I hope so.

I didn't want to have to call Monty, especially knowing how much it would bother Hayes. But when it came down to it, he was the only option we had. Hayes even tried calling Marc instead, to see if there was anything he could do, but there wasn't. Monty was our only option.

The way he stepped up so easily, even after not talking to him for a few weeks, it really showed he cares. Sure, technically he owed me after he involved himself in my and Hayes's relationship, but he still could have told me to fuck myself. Plus, it's a lot harder to stay mad about what he did when Hayes and I are in such a good place.

"Brent," Monty says as the lawyer comes over to us. "This is Laiken, Mali, and Hayes. Laiken is Cam's sister."

He extends his hand toward me specifically. "Brent Waldorf. It's nice to meet you."

"You, too," I reply. "Thank you so much for doing this."

"It's my pleasure. Your brother is in good hands." It looks like things are about to get started, and Brent gives me a small smile as he has to take his place. "Excuse me."

It's one thing knowing your brother is currently in jail.

It's hard, but you can block it out in a way so that it's not so bad. Seeing him in handcuffs and an orange jumpsuit, however, is an image I will never be able to remove from my memory.

With the last case, that polyester never even touched his skin. He didn't spend so much as one night in jail because we were able to bail him out and bring him home until his trial. At least then I knew he was safe. But this time hasn't been anything like that.

It's been worrying about him constantly.

It's been missing his sarcastic commentary.

It's even been missing the way he hogs my boyfriend because *he had him first*.

Cam's gaze meets mine, and the bags under his eyes tell me all I need to know about what he's been through. My grip on Hayes's hand tightens as my brother nods at him, and then he masks all emotions and smiles at Mali. I glance over at her and see the look on her face.

"Stop doing that," I whisper.

"Doing what?"

Exhaling slowly, I pull her into my side. "Blaming yourself. This wasn't your doing."

My parents come to sit on the other side of her, and you can tell my mom is struggling with seeing her son this way. My dad has always been a hard man to read, but not Mom. She wears her emotions like an outfit.

We all stand as the judge is brought into the room, only sitting after he does.

"Okay, let's see what we have here," he says as he reads over the case in front of him. "Mr. Cameron Blanchard viciously and violently assaulted Mr. Isaac Morrison, causing extensive injury, and thus violating the terms of his probation. What is the state's position on bail?"

The prosecutor stands. "We request that the defendant be

held without bail, your honor. This is his second offense within the last year, and only a few months after he was put on probation to begin with. There's no way to guarantee that he is not a risk to others or a flight risk, given the severity of violating his probation."

The judge nods in understanding. "Does the defense object to that stance?"

Brent rises to his feet. "We do, your honor. My client is a good person who shouldn't even be on probation in the first place. The first offense was unreasonable nonsense, and if I had been his representation at the time, I would have gotten it thrown out. It came down to subpar counsel and an ex-girlfriend who was never subpoenaed."

"Not saying I disagree with you, councilman," the judge says. "But that is not the case we're discussing here."

"Correct, but it speaks to the violation of probation. In *this* case, this is someone who wants revenge on my client for having him removed from their shared hockey team after the victim assaulted one of his teammates."

"Your honor, we have a video of the assault taken by the victim's brother," the prosecution adds.

Brent hums. "Well, you make sure to have that sent to my office."

The judge keeps his eyes focused on his desk for a moment while he reads Cam's casefile. We wait with bated breath for his decision, until he sighs.

"While I understand the state's view on this, I agree with Mr. Waldorf in that the first offense was not properly tried. Mr. Blanchard, if you would like to appeal the decision in that case, that is your right, and you are free to do so. As for this one, I am hereby granting bail for Mr. Blanchard in the amount of fifty thousand dollars."

There's an audible sigh from this entire side of the courtroom, and I watch Cam's shoulders relax as Brent thanks the judge for his decision. We all stand, and Brent shakes Cam's hand before the bailiff takes him away again.

"So, what happens now?" Mali asks.

Brent straightens his suit jacket. "Now, we bring the bail money to the court and then Cam will be released from the county jail."

"But we don't have—" my mom starts, but Hayes interrupts.

"That's me," he tells Brent. "I've got it."

Brent nods. "Great. Come with me and we'll get this taken care of. Get him out of there as soon as possible."

As Hayes walks past my mom, she wraps her arms around him and hugs him tightly. "Thank you."

My dad pats his shoulder. "You're a good man, Hayes. My son is lucky to have you. As is my daughter."

It's the first time my dad has outright acknowledged our relationship, and I watch the way Hayes's eyes light up because of it. He was always worried about Cam, but I think a part of him secretly stressed over my parents' views on us dating. After all, they've known him since he was an unruly teenager—acting like his second family at times.

Hayes glances at me, and we share a smile before he leaves with Brent. Meanwhile, I turn to Monty with the utmost appreciation and gratitude.

"Thank you so much," I tell him, going in for a hug.

He wraps his arms around me for a short moment. "You're welcome. He's not out of the woods yet, but I have a few people working on something. We're hoping to get the whole case thrown out."

"What would that mean for his probation?" my mother asks.

"You would have to ask Brent," he answers. "But I believe he would go back to abiding by the original terms of his probation, as if this arrest never happened. Unless, of course, he appeals that decision."

"I think we should worry about this one first," my dad says.

Monty nods. "Agreed."

His phone starts to vibrate as he gets a call, and he excuses himself to take it—telling us that he will keep us updated before he leaves.

"Where did you meet him again?" my father questions.

Mali chuckles. "A club. Laiken accidentally spilled a drink on him."

Both my parents laugh, showing their relief, and my dad shakes his head at me playfully. "I've never been so grateful for your clumsiness."

THERE'S NOTHING PRETTY ABOUT the jail. Not the towers that hold armed guards. Not the barbed wire that lines the top of the fences. Not a damn thing. Just knowing that Cam has been here for the past five days makes me sick to my stomach. We wait outside the gate for him to come out, and the second I see him back in the clothes he was wearing when he was arrested, I feel like I can breathe a little easier.

"Thank fuck," Hayes murmurs as they let Cam out of the gate.

He goes over and hugs my parents first, then comes to

me. I wrap my arms tightly around my brother. We've never been the affectionate kind of siblings. Normally his version of saying he loves me is threatening to kick his friends' asses for hitting on me, and mine is by flipping him off while smiling sweetly. But today, I don't care. Today, I hug my brother because I wasn't allowed to for almost the last week.

Hayes is next, and you can see the relief on them both as Cam thanks him for being there, not just for him but for me. I feel like the latter means more. It's the first supportive thing he's said about our relationship, and I can't help but smile at it.

Finally, he goes to Mali. There's something different about the way he embraces her. He's speaking softly, straight into her ear. I can't hear what he's saying, but I see the way she nods against him. When he finally pulls away, he looks her in the eyes.

"I mean it," he says.

An involuntary smile forces its way through. "I know."

"I am so glad you're out of there," I tell Cam while we all climb into my parents' van.

"You and me both," he replies. "But it may not be for long. My preliminary hearing is in a week. Brent said we should know more then."

My head rests against Hayes's shoulder, and he presses a kiss to the top of my head, knowing I need it.

Please, God, let Monty work a miracle soon.

Hayes
CHAPTER TWELVE

WHEN CAM WAS FIRST ARRESTED, ONLY THE DAY after we started the renovations on what will be our future bar, I thought the timing couldn't be worse. But now, as we're waiting for his preliminary hearing and need something to keep all of our minds off it, turns out the timing is perfect. It gives us something to focus on *and* a way to take out our frustrations.

"Damn," Cam says as he looks around. "You guys got a lot done."

Mali snorts. "Not us. Just him."

She's not wrong. With the surf shop being closed, I technically don't have a job at the moment. So, every moment Laiken spent working, I spent here—breaking shit, as Mali would call it. I got the one wall knocked down, the rest of the counter cleared out, and most of the debris into the dumpster we had put out back. The only big thing left to do is rip up the floor, and then we start the rebuild.

"What happened over there?" Cam asks, seeing a hole in one of the walls we didn't intend on taking down.

I chuckle as I rub the back of my neck. "I may have gotten a little carried away."

His brows raise in amusement. "Oh?"

Mali walks over and takes a seat on the stepladder. "What he means is he has anger issues and was raging a bit too hard."

Laiken wraps her arms around me from behind and

presses her face against my back. "Monty isn't his favorite person in the world, but he's dealing with it because he knows it's your best shot. Right, baby?"

"Yes, dear," I murmur.

Cam snickers but something about the hole has his attention. He goes over and inspects it closely before dropping his head.

"Well, you just created a whole shitload of more work for us," he tells me. "But you also saved us from a shitstorm later."

"What? Why?" It's just a small hole. It would only take a patch and a little spackle to repair.

Cam looks back at the hole. "This place was only open from April to October, right?"

"Yeah..."

He forces his hand into the hole and grips the sheetrock, ripping more out so it's wider. "There's no insulation in the walls. With it only being open in warmer months, it didn't need it. But if the bar's going to be open year-round, we need to take off all the drywall and put insulation in. All the walls need to be replaced."

"Fuck," I groan as my head falls back. "I know it's better we know that now rather than after it's all done, but still."

Laiken squeezes me tighter. "Think of it this way, the walls will be all new and pretty when you're done."

"You won't notice a difference," I reply. "But your optimism is still cute."

Meanwhile, Mali is practically vibrating with excitement. "Does that mean I get to break more shit? Because you were a little selfish with the demolition, Mr. Caveman."

I chuckle as I roll my eyes, grabbing the hammer from the tool bag and holding it out to her. "Knock yourself out."

"Are you sure she should be using that?" Cam questions

skeptically. "Could be things behind that wall we don't want to hit."

In any other circumstance, I might side with him on this, but I shake my head. "Marc gave me the blueprints to the place. She's good as long as she stays on that side."

He doesn't look convinced, but he also doesn't fight with me about it.

OKAY, SO MAYBE HAVING multiple high-strung people in the same room for multiple days isn't the best idea I've ever had. Laiken canceled all scheduled lessons between Cam's release and his preliminary hearing, so she's been here just as often as we have—and Mali comes when she's not working. It's only a matter of time before shit goes a little wrong.

Cam is choosing the safe route, carefully making a hole in one part of the wall, and then using the claw of a hammer to break off the rest piece by piece. I, however, have always believed you work smarter, not harder.

I take the hammer in my hands and use it to break through the drywall, the same way I've done with every other part I've removed, just as my phone starts to ring. I pull it out of my back pocket to see Owen calling me.

Answering it, I put it on speaker. "Hey, O."

"Hey. What are you up to?"

"Breaking shit!" Mali yells excitedly

Owen chuckles. "Sounds like a lot of fun. Listen, I wanted to talk to you. It's about Isaac."

At the sound of his name, my hammer slams into the wall, and Cam winces.

"Are you trying to go through the outer wall, too?" he chastises me.

I roll my eyes and drop the hammer, focusing on my phone as everyone comes closer to hear him. "What about him?"

"He bounced," he says. "Literally packed up his shit and peaced out. Claims he found some team in Arkansas that wants him."

Wow. Looks like he has some sense after all. "Good fucking riddance. But wait, what does that mean for Cam's assault case? Is he dropping it?"

"I was hoping for the same thing, but no. He said if he needs to testify, his lawyer said he can do it over webcam."

Motherfucker. I was really hoping that would be the end of it, and we wouldn't need Monty's help. The last thing I want is for that prick to believe we owe him any favors. Unfortunately, it looks like we will anyway.

"Such an asshole," Cam grumbles. "Thanks for letting us know, Owen."

"No problem," he responds. "Keep your head up, man."

"Will do."

Cam hangs up my phone for me and we all stay silent for a minute. Isaac listened when I told him to get the fuck out of town, but of course, the fucker still has to hold his grudge and try to ruin Cam's life anyway.

I feel my blood start to boil and I pick my hammer back up, banging it into the sheetrock over and over again.

"H," Cam says. "You don't want to do that."

"The fuck I don't," I growl.

He shakes his head while looking between me and the blueprints. "No, I'm saying you don't want to do that *there!*"

This dude is lucky he's my best friend because right now I want to hit *him* with this damn hammer. "I know what I'm doing! You want to do it your little pussy way, go for it, but you're holding the blueprints! I'm nowhere near the fucking p—"

The unmistakable sound of the hammer hitting metal meets my ears just before water starts to spray everywhere, soaking all of us and the room. I close my eyes and stand there, just letting it soak me. And when I open them again, Cam is smirking like the irritating know-it-all he is.

"You were looking at them wrong."

I huff, pushing my wet hair out of my face.

Well, fuck.

THERE'S A LEVEL OF tension in the air as we drive to the courthouse. It's like none of us want to say anything for fear we'll jinx it one way or the other. Monty has been rather vague lately. He's told Laiken and Mali that he's working on something, but he hasn't explained what. It wouldn't surprise me if he's just blowing smoke up our asses, honestly.

If I thought Laiken was nervous and fidgety during his bail hearing, it's nothing compared to this. She looks like she may actually vomit this time, but I might be right there with her. This hearing will determine if we're going to trial, and from what Brent has told Cam, their best chance of getting it thrown out is during this hearing.

I pull out to the courthouse and put my truck in park. Laiken and Mali rode with me, while Cam went with his parents. He tried to fight it—personally, I think he wanted to ride with Mali—but they wouldn't budge. And being the mama's boy he is, the moment his mom's eyes started to water, he caved.

"Do you want to go in or wait out here for a bit?" I ask Lai.

She sighs. "Can we stand outside for a second? I think I just need some air."

"Of course."

All three of us get out of the truck and stand near the steps. The only good thing is that we know Cam will be coming home with us today, regardless of the outcome. The preliminary hearing isn't the trial. But that doesn't make us any less nervous. This thing will be hanging over our heads until it's taken care of.

If it's ever taken care of.

Laiken gives a small smile to someone behind me, and I turn around to see Monty. He's walking in with Brent and a few other powerful-looking people. He waves to us, but then I watch as his eyes meet Laiken's, and he winks. Just like that, I'm imagining what my odds are for getting away with murder if it's committed on the steps of the courthouse.

"You've got to be fucking kidding me," I growl.

Laiken acts fast, grabbing my hand and holding it tightly. "Hey. Relax."

"Relax?" I scoff. "Fuck that. He just—"

"He wasn't winking about her, dumbass," Mali tells me. "He was winking about the status of Cam's case."

"She's right," Laiken says softly, her hand on my cheek to make me look only at her. "Hopefully, it's a good sign."

I'm not entirely convinced. Not after he recorded us having sex for the sole purpose of blackmailing me with it. But Laiken doesn't know that, and if I have anything to say about it, she never will. After the incident with Craig holding pictures of her over her head like a guillotine, I didn't want her to feel like she's constantly being exploited. And there's nothing more demeaning than knowing someone watched such an intimate moment without your consent.

The sick fuck probably jerks off to it, but he'll never get to experience the real thing. The closest he'll ever get is by imagining he's me.

"A thumbs up would suffice just fine," I mutter.

Laiken chuckles. "It's too obvious."

No. *Obvious* is the fact that he basically fucking drools over her every time she's around. But apparently, I'm the only one who sees it.

I take a deep breath and let it out slowly before throwing my arm around Laiken and heading inside. Mali, however, isn't someone to let things go as easily.

"Your boyfriend is going to piss on you to claim his territory," she teases Laiken.

Lai giggles and leans closer into me. "He knows I'd never let his dick come anywhere near me again."

I didn't, but that's good to know. Golden showers aren't my thing, but I've done some crazy things when I'm drunk so it's nice to have a mental list of don'ts—just in case.

IT'S A LONG DAY of listening to other peoples' cases. We hear one with a woman who purposely crashed her car into some woman's house because her husband was having an affair. Another where a guy punched his girlfriend in the face because of a prank—he thought she threw his PlayStation into the pool when in reality, it was a broken one, so she could give him the new PS5. Needless to say, he didn't get the new one, and she threw the actual old one into the pool, too.

And I have to agree with the *yes, bitch* Mali muttered in solidarity under her breath.

When it's finally time for Cam's case, Laiken grabs both mine and Mali's hand—mine for her own comfort, and Mali's for *hers*. I could mention that to anyone around, we probably look like a throuple, but there's a time and place for everything, and now is not it.

"The court calls the case of the State of North Carolina versus Cameron Blanchard."

Brent stands from his place next to Cam. "Before we begin, your honor, all of the evidence was not turned over in this case. The disk that they gave to my office with the aforementioned video of the assault is blank. There's nothing on it."

"That's impossible," the prosecution argues.

Brent shrugs, handing them the disk. "See for yourself."

The prosecutor slips it into his laptop and opens the file to see there is nothing there. "Your honor, there seems to be some kind of mistake."

"That's fine," the judge answers. "These things happen. Why don't you just pull up your copy and we'll play it now?"

He nods, but when he goes to find his copy, that's missing, too. "Unfortunately, I don't seem to have it, your honor, but if I could just have five minutes, I'll have it re-sent to me."

The judge reluctantly agrees, and we take a short recess, but when court comes back into session, the prosecutor doesn't appear any more at ease than he did when we left.

"Okay," the judge says. "Let's see this video."

"I still don't have it, your honor," the prosecutor tells him. "I have checked with the police department and the original source of the video. It seems to be missing from all servers."

The judge pinches the bridge of his nose while the prosecutor looks like he's on the verge of a breakdown. Though I probably would be too if I was tanking my case in front of an entire courtroom.

"In light of this new information, I have no choice but to dismiss the case," the judge announces.

Laiken gasps, squeezing my hand tighter, and I feel like my chest is about to burst. But the prosecution still tries to debate.

"With all due respect, your honor, we still have the testimony of the victim, and his brother who witnessed it."

"Well, are either of them here today to testify?" he counters.

The prosecutor sighs, defeated. "I'm sure I could get his brother here, but the victim would have to be through a webcam, as he recently moved to another state."

The judge's eyes widen. "You mean to tell me that the

man accusing Mr. Blanchard of assaulting him cared so little about this case that he moved out of state before it even went to trial?" The prosecutor goes to answer but the judge raises his hand to stop him. "That was rhetorical, prosecutor."

He takes his attention off the state and moves it to Brent and Cam. "Mr. Blanchard, you are free to go, but the original terms of your probation still apply."

"Thank you, your honor." You can practically hear the relief in Cam's voice.

The judge nods once. "And I mean this in the nicest way possible, but I do not want to see you in my courtroom again."

"Yes, sir."

We all file out quietly, but the moment we get outside, Laiken screams and jumps into Cam's arms. He smiles an actual smile for the first time since he got arrested. And I think I speak for everyone when I say that this could not have gone any better.

"Congratulations," Monty tells Cam.

Cam tilts his head at him. "I don't know how you did it, man. But thanks."

Monty looks back at the courthouse and then at Cam. "Hey, we just got lucky they misplaced that video."

His silent message is clear—he made it go away. I wonder if another *video* has gone away yet, but for some reason, I doubt it. But he just got Cam out of a situation that most likely would have sent him to prison, had Monty not intervened. So, whether I like it or not, he's here to stay.

But he better keep his fucking hands, and his twitchy eyes, off my girlfriend.

Laiken
CHAPTER THIRTEEN

WHEN HAYES AND I WERE SNEAKING AROUND, I couldn't stop imagining what things would be like if we were together. Like together-together. The hold-hands-in-public, kiss-me-in-front-of-everyone kind of together. And I pictured everything, or at least I thought.

I didn't picture *this*.

I've been coming to Cam's hockey games for years. At first, it was because I was dragged here by my parents. But as I got older and understood the game more, I came because I wanted to. Because I genuinely love hockey. And because I love my brother.

Okay, I'm full of shit.

It's because his best friend had my attention in a fucking vise grip.

I really did start to love the game, though. The anticipation, the energy. It's everything. But the absolute best part, the part I didn't even think about while we were sneaking around, is being able to wear Hayes's jersey, with his number drawn on my cheek in eyeliner as I cheer him on.

"You're such a supportive girlfriend," Mali says. "It's gross."

I snort. "And here I thought you were being sweet."

"Clearly, you don't know me as well as I thought you did."

Monty chuckles, but he's too sucked into everything to comment. This is the first time he's been to a game—like ever. Apparently, when your dad is in politics, sporting events aren't exactly high on the priority list.

"You know what I *don't* know?" I take my attention off the game to look over at her. "What's going on between you and Cam?"

She rolls her eyes, then nods her head toward the ice. "Boyfriend just got checked into the boards."

"Nuh-uh. Not going to work," I tsk. "Why won't you tell me?"

"Because there's nothing to tell." She shrugs. "He beat the shit out of Isaac for what he did to me. That earns a certain level of my respect."

Usually, I can read Mali like an open book. She doesn't do very well when it comes to hiding her feelings. At least not from me. And it doesn't *look* like she's being anything but truthful. And I mean, I get it. What Cam did for Mali even earned *my* respect.

So, I drop the topic and turn back to the game.

Soon after, Hayes gets the puck and ends up on a breakaway. The whole rink is on their feet, screaming as it's just him and the goalie. And when he shoots it right into the corner of the net, everyone goes wild.

The whole team celebrates by crowding around Hayes, but the second he's free from them, he skates right over to me—high fiving me with both hands even though there's glass separating us. He's done it each time he scored tonight, making this the third. I can already tell this is a thing he started, and to be honest, I love it.

Mali snickers and when I look back at her, she nods toward a group of puck bunnies that have had a thing for Hayes. I guess they all thought they had a chance with him or something. I glance over to see them glaring at me, simply because they're jealous. I give them a finger wave.

Okay, I may have lied. *That* might be the absolute best part.

"I have to admit," Mali says as I sit down again. "I never expected him to be so cute with you. I didn't think he had it in him."

"I'm still wondering how it happened," Monty chimes in. "Last I had heard, you were heartbroken and devastated."

I shrug. "Our breakup showed him what was really worth it to him, I guess."

Monty purses his lips and strokes his chin. "So...in a way...you could say that I am the one to thank for your relationship."

"Ooh," Mali coos, looking over at him. "That's a risky little game. Tell Hayes that one."

I give her a dark look. "What is this? *See how many assault charges we can rack up for other people in a summer?*"

She pouts. "You never let me have any fun."

Chuckling, I roll my eyes playfully, and the buzzer sounds, signaling the end of the game. We win four to nothing, and Lucas gets his fifth shutout of the season. The guys all get in the handshake line, saying good game to the other team before skating off the ice. I go over to the railing to meet them there.

Cam fist bumps me as he passes, but when Hayes steps off the ice, I lean over the railing, and he pulls himself up the rest of the way to give me a chaste kiss. When he goes to walk away, Lucas comes out next.

"Hey, let me get one of those."

I don't know if he thought Hayes couldn't hear him or if he genuinely has a death wish, but nothing beats the way Hayes turns around to glare at him.

"You know, you made a lot of great saves tonight," he tells him. "But if you don't get the fuck away from my girlfriend, there will be no blocking me from shoving my stick up your ass."

Lucas cringes and looks up at me. "You really find that attractive? The whole *I'm a possessive asshole* bit?"

My gaze meets Hayes's, and I bite my lip. "There's nothing he does that *isn't* attractive."

HAVE YOU EVER STEPPED back and just looked at your man, thinking *I am so goddamn lucky*? Like really gave yourself permission to check him out the same way you did during your first date? Hayes has always managed to melt me with a single look, but I don't think there is anything sexier than watching him work on the bar.

The guys that have the money to wine and dine you are nice, but the guys that aren't afraid to get their hands dirty —*those* are the men you want. They're the ones who will fuck you until three in the morning, when you're so spent from orgasming over and over that you can hardly move.

I watch Hayes's muscles flex as he hammers nails into the wood. Beads of sweat drip down his back, glistening in the light that shines through the window. Apparently, building a wall requires a lot of exertion, so it was only a matter of time before his shirt came off—but fuck, I'm not complaining.

Mali comes to sit next to me on the floor as I lean back against the wall.

Chapter 13

"You've got a little…" She points to the corner of her own mouth.

I don't, and I don't even need to check. "If I did, could you blame me? Look at him."

She tilts her head and hums. "Yeah, you're my girl, but I'm not eye-fucking your boyfriend."

Even if she did, it wouldn't be anywhere close to the real thing. Hayes has a way of knowing exactly where to touch, and exactly how to move, to make me feel like my whole body is in ecstasy. Like every inch of me is his own personal wonderland and he wants nothing more than to get lost in it. Lost in me.

I squirm as my pussy clenches desperately, and when I let out a quiet whine, Mali laughs. "How you went from virgin to sex-fiend in a single summer is a mystery to me."

"You'd understand if you felt what he can do with his tongue," I tell her, not looking away from H.

As if he can read my mind, he glances over at me and smirks. "Are you just going to sit there and watch?"

"Mm-hm," I say, nodding.

He barks out a laugh, putting the hammer back into his toolbelt as he walks over and bends down in front of me. I watch as his eyes rake over me slowly, like he's getting his fill. And when they stare back at me again, his pupils are blown.

"That means I get to watch *you* later," he murmurs, just before he grabs my chin and kisses me—immediately licking into my mouth.

It's so quick, so effortless, but I'm breathless by the end of it.

"Great," Mali scoffs. "I'm jealous of my best friend's sex life. That's just fan-fucking-tastic."

Hayes and I both chuckle, and when he stands up and steps back, he winks at me. I'm so lost in him and everything he is that I don't even remember my brother is in the room until his voice echoes through the room.

"Okay, I've been accepting of"—he waves his finger between Hayes and me—"this, but spending my day in a live-action porno of you two? Not on my list of fucking shit I want to do." All of his attention turns to Hayes. "H, put a goddamn shirt on."

"Screw that," he argues. "It's hot as fuck in here."

Cam's brows furrow. "It *is* hot in here." He walks over to the thermostat and his jaw drops. "Jesus Christ. Who set the heat at eighty-nine degrees?"

Mali looks up at the ceiling, over at the wall, and down at the floor—anywhere but at Cam—and I look at her like she's the hero I didn't know we needed.

"I love you so hard right now that if I wasn't so possessive, I'd let you borrow Hayes," I say, gaping at her.

She throws her head back and laughs, just as Hayes's phone starts to ring. He pulls it out of his pocket and what looks like nervousness fills his eyes. He looks over at me for only a second, trying to play it off like it's nothing, but then he goes outside to take the call.

What the hell?

He's never done that. Never been afraid to answer his phone around me. Not even when we were sneaking around. Don't get me wrong, I have no reason *not* to trust him. It very well could be nothing. But something about it rubs me the wrong way, and I'm not the only one.

"What was that about?" Mali asks me.

My gaze stays focused on Hayes as he puts the phone to his ear but makes sure he's facing the other way so I can't read his lips. "I don't know."

Chapter 13

I'VE ALWAYS TOLD MYSELF to trust my gut. It's never been wrong before. But right now, I can't figure out exactly what it's saying. I don't think I honestly believe Hayes would ever cheat on me, but as the secretive phone calls occur more often over the next few days, I can't help but wonder.

I tried asking him about them, but he just claims it's something for the bar. Something about the paperwork or the permits. But Marc is the one handling all of that, and even if that were the case, I don't see him needing to take it outside.

He's going over different floor choices with Cam, debating between the lighter wood or the darker, when it happens again. He glances at it and tells Cam he'll be right back, then walks out the door. My brother doesn't seem concerned, but it's getting under my skin.

"You don't think he's cheating, do you?" My heart sinks at the mere idea.

Mali hums. "I don't know, babe. You two are together all the time."

"Except when we're not." I look over at Cam. "Is he here all day when I'm at work or does he leave?"

Cam snorts. "Are you asking me as your brother or his best friend?"

"It can't be both?"

"No," he answers. "But then again, I don't think I'm going to answer, regardless. If you honestly believe he's cheating, that's between the two of you. But if you think that I would stand by while he fucks around on my sister, you haven't been paying enough attention."

He's right. Cam is the most protective person I know when it comes to the ones he loves, and Hayes is included in that, but there are two versions of Hayes in his mind—the one that's his best friend and the one that's dating his sister. Protective brother would trump best friend, always.

"Okay," I sigh. "Then my next question. Is he just not into me anymore?"

Honestly, I don't know which would be worse. I'd be devastated either way. But Mali immediately shakes her head.

"With the way he looks at you?" she asks. "Not a chance."

Hayes comes back in but stops when he sees Mali and me staring at him. "Something wrong?"

I shake my head and look away, but Mali isn't the type to keep her mouth shut as she crosses her arms over her chest. "That's what I'm trying to figure out."

"Okay," Hayes says hesitantly. "Do you want to fill me in on what it might be?"

Cam lets out an annoyed sigh. "They want to know if you're cheating or if you're just not into Laiken anymore."

"Dude," I hiss.

But my brother only shrugs. "What? There are way too many dangerous tools in here for Mali to be contemplating whether to kill him or not."

My stomach is in knots, and I can't even bring myself to look at Hayes. I never wanted to be *that* girl. The one who doesn't trust her boyfriend or is insecure about her relationship. But as Hayes slowly comes over to me and puts his hand on my cheek to make me look at him, I realize I may not be completely rid of the feeling that he's in this for a good time, not a long time.

"Lai," he says softly. "You have me. All of me. Forever."

It could be the honesty in his voice or the way he stares into my eyes to make sure I'm hearing him, but my breath hitches and my mind rests. There's no one else. Not for him. Not for me. It'll always be him and me.

"I love you," I tell him.

He smirks, bending down to kiss me. "I more than love you."

Mali gags and Cam mumbles something about never getting this shit done, but the two of us just stay there for a moment—lost in each other when I need it the most.

MY FEET SWING BACK and forth as I sit on the stool, eating ice cream while Cam makes Mali help him hold the new sheets of drywall in place. It would usually be Hayes, but he's not here. He said he had something to take care of this morning and he would meet me at the bar after. It instantly made me worry, the same way I do when he refuses to let his phone out of his sight, but then I closed my eyes and remembered how the day Cam revealed my insecurities, Hayes made sure to show me how he feels every chance he got.

And just like that, all my worries dissipated into thin air.

"That piece is crooked," I say, watching as they struggle to hold it straight.

Chapter 13

Cam turns around to glare at me. "It wouldn't be if *someone* were helping us."

"I *am* helping," I tell him. "I'm helping by telling you it's crooked."

Mali chuckles, while my brother looks like he's contemplating shooting me with the nail gun he's holding. But before he can fully plan out my murder, Hayes walks through the door.

"Thank God," Cam grumbles. "I need your help. Laiken is useless."

"I'm supervising!" I argue.

His patience is definitely being tested as his jaw locks. "You're not helping!"

I puff out my bottom lip. "Aww, are you going to tell Mommy on me?"

Hayes snickers and looks at Cam. "Take a break. I'll help you when I get back."

"You just got here," I whine. "Where are you going now?"

He smiles fondly at me. "Don't worry, I'm taking you with me. I have something to show you."

"It's done?" Cam asks.

Mali and I speak in unison. "What's done?"

But Hayes only nods as he puts out his hand for me to take. "Don't worry about it. Come on."

THE WHOLE TIME I'M in the truck is spent trying to

figure out where he could possibly be taking me. It's too early for a date, unless we're going out to eat—but he's not a brunch kind of guy. And besides, he said he has something to *show* me.

"Can you please tell me where we're going?" I beg. "Not knowing is torturing me."

He pulls up to the red light and stops. "Nope. Actually, I need you to close your eyes."

Instead, they narrow to slits. "Seriously?"

But he gives me the smile that turns me into mush and I sigh as I listen, closing my eyes and covering them with my hands. And when I feel him toss a sweatshirt over my head for good measure, I can almost feel how much he's enjoying this.

"Overkill, much?"

He chuckles. "As if you weren't going to peek."

Okay, so maybe he has a point, but who wouldn't? He's been acting secretive and now he's got me practically blindfolded in his truck. I tend to lack patience on a normal day, but this is testing my limits.

"If you're taking me to have a threesome with the girl you're sneaking around with, it's never going to happen," I grumble.

His response flows out without even needing to think about it. "That's okay. She has friends who are willing."

My eyes shoot open but all I see is the sweatshirt. "You know, I started the joke but now I'm not really finding it funny."

A bark of laughter shoots out of his mouth. "Good."

We must have been close because within a few minutes, the truck turns and then comes to a halt. He turns off the engine and tells me not to move as he hops out. A moment later, my door opens, and he helps me out. He takes the hoodie off my head but covers my eyes with his hand.

"I still can't look?"

"Nope."

Hayes holds onto me as he leads us onto what feels like grass. The only thing I can think of is maybe a picnic or some incredible view he found, but none of those seem to click. As we come to a stop, he holds me close and removes his hands from my eyes.

"Okay, *now* you can look."

I blink, adjusting to the light, and then I notice we're standing in front of a house. More specifically, my favorite house out of all the ones we've seen. And when he pulls the key out of his pocket and shows it to me, it all falls into place.

"You bought it?" I ask in disbelief.

"Mm-hm," he hums against my ear. "You want to go in?"

I nod rapidly. "I really do."

I'm not naive. I know this isn't *my* house. It's Hayes's. But there's something about the fact that he picked my favorite of all the houses to buy...something that tells me he sees the same future for us that I do.

We walk up the steps and onto the porch, and I look around as it starts to set in. He opens the front door and gestures for me to enter.

This place is just as perfect as I remember it being. It's not too big, but has plenty of room to raise a family. And I can just picture curling up next to the fireplace and reading a book on cold winter days.

"I love this place so much," I tell him.

He smiles, staring down at me. "I know you do."

My heart jumps at the intensity of his gaze, but just before I let myself fall into him, I see the mantle out of the corner of my eye. Where it was empty before, it's now decorated with pictures of Hayes and me. I walk closer to get a better look.

There's the one Mali took before the Thomas Rhett concert, and another that I snapped the morning after we got back together—when we woke up on our beach and decided to stay tangled up together while we listened to the waves crash on the shore. When we first saw this place, I remember rambling about how beautiful this mantel would look with some picture frames on it.

"You listened," I breathe.

He moves to stand in front of me, sliding his hand to the back of my neck and rubbing behind my ear. "I hang on every single word you say."

All the air leaves my lungs as I arch up and kiss him. This whole thing feels like a dream. I spent years mentally wrapped up in everything he is, and now he's here, holding me and loving me the way I always hoped he would. It's like I painted my own little fairy tale in my mind and made it come to life.

Pulling away, I break the kiss and rest my head against his chest. Sometimes, I love him so much I feel dizzy. But he wraps his arms around me, kissing the top of my head and rubbing my back. I could spend the rest of my life right here and never have a single complaint.

We end up venturing into the rest of the house, talking about what he could do with each room. There's no garage for him to work on his boards, but there's a shed out back that would suffice. He mentions wanting to turn the downstairs bedroom into an office, so he has somewhere to keep all the paperwork for the bar, and that he wants to paint each room a different color.

Because white is boring.

I listen, giving my input when I have some, until we finally end in the kitchen.

Honestly, this was one of my favorite rooms. It was the one where I could picture us so vividly—cooking dinner together and laughing when I tease him about the dishes. Even now, I can see it. And I want it more than the air I breathe.

"I can't believe this is your house," I tell him.

He steps closer, and my hips are pinned against the island.

"Believe it, baby. It's all mine." He bends down to kiss my neck. "And I plan to worship your body on every...fucking... inch of it. Starting right here."

His hand slides up inside my shorts and pushes my panties to the side. He bends his fingers and goes right for my clit, rubbing circles into it like his sole intention is to make me cum as fast as possible.

"Fuck," I moan softly.

He pulls his head back to look at me. "We're not hiding here, baby. There's no one else in this place. It's just us. And I want to hear you scream."

Pleasure builds inside of me. From his words, from the feel of his skilled fingers, from the way he watches me. And as my head falls back and I stop holding myself back, he smirks.

"That's it," he tells me. "That's my good girl."

His hands move to my hips, and he undresses me quickly, like he's desperate for it. He grips my waist and sits me on the island. The feeling of the cold granite makes me squeak, but the heat of his gaze warms me to the point where I don't care.

He drops down to his knees and hooks my legs over his shoulders. "Let's see just how loud you can be."

There's no teasing in the way he dives right in, licking my pussy and sucking on my clit. I lean back and hold myself up with my hands as he eats me out with so much skill that I'm already on edge. He grips at the skin on my thighs, pulling me closer as if he can't get enough. He needs it all. Every last bit of my pleasure is his and he won't stop until he gets it.

As he presses two fingers into me, I move one hand to the back of his head and grip his hair. He growls against me while I pull him closer, letting the sound of my moans fill the room. Nothing else exists anymore. Just him and me and the way he sucks on my clit while I sit on the island that I pictured us preparing dinner on.

I don't think any part of him was bluffing. He really will fuck me in every inch of this house, and just the thought of it has me squeezing my thighs against his head. That only spurs him on more. His movements quicken, and his fingers find that spot inside me that makes me see stars.

"Give me it, Laiken," he demands. "Come all over my tongue so I can bury myself deep inside of you."

There's no use even trying to deny him. My body is his, and it knows it better than anything else. Everything he wants, he gets—including my orgasm. The pressure is so intense that when he sucks on my clit once more and drives his fingers into my g-spot, I scream his name and fall back onto the counter.

He follows my body, not relenting for a second as he sucks up every bit of what I give him. And the way he moans at the taste of my high is the hottest fucking thing I've ever seen.

The moment my body relaxes, he stands up and his eyes rake over me while he slowly pushes down his pants. He grips his cock and slides his hand over it as he watches me.

"You are a fucking dream," he murmurs. "I will never get enough of you."

My chest rises and falls with heavy breaths as he rubs his dick over my clit. I'm so sensitive and so stimulated from the orgasm that just rocked me that I instantly start to squirm.

And when I feel him starting to slip in bare, it only makes me want him more.

"This okay?" he asks.

I nod. "I need to feel you. All of you."

His eyes darken, and he bites his lip as he presses his cock into me.

There are no words for this. No way to explain how amazing it feels to have him inside me like this. In the water was one thing, but this? This is sexual fucking paradise.

Hayes's muscles flex and his eyes fall closed, overtaken by the feeling. It forces a thought through my mind, and I can't stop myself from asking.

"Have you never…" my voice fades out, but he knows what I'm asking.

He looks at me with the same vulnerability he had that day on the boat. When we were both in the middle of a freefall that neither one of us could deny.

"Only you," he confesses. "Only ever you."

Fuck. There's something about knowing I'm the only one he's ever been with like this that has me clenching around him and using my heels on his ass to pull him in deeper. It's so strong. So powerful. Feeling him fucking me raw like this makes me want to have him deep inside of me forever.

"God, that feels so good," I moan. "So fucking good."

His jaw falls open as he pulls out just to slam back in. "You're mine, Laiken. This pussy. This *body*. It's all mine."

"All yours," I agree.

He lets out a mix between a hum and a moan. "Good girl. Come here."

Sliding his arm under my back, he helps me sit up and lifts me off the counter—still with his dick inside of me. He presses me against the doorway to the kitchen, thrusting into me a few times before carrying me over to the stairs. He slips out of me and places my feet on the ground.

"Turn around," he orders me, and I do as I'm told. "Now bend over and grip the banister."

The heel of his hand slides up my spine, guiding me into position and he lines back up at my entrance.

"Do you want me to put a condom on?"

I shake my head. "Just tell me right before you're about to come."

He slides into me, his hands gripping my waist, and I turn to look back at him. He watches as his cock slips in and out of my pussy. One day, I might even have him record it so I can see what it looks like too from that angle.

His movements start to become faster. Harder. His grip tightens as his fingertips bite into the flesh on my hips. And as my head falls forward again, I realize we're standing right in front of the large living room window.

"H," I pant. "There's no blinds. Someone could see us."

But no part of him seems to care as he fucks into me.

"Let them," he growls. "Let them watch how I make your whole body tense up as you scream my name for the whole world to hear. I want everyone to know just who you belong to."

He bends forward, sliding his hand around to the front of me and playing with my clit. With each circular motion, he thrusts in and out of me. I'm so obsessed with the feeling of every last inch of him that it's only moments before I'm getting closer and closer to the edge. The pressure builds once more, and Hayes can tell because he's chasing it.

He's chasing it for the both of us.

"Fuck," he moans. "I don't want to pull out. I want to fill you up and watch as my cum drips from your pussy."

God, I want that, too. And it's so fucking tempting. But I'm not on birth control, and neither one of us are nowhere near ready for the kind of responsibility that risk brings.

177

"Not today," I tell him. "Today I want you to come down my throat."

"But I'm—"

I turn my head to look at him. "I know."

He licks his lips and adds just enough more pressure to my clit to push me over the edge. His cock is as deep as possible as I clench around him, letting him feel my orgasm with me—with nothing keeping us apart.

As I start to come down, he slams into me once, twice, three times.

"Shit," he curses.

He pulls out of me, and I spin around, falling to my knees and opening my mouth for him to slip inside. I taste my own cum all over him as he thrusts into the back of my throat. I choke and gag around him, and it's just enough to have him spilling everything he has into my mouth.

I stroke his dick as my cheeks hollow and I swallow around him. His hand flies to the railing, gripping it tightly. I look up at him through hooded lashes and do it again, just to see the look of sexual bliss on his face. And after I finally suck him clean, I pull off him with a pop and he smirks down at me.

"You're incredible," he says, as his thumb cleans some of his cum off the corner of my mouth. "I'm so fucking addicted to you."

I smile because I feel it, too. Every time he kisses me. Every time he says my name. Every time I even look at him. He's the only man I've ever loved, and he's the only one I ever *will* love. Because this kind of addiction—it stays. It never fades. There's no recovery. No chance of stopping.

It runs through my veins and claims me from the inside out.

Hayes
CHAPTER FOURTEEN

MOVING EVERYTHING OUT OF MY BEDROOM AT MY mom's house is bittersweet. On one hand, it's going to be so strange not living in the same house as my mom and sister. Not cracking on each other in passing or when we occasionally eat dinner together. But on the other hand, I can't wait for all of the alone time it'll give me with Laiken.

Ever since the first night we spent together, I've had trouble sleeping without her. If I don't have the weight of her head on my chest, or the sound of her breathing lulling me to sleep, I toss and turn all night. Thankfully, my mom never cares if she sleeps over. But Laiken's parents? I have to set an alarm for five in the morning so I could sneak back into Cam's room.

And of course, then I can't fall back asleep because she's not in my arms.

Cam grabs the last box and carries it out to my truck while I stand in the doorway, looking at the empty room. My mom comes over to stand beside me, and I can see her trying to keep from getting choked up.

"I'm proud of you, you know," she says. "You were questionable for a little bit there, but the man you've grown into is just the man I hoped you would become."

I make a noise of disgust. "Do we have to do the sob fest right now?"

She looks up at me and my facade cracks wide open. I

smile, wrapping an arm around her and pulling her close to me.

"Thanks, Mom," I tell her. "For everything."

Her hand comes to cover her mouth as she starts to cry. "Now you're the one making this a sob fest."

I chuckle. "You started it."

"Oh, gross," Devin says as she turns the corner. "You two are being sappy. Excuse me while I leave."

"Come here," I tell her.

She grumbles but does it anyway and I hold two of the most important women in my life close to me. The fact that they won't have a man in the house anymore sits in the back of my mind, but I know they'll be fine. The two of them scare the ever living shit out of *me*. If anyone decides to break in, that's between them and God.

"Don't be a stranger," my mom tells me.

I snort. "I'm only moving a few miles away. It'll be like I never even left."

"That's depressing," Devin teases. "I was looking forward to not having to see your ugly mug anymore."

My eyes roll. "Shut up. You know you're going to miss me."

She tries to play tough, but I can see right through it as she starts to tear up. "Fuck, fine. I'll miss you a little."

Cam up-nods at me through the front door and I know we're all set to go. The guys are on their way back to my house to help unload, and Laiken and Mali are there to unpack and wait for the people delivering my furniture. Apparently, when all you have is a bedroom, you need to buy a lot of shit.

"Hey," I say to Devin, getting an idea. "You busy today?"

Her lips purse before she shakes her head. "No, why?"

"Want to come back to the house with me?" I suggest. "Laiken and Mali are there. You can hang out with them."

She smiles and looks over at Mom. "Will you be okay?"

"I'll be fine," she assures her. "You go have fun and help your brother."

Devin goes to get her shoes on while I turn to my mom.

"If you ever need me, you promise you'll call," I tell her. She tries to wave it off, but I don't allow it. "I'm serious. I don't care what it is, or if it's two in the damn morning. You call me and I'm here."

Her eyes soften and she nods. "I promise. I love you, Hayes."

"I love you, too."

I hug her once more, trying to show her how much I care about her and appreciate how hard she's always worked to provide for us. I know it wasn't easy, raising two teenagers alone, but she never once even thought about giving up on us. Laiken is my future, and I love her more than I ever knew was possible. But everything I am, and the man I've grown to be, I owe to the woman standing in front of me.

With one more goodbye, all three of us step onto the porch. Devin skips ahead to get in my truck, and I turn around, walking backward as I talk to my mom.

"I'll bring her back later," I tell her.

She scrunches her nose. "Do you have to?"

I chuckle as I get in my truck, waving one more time as I pull out of the driveway.

There's a weight in my chest from knowing she's going to go back inside and cry. Memories of when my dad left play through my mind, but I push them away. Unlike him, I'm not abandoning her with two kids and no idea how to get by. I'm not abandoning her at all. If she were to need me, I could be there in under ten minutes.

She'll always have me.

WE GET BACK TO the house and I walk in to see the girls must have gotten bored. They unpacked what we brought back so far, and while I don't know where anything is, I'm just glad it's done. I'm not sure how I feel about them putting together the end tables and the coffee table though.

"Are you sure they're not going to fall apart?" I ask skeptically.

Laiken glares at me. "Yes, prick. We followed the instructions."

Owen picks up the one end table and shakes it. "Seems sturdy to me. Hey, Aid! Come stand on this thing."

"Let's not," I stop him and give Laiken a small smile. "It looks great, babe."

"Thanks," she says, grinning happily.

Mali has her *I'm about to stir some shit* look on her face. "Lai, tell him about your new business idea."

Laiken chuckles, and already, I'm scared. "I've had so much experience in manual labor lately, I should start my own handyman business."

Cam barks out a laugh. "Manual labor? You sit there gawking at your boyfriend all damn day!"

Her jaw drops. "I just put together three tables! And besides, would *you* be able to get any work done with him around? Look at him."

All emotion drops right off Cam's face as he shakes his

head slowly. "There is so much wrong with what you just said."

Devin cringes. "Agreed."

My sister looks at me like I'm diseased, and I flip her off before focusing on my girlfriend. "You're not becoming a handyman, babe."

"Why not?" she presses playfully. "I could make a killing —especially if I do it topless."

That gets Mali's attention. "Ooh, you might be onto something."

When Devin goes to open her mouth is when I draw the line and point my finger at her. "One word out of you and Cam is bringing your ass right home."

Her lips clamp shut, meanwhile Lucas is frantically searching his pockets. Owen's brows furrow as he watches him.

"Dude, what the fuck are you doing?" he asks.

He keeps patting everywhere on his body and looking around. "I can't find my damn keys."

"We're not done bringing shit in," Cam tells him. "Where are you trying to go?"

"IKEA," he says, as if it's obvious.

Everyone chuckles, but I'm too busy in a staring contest with Laiken. She just loves pushing my buttons, and mentioning herself topless in front of Lucas, she knew he would bite. Neither one of us looks away as Mali groans.

"They're doing that thing again."

"Doing what thing?" Aiden questions.

Cam sighs and answers for her. "That thing where they forget the rest of the room exists and live in their own little world."

"It's nauseating," Mali grumbles.

I ignore them and tilt my head to the side a little, giving her a certain look. She knows exactly what it means, and she gets up without a word. As she walks straight into me, I wrap my arms around her.

"Mine," I growl, mostly for Lucas's benefit.

But it's Mali that answers, rolling her eyes. "Yeah, we know, caveman. No need to brand her to clarify."

"It's so weird seeing him like this with a chick," Owen says.

Cam grunts. "How do you think *I* feel? Being around the two of them almost makes me miss jail."

But none of their opinions matter as Laiken looks up at me and my eyes meet hers—because she's the best thing to ever happen to me. And I will spend the rest of my life being hopelessly in love with her.

LATER THAT NIGHT, AFTER everyone goes home, it's just Laiken and me. I'm hanging up a few things she picked out at the store, letting her leave her own personal touches all over the place. I've thought about asking her to move in with me—more than I'd like to admit, actually—but something keeps holding me back. Every time I go to say the words, they just won't come out.

She's sitting on the couch, humming to herself as she works on a song she's writing, and I can't help but smile. She looks so at home, wearing nothing but one of my shirts after I took a break for the sole purpose of fucking her. After her topless handyman shit, I needed to remind her why no one else gets to see her the way I do. And if I paid extra attention to her tits out of pure jealousy, that's no one's business but my own.

Watching her like this, I get a warmth that spreads throughout my whole body. It starts in my chest and slowly makes its way through me. And the way she looks up and smiles at me reminds me of how my mom used to smile at my dad before everything went to shit. I slip my phone out of my pocket, setting it on the mantel and pressing a couple buttons until "Blessed" by Thomas Rhett plays from the speaker.

Laiken looks intrigued as I walk over to her and hold out my hand.

"Dance with me," I tell her.

She giggles. "Babe, there's no room."

I glance around a moment before sliding the coffee table right out of the way. "There. Now, dance with me."

Her hand slips in mine and she stands. "Oh, right. I forgot about your secret love for chick flicks."

Our fingers interlace, and my other hand comes to rest on her lower back as we sway to the music. "Remind me to kill Devin for telling you that."

She chuckles, only to squeal as I spin her away and then back to me. "But then where would I get all of my intel?"

"Me," I answer simply. "There isn't a single part of me I don't want you to know. You can ask me anything."

Her brows raise. "That sounds dangerous for you."

"Do your worst."

We slow dance around the living room while she thinks. "When did you lose your virginity?"

Ha. "And you say I have a one-track mind."

"Yours is caused by perpetual sexual frustration. Mine is caused by jealousy. We are not the same."

I snicker, spinning her again before answering. "Okay...I was sixteen. We were at a party. And I only did it because all my friends already had."

"That's a horrible reason," she chides.

My one shoulder raises in a non-committal shrug. "I was a stupid kid. I didn't know any better."

I don't regret my sexual experiences. Would it have been nice if it was only Laiken who knew that part of me? Sure. But then I'd be the same inexperienced fuck I was. Over the years, I taught myself all the things that she enjoys so much now. Taking that into account, all of it was worth it.

"Fine, you get a pass," she says and moves on. "What went through your head on Monty's boat that one day? You know what I'm talking about."

That question makes my breath pause for a moment, and I huff in amusement. "That I was falling in love with you. I tried so hard to keep you out, but I couldn't. It was beyond my control."

She bites her lip, but her grin widens anyway. "And you tried to say we aren't meant to be."

"Biggest regret of my life," I reply honestly. "You are the *only* one I'm ever meant to be with."

Her head rests against my chest, and we hold each other close as we keep dancing, even long after the song has changed to something more upbeat.

LEAVE IT TO MY friends to look for any excuse to throw a party—even if it's not their house. They say it's my housewarming party, but not a single person has brought me a gift. Except Owen. He brought me a beer.

Just one.

But I'm not complaining. Not when I've got all my friends around me and Laiken by my side. And it's nice knowing I can drink tonight and not worry about how I'm getting home afterward. Or sleep on Cam's floor, for that matter.

It isn't until an unfortunately familiar piece of shit walks in that my mood plummets.

"Fuck, no," I growl, pushing through people on my way to the door. "Out. *Now.*"

Craig scoffs, smiling at his friends like I'm joking. "Come on, man. It's the biggest party of the summer."

"I don't give a shit. Get the fuck out of my house."

Laiken comes over and stands beside me, and when Craig's eyes land on her, I can tell he still has feelings for her. Can't blame him there. He's the dumbass that lost her.

As I put my arm around her, he masks his hurt with irritation. "People said you were together, but I didn't believe it. Never thought *Hayes Wilder* would want my sloppy seconds."

"Hey," I snap. "You don't get to talk to her. You don't even get to look at her. Keep your fucking eyes on me."

Craig laughs dryly. "Okay. Tell me, how's her pussy feel? Or does she keep you at third base, too? Never knew she was a prude until I started dating her."

The whole party is silent, except for Mali in the background trying to keep Cam from coming over here. It's smart. Keeping him over there keeps him out of trouble. But my freedom isn't at risk here, and he's in *my* house.

"See, that's the difference between you and me," I sneer. "I don't feel the need to broadcast my sex life to all my friends. But I get that you have a lot to overcompensate for. Laiken told me all about your little…well, you know."

Lai tries and fails not to laugh. We've never talked about Craig's dick, for obvious reasons. But judging by the way his face turns red, I'm spot on. How unfortunate for him.

"Get out of here, Craig," I demand. "And keep my girlfriend's name out of your mouth."

It's probably the first time half this room has heard me refer to anyone as my girlfriend, but my only focus is getting this shithead as far away from Laiken as possible. Just knowing he's seen her *almost* naked is enough to make me want to deck him.

"No can do, man," he tells me. "It's on my tongue every time I jerk off while I picture her mouth on my dick."

My fist clenches and I go to lunge at him, but Laiken moves faster. She slips in front of me and holds me back with everything she has. Her hands come up to touch my face as she desperately tries to get my attention.

"Babe," she tries again. "Stop. He's just trying to goad you. Don't listen to him."

I take my attention off Craig and put it on her, exactly where it should be. She smiles in relief and slides her hands to the back of my neck.

"Don't listen to him," she repeats. "Just focus on me."

And I can do that just fine. If he didn't like seeing my arm around her, he's really going to hate this.

Pulling her in, I press my lips to hers and feel as she melts into me. It may start all for Craig's benefit, but it quickly takes a turn—becoming entirely for me. Because she keeps me grounded. Because she keeps me sane.

Because she's the only person I ever want to kiss again.

"Get a room!" Owen jokes.

I pull away and my brows raise. "I have three, actually. Thanks for the reminder." Focusing on Craig once more, I smirk. "Now, if you'll excuse me, I'm going to enjoy my party and then fuck my girlfriend the way she never let you."

Taking a step toward him, he takes one back. With a few more, he ends up on the front porch and I swing the door shut in his face. The music starts to play again, and everyone goes back to the party like nothing ever happened. Laiken and I go over to the kitchen, and I grab another beer from the fridge.

"That guy is such a dick," Lucas growls. "How did you ever date him?"

Laiken's nose scrunches. "I was young and stupid. I didn't know any better."

I can't help but laugh, recognizing her words as the ones I used while we danced in the living room. Mali comes back in from the dining room with Cam trailing behind her. My first assumption is that she brought him in there to keep him away from Craig, but as he zones out while staring at her, I think it may have been more than that.

"Cam!" Aiden shouts. "Funnel a beer with me!"

He chuckles, but there's something off about it. "Do I look like I want to vomit tonight?"

"You're no fun." He looks around. "Mali?"

She shrugs. "Yeah, sure. Fuck it."

"Yes!"

Everyone watches the two of them race to see who can drink it faster, but my attention is drawn to the door—where Monty has strolled in and is in the middle of a bro-shake with Owen, like they've been friends for years. I had no idea they even knew each other. And the way Monty quickly excuses himself when he sees me watching, I don't think I was meant to know.

"You okay?" Laiken asks me.

I pull my focus back to her. "Yeah. Yeah, I'm good."

She celebrates with Mali after she beats Aiden with ease,

but I'm still stuck on Monty. There's something about him that rubs me the wrong way. And I don't think it has anything to do with him threatening me. She's mine now. That's not changing.

If he hadn't saved Cam from spending the next few years in prison, I'd say something to Laiken about it. Or even Cam himself. But he earned both of their respect with what he did, and Laiken has become better friends with him since. Because of that, I don't have a leg to stand on when it comes to him.

Not unless I find out what his ulterior motive is.

IT ISN'T UNTIL LATER that I even have a chance to ask Owen about it. I'm outside smoking a cigarette when he comes out for some fresh air. Some people have left. Some are still lingering. Most are drunk. But Monty has stayed sober, and I have a feeling there's a reason for it.

"Oh, hey, H," Owen says. "I didn't realize you were out here."

I hold up the cigarette. "Laiken doesn't want me smoking in the house."

He snickers. "You two shacking up now?"

"Nah," I shake my head. "Not yet, anyway. I don't know. I'll get to that eventually, I'm sure."

His eyes widen in both disbelief and amazement. "That's crazy. I never thought I'd see the day that *you* settle down."

"Yeah, well," I glance inside to see Laiken laughing at something Mali said. "She's amazing."

"Damn," he breathes. "Good for you. Seriously. I'm happy for you."

"Thanks." I take another hit of my cigarette. "Hey, I noticed you were talking to Monty earlier. I didn't know you two knew each other."

His brows furrow until they raise in realization. "Oh, Rollins? Yeah, we've hung out at Isaac's a few times."

"Isaac's?" Now *that* is interesting.

He nods. "Yeah. Those two are pretty close. Grew up in the same social class and all that. I think they met at boarding school."

Funny, throughout all the time Monty was helping us with Cam's case, he never once mentioned that he even knew Isaac—let alone used to be friends with him. And something tells me it's not because it slipped his mind.

"Wow. Guess you learn something new every day."

Owen hums just as Lucas comes out with Aiden. The three of them rode here together. Aiden was supposed to be their DD, but that was shot to shit as he funneled three beers. So, Lucas switched to water.

"Ready?" Lucas asks Owen.

"Yeah." He turns to me. "I'll see you later, H."

I raise my hand for a second in a half-assed wave to all three of them, but my mind is laser focused on Monty. I feel like everything with him is a trick. An illusion. He knows how to make people believe he's got nothing up his sleeve, but I see right through him.

There's something he's hiding, and I'm going to figure it out.

CHAPTER FIFTEEN

Laiken

LET THE RECORD STATE THAT MALI IS MAKING A liar out of me. I was a completely unwilling participant. Okay, that's a lie, too. I didn't exactly object when she told Hayes and Cam that we had to go to her job to take care of a massive issue. But come on. There's only so long we can help them work on that bar before we start to lose our minds.

The only thing that makes it all worth it is seeing how happy it makes Hayes. Sometimes, while we're hanging out at his house, he gets lost in talking about all the ideas he has. Seeing him talk about something with that much passion makes me smile. Because he deserves all the best things.

And I deserve to take a break from paint, spackle, and all things renovations.

"This one," Mali says, holding up what's supposed to be lingerie but really just looks like scraps of lace fabric strung together.

I shake my head. "Absolutely not."

"You would look so hot!"

My arms cross in front of my chest. "Are you saying I don't look hot otherwise?"

She narrows her eyes at me. "Oh, yes. That's exactly what I'm saying. You're a complete toad. It's a wonder you scored one of the hottest guys in town."

"Great!" I throw my hands in the air. "Now you're calling my boyfriend hot, too. Some best friend you are."

The look she gives me tells me she's totally over my shit right now, but all I can do is laugh. After I've spent the last hour listening to her try to talk me into wearing "something slutty" as she put it, she can take a little payback.

"I hate you so much," she tells me.

But I smile sweetly back at her. "That's so cute. You even lie to yourself."

She flips me off and goes back to browsing the store. What she doesn't realize is that nothing in here really interests me. I'm not a lingerie kind of girl. Honestly, I don't even know that I have the confidence to try it. Not that I'm insecure. But everything with Hayes makes me nervous—in a good way, but still nervous.

"Okay, what about this?" Mali suggests.

I turn around with the no already on the tip of my tongue but stop when I see what she's holding. It's sexy, but in a cute kind of way. The white lacy fabric looks soft to the touch, and instead of looking like my clothes got mauled by a bear, it's more of a bathing suit type. I purse my lips and walk closer to get a better look, and Mali is practically gleaming at the fact that I haven't turned it down yet.

"When would I wear it?" I question.

She stares back at me, her mouth opening and closing before she decides on what to say. "Are you serious? Before you have sex. When the fuck else would you wear it?"

My eyes roll. "No. I know that. But I mean like, for what? Because it's a Tuesday?"

"It's Thursday," she corrects me.

I huff. "You know what I mean!"

"Lai, you're putting too much thought into this. It's just something to wear that Hayes would love and would make you feel good about yourself."

"He makes me feel good about myself."

She chuckles. "Gag me. Stay on the topic, please."

Grabbing it from the bottom, I pull it up to have a closer look. It really is pretty, and even if I don't wear it right away, at least I'll have it for when I want to. His birthday *is* next month. That would be a good time for it.

"Okay," I cave. "I'll take it."

And that's when a brilliant idea comes to mind.

I need to go shopping for something else.

IT'S LATE BY THE time we get back to the bar. I half-expected Hayes to text me a few times, asking where I am and when we're coming back, but he's been relatively quiet. It isn't until we go inside that I see why.

There's a stack of empty beer cans strategically placed into a pyramid. It has to consist of at least thirty cans, and that's not counting the random ones lying around. Being as it's just the two of them, you can imagine the state they're in.

Mali and I stop right inside the door, just in time to see Cam ride his skateboard into the tower. The whole thing collapses, but the best part is when one of them gets caught under the wheel and he busts his ass. Hayes loses it, laughing until he's short of breath and crying. And Cam? I think his ego is more bruised than his body.

"What are you doing?" I ask, more amused than anything.

Cam stands up and runs his fingers through his hair. "Nothing. Just…you know…chillin'."

He's trying to seem nonchalant but he's failing miserably. Especially when he goes cross-eyed as he looks at me. I give him a knowing look and he shakes himself out of it, blowing raspberries at me with his tongue. Then he tries to kick one of the cans and falls flat on his ass again.

Mali's hand comes up to cover her mouth as I pinch the bridge of my nose. Hayes is practically wheezing over in the corner. I don't know what I expected to come back to, but it definitely wasn't this.

"What the hell happened after we left?" I ask through a laugh.

"Funny story," Cam slurs. "We were exhausted. And overworked. We were exhaustitworked."

Hayes gasps. "I know how to twerk!" *Oh God.* "Really! Devin taught me!"

He gets up, putting his hands on his knees and starting to twerk. It's surprisingly not as bad as I thought it would be, but there's something about his long, lean form hunched over and doing pelvic thrusts that absolutely destroys me. Mali scrambles for her phone while I watch him lose his balance and fall face first to the floor—turning his head just in time.

"I'm okay!" he calls out but doesn't bother moving from the floor. "Oh, this is comfortable. Why haven't I done this before?"

"No," I whine. "Don't fall asleep on the floor. I'm going to take you home."

Cam goes over and lies beside him. "This *is* comfortable. We should hang funnels from the ceiling and make it a lay-down bar."

"Good idea!" Hayes drunkenly agrees.

Mali snorts. "People would think they'll get a blowjob or some chick riding cowgirl while they drink."

Both their eyes double in size as their heads whip toward

each other—smiling like idiots and nodding. Then Cam turns toward Mali and sighs heavily.

"You can't be that hot *and* have better ideas than me," he tells her. "It's not fair."

She smirks, popping a piece of gum into her mouth. "I'd say I'm sorry, but I'm not."

"All right," I say, putting an end to this. "You're not opening up a sex bar."

Hayes pouts. "Why not?"

"Because I'm not about to let you around naked women all day." I grab both his hands and pull him upright. "Time to get up. We have to drop Cam off at home and then I'll take you to your house."

"Boo!" Cam groans, giving me a thumbs down. "You're not the boss of me."

"No, but technically, Marc is," I counter. "Should I call him?"

Hayes and Cam gasp and look at each other before forming a united front against me. Cam crosses his arms over his chest while Hayes glares at me.

"You would tell *Dad* on us?" Hayes asks indignantly.

Mali chuckles. "Damn. If I had known they were going to be this fun, I never would have made an excuse for us to get out of here."

"Mali!" I hiss through gritted teeth.

Both Hayes's and Cam's jaws drop, and Cam shakes his head. "You lying liars who lie!"

"For the love of fuck," I grumble at my best friend. "Was that really necessary?"

"Absolutely. Look at them!"

She's enjoying this, and I get it. The two of them rarely get this drunk, and when they do, it always gives us material to hold against them later. It's my favorite part. But right now, I want nothing more than to go curl up in bed with Hayes.

"Well, for that, *you* can be the one to get Cam home," I tell her.

Rolling her eyes, she shrugs. I help Hayes stand up the rest of the way and catch him as he stumbles. With an arm around him, I glance at Cam once more before leaving with Hayes.

"You're really pretty," he slurs. "Do you have a boyfriend?"

Jesus Christ. "Yep."

He exhales sadly. "Damn. He's really lucky."

I walk him over to his truck and slip my hand in his pocket to grab his keys. He jumps at the contact and spins around, putting his hands up.

"Whoa. How will your boyfriend feel about you touching me like that?"

Seriously, this is the last time I leave the two of them alone for a few hours. Like, ever.

"Hayes, baby," I say sweetly. "You *are* my boyfriend."

His eyes light up. "Really? Me?" I nod. "That's fucking sweet!"

If he wasn't so damn adorable right now, I'd probably be pissed. But all I can seem to do is chuckle as I get him to climb into the passenger seat.

A task that takes three attempts, mind you.

Making sure his seatbelt is buckled, I walk around to get in the driver's side. He's already passed out with his head against the window by the time I pull out of the parking lot. But at least this way he won't need me to stop so he can puke.

As I drive back to his place, I think about how tomorrow night is going to suck. Since Hayes moved into his own house, I've been sleeping at his place. My parents think I'm at Mali's—that she's been helping me with new ideas for work. But tomorrow, I have no choice but to sleep at home. And I'm already hating it.

IT TAKES SOME TIME, but I manage to get Hayes inside and up to bed. Though, I did consider leaving him on the couch. If I didn't know I won't get to sleep with him tomorrow night, I would have. There's still the dilemma of getting him undressed, but I decide to change and tie my hair up first.

The stairs were enough of a workout. I can only imagine what this will be like.

He doesn't move as I take his shoes off, but the second I start to undo his belt, he wakes up. His brows furrow as he looks at me, then he smiles.

"Hi."

I giggle softly. "Hi. We have to get you undressed."

He nods. "Okay, but then you have to leave."

"What? Why?"

"Because I have a girlfriend." It looks like he's trying to focus, but it's not going well. "And I'm sure you're great, but she's the only one that's allowed to ride my dick like a rodeo."

"Well, that's good," I say through a laugh. "But H, I told you. I *am* your girlfriend."

He thrashes his head from side to side and then stops, eyes widening like he realized how bad of an idea that is.

"Hayes," I say, taking his face in my hands. "Look at me."

His gaze meets mine, and it takes a moment to process, but then his face lights up. "You *are* my Laiken!" He scrambles with his belt and shoves his pants and boxers down in one go, freeing his cock—which is definitely suffering from whiskey dick at the moment.

"Hop on, cowgirl! This bull is all yours."

I fall onto the bed, unable to contain myself as Hayes smiles proudly back at me. "It's a great bull, babe, but you're too drunk. There's no way you're getting that thing up. How about we get some sleep first, and we'll have sex in the morning when you're not as likely to vomit all over me?"

He pouts as I pull his boxers back up, but once I slip into bed and cuddle up next to him, he wraps his arms around me and falls asleep with ease.

I WAKE IN THE morning to the feeling of soft kisses being pressed against the back of my neck. Hayes slips his hand under my shirt, sliding it up to tweak my nipple between his fingers. I arch into him and moan quietly.

"Good morning," he murmurs.

Honestly, I'm surprised. I thought he would be more hungover than he is.

"Morning," I say breathlessly. "Someone woke up on the right side of the bed this morning."

He hums, pressing another kiss just behind my ear. "How could I not? I get to wake up next to you."

I chuckle. "You're quite the sweet talker for someone who didn't even remember who I was last night. Though, it was good to hear you say I had to leave because you have a girlfriend."

"I did not." All his teasing stops and he groans against his pillow. "Tell me you're lying."

I turn over in his arms to face him. "You did. I believe you said that I'm the only one who's allowed to *ride your dick like a rodeo*."

"For fuck's sake."

I could go on to tell him that he told me to *hop on* while his dick was completely flaccid, but I don't think his ego could take another hit right now. Not when he already looks mortified.

Grabbing my phone, I notice a text from Mali letting me know she got Cam home safely, and another from my mother making sure that I don't forget my grandmother's birthday dinner tonight. Dread runs through me at the reminder. Don't get me wrong, I love my grandmother. But I also love sleeping in bed with Hayes, in a place where we don't need to worry about anyone but each other. And the idea of sleeping without him is not my favorite.

"Ugh," I whine. "I don't want to move from this bed."

"So, don't," Hayes suggests. "Let's stay here and ignore the world together."

God, it's so fucking tempting. It feels like we've been constantly on the go lately. Between my job and Hayes working on the bar, we haven't gotten much time to just enjoy each other. But as much as I'd love to take him up on that, it's too late to cancel the private lessons I have scheduled this morning.

"I really wish I could, especially knowing I'm not sleeping here tonight, but—"

"Wait," he interrupts me. "Why aren't you sleeping here tonight?"

I turn my head to look at him. "I have my grandmother's birthday dinner. I told you that already."

"No, I know. I just thought you'd come here after."

"I would, but I don't know how late it'll run, and I'm not sure my parents will believe me if I say I'm going to Mali's *again*. They're probably already suspicious after the last week and a half."

He doesn't look happy, but he gets it. "Is it bad that I just want to keep you to myself in here?"

I shake my head. "No, because I want that, too. I'll come over tomorrow morning before you go to practice, though."

That's the other thing that sucks this weekend—our schedules do not match well. I won't see him all day today, or all night tonight, and then tomorrow I only get the morning and overnight with him. If Mali wasn't already on me about our codependency issues, I'd cancel going to dinner with her tomorrow so I could have more time with him.

But she would annihilate me.

"If I'm still sleeping, feel free to wake me up with a blowjob," he murmurs tiredly.

Rolling my eyes, I kiss his cheek and sit up. It isn't until he tries to do the same that he hisses, holding his head in pain. I smile as he realizes the mistake of drinking so much with Cam last night.

"I was waiting for that," I tell him, smirking playfully. "I'll get the Advil."

He hums as he lies back down. "See? You can't go anywhere. It'll be like leaving me here to die."

"I could always call your mom to come take care of you."

His eyes fly open as I stand next to his side of the bed. "You wouldn't dare."

I hand him the medicine and the glass of water I grabbed from the bathroom. "Yeah, I didn't think you'd want that. Take these and go back to sleep for an hour. Something tells me I don't think Cam will be at the bar early this morning either."

"Oh, God," he groans. "The banging of hammers!"

Yeah, now he's starting to understand the consequences of his actions.

EVER SINCE I'VE BEEN spending every night with Hayes, my bedroom just doesn't feel the same. It lacks the comfort that it used to bring me. It still looks exactly as it always has, but it's missing something.

It's missing *him*.

I sound crazy. I know that. We've only been dating a few months, openly for less, but I love him. I'm hands down, without a doubt, desperately in love with him. And I won't ever apologize for diving all in with him.

"Cam! Laiken!" Mom calls. "We're leaving! Let's go!"

"Coming!" I shout back as I head down the stairs, only to see Cam wince.

He stares at me in a way that shows how hungover he is. "Must you yell?"

I grin sheepishly and mumble an apology as I slip past him. Our parents are waiting for us by the front door, all dressed up and ready to go. My mom smiles as she sees me and tucks my hair behind my ear.

"You're so pretty," she tells me. "It feels like I never get to see you anymore."

The sadness in her voice hits a soft spot. I mean, it's not like she went out of her way to spend time with me when I wasn't spending every possible moment wrapped up in Hayes. But it's nice to know that I'm missed.

"I've been meaning to go get a pedicure," I reply. "We could both go next week."

A smile spreads across her face. "I'd love that, sweetie."

Cam finally saunters into the living room, taking his sweet ass time, and the four of us head out.

I don't remember the last time all of us were in the same car. Sitting in the backseat has a way of making Cam and me feel like children. Then again, it could also be the fact that Cam *acts* like a child when we're sitting back here.

"Put your window up," he murmurs. "The wind is giving me a headache."

"No. You know the backseat makes me nauseous," I tell him.

"Your face makes me nauseous, but you don't see me complaining."

"Well, your best friend seems to like it just fine."

My dad sighs. "Is the arguing really necessary? You've hardly been around each other lately."

Fuck.

I can already tell by the look on my brother's face that I'm going to regret bringing Hayes into it. He grins deviously and tilts his head to the side.

"Yes, dear sister," he drawls. "Where *have* you been lately?"

The last thing I should do right now is poke the bear, but the arrogance plastered all over his face is grinding on my nerves. I glance down and scream, swatting at something that isn't actually there. Cam's hands fly to his head, and he looks absolutely miserable, which means my plan worked exactly how I hoped.

"Sorry," I say to my parents. "I thought I saw a bug."

They chuckle to themselves, but I'm too busy at watching the way Cam glares at me. He'd never out the fact that I haven't really been at Mali's because he'd catch hell for knowing about it and not saying anything sooner. He may get some kind of revenge later, but at least for right now, the win is mine.

Checkmate, brother.

YOU WOULD THINK THAT when making a product that goes on your lips, they would take into consideration what you're going to touch *with* those lips. Clearly, they haven't done that. If they had, I wouldn't be scrubbing my grandmother's lipstick off my cheek like I need to remove a whole layer of skin to get it off.

She's the sweetest lady, and for a long time she was my favorite person. But the number of times she feels the need to kiss my cheek is unnecessary given the fact that I'm grown now. No matter how much older I get, she still treats me like the six-year-old little girl who thought the bowl of expired candies on her kitchen table tasted good.

Dinner was nice, though, and getting to spend time with my family was great. But I couldn't help wishing Hayes was there. It never even occurred to me to invite him. Not that my parents would have gone for it anyway. Nan has met Hayes numerous times but reintroducing him to her as my boyfriend is a step that I'm sure they don't think we're ready for yet.

As I finish removing the red stains from my cheeks, I climb into bed and grab my phone off the nightstand. A text from Hayes is already waiting for me.

> This bed is too cold without you.

> Says the guy who loves it when the sheets are cold.

I watch as the three dots appear, until his response comes through.

> But I love you more.

Before I can type my reply, Hayes's picture covers my screen.

Facetime Call.

Hitting accept, my very exhausted, *and very shirtless,* boyfriend appears. Just looking at him like this makes my bed feel so empty. He should be here. Or I should be there. But being apart is not it.

Not for us.

"God, how do you do that?" he asks.

My brows furrow. "Do what?"

"Look so damn gorgeous even when you're going to bed."

I chuckle, rolling over and propping my phone up. "You

should have seen me before. There had to be at least three lipstick marks on each cheek."

He hums tiredly. "Someone needs to tell Nan that the only person allowed to mark you is me."

"Jealous of my grandmother now, are you?" I tease.

But his eyes soften as he looks at me through the screen. "Baby, I'm jealous of anyone who gets to be around you while I can't be."

My breathing stutters, the same way it always does when he says things like that. It's like he has direct access to all my heartstrings, and he's wrapping each one of them around his finger.

"I miss you," I say honestly.

A small smile spreads across his face. "I miss you, too."

We both lie there, just staring at each other the only way we can right now. It's not nearly close enough, but it's better than not being able to see him at all. I'm starting to think maybe Mali has a point.

"Is it a red flag how codependent we are?" I question.

He barely considers it for a second. "Not to me."

Well, that's all that matters.

The two of us stay on Facetime—not really saying much but both needing to know the other is there—and I manage to finally doze off to the sound of his breathing.

SATURDAY MORNINGS ARE SUPPOSED to be the

one morning I have to sleep in. With the guys having an early practice, it pushes my lessons back by at least two extra hours. During the playoffs, it's even longer. But no matter how hard I try, I just can't seem to stay asleep once the sun peeks above the horizon.

It's like my body knows that Hayes isn't beside me.

So, after a quick shower and a stop for donuts, I head straight for his house. I'm half expecting him to still be asleep when I get there. Waking up early never has been his thing. But to my surprise, I open the door to find him in the kitchen, brewing a pot of coffee.

He turns to look at me, and the moment I put the box of donuts on the island, he crashes into me and wraps his arms around my body. It's all the confirmation I needed to know that he missed me just as much as I missed him. And even with everything Mali has been saying about one night apart every now and then being healthy for couples, I don't care enough to stop.

Being around him makes me happy. Why does that have to be a bad thing?

"I brought donuts," I say, not moving.

He breathes me in and kisses the top of my head. "I see that. Thank you."

"I don't want to let go yet though."

"Good," he answers through a chuckle. "Because I don't either."

We stay there, sharing lazy kisses and just being close until the coffee pot beeps, signaling it's done. Only then do we let go, but the way he keeps glancing over at me tells me he hasn't had enough yet.

I hop up onto the island and pull a donut out of the box, while Hayes sits on one of the barstools. He looks up at me with that perfect smirk on his face, and I just know he's thinking about how he ate me out in this very spot. My thighs press together involuntarily at the memory.

"I couldn't sleep last night," he tells me as he grabs his own donut.

"No?"

"Nope, and it's all your fault."

A frown forces its way through. *My* fault?

He takes a bite and nods. "Mm-hm. So, I'm going to need you to make arrangements to be here every night for the foreseeable future." My jaw falls open as I stare at him. "May as well bring all your shit with you, too. Thanks."

I sit here, gaping at him and wondering if I heard him wrong. The words that just came out of his mouth were spoken with such casualness that you would think we were talking about what we have planned today. Not some major life choice.

When he notices I haven't said anything, he looks up at me. "What?"

"D-did you just ask me to move in with you?"

"No," he says with a mouthful of donut, and my stomach drops for a second. "I *told* you to move in with me. There's a difference."

My brows raise as I chuckle. "Oh, well in that case, I'm going to pass. You know, in the name of women everywhere who don't let men tell them what to do."

He rolls his eyes playfully, dropping his half-eaten donut into the open box and standing up. His hands come to rest on either side of me, his face only inches from mine, and the way he licks his lips has my attention so locked on him, it's pathetic.

"Laiken," he says seriously. "Will you please move in with me so that I don't have to spend another cold and lonely night without you for the rest of my life?"

My heart is trying to beat out of my chest as I smile. Trust me when I say that there is nothing I'd love more than to live here with him. Making this place *ours*. Our own little space where the smell of his cologne and my perfume constantly linger in the air—I want that so bad. The *yes* is right there on the tip of my tongue. It would be so easy to say it. But...

"I'd love to," I tell him, and his grin widens as he exhales. "But I can't. My parents would literally off us both. I mean, we've only been together for a few months. I can only imagine the conniption they would have if I told them I was moving in with you out of wedlock."

His joy is replaced, but not by disappointment. He looks more thoughtful than anything as he stares into my eyes. God, sometimes I wish I could just read his mind.

Whatever conclusion he comes to, it doesn't take him long, because he hums, dropping a quick kiss on my lips. "I can work with that."

Hang on. "Work with *what*?"

But he doesn't answer as he grabs his donut and holds it with his mouth before picking up his phone and car keys off the counter. Then he heads for the front door without a second glance.

"H, what does that mean?" Still silence. "Hayes!"

He takes the donut out of his mouth as he opens the door. "Love you!"

And then he's just gone, leaving me to wonder what the actual fuck just happened.

Chapter 15

HAVE YOU EVER TRIED teaching someone how to do something while your brain is laser focused on something else? It's practically impossible. I spend most of the day in a daze, trying to figure out what the hell he meant by that. I've racked my brain for hours, and the only plausible thing I've come up with is that he's going to try getting my parent's permission to move me in with him. It would be totally out of character for him, but nothing about the way he's been since we became official has been anything like he used to be —not when it comes to me, anyway.

I'm sitting at dinner with Mali, pushing the salad around my plate while she rambles about how Cam freaked when he realized she drove his Jeep the other night. Normally, I would be completely immersed in everything she's saying. But normally, I don't have a bomb dropped on me at breakfast that has me trying to solve the world's hardest puzzle all day.

Whatever it is he plans on doing, I hope it works. Because even the thought of getting to wake up next to him every single morning makes me feel like I'm floating. I'd be lying if I said I haven't pictured it while we've played house over the last week. I just never let myself believe that was something he wants, too. Never until now.

"For some reason I always thought your brother had an average sized dick, so I was pleasantly surprised."

I snap myself out of it with a shake of my head. "Wait, what the fuck?"

She leans back and crosses her arms over her chest. "Exactly. You weren't paying attention to a single word I said."

"I know it was about my brother and his Jeep."

"Lai, that was just the lead-in to the story," she tells me.

I cringe. "Oops?"

"Yeah, oops." She runs her fingers through her hair. "What's on your mind?"

213

I take a deep breath, wondering if it's better to slowly lead into this or just spit it out. But something tells me trying to beat around the bush with this will only lead to Mali making her own assumptions.

"Hayes asked me to move in with him this morning," I admit.

Mali is mid sip as the words spill from my mouth, and she chokes on her soda, coughing violently. "Fucking hell, we need to work on your timing."

"I'd say I'm sorry, but I'm really not."

She flips me off. "What the hell did you say to that?"

I sigh. "I said no...I think."

"You *think*?"

"Yeah. I mean, I wanted to say yes. *So fucking badly*. But you know how my parents are. They're lenient with a lot of the rules the church believes they should have us abide by, but living with Hayes when we're not married? Something tells me that's not going to make the list."

"Jesus," she breathes, leaning back against the seat. "Was he upset?"

"That's the strangest part," I tell her. "He wasn't at all. I explained why I couldn't, and I thought he would feel rejected, but he just kissed me and told me he can work with that. Then he left and I haven't talked to him much since. He's barely even responding to my texts."

"He can work with that?" Mali repeats back to me. "What the hell is that supposed to mean?"

"Exactly!" I nearly shout. "I can't figure it out, and the fact that he's barely answering me isn't helping either."

She tilts her head to the side as she thinks. "Maybe he *does* feel rejected, but he understands your reasoning so he's working on getting over it on his own."

"Then why would he say he can work with that? What's that even mean?"

"Maybe that he can work with knowing you're not exactly saying no, but more saying *not right now*."

That's a possibility that never occurred to me. But if he's upset about it, I'd rather he tell me than disappear to deal with it on his own. I don't want him having any doubts about our relationship. There's no reason for any.

"Yeah," I murmur. "Yeah, you're probably right."

She snickers. "I mean, it's either that or he's going to propose, but it took that man months just to come to terms with the idea of a relationship. You're probably looking at five years *minimum* before he can even Google *jewelry stores near me*."

His words from this morning play through my mind.

"Will you please move in with me so that I don't have to spend another cold and lonely night without you for the rest of my life?"

For. The. Rest. Of. My. Life.

"But hey," Mali continues, keeping me from falling down that rabbit hole. "You *are* nineteen. If you want to move in with him, legally your parents can't stop you."

I chuckle and give her a knowing look. "Sure, if I wanted to be disowned."

"Point taken."

Grabbing a crouton from my plate, I toss it into my mouth—wondering what kind of mood Hayes will be in when I see him tonight.

CHAPTER SIXTEEN

Hayes

I'VE NEVER BEEN A NERVOUS PERSON. THE confidence I've possessed has become a well-known staple in my reputation. Some might choose to call it cockiness instead, and I once heard Mali refer to it as big dick energy, but it's all the same thing. I'm not the kind of guy who shies away from a challenge or backs down from what he wants—apart from when I bitched out about telling Cam about Laiken and me that one day.

But right now, I've never been more anxious.

The day my dad left, I told myself that happily ever afters don't exist. That fairy tales are for books, and no one ever really loves someone more than they love themselves. And for years, all that has been true for me. I never found someone that made me second guess what I believed—until Laiken.

In just a few months, she's proven me wrong at every turn and shown me things completely different from what I thought I knew. With her, I have a relationship that is just as much about friendship as it is being in love. I have a person that doesn't only make my day better but makes me look forward to every day after it. I have someone who has taught me what it feels like to care about another person more than I could ever care about myself.

My other half.

My favorite person.

My once-in-a-lifetime kind of love.

So, as I walk out with a little velvet box bulging from my pocket, there isn't a doubt in my mind that it was always going to come to this.

I STAND IN THE mirror, putting more effort into my hair than I have in months. The thought of wearing a suit passed through my mind for a second, but I decided against it. I can still look good without making her feel underdressed.

My heart feels like a damn hummingbird inside my chest, beating a million times a minute. I could take a shot to calm my nerves, but I don't want to. I want to feel every second of it. After all, I'm hoping this is a one and done.

Headlights shine through the windows and into the house as Laiken pulls into the driveway, and I know it's time. Everything that's running through my mind intensifies—red lights and warning sirens from the part of me that wants to run. But I'm not going anywhere. Not tonight. Not tomorrow. Not ever.

Taking a shaky, deep breath, I let it out slowly and then head downstairs. Everything looks perfect, with lit candles all over the first floor of the house, a bottle of wine in an ice bucket with a couple of glasses on the table, and the most important question I've ever asked spelled out in rose petals on the floor. I just hope it's enough.

As I hear her step up onto the porch, I know that this is it. This is the moment that I lay it all on the line. I'm handing over my heart, my whole heart, for Laiken to do whatever she wants with. And regardless of the outcome, I know I'm never going to get it back.

The door opens and Laiken walks in, freezing as soon as she sees the scene in front of her. I'm honestly not sure I'm breathing at all as she drops her bag and looks around. Finally, her eyes land on me, but I can't seem to get a read on them.

"Did you hit your head recently?" she asks.

I chuckle because I expected this. "No."

"Drugs?"

Taking a step toward her, I shake my head slowly. "Nope."

"Some kind of fucked-up dare where the guys are going to jump out and say I've been Punk'd, like you all used to do a few years ago?"

My grin widens as I pull the ring box from my pocket and open it in front of her. All of the air leaves her lungs in one breath and she stares at the gorgeous diamond in disbelief.

"You're seriously proposing to me right now?"

Yes. "You say that like it's such an outrageous concept."

She looks a little skeptical. "Not *outrageous*, just not like you."

Her words instantly make me wonder if I haven't done nearly enough to prove to her how much she means to me. How important she is.

"What do you mean?" I ask nervously.

"Hayes," she sighs. "It took you until a month ago just to say *I love you*."

I huff out a laugh. "Yeah, because I'm a pussy. Not because I haven't been completely fucking gone for you from the start."

The way she smiles gives me a little hope. "I just don't want you to feel like you need to rush into this. I'm not going anywhere. Okay? Just because I can't live with you right now doesn't mean I'm not going to be here every day."

"No," I say, cutting her off from saying anything else. "Let me make something very clear here, because I'm not sure you fully understand."

Taking a step closer, I rest my arms on her shoulders and stare into her eyes—really making sure she's listening to every word coming out of my mouth.

"You're it for me, Laiken. I don't care if it's been a few months or thirty goddamn years. That isn't going to change. So, you can say no and we can play the long game if that's what you want. We can take it slow. But I'm going to spend the rest of my life loving you, regardless." A single tear slides down her cheek and I gently wipe it away. "This isn't me trying to rush into something to get my way. This is me acting on what I want with absolute certainty that it's the right move—because you are the *best thing* that has ever happened to me. And I don't need to wait in order to know that you're the one I want to grow old with."

Her bottom lip quivers, and her gaze doesn't leave mine as she swats away each tear that slips out. "Okay."

"Okay?" I question, hope swelling inside my chest.

She nods and a smile spreads over her face. "Okay. Ask me."

My heart jolts, nearly lunging from my chest and throwing itself at her feet. The future is always a crapshoot. There's no way of knowing what will happen. But the one thing I do know is that this woman will forever be the one for me. There will never be a time where I don't love her with everything I have.

I grin, trying not to tear up myself as I drop down onto one knee in front of her. She giggles as she cries happily and watches as I open the box once more.

"Laiken Rose," I say, looking up at her and almost swaying from the intensity of my feelings for her. "If I've learned anything over the last few months, it's that this life isn't worth living if I don't have you by my side. I'm already the luckiest man in the world for getting any time with you at all, but I'm greedy and I want every second you have to give. So, for the love of God, marry me, because anything less than forever with you just isn't enough for me."

She's a mess by the end of it, letting the tears drip from her face and onto her shirt, but she's still the most beautiful woman I've ever seen. And when she manages to nod up and down, I know this image is going to be burned into my mind until the end of time.

"Yes?" I double-check.

She nods. "Yes, I'll marry you."

I have heard a lot of amazing things in my life, but the sound of those words coming out of her mouth easily takes the top spot. With one sentence, she makes me the happiest I've ever been in my entire life. I stand up and wrap my arms around her, kissing her with every possible thing I've got.

She's been my best friend's sister, my only secret, and my girlfriend. Now, she's my fiancée. And I can't fucking wait for the day where she becomes my wife.

Pulling the ring out of the box, the two of us are all happiness and smiles as I slide it onto her finger. Just seeing it there, knowing she's mine, it does things to me. It sets me on fire and makes me feel safe all at once.

She fucking said yes.

The two of us stare at it, seeing how perfect it looks on her finger, and when she looks up at me, I somehow manage to fall a little harder.

"I love you, so much," she tells me.

I exhale with a smile. "I love you more."

And as I cover her mouth with my own and pull her into me, I plan on showing her just how much I mean those words.

I LIE ON MY side, propping myself up on my elbow and resting my head in my hands. I can't look away from my new fiancée—though I wouldn't even if I could. I'm too busy admiring just how beautiful she really is. Her chest rises and falls as she waits for her breathing to calm. Her lips are a deep red and a little swollen from all of the kissing. And the mark I left just below her right breast speaks straight to the part of me that wants to scream from the rooftops that she's mine.

Her hair is splayed out on the floor, and I reach up to pull a rose petal out of it. She giggles, taking it from me and blowing it away.

"You've really turned into one hell of a romantic," she teases.

I chuckle and dip down to kiss her once more. "Tell

anyone and I'll say you're full of shit. My reputation has no room for a Sappy Fucker title."

"Okay, totally changing your name in my phone to Sappy Fucker now," she jokes. "But no, I won't be telling anyone. Are you kidding? All the girls that try hitting on you are only looking for a hookup because they're convinced that you're not *boyfriend material*. No way in hell am I correcting that. They'll break our damn door down."

There's only one part of what she just said that has all of my attention. "*Our* door? I like the sound of that."

She bites her lip as she smiles. "Me too."

My hand rests on her stomach, my thumb moving back and forth across her skin. "God, I can't believe I'm marrying you."

"How are we going to do it?" she asks. "I don't think either of us has the patience for a long engagement."

I shake my head. "Definitely not. I want you to be my wife as soon as humanly possible. I want you where you belong—infiltrating all of my space and sleeping beside me every night."

That makes her smile just a little brighter. "So, courthouse in the morning? A flight to Vegas within the next couple days to elope?"

It's tempting, honestly. There's no doubt I'm about to walk us right into a shitshow. But I don't want her to think that I'm trying to hide her, or us, or what she means to me. Not anymore.

"No," I tell her. "I respect both of our mothers way too much to do that to them."

Laiken's brows furrow. "Okay...what are you thinking instead?"

"I'm thinking I want to marry you in front of the ones we love. Nothing crazy. Just you, me, and the most important people in our lives. And that includes your parents."

Realization crosses her face, and she nods. "Ah, so this is a suicide mission. Got it. I'm clued in now."

My eyes roll playfully and I tickle her side, sending her into a fit of giggles.

Whatever we have to deal with, it'll be worth it.

Hayes

CHAPTER SEVENTEEN

My mom has always been the one person to consistently have my back. It never mattered if I was in the right or the wrong. She would make me own up for my mistakes, but she would do it in a way where I knew she was just looking out for me. I've never been afraid to tell her anything.

Until now.

It's not like she won't be supportive. I know she will. But I think a part of me is afraid to tell her that I'm getting my happy-ever-after, when she was cheated out of her own.

Laiken sits beside me at my mom's kitchen table, her left hand tucked into the sleeve of her hoodie to hide the ring. I suggested she could just take it off and keep it in her pocket for now, but she refused. Said that if that ring ever leaves her finger, it won't be on her own free will.

"H," my mom says. "You've got to say something. You're starting to worry me here."

I can see the way Laiken smirks out of the corner of my eye and I take a deep breath. "I know. Nothing's wrong. Just give me a second."

And then, as if it's the most natural thing in the world, Lai reaches over and laces her fingers with mine. We've never shown affection in front of either of our parents, but this is different. This is her knowing that I need her.

A silent message to tell me that she's right here, and she's not going anywhere. Even if today goes to complete shit.

Her hand squeezes mine three times, and I reply with four back.

"Mom," I say calmly. "I love Laiken."

"Okay...this isn't something I haven't already known," she replies.

"I know, but I need you to understand just how much I love her. How strong it is and how I would do absolutely anything to be with her."

"H," Mom says through a chuckle. "She's the only girl you've *ever* brought home. I may not have ever asked you about this stuff, but don't think for a second that I don't know you. I could see it in the way you looked at her the first morning I saw you two together. She's your one."

This. This right here is one of the things I appreciate most about my mother. I look over at Laiken to find a light blush on her cheeks. And when her eyes meet mine, we both smile.

"Don't worry. It's mutual," Mom tells me.

"I know it is," I reply. "Because I asked her to marry me, and she said yes."

My mom's eyes widen. "Okay, I didn't see *that* coming."

"It's fast. I know."

"It's NASCAR," she corrects.

I nod. "But Mom, I've never been so sure of anything in my entire life. She's everything to me, and I know what you're thinking. That there's no rush. And that if we're meant to spend the rest of our lives together, we're already doing it. But every time I think about her, the word *girlfriend* never seems to fit. She's so much more than that. So, I don't want to wait just because society set some kind of standard timeline on this shit. I want to make her mine, legally and as officially as possible."

My mom sighs, a soft smile on her face as she turns to Laiken. "And what about you? I'm sure your parents are going to have their reservations about this."

"Let them," she answers simply, then her gaze locks with mine. "We'll deal with it the same way we'll deal with everything else—together."

I've never kissed a girl in front of my mom. I've never had someone *worthy* of being kissed in front of my mom. But with Laiken, she's worth the whole damn world, and nothing can stop me from pressing my lips to hers.

My mom sniffles, wiping a tear from her cheek. "Dammit, sorry. It's just really nice to see you so happy."

"I *am* happy. I get to spend the rest of my life with someone who makes me the best version of myself."

"That's all I've ever wanted for you," she says. "Congratulations to you both. The only advice I can give you is to remember this feeling. Hold onto it and never let it go."

I pull Laiken in and kiss the top of her head. "That's exactly what I'm doing."

The front door opens behind me, and my sister stops when she sees us all sitting at the table.

"Oh God," Dev groans. "Who died *now*?"

My mom chuckles and up-nods at me to tell her. I turn around to see the reaction on her face. She's holding a McDonald's cup in one hand and her wallet in the other, and she stares back at me curiously.

"What?"

"How would you like to have a sister-in-law?"

Everything immediately falls out of her hands, the cup spilling on the floor, as she throws her hands over her mouth. Tears fill her eyes, and she glances between Laiken and me, nodding excitedly.

That's when the whole mood changes. The weight lifts off my chest, and I watch as my mom and sister hug Laiken, demanding to see the ring. I even manage to get a nod of approval from Devin—though I'm pretty sure she's taking partial credit for Laiken and me.

Brat.

By the time we head out the door, I feel a million times better.

"See?" I ask Laiken. "That wasn't so bad."

She chuckles. "Are you kidding? That was just a practice run."

I climb into my truck as she gets in the passenger side. Looking over at me, she knows where we're headed next. And maybe I shouldn't get ahead of myself, thinking that everyone will be happy for us.

Lai smirks at me as she buckles her seatbelt. "You have a living will, right?"

Fuck.

OKAY, SO MAYBE SHE was right. My mom *was* the practice run. And it went really well. But as I sit here, staring across the couch from Laiken's parents, I feel like there isn't enough oxygen in this room. My hands are sweating. My collar seems too tight. There's a good possibility that I'm choking on my own saliva right now.

Everything was going well. They were happy to see us both when we got here. But the tension started to grow the second Laiken asked if we could all sit down and talk. And now, as I look over at her, she raises her brows at me.

"This was your idea, Casanova," she teases. "I'm just here for entertainment purposes."

Well, she has a point. She *was* completely on Team Vegas. She may have been onto something. A part of me wonders if it's too late to choose differently. But I meant what I told her. I respect our mothers, and her father for that matter, way too much to marry her without them there to see it.

I breathe in deeply and let it out slowly, looking at the people who have become a second set of parents for me over the last third of my life. "Mr. and Mrs. Blanchard, I would like to marry your daughter."

Her dad's mouth opens and shuts multiple times as he swings between confused and outraged, while her mom puts a hand to her chest to clutch her metaphorical pearls.

"I'm going to be a grandmother?" she asks tearfully.

"No!" Laiken and I answer, urgently and in unison.

Mr. Blanchard's face turns beet red. "You knocked up my daughter?"

"No," Laiken stops him. "Dad. No. I'm not pregnant."

Both her parents sigh—her father in relief and her mom out of what looks a lot like disappointment. Laiken tilts her head at her for a second before shaking it off.

"Okay," Mr. Blanchard says. "So, what's with the shotgun wedding?"

I sit up a little straighter. "Well, as you know, there have been some big changes in my life lately, and they revealed things to me that I didn't even realize I wanted—the main one being your daughter, officially and permanently," I explain. "So, with your permission, and respectfully, even without it, I plan on marrying her and making her my wife."

"The fuck you are!" Cam's angry voice echoes through the room.

And okay, I probably should have talked to him about this first. But I was afraid he would try to talk me out of it.

Judging by his reaction right now, I think that was a pretty accurate assumption.

"Cameron!" his mom chastises. "Language!"

Cam scoffs. "No. Fuck that. It was one thing when they started dating, but I'm not going to sit around and watch him legally lock her down because he wants pussy on demand."

"Sweet Lord," Mrs. Blanchard says, mortified.

Meanwhile, Mr. Blanchard looks like he's plotting my murder—and it's going to be a violent one. "Is that true? Is that all you're trying to get out of my little girl?"

All Laiken is lacking right now is popcorn as she rests her chin in her hands and leans toward me. "This is going well."

Jesus fucking Christ.

"No!" I tell her dad, then turn to Cam and repeat it. "No."

But he doesn't want to hear it, and he storms out of the room, leaving us to clean up the mess he just made. I know that's something I'll need to deal with in a bit. The last thing I want is for him to be pissed at me again. Especially when we're in the process of opening a bar together. Right now, however, I have to focus on Mr. Blanchard before he kills me and buries my body in the backyard.

"That's not at all true. Not even remotely."

He looks me up and down, judging me more than he ever has in the last seven years, and I don't blame him for it. "Then what? Why do you want to marry my daughter?"

"Because I love her more than I've ever loved anything," I answer immediately. "She has very quickly become the center of my entire universe. The one person I cannot live without. And if I can spend the rest of my life making her feel for me, even *half* of what I feel for her, that would be a life worth living."

Laiken's eyes meet mine, and she smiles in the way that's reserved only for me. I take her hand in my own, kissing the back of it. If I die today at the hands of her father, it would still all be worth it.

But he seems to be calming down, so maybe I'll survive another day. He watches the two of us skeptically and then sighs as he focuses solely on his daughter.

"And what about you?" he questions. "Is this what *you* want?"

She reveals her left hand, with the diamond ring sparkling on her finger. "Would I be wearing the ring if I didn't?"

Her mom's eyes widen as she comes closer. "Oh, sweetie. It's gorgeous."

She's right. It is a very pretty ring. I knew it was the one the moment I saw it. But even so, it pales in comparison to the woman wearing it.

Laiken smiles at her father. "I love him, Dad. I know it seems fast. I get that. And it is…for you. But I've been in love with him since I was fifteen years old." She glances over and nudges me with her elbow. "He just took a little while to get up to speed."

I chuckle, rolling my eyes fondly. Leave it to her to make me laugh in the middle of a situation as tense as this one. But that's the thing about her. I could be in the center of my own personal nightmare, and with her by my side, there's nothing that can bring me down. She makes me stronger. Better. Worthy of being loved the way she loves me.

"I'll be honest," Mr. Blanchard begins. "It's not my favorite thing to ever happen. Nothing against you, Hayes. We love you like a son. You know that. You're a good guy, and you've always been a great friend to Cam. But Laiken getting married at nineteen was never what we pictured for her."

My heart sinks inside of my chest. I know I said I would marry her without his blessing, but honestly, I don't know that I have it in me to betray him like that. I don't know that I could do that to Laiken.

"With that being said," he continues. "While I may not love the idea of you two getting married so young, I *do* love my daughter. Her happiness is and always has been very important to me. So, if this is genuinely what you two want to do, you have my blessing. But you need to promise me that you will always take care of her, putting her needs before your own."

"I promise," I say honestly. "She's in good hands."

"Now *that* I believe."

Here I go again, feeling breathless, but this time it's in the best way. We all stand up. Laiken goes to hug her mom, while I shake her dad's hand. These people, who have been there for me during some of the toughest times of my life, are going to be my in-laws. Not only am I getting the best person I know as my wife, but they will legally be my family.

I don't think I've ever felt so blessed.

But before I can fully enjoy the moment, I have something else that needs to be dealt with first.

"Excuse me," I tell the three of them. "I'll be back."

They all understand, knowing exactly where I'm going. And as Laiken sits down with her mom and explains what we were thinking for a wedding, I head through the kitchen and up the stairs. I consider just walking in, but then I remember the hockey puck that flew at my head the night I told him about Laiken and me, and I decide against it.

I knock twice, then open the door—standing back a little. When nothing gets thrown, I peek my head in and see Cam sitting on his bed. He rolls his eyes, but doesn't tell me to get out, so I walk in and sit beside him.

"Does the offer to stab you still stand?" he grumbles. I pull the switchblade out of my pocket and hold it out for him, but he just scoffs. "Smartass."

It's quiet for a moment while I choose my words carefully.

"You think the worst of me when it comes to your sister," I tell him. "And I don't blame you for it. I've never given you any reason to think differently. All you've known when it comes to me and girls are meaningless hookups and one-night stands. But I need you to trust me when I say that this is different."

"Oh, fuck off with that shit," he sneers. "You two have been together for what? Like three and a half months? You barely even know her."

I smile down at my lap. "I know she talks in her sleep if she drinks caffeine before bed. And that while she acts like a badass, and a part of her is, she's also fragile and would throw herself on a blade to protect those she loves. I know that she doubts herself on a constant basis, even though she's the most amazing person I've ever met." As a distraction, I pick at a string on my jeans while Cam stays completely silent. "And I know her older brother is one of her favorite people in the world, and if he won't be at our wedding, there won't be one because he's one of the most important people in her life...and in mine."

He exhales, showing he's listening, but I haven't won him over yet.

"Answer me this," I tell him. "When have you ever seen me even let a girl stay the night, let alone want to spend every single moment with one—awake or asleep?"

The phone he was flipping in his hand stops and he sighs. "Fucking hell. This really isn't just a fling, is it?"

I shake my head. "I want to spend the rest of my life with her."

He snorts. "You really hate yourself that much?"

The two of us chuckle, and I feel better knowing that we're going to be okay. He's always been like a brother to me, and now he's going to be my brother-in-law. When we were younger, we used to talk about how cool it would be if we were brothers. But I don't think he ever thought that would happen by me marrying his sister.

Though it did pass through my mind, even then.

"So, what do you say?" I ask. "Will you be my best man?"

He huffs out a laugh, shaking his head in disbelief. "Yes, but on one condition."

"What's that?"

"Stop asking me important questions right after I stop being pissed at you."

My head rests back against the wall. "Aw, man. I was planning on arguing with you right before I ask you to be the godfather of our future kid."

He turns and gives me a knowing look. "As if you want *me* raising your kid if anything ever happens to you two."

Fair point. "Eh, with a certain spitfire, I think you'd do just fine. And speaking of...when are you going to do something about that?"

Cam instantly looks away, letting out a heavy exhale. "I don't know, man. That's a five-beers- deep conversation."

"It's a good thing we're opening a bar, isn't it?"

CHAPTER EIGHTEEN

LITTLE GIRLS DREAM ABOUT THEIR WEDDING DAY. They imagine what it's going to look like, the kind of dress they'll be wearing, and who they'll invite. But me? I always pictured who was at the other end of the aisle. And since I was fifteen, I pictured Hayes.

Granted, I told myself it was never going to happen. That he would never see me as anything other than his best friend's little sister. But it was still fun to fantasize about it and wonder what it would be like.

If only that girl could see me now—in my mom's wedding dress, with my hair curled and a veil sitting on top of my head.

Hayes wasn't kidding when he said he wanted to marry me as soon as humanly possible. He's nothing if not impatient. When we went to the courthouse two days ago to get our marriage license, he almost tried to marry me there. But if we were going to do it that way, there was no point in telling our parents beforehand.

Besides, this feels more special.

"Do I look okay?" I ask my mom.

She dabs under her eyes with a tissue for what feels like the millionth time since she walked in. "You look beautiful, sweetheart. I always knew you would make such a gorgeous bride."

I smile, looking at myself in the mirror once more. Honestly, I can't believe we're here. Even at dinner that night with Mali, we barely even considered the possibility that proposing was what he meant by *I can work with that*. And speaking of...

As I hear the sound of footsteps climbing the stairs, I also hear Mali grumbling to herself. And I should probably mention that I haven't told her about *any* of this yet. Partly because I didn't want her trying to talk me out of it, and also because this way is much more fun.

"Your boyfriend is fucking weird," she says as she walks in the room, her eyes focused on her phone. "He wouldn't let me come in the front door. Insisted that I come in the back and straight upstairs for some rea—" Her head raises to look at me and she freezes. "You're in a wedding dress."

I smirk. "Nothing gets past you, does it?"

That's when she sees my mom sitting in the chair, also dressed up, and her eyes widen as she looks at me once more. "Y-you're getting married? Like, today? Right now?"

"Yes," I say slowly. "And if you'll be my maid of honor, your dress is hanging in the bathroom."

She goes into the bathroom and grabs the dress, then comes back out, still looking at me like I'm crazy. "How pregnant are you, exactly?"

"She's not," my mom tells her, complete with air quotes.

Jesus Christ. "Mom, really. I'm *not* pregnant."

But she just sighs, as if she knows more about whether or not I'm with child than I do. "It's okay, sweetie. I understand the importance of waiting until you're three months along to tell people."

Oh, for fuck's sake.

My eyes meet Mali's, and she must be able to see that I'm at my wits end with her about this, because she presses her fist to her mouth to keep from laughing, then distracts herself with getting dressed.

I NEVER REALLY UNDERSTOOD the whole *something old, something new* tradition. Who decided that a bunch of random shit is necessary in order to have a good marriage? Did they poll the people who didn't have it all and see how many got divorced? Hell, half of the couples who get married these days get divorced. There must not be enough *something blue* to go around.

Still, as my mom checks to make sure I have everything, I don't try to stop her. It's little things like this that make her happy. Though, when she puts her hand on my lower belly when she says *something new*, that's it for me.

"Mom!" I push her hand away. "Again, not pregnant."

She chuckles. "Sure, honey."

My eyes roll as she grabs my bouquet and hands it to me, showing me the blue flower in the center—the one I don't have the heart to tell her is actually teal. But it's fine. Mali subtly grabs a blue hair clip from her bag and clips it to the side of the bouquet.

"Okay," Mom says, looking me over once more and fanning her eyes when she starts to cry again. "I'll see you downstairs. I love you so much."

I can't help but smile. "I love you, too, Mom."

The second she's out of the room, Mali looks at me with narrowed eyes. "Seriously, not even a little pregnant?"

"Nope."

She hums amusedly. "Huh. Your mom is going to be

devastatingly disappointed in a few months." I giggle just before she finally says what she's been dying to since she walked in. "But if you're not pregnant, do you mind telling me what the fuck is going on? Since when are you getting *married*?"

"Since a few nights ago," I confess. "That conversation you and I had at dinner Saturday night? Yeah, I came over that night, and he asked me to marry him."

"Holy fucking shit. This was *Hayes's* idea?"

"Yeah," I breathe. "And I tried to tell him he didn't need to do this. I gave him an out. But he practically convinced me into it. Not that I wouldn't have said yes immediately if I'd known he was serious."

Mali looks utterly shocked as she tries to make sense of it. "Damn, babe. What kind of magical pussy do you have?"

I chuckle, just as my dad knocks twice and opens the door. The moment his gaze lands on me, his eyes start to water. I'm used to my mom crying. Once, I took my time wishing on my birthday candles, and she cried because I *put so much thought into it*. But I've never seen my dad shed a single tear until now, and it instantly gets to me.

"Wow," he chokes out. "I've thought about this moment since the day you were born. You're a lot younger than I thought you would be, but you're just as beautiful. Hayes is a very lucky man."

Pressing my lips in a line to try to keep from crying, I walk toward my dad and hug him. He lightly kisses my cheek and then moves his mouth to right by my ear.

"And if he ever hurts you, he's going to be a very *dead* man."

Laughter bubbles out of me. "Thanks, Dad."

He rubs my back and looks over at Mali. "You look good, Mal."

"Thank you, Daddy B," she says, then cringes. "Mm,

nope. Can't call you that anymore. Hook up with a guy with a daddy kink one time and everything changes..."

My dad chokes on air. "Still lacking that filter, I see."

As if she just realized what she said, her eyes fall closed, and she pinches the bridge of her nose. "Yep. Sure am."

Meanwhile, I'm laughing so hard my stomach hurts, because *what the actual fuck* did she just say to my dad. She looks completely mortified, and so does my dad, for that matter. Thankfully, Cam peeks his head in the door.

"You guys ready?" But when he sees me, he smiles. "Look at you."

"How is he?" I ask nervously. "Is he still going to be there when I get downstairs?"

Cam rolls his eyes. "Are you kidding? Why do you think I'm up here? He's ready to drag Pastor Todd up here and marry you in the bedroom."

Well, that would save us time later. But *unlike Mali,* I have a filter, so that thought stays tucked away inside my brain.

"Okay, good," I say, relieved. "Yeah, we're ready."

Cam nods, and before he leaves, he comes over to give me a hug. "I'm happy for you, sis, even if you *are* stealing my best friend."

"Please. You're opening a bar together," I tell him. "You're going to get more time with him than I will."

"Rightfully so. He was mine first."

I stick my tongue out at him, and he chuckles before leaving the room.

As I hear the music start to play downstairs, I know that it's time. My dad, Mali, and I walk over to the stop of the stairs. In a few minutes, I will be Mrs. Laiken Wilder. And *oh my God*, that just hit me.

Mali goes down one step and then turns around. "You're sure about this? Because we can go out the backdoor—be in Bora Bora by noon tomorrow. No one will find us."

I smile at the offer as my dad tilts his head toward me. "I hear it's beautiful there this time of year."

"You are both impossible," I say with a sigh and then I nod at Mali. "I'm sure. Go."

"All right," she says skeptically. "Let's go get you a ball and chain."

I watch as she carefully walks down the stairs and turns, winking at me before she steps out of view. Holding onto my dad's arm, I take a deep breath as we head down together. All I can do is focus on not tumbling all the way down the stairs, but once we reach the bottom and turn toward the living room, I look up and my gaze locks with Hayes's.

Any nerves I had dissipate immediately. Just like that, nothing else matters. I love him and I want to spend the rest of my life with him. People can think I'm crazy, or assume I must be knocked up. I don't care. Because if they had what we do, they'd make the same exact decision.

He stares back at me with the biggest smile plastered across his face and tears in his eyes, and I don't stand a chance at holding back now. My lips purse as I try not to cry. He drops his head as he laughs and wipes away a stray tear.

What feels like ages later, we finally get up to him. He steps forward and shakes my dad's hand.

"If you ever do her wrong, I *will* kill you," my dad tells him.

Hayes looks at me with nothing but admiration in his eyes, but his words are meant for my dad. "If that ever happens, I'll let you."

He seems to like that answer, because he kisses my cheek and passes me to Hayes—officially giving me away. Leaning forward, Hayes brings his lips to my ear.

"You are breathtaking."

Butterflies erupt in my stomach, and I hand Mali my bouquet as I step in front of the pastor who has watched

Cam and me grow up. Mali stands behind me while Cam stands behind Hayes. The rest of the room is filled with my parents, Hayes's mom, and Devin.

It may not be a traditional wedding, being in the middle of our living room, but it's ours. And all the flowers and decorations that our moms put around the room, it goes to show how supported we are. Most of the people we know might think we're crazy, but the ones who matter are right here—watching us promise the rest of our lives to each other.

Pastor Todd starts talking, giving the pre-vow speech about why we're all gathered here today—as if people may have thought it was something else. But most of what he says fades into the distance as I get lost in Hayes's eyes. The man standing in front of me is everything I have ever wanted and more. I couldn't have dreamed him up if I tried. And all of the things we went through that brought us here, they showed us what's really important. For that, I'm thankful.

I'm thankful for *him*.

"The couple has prepared their own vows that they will read now," the pastor announces. "Hayes, if you'd like to go first?"

He smiles as he nods, pulling a folded piece of paper from his back pocket. "Laiken. I don't know how I'm supposed to put how I feel for you into words, but you wanted us to write our own vows, so I'm going to try."

Pausing to look at me, he swallows, crumpling the paper and tossing it to the side.

"Yeah, nothing on that would do you any justice. There *aren't* any words for how much I love you, because *my God*, it makes me dizzy. You are the reason I get up in the morning. The first person I want to go to when I'm having a bad day, and when I'm having a good one. We may not have started like any other couple, but I think that only makes us stronger.

You were the biggest risk I've ever taken, and you were the *best* risk I've ever taken.

"There's no one else who loves the way you do—so unforgivingly and without anything holding you back. And to know that I get to sit in your light and admire you for the rest of my life is all I could ever ask for. So, this is me promising to love you, to be there for you, and to support you with everything I have until the world explodes, and probably even then. Thank you, not only for loving me, but for never giving up on me."

My heart feels like a puddle of mush, barely beating because he took it—stole it straight from my chest. Tears are flowing down my cheeks as I silently mouth *I love you* to him. But the only sound we hear is the sniffling behind me. Hayes leans to the side and gives Mali a look.

"Really, Mal?" he asks.

She huffs out a wet laugh. "Shut up. My best friend is getting married and she didn't even give me a heads-up so I could get this out of my system."

Everyone chuckles, and I take my attention off Hayes for a moment to hug my best friend. In hindsight, I should've told her, especially now that I know she wasn't going to try talking me out of it. But the last few days have been such a whirlwind in the best possible way. And besides, her reaction was fantastic.

"He's stealing you from me," she whispers loudly.

I giggle and pat her head. "No one can ever steal me from you."

She looks up to glare at Hayes. "Hear that? *No one.*"

Thankfully, Mali is the one person he isn't possessive over me with. I mean, it's probably because he knows she would knock him over the head so hard he wouldn't even remember who I am, but still.

Hayes snickers as I release Mali and turn to face him again.

"Laiken," Pastor Todd says, nodding for me to go ahead.

I take a deep breath.

I've got this.

"Hayes. I stand here in front of you and our families, tasked with explaining how much you mean to me, but you were right. It's not possible, like taking a picture of the moon—the outcome is never anywhere near as good as the real thing.

"Three years ago, I fell in love with the boy who insisted on wearing a backward hat instead of a helmet during hockey. Since then, my feelings for you have only grown, never lessened. You're the one I want to share my good days with, and the one I want holding me through the bad.

"I promise to spend the rest of my life believing in you and supporting your dreams. I promise to cheer you on at your games, only ever wearing your jersey. And I promise to always put you in your place, the way you love so much."

He chuckles, and I can't help but smile at the sound of it.

"The fact that I'm going to spend forever loving you is nothing new to me. I've known that for years. But knowing I get to do it while having your last name is a dream that I never thought would come true. It's always been you for me, H. That won't ever change."

The look in his eyes, the way he wipes away a tear the second it escapes, shows me just how important I am to him. That vulnerability he tries to hide from the world in an effort to protect himself—he shows to me. I'm the only one who gets to see the real him, exposed and open, and the fact that he trusts me enough for that means everything.

"Beautifully said," Pastor Todd tells us both. "You two will have a beautiful life together."

"That's the plan," Hayes jokes.

He laughs along with everyone else then gets back to business. "Hayes. Do you take Laiken Rose Blanchard to be your wife? To have and to hold, in sickness and in health, for richer or poorer, keeping yourself unto her for as long as you both shall live?"

Hayes's brows furrow as he cranes his neck to see into the book Pastor Todd is holding. "You got anything longer than that in there?"

God, I love this man.

The pastor smiles as he snickers. "Afraid not."

"Fine then." Hayes looks me in the eyes. "I do, even after *we both shall live.*"

"And Laiken, do you take Hayes Beckett Wilder to be your husband? To have and to hold, in sickness and in health, for richer or poorer, keeping yourself unto him for as long as you both shall live?"

"I do," I say confidently.

I don't think I've ever meant two words more in my life. Once again, I'm lost in staring at him—acknowledging just how unfairly gorgeous he is as he tells him to skip the rings because we don't have them. We had another idea in mind for that, and trust me...

I am *all* for it.

Pastor Todd smiles. "Then by the power vested in me by the state of North Carolina, I now pronounce you husband and wife. You may kiss the bride."

Hayes smirks, grabbing the back of my neck and pulling me in like he's been waiting on this forever. His mouth covers my own and with a hand holding me in place, he dips me back. And as we kiss for the first time as Mr. and Mrs. Hayes Wilder, it hits me.

I get to spend the rest of my life doing this.

Hayes
CHAPTER NINETEEN

LAIKEN'S HEAD RESTS AGAINST MY CHEST AS WE sway to "Take My Name" by Parmalee. The slow sound of the wedding version is perfect, and the lyrics are so accurate, you'd think it was written about us. Our wedding may have essentially been a sprint down the aisle, but this is one thing I wouldn't skip.

To have her in my arms, dancing to the song that comes the closest to portraying how I feel about her—nothing can beat this. Her vows replay on a loop inside my head, and a part of me considers tattooing every word on my chest. Right over the heart that will never belong to anyone else.

"I love you, Mrs. Wilder," I tell her softly.

She lifts her head and looks up at me with a smile. "I love you, too."

LET ME PREFACE THIS by saying I love my family. The people in this house that watched and supported us as we got married, they're the best family I could ask for. But they need to get the fuck out.

You see, from the second Laiken came down the stairs in that dress, the only thing I've been able to think about is getting her alone. And after spending the last few hours celebrating us, all I want to do is love her in the best way I know how.

"Do I *look* pregnant or something?" Laiken huffs.

I scratch the back of my neck and squint. "This feels like a trap."

She glares at me as Mali laughs. "Easy. You have to wait until *after* the marriage is filed with the court before you kill him. Otherwise, you're just a homicidal bride."

My head tilts to the side as I look at Mali. "Do you contemplate my murder often?"

"Are you kidding? That's my *best friend*," she scoffs. "I've thought of every last angle. Hurt her and everyone will think you're on a coke binge in Vegas with a couple of hookers."

"Is that something I would do?"

She smirks and winks at me, while Laiken rolls her eyes.

"Can you two focus? Pastor Todd just told me to make sure I reach out when we're ready to get the baby baptized!"

Wow. Her mom really is dead set on this pregnancy thing. "Relax, babe. Everyone will realize you're not pregnant eventually."

"Great. In the meantime, they all think I'm with child."

Having a family of my own was never something I imagined being in my future. After all, that requires being with someone for longer than a couple hookups. But for the first time, that thought doesn't scare the shit out of me.

I wrap my arms around Laiken's waist and pull her against me. "Get all these people to leave before I drag you upstairs and fuck you anyway."

"My dad and Cam would literally kill you," she drawls.

Pressing a light kiss to the back of her shoulder, I hum. "Guess you're going to be a widow then."

She leans back and turns her head to smile at me, kissing my forehead. It's such a simple move, one she probably didn't think twice about, but it sets me on fire. Because that's what she does. Everything I am and everything I want to be revolves around her.

WE STAND AT THE front door, with my arm around Laiken as we wave goodbye. The minute the car pulls out of view, I turn and pin her against the doorway—covering her mouth with my own. The kiss we shared when we said I do, along with each one after that, they weren't enough.

Her hands come around to my back and she drags her nails down it, moaning breathlessly. "Is this where you steal my virtue?"

Grabbing her ass, I pull her into me and grind against her. "This is where I make you feel so good the *neighbors* will need earplugs."

"Yes, please," she says, kissing me again.

I groan into her mouth. "That's my good girl."

She squeals as I bend down and lift her up bridal style. I carry her up the stairs and into our bedroom. But when I go to lay her on the bed, she stops me.

"I have a surprise for you," she says.

I'm thrown by the slight edge of nerves in her voice, but she doesn't give me a chance to question it before she goes into the bathroom and shuts the door. While I wait, I take off my shirt and toss it into the laundry basket.

Lying on the bed, I let the events of today play through my mind. If someone told me at the beginning of this summer that I would be married by the end of it, I'd ask for some of whatever they were taking. But now that I'm here, I wouldn't trade it for the world. I fell for her so damn fast it makes my head spin. Or maybe the feelings I swore I didn't have all those years ago just never really went away—they grew in the background instead.

It's almost funny to think that I actually tried to keep things between us casual. I should've known I never stood a chance at that.

"What's my surprise?" I call out.

She opens the door a crack and sticks her head out. "Don't be impatient."

"Know who you married. I don't have a patient bone in my body when it comes to getting you beneath me."

Her eyes roll. "Okay, okay. One more minute."

I grab my phone and respond to a text from my mom, telling me how happy she is for Laiken and me. Just as I hit send, the bathroom door opens once more.

"Okay," Laiken murmurs.

Glancing up from my phone, the biggest grin immediately spreads across my face when I see her. She's leaning against the doorway, dressed in a fucking trench coat. It's been a running joke since the night I finally stopped fighting this, and as my eyes rake over her, I realize there isn't anything she *doesn't* look sinful in.

"Please tell me you have nothing on under that," I beg.

She bites on her bottom lip. "Why don't you come find out for yourself?"

I definitely don't need to be told twice. Standing up, I stalk toward her—keeping my gaze locked with hers. Once I'm close enough, I slowly undo the coat and slide it off her shoulders, but the moment I do, I'm fucking speechless.

She's wearing white, lacy lingerie. It looks like she tapped into a fantasy I didn't even realize I had and replicated it perfectly. The bodysuit hugs her in all the right places. And as I slide my hands down over the soft material, she arches into my touch.

"You like it?" she questions, looking up at me through hooded lashes.

I exhale, not even able to make a joke right now. "I love it. God, you're stunning." Pulling her closer into me, I put my lips to the shell of her ear. "I am going to worship every last inch of your body."

"It's all yours."

Fuck. "Damn right it is."

My lips meet the skin between her neck and her shoulders first, kissing it softly. I meant what I said—I'm going to take my time with her tonight. She lets out a breath and arches her neck to give me more space, while I drag my fingertips up the inside of her thigh.

The good thing about these bodysuit things is it's so simple to slide it right out of the way. And when my fingers brush across her clit, she looks more than pleased with her decision. Her back is against the bathroom doorway, and I lift her right leg just enough to give me the right angle.

It's so fucking hot to see her like this, instantly starting to come apart on my fingers. But what she doesn't know is I don't plan on stopping until she's begging me. Her head falls back as she gives me the first orgasm of the night and she bites her lip, but never again does she need to be quiet. Not in here. Not with me.

"Nuh-uh," I tell her. "You're going to let me hear *all* of it. I want you screaming until your throat is raw."

Dropping down to my knees, I move her leg so it's draped over my shoulder. She watches me as I smirk at her, and dive into something much more delicious than the wedding cake she fed me earlier. A breathy moan leaves her mouth while I suck on her clit and slip two fingers inside.

"Oh my God," she pants. "Your mouth should be illegal."

I smirk against her pussy. That's one thing I love about her—she's always so damn responsive. Just one flick of my tongue is enough to have her squirming, and she doesn't even realize how much it turns me on.

"Mali can get you another one of these things, right?" I ask, referring to the bodysuit.

She nods, and that's all I need to know before I rip the bottom of it in half, freeing her completely to me.

"That's better."

A soft laugh leaves her mouth, but the second I'm on her again it turns to a moan. Her fingers come down to lace into my hair, and she arches her hips to grind herself against my face. The taste of her is so addictive I can't get close enough. I want to fucking suffocate on her.

Gripping her waist, I lift her up. Her other leg goes over my shoulder as I carry her over to the bed and lie back with her on my face. She instantly tries to hover, but when I grip her and pull her down, she gets the point.

"Fuck," she breathes. "Hayes."

That's it, baby.

Her hips start to move as she grinds on my face, until she's desperately chasing her own high for the second time. And when she lets go, she fills the room with the sound of it as my mouth carries her through it, her whole body trembling from the sensation.

"Look at you. So fucking good for me."

She climbs off and starts undoing my pants. "Always good for you."

"You are, baby," I tell her. "You're always perfect for me. So perfect."

Sliding my pants and boxers down in one move, my cock springs free. She wraps her hand around the base and drops down to kiss the tip. Her mouth opens slightly as she licks the precum off and hums. It shouldn't be nearly as hot as it is, but everything about her is so damn sinful.

"God, Lai. You're incredible." My eyes stay focused on her as she kisses and sucks on the shaft. "Such a pretty mouth on my cock."

Her tongue slides up the underside before she takes me completely into her mouth. I feel myself hit the back of her throat and she chokes on my dick, only to pull back and do it again. It's so intense, the way she wraps her lips around me, I press my head back into the pillow.

And when she takes my hand and puts it on her head, a silent message to fuck her mouth, I'm in complete awe of her.

I grip her hair and arch my hips, pulling her down and feeling her gag on me. Her eyes find mine and she looks just as turned on as I am right now. Because that's how we are— not only does our own pleasure get us going, but so does the other's.

As I thrust up into her mouth, I keep my gaze locked with hers. She's so fucking hot like this, with tears in her eyes from gagging on my cock as I slide deep into her throat. But if I keep going, I'm not going to be able to stop myself, and I'm not done with her yet.

I pull her off me and go to move, but she places a hand on my chest and pushes me back down. Throwing one leg over me, she holds my dick in place and lowers herself onto me. And holy shit, I get so deep like this.

She starts to bounce on my cock, still wearing the lingerie, but it's getting in the way of my view. My hands slide up her side, pulling it with me until she takes it off and discards it on the floor.

"You're so beautiful," I tell her as I tweak one nipple between my fingers. Then I sit up and take the other into my mouth. "So goddamn gorgeous."

Her head falls back as she starts to move her hips in circles. Between the fact that her pussy is taking all of me and that I'm in her bare, it all makes it that much more intense. I can't wait for the day I can empty myself inside her. To come with her, feeling her clench around me while my cock pulses. *That* is what I imagine heaven feels like.

Falling back onto the bed, I watch as she rides me with such skill. And the hottest part is that she's not even trying to get me off—she's doing this for herself. I grip her hips, pulling her down a little harder as I thrust up into her. She's so close, and her nails are digging into the skin on my chest. Her hair falls in front of her, outlining her face and blocking anything else from view.

"Do it, baby," I order her. "Come all over my cock like a good girl. You feel so good like this. Can only imagine how you'll feel when you come."

Her movements get sloppy as my words push her that much closer to the edge. She rocks back and forth frantically until she finally explodes, falling forward on top of me as I feel her pussy clench around me, and I fuck her through it.

She's completely boneless, spent from three orgasms, but I want more. I want every last ounce of pleasure she has tonight.

Lifting her off me, she rolls on her back. I flip over and bend down to taste her some more. The sensitivity is so overwhelming that she screams out when I suck on her clit.

"I can't," she says through heavy breaths. "It's too much."

I straighten up and take my cock, rubbing it against her. "You can."

It looks like she wants to fight it, but a bigger part of her is excited by the idea of coming again. To let me take everything she has to give.

As I slip back inside of her, she lets her eyes fall closed and she sighs blissfully. This is right where we belong, just like this.

Bringing my hand down, I press my thumb against her clit and start rubbing it in circles. And as I lean forward, using my body to apply more pressure, her eyes shoot open and I know I've got the right spot. My cock rubs against her g-spot while my thumb takes care of her clit, and it's enough to have her screaming—loudly.

I fuck into her as I watch her come over and over again. Every time I think she's done, another one rips through her. It's unlike anything I've ever seen before, but she's always been one to surprise me at every turn.

"Fuck, fuck, fuck!" she screams.

I know if I don't pull out soon, I'm going to fill her up, but seeing her like this, I don't want to stop. I *can't* stop. My jaw locks as I hold it back and feel her go through the seventh orgasm of the night. And when she finally pulls my hand off her, I pull out at the last second and cover her stomach in my cum.

Her chest rises and falls as she tries to catch her breath, and I crash on the bed beside her. I never understood why guys find it hot when a girl is covered in cum—until now. Seeing me all over her, it makes me want her all over again, but I'm thinking she might castrate me if I try.

"Holy shit," she breathes, her head slumping to the side to look at me. "Holy fucking shit."

I bite my lip to conceal my smile, thoroughly pleased with

myself, and I kiss the tip of her nose before I go to get her a warm washcloth.

And they say that married life is when the sex stops.

Something tells me we won't have that issue.

THE NEEDLES PIERCE MY skin repeatedly as they drill ink beneath it. All you can hear is the sound of the two tattoo guns going at once. Typical couples may decide to go the traditional route, using rings to show they're married, but I'm not interested in anything removable.

"I still can't believe you're married now," Zack tells me. He's the only one I've ever let tattoo me. "I didn't even know you were dating anyone."

Looking over at Laiken, she smiles and winks at me.

The fact that she is currently getting an H inked onto her ring finger speaks to the possessive side of me. The side of me that wants to knock a guy out just for looking at her too long. She will forever be marked with my initial, and so will I —with the L on my ring finger to match.

"It surprised me, too," I admit. "But fuck, man. I've never felt anything like this before."

He chuckles. "I can tell. You're different with her."

It's not the first time I've heard that, and I'm sure it won't be the last, because I *am* different with her. She makes me want to be a better person. Someone deserving of her.

Someone worth spending a life with. And I don't know if I'm ever going to fully get there, but I do know that I'll never stop trying.

"You doing okay?" I call across the room.

Laiken nods. "Yep, but you might not be when Mali sees that you branded me."

Yeah, maybe I should've thought of that beforehand.

THEORETICALLY, I SHOULD BE somewhere tropical right now. With Laiken in my lap and a drink in my hand, living the good life of being on a honeymoon. But when you're in the process of turning a former surf shop into a bar, and you all but sprinted down the aisle, there isn't much time for that.

The place is finally coming along, though. We found a guy who could build the bar exactly how I want it, and while it may have cost me more than I would have liked, it'll be worth it. Cam and I have the same vision when it comes to this place, and we're not willing to sacrifice that because the price is a little higher.

We're going through which kinds of beer we want to carry when Laiken storms in, clearly frustrated. She throws her bag down and crosses her arms while she glares at Cam.

"Dude, what did you do?" I ask him.

He's just as clueless as I am. "Fuck if I know."

She's not saying anything, but she looks pissed. Livid, even. Like she's ready to burn the whole world to the ground. Meanwhile, neither one of us seem to want to poke the bear.

"You ask her," I say, nudging him.

He shakes his head. "Fuck that. She's *your* wife."

Hell yeah she is, but I prefer calm and happy Laiken—this demon version he can keep. "It's not me she's murdering with her eyes." She glances at me and I wince. "Or at least it wasn't."

Cam sighs and gives in before she paints the walls red. "What's wrong with you?"

"Your mother is a crazy person, that's what," she snaps.

He purses his lips, looking even more confused. "That's funny. I always thought we had the same mother."

"Nuh-uh. No." She shakes her head. "I'm not taking ownership for this woman."

Grabbing the laptop from us, she slams her fingers on a few keys and then spins it back around. Cam tries not to laugh as his mom's picture sits above a plethora of nursery images.

"She has a whole Pinterest board! And it's *public!*" she shrieks. "All throughout today's lessons, the parents were congratulating me on my bundle of joy. One even told me I shouldn't be ice skating in *my condition.*"

Cam snorts, going back to beer selections, while I walk around the table. I gently place my hands on her waist, and she melts into me. Pouting, she rests her head on my chest.

"I had to run out of there when Mrs. Timmons started telling me how her vagina ripped all the way to her asshole."

I freeze for a moment. That's…disturbing. My fingers lace into her hair as I kiss the top of her head, and once again, the thought of her all big and pregnant with my baby doesn't make me want to run for the hills. Hell, the idea of having a family is even a little appealing.

"Would it really be the worst idea?" I ask softly. "Having a baby?"

She backs away and raises her brows at me. "Did you not hear me? *Her vagina ripped to her asshole.* What part of that doesn't sound like the worst idea of all time?"

Chuckling, I shrug. "I don't know. I kind of like the idea of you all cute and knocked up with my baby."

I step closer and rest my hand on her belly, and she leaves it there for a second, until she doesn't. "You don't want a baby."

"Why not?"

"Because you're too selfish to share me," she says simply. "And a baby is almost a constant cockblock."

Shit. Yep, definitely didn't think of that. I look around, finding my keys on the counter and grabbing them before heading to the door.

"Where are you going?" she calls.

"We need more condoms."

JUST WHEN YOU THINK everything is going perfectly, it goes wrong. It's practically a law. We should've known it would happen with the bar. But as Cam and I stand here, looking at the mold the inspector found inside one of the upstairs walls, neither one of us saw it coming.

"We're going to have to tear out all the drywall up here,"

Cam says. "We'll get it all cleared out and then have someone come to take care of the mold."

"May as well insulate it after," I add.

He nods. "It'll tack on some time, but you're right. It'll help keep it warm downstairs in the winter."

Sighing, I take out my phone and send a text to Laiken. We had planned to go out later, but it looks like I'm going to be here for the rest of the day. And every day this week, for that matter.

> Enjoy lunch with Mali, babe. Looks like I'm going to be stuck at the bar. We have to rip out the upstairs walls. Feel free to join us if you want. 😉

So much for almost being done with this place.

Laiken
CHAPTER TWENTY

EVERYTHING IS CHANGING. SOMEHOW, I WENT FROM crushing on my brother's best friend, to being married to him all in the course of a summer. I wouldn't trade the life I live for the world. I have everything I've ever wanted falling right into my lap. But it's still nice to have one thing that isn't any different—and that's my friendship with Mali.

I love Hayes with all of my heart, and truly believe I'm meant to spend the rest of my life with him. But Mali is my soulmate. She's that one person who will have my back, no matter what it is or how much I fucked up. She's my forever friend. The one who always seems to amaze me with her strength and resilience. Though I will say, I do still worry about her. She's the strongest person I know, but even diamonds have a weak spot.

Pulling into her driveway, I notice Monty's car. He must be back from Aspen. Apparently, his family has a house out there, and they always go this time of year. I'm surprised he didn't reach out when he got home, but as I get out and notice the flowers in Mali's hands, I'm starting to understand why.

"Hey, babes," Mali says to me.

"Hey. We still going to lunch?"

She nods. "Let me just go get my purse."

"Okay," I tell her, and she leaves me outside with Monty. "How was your trip?"

Chapter 20

"It was really good," he replies. "Put a lot into perspective. The mountains have a way of doing that."

Whatever *that's* supposed to mean. "That's great! I'm glad you enjoyed it. You deserve good things."

His grin widens. "I do, don't I?"

Only a second later, Mali comes out and smiles at me. "Ready to go?"

"Yep," I answer, then look at Monty. "Are you coming with us?"

He shakes his head. "I have a few things to take care of. Unpacking and all that."

That's weird. He just got back, and he came straight here? But as we go to leave, he gives me a quick hug and then plants one right on Mali's lips.

What. The. Fuck.

My eyes widen, and Mali subtly flips me off. Having been her best friend since we were old enough to know what a best friend is, I've seen my fair share of her hooking up with someone. And I can tell that *this* is not something she's into. But she goes with it, forcing a smile on her face as he pulls away.

"I'll see you later, babe," he tells her.

My lips press together as I try to keep from both laughing and freaking out. He and I wave at each other, and he smiles at Mali once more before getting into his Range Rover and driving off. The second he's gone, I turn to her.

"Okay, what the actual fuck was that?"

Honestly, for the last month, I thought she was harboring secret feelings for my brother. Once everything with the bar died down, I was going to ask her about it. But this throws a wrench into that.

She sighs, walking around to the passenger side of my car and climbing in. "I don't know. He texted me and said he needed to talk to me about something, and when I came

268

outside, he handed me a bouquet of flowers and asked me out."

"And you said *yes?*" I balk.

She throws her hands in the air. "Well, what was I supposed to say? Cam almost went to prison because of me. And don't start with the *you're not to blame* shit. The *only* reason he's not locked up right now, is because Monty saved his ass."

Okay, so she's pity dating him, but that still doesn't sound like her. "So, you're just going to date him as what? Payment for his services?"

She shrugs. "I owe him at least a chance. Besides, he's a good guy."

Her words say one thing, but the underlying meaning behind the last sentence comes through clear. She said yes because he's *safe*. He won't try to force her into something she doesn't want to do, and no one is going to fuck with her when she's dating a Rollins.

If this is what helps her, what makes her feel better after everything that happened, then so be it.

I swallow down anything else I was going to say and put my car into reverse. "I can't believe you're dating *Monty*."

She hums. "Honestly, I always thought he was into you."

Don't let Hayes hear that. "I thought he was gay."

We both look at each other, shrug at the same time, then break into giggles.

Chapter 20

SO MUCH FOR BEING done with all the loud banging at the bar. At least *that* kind of banging, and at least for now. There will be no promises about the other kind of banging once this place is open. We walk in the door to find Hayes talking to Grant, the guy they hired to design and build the counter.

"Hey, babe." I arch up and kiss him. "How's it going?"

He pinches his eyes shut and groans. "It's a nightmare. We can't pass inspection until we redo the walls upstairs. And since we have to do it anyway, we're going to add insulation like we did down here. It's probably for the best, but right now it's just frustrating. I thought we'd be ready to open by my birthday."

My bottom lip juts out. "That sucks. I'm sorry."

"It's fine." He wraps his arms around me. "I feel better now that you're here."

Mali makes a noise of disgust. "Marriage made you two even more nauseating."

I chuckle, turning in his hold. "Aw, don't worry, Mal. I'm sure your new boyfriend will be a sweetheart to you. Hell, he might even buy you a car for a random Tuesday."

Mali glares at me while Hayes looks confused. "Wait, what new boyfriend?"

"I hate you," she tells me. "Like really, genuinely, hate you."

My nose scrunches. "You can't. Besides, now we can double."

She snorts. "Yeah, okay. I see how it is. You want Hayes to ban me for life."

"What's going on?" Cam says as he comes to grab some more tools.

Hayes glances at him. "That's what I'm trying to figure out."

Mali rolls her eyes. "It's not that big of a deal."

"Okay, then tell them."

Don't get me wrong, I totally understand why she's doing this, but that doesn't mean it feels good to watch her settle out of fear. Mali is the greatest person I know, and I like Monty, but he doesn't deserve her—nor do I think he could handle her, if I'm honest. He's just not the guy for her.

"Fine," she murmurs, focusing her attention on the ground. "I'm dating Monty."

Cam's back is to us, so I can't see his face, but the way he stills makes me think he's not happy about it. Meanwhile, Hayes's brows raise.

"I'm sorry," he says through a laugh. "All the banging must have damaged my hearing, because it sounded like you said you're *dating* Monty." When neither of us say anything, it clicks. "Oh my God, you're dating Monty."

"Can we not make this a thing?" she pleads.

But Hayes isn't going to let it go that easily. "How can we not? It's Monty. You are *dating* Montgomery Rollins."

She scoffs. "Thank you for that information. I thought I was dating Monty Python."

"All of them?" I question, but she just flips me off.

Mali looks over at Cam with a solemn expression on her face. "Cam?"

He finally turns around. "Huh?"

"You're quiet," she murmurs.

My brother forces out a laugh. "Sorry, I was trying to figure out which hammer I want to use. That's great, Mal." He comes over and wraps his arms around her. "I'm really happy for you."

Her eyes fall closed as she hugs him, and when he pulls away, she runs her fingers through her hair. "Thanks."

Grabbing a hammer off the table, he goes back upstairs. It stays quiet for a moment, the tension in the air too thick to speak, and then we hear it—the sound of Cam slamming the hammer into the wall with force. He's always been so careful, and when Hayes hit a pipe, he lectured him on why using a hammer is a bad idea for hours while they fixed it. He's pissed, that much is clear, but what I can't understand is if he wanted Mali, why has he never asked her out?

The sound of something cracking follows, with Cam screaming, "Motherfucker!" at the top of his lungs. We all cringe.

"I should..." Hayes starts, but Mali stops him.

"No," she says. "Let me."

With a deep breath, she heads toward the back room and upstairs, while Hayes nods to the door. "We should go for a walk."

He holds the door open for me and then laces my fingers with his. The temperature is starting to cool, but in the best way. It's not as hot and humid as it was a month ago. Instead, it's the perfect temperature.

The waves crash, sending water up the beach. It almost hits us, but we walk just outside of it.

"I still can't believe she's dating Monty," I tell him.

It's hard to wrap my mind around it. Mali might love money, but she's not the kind of girl to settle because a guy has a lot of it. She's a lot of things, but a gold digger is not one of them.

"About that." He pauses for a second. "Do you think he's with her for the right reasons?"

"What do you mean?"

"I don't know. Do you think he's just using her because he knows she would do it? Is he taking advantage of the opportunity?"

I let go of his hand. "Are you kidding me? You're *still* holding that shit against him?"

He looks at me like I've lost my mind. "Uh, yeah, and it's a little frustrating that you're not. He broke us up."

"No," I correct him. "*You* broke us up. He just gave you a reason to."

"He threatened to tell Cam about us."

"Because you weren't going to!" I cross my arms over my chest. "You might not like it, but if it weren't for what he did, we'd still be sneaking around and I'd still be grasping for whatever parts of yourself you were willing to give me at the time."

He huffs. "What I *don't like* is him. The way he watches you? I'm telling you, Laiken. I get a bad vibe about that guy."

I look away for a second, muttering that this is bullshit. "You get a bad vibe about any guy that comes within ten feet of me. And yeah, sometimes it's hot when you go all caveman, but right now, it's just annoying. I *married* you. Literally swapped my last name for yours. I don't know how else to show you that no other guy even exists on my radar anymore."

His shoulders sag, and he tries to reach out for me. "I don't want to fight with you. Not over him. That prick doesn't get to rip us apart again."

But his words aren't making me feel any better. "Might I remind you *that prick* is the one who saved my brother from prison? Your *best friend*?"

"Oh, so that just makes him a good guy? You're seriously defending him right now after what he did?"

"I thought he made up for it after he helped us when he didn't have to." But before I say anything else, I stop and take a step backward, chuckling dryly as I shake my head. "No. You know what? I'm not doing this right now. Come home after you sort your shit out and realize that one mistake does not define someone. You of all people should be grateful for that."

I turn around and leave him standing there.

So much for newlywed bliss.

CHAPTER TWENTY ONE

WHY IS IT THAT EVERY TIME LAIKEN AND I ARE truly happy, this fucker has to come in and ruin it? He has enough money to be dating a goddamn supermodel, and he chooses my wife's best friend? I don't fucking buy it. He's up to something, and he's using Mali. There's no other explanation.

Laiken pushes past me as she and Mali leave. I don't try to stop her. Right now, she's angry. And for what it's worth, so am I. She knows everything he did, and yeah, he may have helped Cam out, but if what Owen said was right and he's friends with Isaac, who's to say he didn't have a hand in what happened in the first place?

I go upstairs to find Cam leaning against the wall. He's frustrated—at himself probably, or at Mali for not turning Monty down. Who really knows? But I'm too pissed to handle him with kid gloves right now.

"You just had to be all sensitive and worry about if you're the right guy for her or not, didn't you?" *Yeah, I know. I'm a fucking hypocrite.* "Couldn't have just made a move on her when I told you to?"

"Fuck off, Wilder," he growls.

"Why? Because you know I'm right?" I sneer. "If you had grown a pair and asked her out, she wouldn't be dating Mr. Moneybags."

"You think I don't know that?" he snaps, throwing the hammer to the floor. "You think I'm not kicking myself in the ass for it? But what the fuck am I supposed to do? I can't even be angry about it, because the guy might be a douchebag, but I owe him my freedom."

I scoff, throwing my hands in the air. "What the fuck is with you Blanchards and thinking that prick is some knight in shining armor? Shit like this is the reason he has a goddamn complex to begin with."

Cam's brows furrow. "Why are you even so pissed off about this? I know why I don't like him, but I can't wrap my head around why you don't."

"Because he wants Laiken. That's why he threatened me and told me to break up with her or he was going to tell you."

"Okay. That's a dick move on his part, sure. But that led to you telling me and now you two are fucking married. You're still friends with Lucas, and he openly wants her. So why do you hate Monty so damn much?"

I pinch the bridge of my nose, exhaling heavily. The truth about the sex tape is on the tip of my tongue, but I hold it back. Nothing good would come from him knowing about that. Especially right after learning that Mali is dating him now.

He would kill him, and we're trying to keep him *out* of prison, not look for reasons to put him in it.

"You're right." He's not, but I pretend to cave to end this shitshow. "I should just let it go."

Cam hums. "You should. At least you won...unlike me."

"Could always go after her anyway," I suggest. "Be honest with her."

He shakes his head. "Nah. He's the better guy for her, even if he is a tool. He'll make her happy."

That's bullshit and we both know it. It was all over both their faces today. She didn't look the slightest bit happy about her new relationship status, and if she didn't have feelings for Cam, she wouldn't have looked to him for his approval.

A part of her wanted him to fight for her.

To tell her to be with him instead.

To tell her *anything* except what he did.

But there's no getting through to him right now. Not when the wound is still fresh. Besides, Mali is a smart girl. Whatever Monty is up to, she'll figure it out and dump his ass when she does.

I just hope it happens sooner rather than later.

HAVING TO APOLOGIZE FOR hating a guy that would end my marriage if given the chance feels a lot like cruel torture. It's still grinding on my nerves that Laiken defended him to me after what he did. But then again, she doesn't know the full story.

And I can't tell her.

Monty is dangerous. That much is clear. There's no way to be sure how far that psycho is willing to take this, or what I'll need to do to keep her safe. Keeping her in the dark on this is what's best for her because if something goes wrong, I can't have her caught in the crossfire.

As I pull into the driveway, I see her car in the driveway and the downstairs lights are on. A small rush of relief floods through me when I realize she's home. Not that I thought she wouldn't be, but today threw me for a loop.

I unlock the door and step inside. Laiken is sitting on the couch, reading a book, and she glances up at me when I come in. The fact that she doesn't look happy to see me stings, I'm not going to lie. I've never been able to stand when she's mad at me, and that doesn't seem to be changing any time soon. So, instead of dragging this out, I walk over to her and sit on the floor beside the couch—resting my head on her stomach and sighing.

"I'm sorry," I tell her. "I know I'm a lot sometimes, but the thought of losing you scares the shit out of me."

She puts down the book and runs her fingers through my hair. "I'm sorry, too, but you need to learn that I'm not going anywhere. Your initial on my ring finger and the marriage certificate you have framed on the wall like a damn certificate of ownership is proof of that."

I chuckle. "It's not a certificate of ownership. I just like looking at it and knowing it wasn't a dream. That you really married me."

"Of course I did," she replies. "I love you, even when you're a pain in the ass."

Nuzzling my nose into her stomach, I breathe in the scent of her. It has a way of bringing me from on edge to calm in seconds. Just another magical thing she does. Lord knows there's a lot of them.

"I love you, too. God, fighting with you is the worst."

She hums. "Well, I thought of a way we could stop Monty from being a problem between us, but you have to stay open minded."

Oh God. This should be good. "I'm listening."

"I want us to go on a double date with him and Mali."

Great, she *wants* to tempt me with the ability to kick his ass. "Do we have to?"

"Well, no," she says sadly. "We don't *have* to do anything, but I'd like to. I think you and Monty got off on the wrong foot."

"You mean the foot where he threatened to out us if I didn't break up with you. That foot?"

Her eyes narrow. "All I'm saying is I think you should give him another chance. He's dating Mali. It's not me he wants."

Somehow, I doubt that. She's blinded by the version of him that helped her brother, and I hate that. From the moment he got Cam's case thrown out, I knew this shit was going to be held over my head. She might say we don't have to go, but I know that if I refuse, she's going to get mad at me again. And we are too early into this marriage for one of us to be sleeping on the couch tonight.

"Okay," I agree reluctantly. "For you, I'll go."

A smile spreads across her face, the one I'd do literally anything to put there. *Case and point.* Her hand moves to the back of my neck, and she pulls me in, breathing life back into me with a kiss. I can't help but sigh into it.

"Thank you," she tells me. "I know you don't like him, but I appreciate you giving him another chance."

Like I had any other choice. "The chances of me changing my mind about him are slim."

"I get that, but I still appreciate it."

"Yeah?" I bounce my brows. "How much?"

You know what they say, makeup sex is the best sex.

She takes her bottom lip between her teeth and it's on. I'm going to make sure Moneybags isn't even a thought in her mind for the rest of the night.

COFFEE IS A NECESSARY evil. I hate the taste of it, but when you were up late the night before checking positions off the *Kama Sutra* like it's your own personal bucket list, it's the only thing that might save me from dragging ass all day. Between the extra renovations needed at the bar and the research I'm currently doing on Monty, I can't afford to be tired.

I'm sitting at the island, scrolling through my laptop. There has to be other crooked shit he's getting away with. He made the video of Cam fighting Isaac disappear like it was nothing. A video that was not just on the defense attorney's computer, but also the prosecutor's and the police department servers. And then it was gone, without a trace of it ever existing. Even Craig couldn't find it on his phone anymore. It's like it never even happened.

Motherfucker covers his tracks well, because I can't find a damn thing on him. Not even his name in a school yearbook. All the articles just reference him as being Senator Rollins's son. It wouldn't surprise me if Montgomery Rollins wasn't even his real name. If Laiken didn't personally meet his dad, I'd wonder if he was lying about that, too.

"God, I love that showerhead," Laiken says as she comes into the kitchen.

With a press of a single button, all the windows disappear, leaving only the beer selections that Cam and I are still deciding on. She comes over and kisses me before getting her own cup of coffee.

"It's because when I moved in, I drilled a hole in it to stop it from regulating the water pressure," I explain.

She smiles. "Well, you're a genius. If only it was a handheld."

"Oh, I'm sorry. Were three orgasms not enough for you last night, princess?"

"I can never get enough of you or the things you do to me."

I smirk. "Our wedding night proves otherwise."

She throws her head back, laughing. "Okay, fine. But in my defense, if you kept going, you weren't going to pull out in time."

"Get on birth control and I won't have to pull out at all," I counter.

"That's exactly why I made an appointment to get the shot," she tells me. "But it's not for another month. Apparently, they're really booked out. Good vagina health must be all the rage these days."

Just the thought of being able to have her like that all the time has me half-hard in my jeans. To see my cum leaking out of her pussy—fucking hell. I shake myself out of it and watch as Laiken smirks, knowing exactly what she just caused.

"Oh, by the way. Monty made reservations for tonight."

And there goes any boner I had. "Was that your plan? Make me think about sex so it wouldn't irritate me when you mention him?"

"That depends. Did it work?"

I grab her waist and pull her into me, putting her mug down on the counter. "You don't play fair."

She smiles. "I never said I would." Kissing me for a moment, she steps away. "But seriously. We're going to some five-star gourmet place a half hour from here. He said that reservations are normally booked out for six months, but he knows the owner."

Of fucking course he does. "Sounds good, babe. I've got to go, though. Marc is stopping by the bar this morning to see how everything is coming along."

She nods, coming over to kiss me once more. "Have a good day. I love you."

"I love you more."

And as I walk out the door, I wonder if she has any idea how much. That if this fucker tries to come between us again, I won't hesitate to make sure he never shows his face around here again. Because I will *not* lose her.

I can't.

I don't think I'd survive it.

IN ALL THE TIME that I've known Marc, I don't think I've ever been nervous around him. Until now. But then again, I've never been business partners with him. I was just his previously troubled employee. A charity case of sorts. Now, I'm watching him look around the bar and holding my breath as I wait for his critiques.

"Okay," I groan. "Put me out of my misery please."

He chuckles and purses his lips. "It looks amazing."

Thank fuck. "Seriously?"

"Yes, seriously. I'm really impressed. You guys really brought your vision to life in here. I can see all of the little details you were explaining, and they finally make sense to me."

Turning to Cam, we bump fists.

"The failed inspection was a little inconvenient," he tells Marc. "But we should be done with that by tomorrow afternoon and the inspector is going to come back the day after."

Marc nods in understanding. "It's frustrating, I'm sure, but it's a good thing they caught that. Otherwise, it would've spread and put you out of business while you gutted the place *again* just to get rid of it."

"I hadn't thought about that," I say. "That's a decent silver lining."

Marc checks out the handiwork on the new wall we put up. "I'm really liking this backroom."

Cam grins proudly. "Yeah. Cases of beer are heavy. We didn't want to have to carry them up and down the stairs, so we made a storage room."

"Smart thinking," he responds. "So, what do you think you'll end up doing with the upstairs?"

"We haven't really figured that out yet," I admit. "It's big enough to be a damn apartment, though, so the opportunities are endless."

Cam snickers. "Maybe I'll move up there. Get the fuck out of my parents' house."

It's not a bad idea, honestly. The location is perfect, and his commute to work would consist of walking down the stairs. There's just one problem.

"We don't have a kitchen, my guy. And you eat more than anyone I know."

He looks disappointed, but only for a second. "Eh, so I'll live on takeout. You do it."

"Not anymore," I correct him. "I'm a married man now. Went all domesticated and got myself a wife."

"Get the fuck out of here," Marc shouts. "*You* got married?"

I run my thumb over the L that's permanently inked into my skin. "Yep. Asked Laiken to marry me and we had a tiny ceremony in our living room a few days later."

He chuckles. "You knock her up or something?"

Cam cringes. "Don't ask *her* that. She'll rip your head right off."

He's not lying. "Nah. Just knew what I wanted and went for it. Life's short and all that shit."

"Yeah, right." Cam rolls his eyes. "It was a cross between his tendency to become a possessive caveman when it comes to her and wanting to be my brother-in-law so badly he was willing to sell his soul to the devil for it to happen."

I snort. "Did you just insinuate that your sister is the devil?"

"Absolutely. I love her, but she's ruthless." He puts his hand on my shoulder. "Best of luck to you. Please know there are no returns. All sales are final."

Marc leans against the wall and crosses his arms over his chest. "It's going to be fun to see you two running this place together. You should serve popcorn."

But all I can think is that if he thinks we're entertaining, wait until he sees Laiken and Mali together. Now *that* deserves popcorn.

THE ONLY THING WORSE than having to do on this double date is having to wear a suit to it. I don't do formalwear. Hell, I didn't even wear a full suit at our wedding, and that's not because it was in our house. It may be September, but that doesn't mean it's not fucking hot out. No one wants to wear a jacket in this shit. But the place Monty chose has a dress code we have to abide by.

Monty's suit looks like it costs more than my house, and the diamond necklace Mali is wearing tells me he thinks her affection is up for sale and he's going to be the highest bidder. As Laiken and I got closer, Mali started to become one of my closest friends. It's not just Laiken I'm looking out for.

It's her, too.

The hostess leads us to our table in the VIP section. I mean, really, he couldn't be showing off any more if he tried. We all sit down and I barely get to look at the menu before a man comes over to say hello.

"Montgomery Rollins," he greets him. "It's great to see you again. How's your dad?"

Monty smiles at him. "He's great. Making some great changes in the political world."

"I've noticed. That's fantastic." He looks around the table. "So, who are the fine people you have with you tonight?"

He puts an arm around Mali. "This is my girlfriend, Mali, my friend Laiken, and her boyfriend, Hayes."

His words surprise me. Either he did it on purpose to undermine our relationship, or he doesn't know. And judging by how Laiken makes no move to correct him, I'm guessing it's the latter.

"Husband, actually," I say, putting out my hand. "It's nice to meet you, Mister…"

"Augustus," he fills in and shakes my head. "The pleasure is mine."

He and Monty share pleasantries before he tells us that he's assigned his best waiter and the head chef to our table, and to let him know if anything isn't mouthwatering perfection. We all thank him and as soon as he walks away, Monty's brows raise.

"So, you two got married?" he asks, taking a sip of his water.

I nod, taking Laiken's hand in my own and resting them on the table. "About a week ago. I'm surprised neither of them mentioned it."

The grin on his face is far from genuine. "I'm a little offended I wasn't invited."

"No one was, really," Laiken answers. "Just family."

"I assume Mali was there."

"Like she said, family," I repeat. "Mali *is* family."

This guy has a lot of nerve, thinking that because he played a part in saving Cam—which I've concluded was more because of his father's connections than it was his—that he deserved to be included in such an intimate moment. If the guys from the team weren't invited, there's no way in hell he would be.

"Well, that's great news," he chokes out. Raising his glass, he nods at us. "Cheers to the happy couple."

I smirk as I clink my glass against his. Laiken looks confused as I subtly drop her hand, but she shouldn't be. She's told everyone who will listen that we got married. Even the cashier in the grocery store heard all about it. But it just so happens that the one friend of hers who played a part in our breakup *didn't?*

Try again.

But for now, I drink my water out of the champagne glass like I belong in this glorified diner.

Shit dipped in gold and overpriced is still just shit.

I STAND AT THE railing that overlooks the dancefloor, watching Laiken and Mali have the time of their lives. They move to the beat and spin around with wide smiles stretched across their faces. There's nothing I love more than seeing Lai just like this—when she's so happy it's infectious.

"She's gorgeous, isn't she?" Monty says as he steps up beside me.

"I don't know, man. I've never looked at Mali that way."

He takes a sip of his beer. "I wasn't talking about Mali."

Son of a bitch. "Keep your eyes off my goddamn wife."

"Or what?" he sneers. "You'll sick big brother on me? Don't want to do that. There's still a cell in Neuse Correctional with his name on it."

"You think I won't do my own dirty work? That I won't enjoy slamming your face repeatedly against the curb? You're not the only one with connections, Rollins. I'll strangle you and make it look like you fucked off to an island somewhere with a man named Ramon."

He doesn't look the least bit scared as he smirks. "Careful, *H.* Look at her. She's happy. You don't want to be the one to ruin that, do you?"

I scoff. "Fuck off. You act like you're all big and powerful, but you're nothing but a little boy with entitlement issues because your parents never paid enough attention to you as a child." I turn to face him, looking down because of our height difference. "I know you're friends with Isaac, or at least you were. Owen told me. It's funny, because you never once mentioned even knowing him while we were dealing with Cam's case."

"I met him at Laiken and Mali's birthday party," he says simply.

Nice try, Moneybags. "Isaac wasn't *at* Laiken's birthday party. Might want to work on rehearsing those lies a little more. Wouldn't want you getting tripped up when it matters most."

His confident demeanor slips. "What's that supposed to mean?"

"It *means* I'm coming for you," I tell him. "I'm going to figure out everything there is to know about you. Your secrets. Your lies. Your wrongdoings. And if I find out you're fucking with the lives of people I care about, I will make destroying you my top priority. Even daddy dearest won't be able to save you from me."

He still tries to maintain his cocky attitude, but I notice how he swallows harshly. "Are you sure you want to do that? I am not a good enemy to have."

"You started this the moment you decided to try to steal her away from me. Put your name right on the top of my shitlist and underlined it in red. You may be the senator's son, but *no one* fucks with my family. What did you think? That Isaac just *chose* to leave?"

I smirk, winking at him as I step back.

"Now, if you'll excuse me. I'm going to go dance with my *wife*. It gets her all hot and bothered when she grinds her ass against me."

With that, I walk away and leave him standing there to watch me have what he never will.

CHAPTER TWENTY TWO

HE'S PISSED OFF. WHY? I HAVE NO IDEA. BUT HE'S been walking around here like he's constantly on edge. At first, I thought it had something to do with the double date the other night, but Mali helped me realize he was fine that night. It wasn't until the next morning that he started acting strangely. And every time I ask him about it, he claims he's fine.

Long story short; my husband has become a PMS-ing preteen.

I'm standing in the bathroom, curling my hair, when he comes into the bedroom. He stops and lets his eyes rake over me, but the part of me that hopes he likes it gets crushed as he huffs, shaking his head.

"What's your problem lately?" I ask, finally having enough of his attitude.

He leans against the doorway. "I don't know, Lai. Why don't you tell me where you got the dress?"

Oh, this should be fun. "It was sent over."

"Moneybags is buying you shit now?"

"No," I say sternly. "This is from the designer and will go back to them after the gala tonight. I'm essentially a walking billboard. I mentioned in our group chat that I had nothing to wear, and Monty connected me with someone who arranges for outfits to be modeled at these events."

He scoffs. "You're in a group chat with your best friend and her boyfriend? And you don't find that weird?"

"Maybe, if I had met him because she's dating him, but it was created long before they became a thing."

There's clearly no reasoning with him as he turns around and goes to lie on our bed—though calling it that right now might be a bit of a stretch. Lately, he's been avoiding me by working on the bar so late that I'm asleep by the time he gets home.

My brows furrow as I look at the time, noting we have to leave in thirty minutes, and he isn't even showered yet.

"Aren't you going to get ready?" I question.

He doesn't look up from his phone. "No, because I'm not going."

My jaw drops. "Seriously?"

"Don't act like you're surprised," he tells me. "You've known all week I wasn't going to end up going to that hoity-toity bullshit."

"No, I didn't, because you haven't talked to me in days. Not really, anyway." I feel like I'm on the verge of breaking. "Why aren't you coming?"

"Because it's not my world! And it's not yours either, no matter how much you may want it to be."

"What the fuck is that supposed to mean?"

He tosses his phone on the bed. "Oh, don't play dumb. You know exactly what I'm talking about."

"I don't!" I shout.

"You don't." He repeats sarcastically. "Really? That's hilarious, because you couldn't seem to stop talking about the fact that we got married, but magically, the one person in all of Calder fucking Bay who didn't know was Monty."

This can't be happening. If I had known he was going to freak out over who knows about our wedding and who doesn't, I would've screamed it from the rooftops. Had it written in the damn sky, even. But I never thought he was the kind of person to worry about that—not after he kept *me* a secret for the first couple months.

It's not even like I intentionally didn't tell Monty. The only time I've been around him since our wedding was the day I found out about him and Mali. Needless to say, that was a little distracting. But before I can tell him that, he smirks like his next words are meant to cause pain.

And they do.

"Why didn't you tell him, Lai?" He presses. "Wanted to keep your options open?"

It feels like he just punched me full force in the stomach. Then again, that would probably be preferable. It would hurt less. Tears spring to my eyes. I don't know who the guy standing in front of me is, but it's not the Hayes that I married.

"Fuck you," I hiss.

If he still thinks that he's not the only guy I've basically *ever* wanted, that's his problem. I'm not about to stand here and let him berate me over it. I turn around and head for the door.

"Where are you going?" he calls out.

"To the gala," I answer. "Without you."

As I reach the bottom of the stairs, I hear him curse followed by the sound of his footsteps on the ceiling above me. "Babe, wait."

But I don't want to hear it. Not right now. He spent the last few days barely speaking to me, and after the shit he just said, he can taste his own medicine for a few hours.

293

I HAVE TO ADMIT, I don't want to be here. Everyone looks so happy, dancing around like their worlds are so perfect. And they probably are. These kinds of people, they come from old money. They've never had to worry about anything a day in their lives. Most of them don't even work. They just show up to events like these and toss their money around like being born is something to be proud of.

Hayes might have had a point—this *isn't* our world. But he was wrong when he assumed that I want it to be. As if any world other than the one with him is something I'd even begin to consider. It makes me feel like I never should've come without him.

A part of me just wants to leave. To go home and work this shit out. We're married. We made vows. And to be here right now instead of home with him feels wrong. But it's not a bad idea to let us both calm down. If we're still angry when we try to talk, it'll only make it worse.

So, I stay, but it doesn't mean I'm having a good time.

Monty keeps a hand on Mali's back, like he has something to prove. And I can't help but notice the way Cam keeps glancing at it. The second he realized Hayes wasn't coming, I could tell he wanted to leave. But it's too late. He's already here.

"I can't believe summer is over," Mali says as she looks around the party.

Cam doesn't agree. "It's locals' summer now."

"Yeah, but that only lasts a few weeks. It's essentially over."

I sigh, thinking about how Hayes's twenty-first birthday is coming up. Our original plan was for the bar to be ready so we could celebrate there, but it doesn't look like that's going to happen yet. In no way does that mean we're going to let it go unrecognized though.

"H's birthday is coming up," I point out.

Cam gasps, feigning shock. "Really? Wow. I had no idea. Thank God you married him so I could find out that useful information."

I flip him off. "I was thinking of throwing him a surprise party. You know, since the bar won't be ready in time."

"Wow," Mali says. "Mad at him and still planning something nice for him? How grown up and mature you are. I'm so proud of you."

Monty only latches onto one part of that. "Mad at him? Is there trouble in Wilder Paradise?"

A pit settles in my stomach. The idea of talking to Monty about our issues when I know Hayes doesn't like him—it doesn't sit well with me. That's why I only told Mali about it while we were alone. I wouldn't want Hayes talking to a girl about the weak spots of our marriage. So, it's only right that I give him the same respect.

"Nope, we're good. Just a *put the toilet seat down, you don't live alone* kind of disagreement." I wave off the topic. "Seriously, though. His birthday. Should we throw it at the house? The rink?"

Cam isn't a fan of the idea. "Nah. He's not the surprise party kind of guy. You want to make him happy? All he wants is to get drunk with a few of his friends."

I purse my lips. He has a point. That's really all Hayes ever wants. I know his mom is planning on having a cake for him in the afternoon. She made sure to mention it the other day in case I was planning something. But to leave that and go somewhere that we can just drink and have fun sounds like a pretty good idea.

"If it's not too many people, we could use my boat," Monty suggests.

Mali snorts, but the moment she goes to open her mouth, I cut her off. "I'll think about it. Thanks Monty."

She's already four glasses deep in champagne. The last thing I need is for her to word vomit Hayes's dislike for Monty in detail. At least Hayes pretends to be nice to his face. And Monty doesn't know him any better to notice it's fake.

"I need a beer," my brother says, then mumbles *or seven* under his breath.

Monty nods over toward the right. "Open bar, my friend. Knock yourself out."

"Thanks," he grumbles, walking away.

Mali's eyes seem to linger on him and there's a hint of sadness on her face, but when Monty kisses her cheek, she tears her attention away from him and smiles. It doesn't reach her eyes though.

It never does with him.

The opening notes of "Take My Name" start to play, and my stomach sinks. *Our wedding song.* The last time I heard it, I was on cloud nine, dancing around my living room like it was the most romantic place in the world. Nothing else mattered because I was in his arms. And now, he's not here to share it with me.

What am I doing?

I shouldn't be here—not while my marriage is in trouble. He's not wrong to be upset. If I thought he was intentionally hiding our wedding from people, I would be, too. And the longer I stand here, the worse I could be making it.

"I have to go," I say in a rush.

But as I turn around to leave, I find Hayes standing there, freshly showered and shaved and wearing a suit that makes him look *so* fucking good.

"May I have this dance?"

The sound of his voice feels like coming home. He puts his hand out and I take it. There might still be a lot to talk about, but right now, I need to be in his arms like I need to breathe.

"I should've told you how beautiful you look before you left," he murmurs softly into my ear.

I sigh and relax into his arms. "I'm sorry. I should've told him. It's not that I'm ashamed of us or want anyone other than you. I honestly just hadn't gotten the chance yet, except for when I found out him and Mali were dating, and that threw me for a loop. But I swear on my life, I was *not* hiding you. I love being married to you more than anything."

He tilts my chin up and kisses me. There's no way to explain the feeling of the relief that rushes through me. And when he pulls away, he stares into my eyes.

"I'm sorry, too," he says sincerely. "The things I said to you today were uncalled for. I'm not proud of the way I acted the last few days. To be honest, I still don't fully believe I'm deserving of you, and I let that insecurity get the better of me. But watching you walk out the door today was devastating. I would never forgive myself if I let you get away."

God, I love this man.

I kiss him again, this time a little slower. "One of these days, I'm going to get you to realize that you have nothing to worry about. I'm yours, H. Always."

"Just don't give up on me," he pleads, his voice laced with vulnerability.

"Never," I promise. "And you can't give up on me, either. You're not the only one who screws up sometimes."

"Oh, I know," he says teasingly. "I can only imagine what I'm in for."

I giggle and my head rests on his chest once more, as we sway to the music. He quietly sings along, and I commit the sound to memory, because there's nothing better than hearing our wedding song in his voice, knowing he means every word.

I GET OUT OF the car, slamming the door behind me— only for Hayes to do the same. Everything was fine. We were all having a great time, drinking and laughing. But I had promised to be Cam's designated driver, so I stayed stone cold sober while Hayes took advantage of the open bar. And the more liquid courage he got, the more of an asshole he became.

"I don't get what the big fucking deal is," he argues. "You know I don't like him."

I throw my hands in the air as I spin around. "You don't have to like him, but you don't have to be an asshole either!"

"I wasn't an asshole. I just wasn't playing nice."

"Hayes, he just wanted a handshake, and you just stared at it and laughed." He's not getting it. "It was fucking rude!"

He scoffs. "No, what's rude is that he wants my fucking wife and knows that I know but acts nice to save face in front of you!"

"Oh my God," I groan. "Not this shit again. He's! Dating! Mali!"

"Yeah, so he can stay around you!"

Staring up at the sky, I can't believe we're having this argument *again*. We literally just got over this a few hours ago. I've experienced my fair share of stubbornness. I grew up with Cam, and damn can he hold a grudge when he wants to. But this is another level.

"You're delusional." I tell him. "Do you even hear yourself?"

"Oh, come on," he growls. "Those two have as much chemistry as Mrs. Garrison and a giraffe."

His words catch me off guard, and I have to hold back my laugh. The mental images running through my head of the sweet florist are disturbing, yet hilarious. And as I smirk at him, I feel my anger subsiding.

"It's the tongue, isn't it?" I tease.

His shoulders sag and he tries to hide his smile. "That's not fair."

"I know!" I agree. "Giraffes have like eighteen-inch tongues!"

I watch his eyes darken as he comes closer, looking down at me. "Do you think that means it would be better than mine?"

Tilting my head to the side, I look away to keep a straight face. "Well…"

Before I can even finish that sentence, he picks me up and carries me into the house. I squeal at the sudden move, but when his lips meet my neck, it quickly changes to a moan.

This.

Right here.

This is what we need—to get lost in each other and forget the rest of the world exists. We haven't had sex in days, and while that might seem reasonable to some, it's not normal for us. We're constantly all over each other when we're alone. I'd blame it on being newlyweds, but I can't. It's just how we are.

Physical touch is our love language, and there's nothing wrong with that.

As he shuts the door behind us, he pins me against it. His tongue tangles with mine and our moans mix as he grinds into me. It's so needy. So desperate. Hands are everywhere and the kisses are rough enough to bruise. He moves down to my collar bone and sucks a mark into my skin harshly. It stings but feels so good as his hands grip my breasts.

"You're infuriating," he rumbles. "So fucking maddening and so fucking mine." His hand comes up to grip my throat as he stares into my eyes. "Say it. Say who you belong to."

"You," I breathe. "I'm yours."

The corner of his mouth raises into a smirk. "There's my good girl."

Fuck. This is what he does. He makes me want him so bad I can't think straight. It's so intense that it blinds me. Turns me into a version of myself that only wants to please him.

Looping his fingers around the straps of the dress, he gently slides it off my shoulders and lets it pool on the floor. I should probably pick it up. After all, it's not mine. It has to go back to the designer. But with the way he licks his lips as he checks me out, I don't dare to move.

He hums, dragging his knuckles down the center of my chest. "You are a work of art. There's no one more gorgeous than you."

Normally, I would feel exposed. Standing here in only panties and heels, it's not comfortable. But he has a way of making me feel sexy. He sees me in a way I've never seen myself.

Gripping my ass, he lifts me. I wrap my legs around his

waist and kiss him deeply. There's nothing I want more than him. I *need* this. Need him.

As we get upstairs, I expect him to go straight to the bed, but instead, he brings us into the bathroom. His lips move against mine as he throws his hand at the wall to turn on the light. Then he carefully puts me down and breaks the kiss, turning me around to face the oversized mirror.

"Look at you," he says, and when I try to look away, he grabs my chin and moves my gaze back where he wants it. "Fucking flawless."

I watch in the reflection as he presses light kisses from my shoulder to my neck. His fingertips graze down my sides until he starts to slide my panties down my legs. When they reach my knees, he stops and undoes his belt.

My breathing quickens as he pulls his cock out and rubs it against my pussy. He's really going to do this. He's going to fuck me and make me watch him do it. And holy shit is it hot.

He presses the heel of his hand between my shoulder blades and bends me forward. My hands rest on the countertop and his eyes lock with mine through the mirror as he enters me. His head falls back as he groans at the pleasure of it.

"You're mine, Laiken," he growls, as if I need to be reminded. "All fucking mine. Every inch of you."

I'm a mumbling mess of moans as I watch him grip my hips, sliding his cock in and out of me. And then I get an idea.

If he wants me to watch him, it's only fair that I make him watch me.

The moment he lifts his head, and his gaze meets mine, I smirk. My hand slides down in front of me and I press two fingers against my clit. It doesn't feel nearly as good as when he does it, but the way he drives himself deeper into me makes it more than worth it.

"Does that feel good, baby?" he murmurs. "You love touching yourself, don't you?"

I bite my lip. "I love imagining it's you. No one does it like you."

My words speak directly to the possessive side of him. He wraps his hand around my throat and pulls me up, pressing his chest against my back. It changes the angle, but the way he rocks his hips, I can feel every inch of him inside of me. His other hand grips one of my tits and he nips at my neck while he watches me play with myself.

"Look at you. Such a sinful little seductress."

He tweaks my nipple and I gasp, letting my head fall back against him. My legs feel weak as they start to tremble, but as they start to give, it only lowers me a little more onto his cock.

I watch as his hand slowly glides down until it's covering mine. It's the morning in my bedroom all over again, except this time it's better.

This time, he's inside me.

This time, he's mine.

"God, baby," he moans as he teases my earlobe. "You're so good. Feels so good like this."

I can't hold it back much longer. The way I can feel his cock in my stomach, it's the hottest fucking thing. He's giving me everything he has, and I'm greedy. I want all of it. I want him everywhere.

"Come in me," I say breathlessly.

He smirks, his eyes meeting mine. "Trust me, babe. I want nothing more than I want that. But you said yourself, I'm too greedy for a baby."

I whimper, moving my hips opposite of his to make him feel good. "I don't care. I need it."

It looks like he's considering it, and I'm hanging on every second. I want to come when he does. But instead, he slides his hand a little lower, sliding two fingers into my pussy beside his dick. It's so much more intense as I stretch around him.

"Give me it, Laiken," he demands. "Soak my cock and my fingers with your cum."

There's no part of me that can deny him as my orgasm rips through me, clenching around him. Loud moans fill the room as they come from both of us. I fall forward as he removes his grip from my neck, and Hayes's hand replaces my own to rub my clit as my whole body trembles. But it's what comes next that I didn't expect.

He removes his fingers from inside of me and his gaze stays locked with mine as they tease the only hole he hasn't taken. I take my bottom lip between my teeth, but I don't dare to tell him no. It's like I have a direct line into his thoughts, and I want what he does.

One finger slides into my ass, lubed up with my cum. It's tight at first, but after a minute, it gets better. He rolls his hips to hit my g-spot, distracting me as he inserts a second finger. It's like he knows exactly what to do, exactly how my body works, and as his fingers start to scissor me open, I'm becoming desperate for it.

"You going to let me fuck your ass, baby?" he asks softly. "Going to be a good girl and take all my cum?"

Holy shit. It's going to hurt. Mali already warned me about how uncomfortable it is, and Hayes is *big*. But knowing he'll get to release inside of me, filling me up with every drop of cum he has, drowns out the voice of concern.

Love and pain are one and the same, right?

"Please," I beg. "I want it. I want you to come in my ass."

He lets his eyes fall closed for a second. "That's my good girl. Always so good for me, giving me everything I want."

His fingers work my hole open a little more before he pulls his cock from my pussy and lines up at my ass. He presses in slightly, and I hiss at the stretch. It feels like I'm being ripped open. But he bends forward and presses a kiss to my back.

"Relax," he coos. "It'll feel better if you're relaxed."

I take a few deep breaths, calming myself, and he slips in a little more. Slowly, he moves until he's fully inside my ass. Mali was right, this fucking hurts, but as he waits for the pain to subside, his fingers rub my clit and the pressure in my core starts to build—masking the pain at first then working with it to build me up.

"Do it," I tell him. "Fuck my ass."

He licks his lips and moans as he starts to move. It's slow at first, barely noticeable, but with each thrust, his movements quicken.

"You feel amazing like this," he groans. "Taking me like such a good little princess."

The more he loses himself in the feeling of me, the more it turns me on. I watch as he chases his own high, fucking me in the ass like he needs it to survive. I rock back against him to meet each thrust. And when he finally slams deep inside of me and releases everything he has, he takes me right over the edge with him.

His cock pulses in my ass as my second orgasm destroys me—no mercy given. I watch his muscles tense and can feel him emptying himself inside of me. A bead of sweat drips off his forehead, and he looks down, admiring the look of him stretching my asshole open.

"We fit so well together," he says. His thumb rubs over the edge of my hole to feel me around him. "You were made just for me."

Slowly, he pulls out and I don't look away from the mirror as his brows furrow. He bites his lip and moans at the sight of his cum leaking out of me. Then he uses his cock to spread it around my pussy.

"Fuck," he groans. "That's the hottest thing I've ever seen."

He admires it for a little longer, then walks over to turn on the shower. Steam fills the room and I straighten myself up, regaining control of my breathing and feeling him everywhere. He comes to stand in front of me, and when I look up at him, I still see that teasing look in his eyes.

"Don't go anywhere. I'm nowhere near done with you yet."

I LIE WITH MY head on his chest, both of us naked and breathless after round three. I can't even count the number of times he's made me come tonight, but my pussy is still tingling. I don't see it stopping any time soon. But there's a little voice in the back of my head reminding me of our fight.

The one that says we can't keep fucking just to avoid talking about it.

Everything has been great from the moment we got back together, but now it feels like we're constantly fighting. Like the shit with Monty lit a fuse we can't put out. And to be brutally and vulnerably honest, it scares me. We've never been like this. Even during the time we were broken up, we were miserable but we weren't fighting.

"Are we going to be okay?" I ask, breaking the silence, and there's no way to hide the hint of fear in my voice.

He sighs and presses a kiss into my hair. "Always. As long as the entire world knows your mine."

"Aw, I kept you a secret and you didn't like that?" I tease, reminding him of a time not too long ago. "Mm-hm. Tell me more, Mr. Kettle."

His fingers dig into my side as he tickles me, and the room fills with laughter while I beg him to stop.

Yeah. We're going to be fine.

CHAPTER TWENTY THREE

IT'S TIME TO CHANGE TACTICS. AFTER HEARING THE tone of Laiken's voice last night, like she genuinely wasn't sure if we're going to be all right, I realized I've been going about this all wrong. There's no way to show her how he really is when he's working so hard to hide that side of him from her. And by me pressing the matter, all it's doing is putting a strain on our marriage.

But I can't do this alone, either. There's strength in numbers, but as far as I'm concerned, there's only one other person I need for this.

It's early, barely past sunrise, when I walk into the gym. Cam used to come here at three in the morning just to get it in before he went to work. But now that we've been renovating the bar, he's able to come a little later. Still early as fuck though.

"Hey," a woman greets me. "Haven't seen you around here. Are you new?"

I don't miss the way she puffs her chest out and licks her lips to make them shine, but if she saw who is currently sleeping in my bed right now, she would know she doesn't stand a chance.

"Nope. Just looking for Cam Blanchard."

She smirks. "Oh, so you're a friend of Cam's, huh?"

Great. We're playing a game of *"tell me you've fucked my best friend without telling me you've fucked my best friend."*

"Yeah, I'm also married to his sister, so you can put your tits away. Thanks."

Maybe it's rude. According to Laiken, I have a tendency of being that way. But in this instance, I don't think she would mind. The woman's smile drops off her face and she looks a little offended, but that's not my problem.

I walk around the counter and further into the gym, finding Cam over by the weights. His eyes widen when he sees me.

"Damn, I never thought I'd see the day," he says.

I chuckle. "Yeah, don't get used to it. I choose to work out in other ways."

He puts the dumbbells down and cringes. "Gross. That was only okay to say when it wasn't my sister you were referring to."

"Fair point. Forget I said that."

"I wish I could." He goes over to a machine and sets the weight. "So, if you're not here to work out, what has you up at the asscrack of dawn?"

Honestly, I haven't slept yet. I laid there for a while, listening to the sound of Laiken's breathing, but no matter how much I tried, I couldn't doze off. My mind is on an endless loop. After hearing the fear in Laiken's voice, I knew that if I don't figure out another way to go about this, there's a chance I could lose her.

And that's not a fucking option for me.

"You need to steal Mali away from Monty," I tell him.

He lets the weight fall and slam down inside the machine. "No."

"Just hear me out."

But he's not even up for that. "I'm not doing it, man. You saw his house. He can literally give her everything she's ever wanted. I can't compete with that, and I'm not about to try."

"Bullshit," I scoff. "She *wants* you. She's always fucking wanted you. You're just too stubborn to let yourself see it.

But that's not even what I'm worried about here. We just need to get her the fuck away from that douchebag."

He sighs, grabbing a towel and using it to wipe his forehead. "I thought you were letting that shit go."

"I tried, but I can't."

There's no other way around this. Nothing I can tell him that will make him understand my hatred for Monty other than the truth. And he's the only one who can help me get rid of that fucker once and for all.

"I'm going to tell you something, but I need you to promise you're not going to go all *Cam the Criminal* on me," I say seriously. "Your ass has to stay out of prison, so no violating your probation. We're going to do this shit the right way. Or at the very least, the discreet and untraceable way."

That gets his attention. "What is it?"

"Cam," I press.

His eyes roll. "Yeah, yeah. No punching anyone. Got it. What is it?"

I take a deep breath and when I let it out, the secret I've been keeping comes with it. "He has a sex tape of Laiken."

"What?" he balks. "What the fuck do you mean he has a sex tape of Laiken? Did *he* touch my sister?"

Shaking my head, I push my hair out of my face. "No. It's of Laiken and me. While we were sneaking around, Monty let us borrow his boat. I should've known he was up to something, but I was too caught up in everything to realize it. Turns out, he had planted a hidden camera on it and recorded the whole thing. *That* is the proof he threatened me with."

Cam's knee bounces, and I can tell he's holding back the urge to go rip him to shreds. "And I'm guessing she doesn't know about it?"

"I didn't tell her," I admit. "I realize now that I should've. She would have never talked to him again if she knew, but it's too late for that. If I bring it up now, she'll just think I'm making it up because I don't like him. Not to mention the fact that I kept it from her."

He huffs out a laugh and looks up at me. "You don't fuck up small, do you?"

"Have I ever?" I joke. "To be honest, though, it's probably better she doesn't know, just in case this gets ugly. Innocence by ignorance."

"No, you're right." His head drops and he's still for a second, then he throws his water bottle across the room. "That fucking prick. He did that shit and then has the nerve to act like we're all friends?"

I need to rein him in, before he does something that makes me regret telling him in the first place. Don't get me wrong, I'd love nothing more than to be rid of that piece of shit, but not at the expense of losing my best friend.

"We've got to be smart about this," I tell him. "He might just be some entitled rich kid with boundary issues, but that doesn't mean he's not connected."

"He can't get away with this shit, though."

"And he won't. We're going to figure out a way to make him pay for it, but it has to be in a way that doesn't jeopardize any of us—especially Mali. I don't know what she's doing or how into him she is, but she's in a dangerous spot."

For the first time since this conversation started, Cam looks less pissed and more worried. He's done pretty well at holding himself back when it comes to her, but that doesn't mean she's not one of the people he cares for most. If I had to guess, after what happened that night with Isaac, I'd say she's tied with Laiken for the top spot.

"If he does anything to her, the rules we just agreed to go out the window." There's no bluffing in the way he's talking to me. Every word coming out of his mouth, he means it. "I don't care if I spend the rest of my life rotting away in a jail cell."

I sigh heavily. "No one is going to jail, and she isn't going to get hurt. We just have to find the right way to go about this."

He nods. "No, I know. You're right. But before we do anything, we need to find a way to erase that video. That way he can't release it and make Laiken collateral damage."

"I've tried. Literally tried every possible thing on the internet."

"What is this, amateur hour?" He reaches forward and grabs my phone out of my hand. "We need an actual hacker. Someone who knows what they're doing. And Monty isn't the only connected person we know."

He holds up my phone, showing me Marc's contact. I really didn't want to get him involved in this. Not when so much is at stake. He has more to lose than any of us. But Cam has a point. We need someone with skills that we don't have, and if anyone would know of someone we can trust, it would be him.

Fuck. I really hope this shit doesn't backfire.

I WALK IN THE door, feeling better than I have in over a week—which is surprising given I still haven't slept. It could be all the sex we had last night. I swear, we just couldn't get enough of each other. But I figure it's more about having Cam on my side now. That I'm not alone in my war against Monty.

We're going to bring that motherfucker to the ground.

Just as we thought, Marc knew exactly who to get in touch with. He didn't want to know any more than the fact that we need a hacker, and I don't blame him. I prefer it that way. Now we're just waiting for a time and place to meet the guy.

I find Laiken sitting at the island, drinking a cup of coffee, and she smiles when she sees me.

"Hey, you. Where'd you run off to? Your note was kind of cryptic."

Shrugging, I kiss her forehead. "Just went to the gym to talk to Cam about some things. Sorry if you were worried."

Her brows furrow as she shakes her head. "No, I just... you seem different today."

"I feel different." I come closer, wrapping my arms around her. "I want you to know that Monty isn't going to be an issue anymore."

She places her hand on my chest and holds me back a bit, and I can tell by the look on her face that she's thinking the worst. It makes me chuckle.

"Don't worry. I didn't do anything to him." *Yet.* "I'm just not going to let him get to me anymore. I still don't like him, or trust him for that matter, but I *do* trust you. And that's all that matters."

The smile that stretches across her face shows her relief. "Thank you." Standing up, she hugs me tightly and then kisses me. "I love you."

"I love you, too."

In the worst timing ever, a yawn pushes its way through and forces me to break the kiss. Laiken giggles as I pout. *I want to kiss my wife, dammit.*

"You okay?" she asks amusedly.

I nod, rolling my eyes as I yawn again. "I'm fine. I just don't sleep very well after we fight."

"I get that. I don't either." She picks up her phone off the island and types something into it, then puts it down. "What do you say we go cuddle in bed and watch a movie? You can take a nap."

"Don't you have work in a few hours?"

Her phone dings and she smiles as she glances at it. "Nope. Just got Blake to fill in for me."

Thank you, Blake.

My grin widens as I grab her wrist and pull her up toward the stairs, since carrying her probably isn't in the best interest of either of us right now. But a day spent in bed with my girl should more than fix that.

And as I lie with my arms wrapped around her, I know there isn't a thing in this world that I wouldn't do to protect her. Even if she doesn't believe she needs protecting.

I FEEL LIKE I'M in some low-budget black ops movie. The kind where you dress in disguise and go to a secret location. When Cam got a reply from the hacker, he called me and pretended to need my help with something at the bar. I hate lying to Laiken, but I had to. If she knew what we were really up to, she'd lose her shit.

And I'd probably lose *her*.

Cam follows the instructions in the message, knocking twice, then three times, then once. It takes a minute or so, but the door finally opens. The guy standing on the other side is not at all what I thought he would look like. You always picture hackers as computer nerds. Not this one, though.

He looks like your average college student, complete with a pair of plaid pajama pants and bed hair. The only thing that tells me we're in the right place is the massive computer setup I can see from the doorway.

"You Marc's friends?" he questions.

Cam nods. "Yeah. I take it you're—"

But he can't finish his sentence because the guy shushes him immediately and gestures for us to come inside. When he shuts the door, it looks like we just walked into some kind of panic room. He locks at least six deadbolts, and three chains.

"Sorry," he murmurs. "When you do what I do, you tend to make some enemies."

Again, low-budget black ops.

"You're fine, man," Cam tells him. "It's when you start locking things we can't unlock that I'll have an issue with.."

The guy forces out a laugh. "Yeah, none of that."

It goes quiet, and it's in no way comfortable. But thankfully, he claps and heads to his computer.

"Right, so." He sits down and starts typing. "I will say that I don't like that you insisted on being here as I do this. *Or* the fact that this guy is a senator's son."

What the fuck? "So, what? You had us come all the way down here to tell us you're not going to do it?"

Turning around, he stares at me with zero emotion on his face. "Yes. I gave away my secret location for something I could have said over a text message."

As he rolls his eyes and goes back to what he was doing, Cam chuckles. "I like this guy."

"Fuck off."

"Lucky for you," the hacker continues. "I hate the government more than I hate to compromise."

Cam and I stand behind him, watching him type a million miles a minute. The computer screen is filled with code in multiple different areas, and we couldn't read what it says if we tried. It's like another language, and this dude is fluent at it.

"You said we're looking for a video?" he asks.

"Yeah," I answer. "It's a sex tape taken from a hidden camera on a boat."

A few minutes and a thousand keystrokes later, he sits up straighter. "Okay, I'm in."

How in the fuck? I tried for hours to figure out a way to hack into his phone, and this guy did it in a matter of five minutes. I really should have paid more attention in school.

"I believe this should be it."

With a click of his mouse, the video appears on the screen. Cam looks away, but the sound of Laiken's moaning flows through the speakers.

"Damn. Who's the babe?"

Both of us glare at him. "My wife," I snap at the same time Cam says, "my sister."

He glances between us, and his brows raise. "Because *that* doesn't sound complicated."

The noise stops as he spins back around and presses the spacebar to pause the video. He pulls open a drawer and takes out a thumb drive, inserting it into the computer.

"Once I erase this, the only place it'll exist is in this drive," he tells us, then he pauses. "Wait a minute."

"What?" I growl. "Don't tell me you can't erase it."

He shakes his head. "No, it's not that. But you should see what else this guy has on his phone."

Cam and I lean in to get a better look. There are tons of pictures and videos—from girls our age to older women. And it doesn't stop as he scrolls down. It's like this guy is just some sick pervert who collects illicit videos of women without their permission.

"Wait," Cam orders. "Scroll back up."

He does, and the moment I see what Cam did, my stomach drops. For Laiken and Mali's eighteenth birthday, they both snuck off to get tattoos. Laiken's is the one that's hidden along her spine, only visible when she's undressed or in a bikini. But Mali's wraps around her side. It's much more obvious.

"That one," I say, pointing to it.

The video starts to play, showing Mali's bedroom. It's empty at the beginning and then she walks in. She closes her door and stretches her neck to each side. She grabs some clothes out of her closet and lays them out on her bed before leaving the room, but when the camera angle switches to the bathroom, my jaw locks.

"This fucker has her whole place bugged," I mutter.

Meanwhile, Cam is gripping the desk so tight it looks like it might break. Mali turns on the shower, but the second she starts to lift her shirt, we both turn away.

"Shut it off," Cam tells him.

I knew this guy was sick, but I didn't realize just how deep it all went. "Add that one to the drive, and then delete them all."

"If I do that, he's going to know someone hacked him," he argues.

"Do I look like I give a fuck?" I roar. "All of them."

He must have some sense of self-preservation because he

sighs heavily but does exactly as I say. "Your goddamn moral compass is going to get me killed."

Once he's done, he pulls the thumb drive out of the computer and holds it out to me. I pull the wad of cash from my pocket and we trade. As I put the only existing copy of the sex tape in my pocket, I know it was well worth the five hundred I had to pay for it.

We're clearly dealing with someone more psychotic than we originally thought. We need to tread carefully, to both protect the girls *and* keep Cam out of prison. But loaded with the proof we got tonight that he's not the guy he says he is, it should be enough to get him out of our lives.

We'll see how much he values the pristine reputation of the Rollins name.

It's time he gets a taste of his own medicine, and I hear blackmail has a bitter taste.

Laiken

CHAPTER TWENTY FOUR

THERE'S NO BETTER BIRTHDAY GIFT THAN WAKING up in the best way possible—with a blowjob. Or that's what I've been told, anyway. I wouldn't know firsthand. But I can't see any better way to be woken up than with Hayes's head between my legs, so it must have some validity.

I carefully slide his boxers down his legs and wrap my hand around his cock. He stirs in his sleep but doesn't wake up. His dick, on the other hand, is another story. Just a few tugs of my hand and it's standing at attention.

Sergeant Boner reporting for duty.

Starting off slow, I lick the tip and swirl my tongue around it. Hayes takes a quick breath in, but still doesn't move. I smirk, watching him as I take him fully into my mouth. He moans in his sleep, until his eyes blink open and he looks down at me.

"Fuck breakfast in bed," he says, his voice groggy with sleep. "This is much better."

Instead of answering, I slip him deep into my throat, and he jolts. His head presses into the pillow and his hips arch as I hollow my cheeks around him. He bites his lip hard while groaning and mumbling how good it feels.

I slide my own panties down and start to play with myself. There's something so exhilarating about the way he reacts to the feeling of my mouth. Like it's the greatest thing he's ever felt in his life. But when he sees me doing it, his eyes darken.

"Spin around," he says. "Lie on top of me."

Pulling my mouth off him with a pop, I shake my head. "Today is all about you."

But he isn't having it. "If you think getting to eat your pussy for breakfast isn't a present, you don't know me at all."

Before I can argue it further, he grabs me and uses his strength to flip me around. My stomach rests on his as my legs straddle his face. And as I take him back into my mouth, he licks over my clit.

We've never done this, and I'm failing to understand why. The vibrations of our moans only make it more intense, for both of us. And the deeper I take him, the more pressure he gives me. It's the perfect give and take.

Hayes's hands grip my ass as he pulls me down against him. It feels so good, the way he goes between licking and sucking on my clit and fucking me with his tongue. I lay my tongue flat against his cock and lower my head, taking him as deep as I can until I can't breathe. I gag around him as I choke, and I gently take his balls into my hand.

"Fuck," he pants.

It's like a game, racing to see who can get the other off first, and I'm a sore loser. Letting him beat me at pool once was just to find out what he would ask for. But there's no reason to let him win this one.

I lift my head for only a second to get some air, then I'm right back down, deep throating him in a way that I know is driving him crazy. His tongue is frantic as he tries to get me to break first, but I can tell he's getting close. The muscles in his legs are tensing and he's bucking up into my mouth.

But he's just as stubborn as I am, and I know he's holding back until I come first. And when he presses his thumb into my ass, it reminds me of the night he filled me there, and I lose it. My orgasm has me grinding against his face, and I moan around him, only for him to shoot everything he has into the back of my throat.

After swallowing it all down, I roll off him and collapse onto the bed. My plan was to blow him and then cook him breakfast, but after that, I'm not sure I can move.

"There is nothing better than getting the taste of you on my tongue first thing in the morning," he tells me.

I chuckle, lifting my head for a second to look at him. "You're filthy."

"No. I'm honest. And you're delicious."

I swear, his mouth is going to be the death of me one day. Whether it's from the magic of his tongue, or the dirty things he says, I'm not sure. But it's going to kill me.

Oh well. At least I'll die satisfied.

Forcing myself to sit up, I smile at him. "Happy Birthday, baby."

"Thank you." He props himself up on his elbow and kisses my cheek. "Can it be my birthday every day?"

My nose scrunches. "Are you sure you want that? You're already getting kind of old."

"Twenty minutes." he chuckles. "You could only go twenty minutes without insulting me on my birthday."

I press my fist to my mouth as I giggle. "You walked right into it."

His eyes roll playfully. "Can we just stay in bed all day? I just want to have you to myself, over and over again."

"Yes," I agree, because there is no part of that I don't like. "But we have to leave by four."

"Where are we going?"

"Your mom's, for dinner and cake with her and Devin," I explain. "And then I think Cam and Mali are going to come over so we can drink. Monty had offered his boat, but I turned him down."

To be honest, I've been trying to distance myself from him

—at least as much as I can, anyway. He's a great friend and I appreciate all he's done to help me, but he's not worth losing my marriage over. I know what it's like when someone wants to steal what's yours, and whether his assumption of Monty is accurate or not, I don't want him to feel threatened in any way.

Hayes's lips purse as he looks at me. "I don't know. Maybe we should take him up on that."

What? "Babe, he would be there. This isn't like last time. He said *we* could take his boat, meaning him included."

"Yeah, so?" He shrugs.

"You hate Monty," I deadpan.

His hand reaches out to take mine. "Yeah, but I have fond memories involving that boat."

I melt, becoming putty in his hands. He can't stand Monty, but spending his birthday on the same boat where he first realized he was falling in love with me is worth the guy being around on his birthday. Just when I think I couldn't possibly love him any more than I already do, he goes and does that.

"Are you sure?" I ask. "Because it can just be the four of us here. He doesn't need to come."

He shakes his head. "Nah, really. It's fine. A night on the boat sounds fun. Besides, soon it'll be too cold for it."

"Okay." I grab my phone off the nightstand. "I'll text him and let him know."

> Hey. Does the offer for your boat tonight still stand? Thinking we'll all meet at the docks around six? That way we're out there for the sunset.

It only takes a minute for him to respond.

> Sounds good. I'll grab Mali and meet you there.

I smile, sending him a quick thank you and putting my phone back where it was. "All set. We'll head out at six and watch the sunset."

"Great," he says, reaching out to grab me. "Now get back over here. I just turned twenty-one, which means you owe me twenty more of your orgasms."

Pretty sure that's not how that works, but no part of me is about to argue.

LET ME TELL YOU, mama's boys are so slept on. They know how to treat you with respect, have someone they can go to if they need ideas on what to buy you for a present, and most of the time, they put your pleasure before their own. Not to mention the way Hayes is with his mom is the fucking cutest. Their bond is unmatched. It's like she's not just his mother, she's also one of his best friends.

She carefully carries the cake over with the lit candles as we sing happy birthday. Devin, of course, adds her own lyrics for the sake of roasting him. But as we get to the end of the song, where he's supposed to make a wish, he smiles at me and pulls me onto his lap, wrapping his arms around me.

"I already have everything I could ever want," he murmurs, kissing me quickly.

Chapter 24

When he goes in for another one, I grab his face. "Nuh-uh. You can't just not make a wish."

His eyes narrow. "Fine."

Turning to the cake, he pinches his eyes closed tightly, like a little kid does when they think about their wish. And then he blows out the candles. When he turns to kiss me again, I let him.

"Ooh. Those things almost never come true."

I chuckle as Devin shoves her finger in her mouth, pretending to gag herself. But his mom just watches us in awe as she takes the cake away to slice it.

"So, how's it feel to be twenty-one?" Devin asks him.

His hand on my waist slips just beneath my shirt, needing to feel my skin against his. "Well, I definitely didn't think I'd be married and opening a bar at this age, but I'm not complaining."

She grins like she's trying not to make fun of him. "It's weird, seeing you all domesticated and shit."

"Especially because the first time I came over, I had to teach you how to do the dishes," I add.

He pouts. "Are you ever going to let me live that down?"

"Absolutely not." I look over at his sister. "He didn't want to leave the fork and plate he used in the sink, so he just threw it in the trash."

Devin loses it, throwing her head back as she laughs, while his mom's jaw drops. "Hayes Beckett Wilder."

"Oh, what? Are you going to ground me? Send me to my room?" He pauses, and I can practically see the gears in his head turning. "On second thought, that's a great idea. You should definitely do that."

She closes her eyes and sighs. "You did not just make a sex reference to your mother."

As if he realizes the line he just crossed, he breaks into a fit of laughter. And all I can do is watch him, thinking about how *this*, right here, is what happiness truly is.

WHEN WE'RE GETTING READY to leave, Hayes brings his sister out to the truck to show her the new sound system he put in it—a joint birthday present from Cam, Mali, and me. Because what else do you get someone who claims he has everything he's ever wanted?

I watch them from the doorway as he excitedly turns up the music and Devin stands there, shaking her head at him. When he starts dancing like an idiot in the front yard, she barks out a laugh and joins him.

"You know, I never did get a chance to thank you," his mom says.

My brows furrow. "For what?"

"Showing him that real love can be selfless and genuine. That not every relationship has to turn out like mine did."

I can see the pain in her eyes, and it hurts my heart. "He doesn't blame you for any of that."

"I know he doesn't," she replies. "But I also know it's the reason he didn't take any relationship seriously. It's why he never brought a girl home. Until you, anyway." She comes over and stands beside me, watching her kids. "You're really good for him, Laiken. And I'll never be able to thank you enough for how happy you've made him."

I've always known that his mom loves me. Hell, she's

Chapter 24

been in my life since I was twelve—not there all the time, but she was there. Some people have horror stories about their mother-in-laws. Not me, though. Mine is an absolute goddess.

"Thank you for raising him to be the man he is," I tell her. "All the good things about him, and how deeply he loves when he finally lets someone in, that's all because of you."

Tears fill her eyes, and she wraps her arms around me. "You're something special. It's no surprise he loves you so much."

Hayes and Devin come back up, and he tilts his head when he sees his mom hugging me. "You trying to steal my mom now, Rochester?"

"Yep," I say with a smirk. "That was my plan all along."

"Went through a lot of work for something you could've done from the start," he jokes. "She would've picked you over me before we hooked up."

His mom rolls her eyes, lightly smacking him in the chest as he laughs. "It's a little true, though." Hayes's jaw drops at her words. "What? She's a lot less of a handful than you are."

He snorts. "Try living with her."

I cross my arms over my chest. "Watch it. There's an empty room here I could easily move my things into."

His bottom lip juts out. "You can't threaten me on my birthday."

Devin cocks a single brow at him. "Are you seriously pouting right now? You're twenty-one years old."

But he doesn't answer. Instead, he covers her face with his whole hand and pushes her away. I've always loved his relationship with his family. Having kids might not be in the immediate plans for us, but sometimes, when I see him with them, it makes me think about what he would be like with a daughter of his own. It warms me from the inside out.

One day.

WE GET TO THE docks to find Cam, Mali, and Monty already waiting for us. They each wish him a happy birthday, and Hayes even shakes Monty's hand. It's surprising to see, especially after what happened the last time Monty attempted that. But he's in a good mood, and I don't think he's going to let anything get in the way of that.

Climbing onto the boat, Cam shows Hayes the massive cooler stocked with beer and liquor. There's enough for an entire frat party in there, and it's only the five of us. Something tells me we're going to need to take an Uber home, but that's fine. We deserve to let loose a little.

"Jesus Christ, man," Hayes says. "Did you raid a liquor store?"

Cam chuckles. "It wasn't me. Monty had it when I got here."

Monty shrugs. "It's no big deal. Not like it broke the bank or anything."

I wince, expecting some smartass remark from Hayes about how he's rubbing his money in our faces, or something about rich people, but one doesn't come.

"Thanks." He puts a hand on his shoulder. "You're a generous man, Rollins."

Leaning closer into Mali, I don't take my attention off them. "What the fuck kind of twilight zone did we just step into?"

"The kind where Hayes can be bribed with alcohol, apparently."

And here I thought sex was the best tool to use against him. Turns out, all I needed to do was get him some beer. Go figure.

Monty gets everything ready to go and we pull away from the dock, raising our drinks in the air to cheers the fact that Hayes is finally twenty-one and can legally obtain the liquor license for the bar.

WE'RE ALL DRINKING AND having a good time as we wait for the sun to start setting. I don't know who suggests it, but we start playing truth or dare. The last time we played this, Cam ended up calling chicken for the first time ever. Thankfully, I don't think anyone is going to dare him to kiss Mali with her boyfriend right there.

Or at least I hope not.

I don't think that would go over too well.

"Cam, truth or dare?" I ask.

He looks bored. "Dare."

"I dare you to jump into the water."

His eyes roll as he scoffs. "Fuck that. It's bad enough I'm already the fifth wheel. I don't want to be soaking wet, too."

I scoff. "Please. You're just afraid you're going to get eaten by a shark. You have no balls."

"Oh, and you do?" he counters.

"Yep!" I answer proudly. "They're just too big to go between my legs, so God put them on my chest."

Hayes sputters on his beer, coughing and gagging dramatically. Mali chuckles while Cam watches him like a circus act he doesn't understand.

"What the fuck is wrong with *you?*"

It takes Hayes a few seconds to catch his breath enough to answer, until he finally chokes out, "They were in my mouth this morning."

Cam looks like he's never regretted a question more in his life as he groans and throws an empty beer can at him.

The rest of us laugh while the two of them roughhouse, only stopping when Hayes almost throws Cam into the ocean. That's when he calls mercy and admits defeat, only to follow it up with the excuse that he wasn't going to kick his ass on his birthday.

It's apparently "rude."

But if those two were to ever really go at it, it's a toss-up as to who would win.

I LEAN BACK AGAINST Hayes, with his arms around me, as we watch the sunset in the same spot we were the day we escaped the rest of the world and just enjoyed each other on the open water. This time, however, I don't think the sunset will be followed up the way it did then. Mali probably wouldn't give a shit, but Cam and Monty might have some complaints.

"Did you have a good birthday?" I ask him.

He lowers his head and drops a kiss on my shoulder. "I had *the best* birthday, and it's all thanks to you. I don't deserve you."

"You do. You just don't realize it yet."

The sunset is beautiful, but instead of admiring it, Mali is too busy watching Monty with an unreadable look in her eyes. I glance over and see him making yet another drink. He's supposed to be driving the boat, and if he's drunk, that doesn't mean good things for us.

"Everything okay, Mal?" I ask softly.

She pulls her attention from her boyfriend. "Yeah."

But while her words say one thing, she silently nods her head toward Monty—a message to keep an eye on him. If need be, Cam and Hayes have been driving boats since they were ten. And even I know how to work one. But for now, we'll just see how this plays out.

Besides, as long as he doesn't crash the boat, the worst that could happen is he gets in some legal trouble for boating while intoxicated. And something tells me he has enough money to get out of it.

I focus back on the sunset and the feeling of Hayes's arms around me. "It's so pretty."

He hums. "It's got nothing on you."

Once the sun is gone and the colors start to fade, Monty begins to turn the boat around, but I don't think any of us are ready for the night to end. There are a few ideas being tossed around, like going back to our house or having a fire at my parents' place. But Mali spots a better idea.

"What's that?" she asks, pointing to the faint outline of something in the distance.

All the guys look, but it's Monty who answers. "That's Slaughter Island."

"*Slaughter* Island?" She repeats, looking skeptical.

He nods. "Some say it got its name from all the dead horseshoe crabs that used to wash ashore, but legend has it there was a family that lived there before the man of the house went crazy from the isolation and slaughtered his entire family. If you go late at night, they say you can still hear their screams."

"Oh, I've heard of that place!" I say as I remember the myth. "I've never been, though."

Mali gets excited. "Can we go now?"

We all exchange glances at each other and when Hayes and Cam both shrug, not pushing to go home, Monty turns the boat toward the island.

THE PLACE LOOKS CREEPY, I will give him that. There's remnants of what used to be a dock but is now just a few pillars—probably destroyed by a storm. An abandoned house is off a little ways in the distance. While I'm not sure I believe Monty's story, the evidence definitely supports the claims.

As he pulls the boat as close to shore as he can, he jumps out and uses the anchor to keep it from floating away. Hayes hops down into the water and helps both Mali and me get down safely. It's already too dark to see, with only the boat lights illuminating the area, but I want to go exploring.

"Monty, do you have any flashlights?" I ask him.

He pauses to think and then climbs up into the boat to look around. "I should."

A few minutes later, with a small *ah-ha*, he pulls a flashlight out from under one of the seats. He passes it to me and I thank him before turning to Hayes.

"Are you coming?"

He shakes his head. "I think I'm going to hang out here."

It's risky, leaving him alone with Monty, but Cam doesn't seem to be coming either. Mali loops her arm with mine and the two of us head off toward the abandoned house.

"Give me the flashlight," she says, putting her hand out.

"Why?"

"Because I don't trust you not to freak me out."

My hand moves to my chest as I clutch my metaphorical pearls. "Mali Elizabeth. I am hurt."

She gives me a look that basically says *I know you too well*, and I chuckle. But I still don't give her the flashlight, because she's right. I do want to freak her out. The girl is such a badass all the time, but she scares so damn easily. How could I possibly pass up the opportunity?

The door squeaks as I push it open and the floor creaks as we step on it. Going in probably isn't the greatest idea we've ever had, but we've already come this far. There's no turning back now.

Cobwebs cover every corner of the inside. Though, how spiders even got here is not something that makes sense to me. We're on a small island about ten miles off the coast. It's not even big enough to show up on a map, and there's nothing around it but miles of water.

The furniture that sits covered in each room makes it look like someone just randomly up and left this place. But the sand spread across the floor and the water damage makes me think that maybe a storm drove them out. I can't wait to get home later and look this place up—find out what really happened here.

Mali sticks right by my side as we look around, until we stumble upon a bedroom. The iron rod bed has been stripped down to just a mattress that has definitely seen better days.

"Imagine having sex on that bed and seeing a ghost watching you," Mali says.

I snort at the idea. "Your boyfriend is right outside. You have fun with that."

It's meant to be a joke, but her demeanor changes a little. "We actually haven't...we're just not very physical."

Her words surprise me, but not as much as I thought they would. After everything that happened, it's totally normal if she doesn't want to go there with him yet. But Mali used to be such a sexual person.

"Because of you or him?"

She shrugs. "Both, I guess. He barely even kisses me, let alone tries to have sex with me."

I hum. "Maybe he really *is* gay."

But she's thinking the reasoning is something else. "Or maybe Hayes is onto something, and he really does have a thing for you."

My head falls back as I groan. "Not you, too."

She snickers at my dramatics. "All I'm saying is he might have a point. I mean, what kind of boyfriend only wants to be with his girlfriend when her best friend is around?"

I look at her, seeing no sign of any lies. Not that she even has a reason to lie. "Seriously? That's the only time you see him?"

She nods. "Even tonight. He told me yesterday that he had plans with a friend, but then magically he was free after you asked about taking the boat out. And the only time he kisses me on the lips is when you're with me. Other than that, he kisses my cheek."

The more she says, the angrier I get. It could just be a misunderstanding. Him just being nervous about being alone with Mali and doing the wrong thing. But if she's right, if he's actually lying and using my best friend, I will fight him. I don't care how powerful and influential he is.

"Dude, look. There's a crib over there." She squints as she gets a little closer. "Wait, is that blood?"

I'm so lost in my thoughts that I'm not looking where I'm going, and I accidentally kick an old metal box. It screeches as it moves across the floor. Mali, of course, startles and screams at the top of her lungs, but it's the loud bang that follows that has my whole body going cold. Our heads whip toward each other and we both move at once, running from the house and back to the boat.

When we get there, Hayes and Cam are looking at each other with wide eyes.

"What the hell was that?" I ask, wondering if they heard it, too.

But before they can answer, Mali lets out a blood curdling scream. It isn't until I see what she's looking at that I realize what happened.

Monty is lying on the ground, blood staining his shirt as it comes from his stomach. His breathing is harsh and unsteady. I throw myself onto the sand beside him as I panic, trying frantically to stop the bleeding.

"What the fuck happened?" I wail.

Cam looks like he's in shock as Hayes answers. "He pulled out a gun and started waving it around like a psycho! I took it from him because he's drunk, and it just went off!"

"Oh my God," I cry. "We need to get him help. Someone call 9-1-1."

Chapter 24

"Laiken," Hayes says, but the only thing I'm worried about right now is my friend bleeding out in front of me.

Mali pulls out her phone. "I don't have any signal."

"Laiken," Hayes repeats, a little louder this time.

I grab my own phone from my pocket and realize the same thing. "Climb onto the boat and use the radio. That's what those things are for, isn't it? See if you can get a hold of the Coast Guard."

Pulling my shirt over my head, I'm left in only my bikini top as I try to press the material onto his stomach to stop the bleeding.

"Laiken!" Hayes shouts.

"What?" I snap.

There's fear in his eyes as he stares back at me. "We have to get out of here."

Nothing about what he's saying makes any sense. "Get out of...what? We can't! He needs to get to a hospital!"

"He won't make it to the hospital," he argues. "And we will all go to jail."

"B-but it was an accident." *Wasn't it?*

He shakes his head. "That's what the manslaughter charge is for. We will *all* go down for this. Think of who his dad is. You really think *Jeremiah Rollins* is just going to let this go? He'll make sure they throw the damn book at us."

Not wanting to hear it, I ignore his every word and turn back to Monty. My vision blurs as tears flow from my eyes, but as I go to wipe them away, I'm only getting his blood on my face. Because it's all over my hands. All over *me*.

The sound of Hayes ordering Mali to get into the boat barely registers in my mind as Cam grabs the anchor and tosses it onto the bow. Then, Hayes's arms wrap around my stomach and he starts pulling me away.

"We have to go, Lai," he says softly.

But this isn't right. "No! We can't just fucking leave him here!"

"We have no choice."

"But he's going to die!" I kick my legs and try my hardest to rip myself from his grasp. "We can't just let him die!"

Hayes sighs. "Laiken, he's already gone! There's nothing we can do!"

"No," I breathe. "No, he's…"

"He's gone," Hayes repeats. "We have to go."

My heart sinks as I notice the way I can't see his chest moving anymore, and his head is slumped to the side. Sobs rack through me and I go to cover my mouth, but I realize I can't. My hands are still stained red and covered in his blood.

Everything goes numb.

I can't feel the rest of my body.

I can't move.

Can't look away from the sight of Monty lying on the sand.

Hayes passes me to Cam who sits me inside the boat, and I can hear the sound of Mali's cries somewhere nearby. But as Hayes pushes the boat off the sand and climbs in, all I can do is watch as we leave Monty behind.

CHAPTER TWENTY FIVE

FUCK.

Fuck!

Adrenaline flows through my veins like a drug, and I hope it doesn't stop any time soon because right now I need it. Tonight was not supposed to go down like this. We we're just going to threaten him. Tell him to leave town or we were going to show the girls all about his sick habit of filming people without their permission.

Who the fuck knew Moneybags had a goddamn gun on the boat?

The ride back to the docks is filled with Mali's cries. Laiken sits right where Cam put her, not moving an inch. She hasn't looked away from the back of the boat, as if she's still staring at the island that has long since vanished in the distance.

"Mal, I need you to breathe," Cam says calmly.

She's trying, but I don't think she can. She's having a panic attack—hyperventilating as she struggles to breathe. Cam is knelt down in front of her, trying to help her through it.

"He's…he's really—"

There's no chance of her even getting the words out as he shushes her and tells her to focus on his breathing. I know Laiken used to have them, so he's pretty skilled on how to work through it. I glance back at her as I drive the boat, but it's like she's mentally not there.

Checked out.

Left on the island with Monty's body.

WE GET BACK TO the docks, and I find Devin waiting there for us. The bag in her hands holds everything I'm going to need. But I can tell by her face that she's confused.

"What's going on?" she asks, watching Mali with a concerned look on her face.

I don't answer. Not yet. Cam helps Mali off the boat while I go over to Laiken.

"Baby," I say softly. "Babe, we need to get you home."

Her eyes look empty, devoid of the life they once held. The only reason I know she's still feeling something are the tears that still flow down her cheeks.

Gently, I lift her up and carry her off the boat. "I'm going to need you to stand, babe."

She does, knowing she has no other choice, but when my sister sees the state Laiken is in, she only grows more concerned.

"Is that blood?" she panics. "Hayes?"

I take a deep breath, pulling my keys from my pocket and handing them to Devin. "Take Laiken and Mali back to my house and stay there until I get back."

My words finally pull Laiken from her daze. "You're leaving?"

Fuck. I toss the bag onto the boat and take her face in my hands, not even paying attention to Monty's dried blood on it. "I have to, baby. I have to go take care of this. But I'll meet you there. I promise."

Pressing a kiss to her lips, I tell her that I love her and pass her to Dev. Normally, my sister would be drilling me with questions, but she does as I ask, knowing there will be time for that later. Right now, there are much more important matters at hand.

I turn to Cam and we share a look before both climbing back onto Monty's boat. Watching until the three of them get into my truck, I press the throttle down and start heading toward where Cam's small fishing boat is stored.

THE RIDE BACK TO Slaughter Island is eerily quiet, with only the sound of both boats' motors. And after a while, that starts to fade into a white noise. Thankfully, the ocean is calm tonight. If it wasn't, Cam's boat would never make it out here.

We finally get back to the scene of the crime. Monty's body lies where we left it, but the change of the tide has the water washing over him as we approach. Cam pulls his boat up next to me and stares wide eyed at Monty. Grabbing a pair of gloves out of the bag, I slip them on and get to work— dousing everything in bleach to get rid of any evidence of us being here. I find a roll of garbage bags in one of the compartments and I toss it off the boat and onto the sand.

Meanwhile, Cam kneels down beside Monty's body, looking like he's on the verge of having a mental breakdown.

"What the fuck did—"

"Dude, you're my brother, but now is not the time," I tell him.

Once all the blood from where Laiken was sitting is gone, and I've covered the rest of the boat in bleach, I grab the bag and hop off the boat. There's a bucket from Cam's boat that I use to grab some water, throwing it all over where the bleach just was. Then, I push the boat off the sand and watch as it starts to float away.

"If they find that, won't they smell all the bleach?" Cam questions.

I shake my head. "There's a storm coming out of the southwest. The chances of them even finding the boat are slim, but if they do, the rain will have washed a lot of it away."

Ripping off a few of the garbage bags, I lay them down inside Cam's boat, then walk over to the body. "Help me lift him."

Cam grabs his ankles while I lift from under his arms. We carry him over to Cam's boat and lay him on top of the area I prepared, keeping any blood from getting anywhere we don't want it. But the sand beneath where he was laying is covered in it. Hopefully, the storm will wash that away too, but just in case, I scoop what I can and throw it into the ocean.

Just before we leave, I spot the gun lying in the sand. The one that fired the bullet right into Monty's stomach. I grab it and toss it into the boat beside the body, then we leave the island I never want to come back to again.

ALL YOU CAN SEE are the stars in the sky as we ride out into the ocean. The handheld depth finder Cam has shows what I'm hoping is big enough sea life to ensure his body is never found, and I stop the boat.

"Here's good," I say.

There's no one around for miles, and the only thing we can hear is the sound of a buoy a little ways off. I move to the front of the boat where Monty's body lies and start filling his pockets with all of the sinkers Cam had on board.

"All right, let's dump him," I tell Cam. "The sharks will take care of the rest."

He does as I ask and the two of us lift the weighted body and heave it into the water.

We both stay completely still, watching as it sinks and knowing that this secret is graver than any one we've kept before it. Reaching down, I pick up the gun and take it apart. Each piece gets doused in bleach before I toss that too.

"Good," I murmur once I'm done. "Let's go."

I have to get back to my wife—or at least whatever is left of her.

Chapter 25

IT TAKES LONGER THAN I would have liked to get back. We wanted to avoid any Coast Guard boats. Technically, Cam's boat isn't even nighttime legal. But my concern was that if they saw us out there, they would attest to us being anywhere but at my house all night.

I drop Cam off at the docks to get his Jeep and drive the boat back to where he stores it. He meets me there and I hop in with him, finally heading to my house.

"If anyone asks, we left the dock when Monty started getting too drunk and snapped at Mali," I tell him as he pulls into my driveway. "We came back here and spent the night drinking and celebrating my birthday. Just the four of us."

Just the four of us. I should've taken Laiken's offer of that. It should have been the plan from the start. But no. I just *had* to take advantage of the opportunity to get around Monty. Wanted to give myself a birthday present of making him go away.

This is not what I had in mind.

Cam nods silently and the two of us get out of the Jeep.

I walk inside to see Laiken sitting on the floor with a towel beneath her, still in shock. Mali is curled up in a ball on the couch, and Devin is in way over her head. If there was anyone else that I could've called, I would have. The last thing I wanted to do was get her involved. But the only people I trust were with me when it happened.

346

"I didn't want her getting blood anywhere, but I didn't know where to put her," my sister explains.

My eyes stay focused on Laiken. "It's okay. Thanks, Dev."

Cam leans against the wall, looking exhausted, while I carefully lift Laiken into my arms. She rests her head against me as I carry her upstairs and into the bathroom. Turning on the shower, I wait for it to heat up and bring us both into it—fully clothed and all.

As I put her down, she stands on her own two feet as I start to wash Monty's blood off her. And when her brows furrow and she tries to look down, to see all the blood rushing down the drain, I stop her.

"Keep looking at me," I say softly. "Just keep your eyes on mine."

And she does, not taking her gaze off me for a second while I clean her up.

Like I said, I will *always* do whatever it takes to protect her.

THE NIGHT IS SLEEPLESS. I lie in bed, staring at the ceiling for hours. My mind is spinning from the events of tonight. The only thing that keeps me calm is the sound of Laiken sleeping beside me. It took a while for her to get there, tossing and turning the same way I did, but she finally managed to doze off.

Once I knew she was safe and at least somewhat okay, I went downstairs and talked to Devin. She's frustrated that I won't give her the whole story, but all she needs to know is that she hasn't seen me since Laiken and I left Mom's. Implicating her any further just isn't a good idea, and something I'm not willing to do.

I watch Laiken sleep, admiring the way she looks so peaceful. It has a way of comforting me. I don't know how the next couple of days are going to go, or even what the future holds for me now, but I do know that I won't let anyone else go down for this. If anyone gets blamed for Monty's murder, it's going to be me. That's it.

THE TENSION IN THE room is thick enough to suffocate you. Everyone is tense, but that's not surprising. We all witnessed someone die yesterday, and definitely not from natural causes. It would be understandable if we were all at each other's throats, but thankfully, we're not.

We're just worried.

Cam spent most of last night talking to Mali and getting her to calm down. I don't know exactly what he told her, but I know whatever it was, it worked. She's not in her normal upbeat, spitfire kind of mood, but she's functioning—which is more than I can say for Laiken.

She won't eat.

She's barely even talking.

If I hadn't forced her out of bed, she would probably still be lying there, staring at the wall.

"Lai, you have to eat something," I tell her.

She shakes her head. "I'm not hungry."

Even her voice is monotone. Like I'm not talking to the love of my life but a robotic replica of her. I can't just let her stay like this, and she can hate me for it later, but she needs something in her stomach.

I pour her a bowl of cereal and place it in front of her. "Just a few bites, babe. Please. That's all."

By the grace of God, she gives in. I sit here watching her like some kind of parent, but I won't be okay if she's not. After she eats half the bowl, she drops the spoon in it and pushes it away. But I'm happy with it. I kiss her forehead, whispering a thank you, and bring the bowl over to the sink.

The sound of Mali's phone ringing grabs my attention and all four of our heads turn to it. She steps forward and looks at it.

"It's his mom," she mutters.

Shit. I'm about to open my mouth, but Cam does it for me. "Hey, you can do this. It's just like we talked about, right?"

He's gentle with her, but firm, and she nods. After taking a breath, she answers the phone and puts it to her ear. We all stay completely silent as we listen to her tell his mom the same story we went over—that we were with Monty until they got into an argument, and then we left.

"I'm sure he's just being Monty, but I'll try calling him, and if I can get ahold of him, I'll tell him to call you," she promises.

A few seconds later she hangs up the phone, but before she can put it down, I stop her. "You have to call Monty now."

Her brows furrow. "What?"

"It has to look believable if they check the phone records."

She swallows harshly, grabbing her phone and scrolling to his contact. "This is so fucked up."

The sound of the outgoing ring is a taunting one as she puts it on speaker. We all watch it, holding our breath as if he's just going to answer, even though we know he won't. And when it goes to voicemail, Laiken's head drops.

"Hey. It's me. Your mom called and said that she can't get ahold of you. So, when you get this, call her. And then call me. We need to talk."

It's a nice touch she adds at the end, letting it corroborate the part of the alibi where they got into a fight. It slightly surprises me that his mom is looking for him already, but then again, my mom would probably panic if she couldn't get ahold of me either.

"Cam, you ready to go?" I ask him.

Laiken looks up at me with fear in her eyes. "Where are you going?"

"Hockey practice," I answer. "We have to make it look like today is just another day."

"Can't you just not show?" she pleads. "Your twenty-first birthday was yesterday. I think Coach basically assumes you're too hungover to skate."

It pains me to leave her, especially when she's so fragile, but I at least have to show up and make it look like everything is business as usual.

I sigh. "Let me attempt to go. I'll have Coach send me home, and I'll be back within the hour."

She wraps her arms around me and holds me close. I press a kiss to the top of her head.

"You're going to stay, right?" I ask Mali.

"All day," she confirms.

Before we leave, Cam asks if she's okay and she nods. Then he kisses her forehead and heads out the door with me. I don't know what happened between them last night, but maybe I should take some notes. She's holding herself together a lot better than Laiken, and Monty was *her* boyfriend.

As we walk out the door, Cam asks if we're taking his Jeep or my truck. But instead of answering, I hold up one finger and rush over to the bushes, emptying the entire contents of my stomach into them. The adrenaline is wearing off, and not needing to be strong for Laiken for right now, my body gives in to the stress of the last twelve hours.

Might not be so hard to get Coach to let me leave after all.

THE NEXT COUPLE NIGHTS go the same way as the first, spent with my mind running wild while I can't sleep. Even the sound of the rain doesn't help, especially after we were all hauled into the police station yesterday morning for questioning. Since then, Laiken has made it a habit of Googling Monty's name. I stop her each time I catch it, but I can only do so much.

When I finally manage to doze off, letting sleep deprivation pull me under, it doesn't last long. A nightmare immediately haunts my mind, picturing myself being charged for murder and pulled away from Laiken as she sobs in Cam's arms.

Monty's face appears in front of me. "I knew you'd fuck up eventually."

I jolt awake, trying to catch my breath and tell myself it was just a dream, but then I notice that Laiken is no longer in bed next to me. Panic immediately sets in, and I look toward the bathroom, but she's not there either.

Climbing out of bed, I go downstairs to find her sitting on the couch. My lungs feel like they can finally take in air again. I don't know when Cam and Mali got here, but all three of them are laser focused on the TV—more specifically on a picture of Monty.

Authorities are searching for Montgomery Rollins, the son of Senator Jeremiah Rollins, after his parents filed a missing person's report early yesterday morning. He was last seen Friday night while at the boat docks with a few friends. According to reports, the friends left after he became intoxicated and got into an argument with his girlfriend. If you have any information on his whereabouts, please contact the Calder Bay Police Department.

They move onto another topic like his disappearance is just another headline. Like it's not the tragic event that has my life hanging in the balance. Cam switches off the TV, and the whole room stays completely silent.

None of us really know what to say anymore.

CHAPTER TWENTY SIX

Laiken

THERE'S A HAZE THAT LINGERS IN THE AFTERMATH of tragedy. A subtle but constant reminder that nothing is ever going to be the same again. You can't rewind. Can't go back. You just have to make sense of the pieces that remain.

I lost a friend. Someone I trusted. Someone I cherished. He wasn't perfect and he made his mistakes, but he made up for them by being there when I needed him the most. What he did to keep Cam out of prison was more than enough to deserve my forgiveness. And that's what he got.

The feeling of my hands being soaked in his blood is something I'll never get out of my head. It's burned into my mind like a horrid memory that will forever leave me traumatized. But as much as I want to scream and cry and rip my hair out, I can't.

I can't *feel* anything except fear.

I'm scared for all of us. For myself. For my brother. For my best friend. For my *husband*. The image of him lying there, with blood pooling from his stomach—it's directly linked with the dread of what comes next. And the worst part is I can't even make sense of it all. I don't understand what happened. All I know is that everything was fine, we were having a great night, and then Monty was dead.

I wasn't lying when I told police I don't have any idea what happened to him. Honest. I don't. Other than the fact that my husband can add *taken a life* to his list of sins, but that's not something I was about to tell them. Hell, it's barely something I can tell myself. It was an accident. I know that.

But there's this little voice in the back of my mind, repeating all the horrible things Hayes has said about Monty.

THERE'S A FINE LINE between calm and chaos when it feels like your entire life is on shaky ground. Just a breeze from the wrong direction could send it all crashing down around us. All we can do is hold on for dear life and hope we make it out alive, and I'm trying to. But that doesn't mean I'm not breaking inside—worried about what could go wrong next.

"Laiken, you have to stop!" Hayes yells at me, his patience hanging on by a thread and ready to snap.

I roll my eyes, holding the remote away from him. "I don't *have* to do anything! We were cleared by the cops, so what fucking harm does it do? It's not like I'm making you watch it."

"Because it's not healthy," he says as he kneels in front of me. "You can't keep obsessing over this. It was an *accident*."

"Then why did we just leave him there? Why not try to get him help if you did nothing wrong?"

His fingers run through his hair as he sighs. "And then what? You think his family would just be okay with it? Say *shit happens* and move on?"

I scoff. "Can you imagine what we're putting his mother through? It must be torture, not knowing where her son is or what happened to him! This is *wrong*, Hayes, and you know it."

The guilt is eating me alive. It's ripping me apart from the inside out. I can barely even look at myself in the mirror anymore. And yet, he's fine. He's the one that shot him, and he's managing to hold it all together. Could he really have hated him *that* much, to the point of not caring that someone died at his hands?

Hayes goes to grab the remote again, just as a picture appears on the screen and my stomach sinks. "Wait, look."

It's Monty's boat, shipwrecked into the rocks. Chunks of it are missing and almost half of it sits under water, with the part that's not only being held up by the rocks it's resting on. I turn the volume up to hear what they're saying.

"We have new information in the case of missing twenty-year-old Montgomery Rollins. His boat was found wrecked almost one hundred miles up the coast from where he was last seen. Police had this to say in a press conference."

The video switches to the chief of police standing at a podium. Other officers and officials stand behind him, but it's the sight of Monty's parents that breaks my heart. His dad holds his mom as she tries to keep herself from crying, but you can see the way she sniffles. They both look absolutely devastated.

"After the discovery of Mr. Rollin's boat, we believe we have enough evidence to declare Montgomery Rollins deceased. After a thorough investigation, it is our professional opinion that the cause of death is accidental drowning. The events that transpired Friday night are believed to be as follows. After an argument with his girlfriend, Mr. Rollins appears to have gotten into his boat and went for a drive to let off steam. At some point, he fell overboard and due to his intoxicated state, was unable to get back to the boat. Our hearts go

out to the Rollins family, and we ask that you respect their privacy as they grieve the loss of their son."

The newscasters come back onto the screen, talking about what a devastating loss it is, and then moving on to his father's campaign as if it's at all relevant. They're not even the slightest bit affected, but why would they be? It's not like they knew him. Or knew what it's like to be in his presence.

Tears flow down my face as I mourn the loss of my friend. I cry for the life that was taken too soon. I cry for the pain his parents are experiencing. I cry for the people that will never know what really happened or have his body so they can lay it to rest.

Hayes wraps his arms around me and holds me while I sob, whispering everything I need to hear as he keeps me together.

It's going to be okay.

We'll get through this.

I've got you.

And I know he does. He always does. But the guilt hurts. It's utterly destroying me. All I can do is lean on Hayes and hope he's enough to get me through this.

AN OVERACHIEVER IN LIFE and in death, it doesn't surprise me that Monty's memorial service is beautiful. The church is decorated in black and pale red flowers, matching the black pews. If he were here, I know he would love it. But he's not here.

There's no casket.

No urn filled with his ashes.

According to Hayes, he's out in the ocean somewhere, becoming a five-course meal for a shark, most likely. So, all we have to honor him and the life we lost is the massive-sized picture of his smiling face front and center.

"Do you want me to go with you?" Hayes asks.

I shake my head. "No."

He sighs but doesn't fight it as he goes to join Cam and Mali who have already made their rounds. It's no surprise to me that he doesn't want to say goodbye. He hated Monty. But he's here for me, and that's what matters.

Stepping up to the picture, I put my hand on it. It doesn't feel real, him being gone. That I'm going to wake up tomorrow to a call from him, asking if Mali and I want to go shopping or just hang out because *"rich kid life is boring sometimes, believe it or not."*

"I'm so sorry," I whisper. "I am so unbelievably sorry. We should have stayed with you. We shouldn't have left you. You didn't deserve this." My eyes fall closed as I try my best not to break down. "I miss you so much, and I will *never* forget you."

Kissing my fingers, I press them to his cheek.

I'm still crying as I go sit between Hayes and Mali. My best friend gives me a sad smile and holds my hand in hers. It's a small act of solidarity, telling me she understands and feels it, too—something I don't have with Hayes. He's trying to be supportive and doing his best to console me, but he doesn't get it like she does. And I can't help but mentally note how unaffected he looks—like he's not part of the reason there's a funeral for him in the first place.

HAVE YOU EVER NOTICED the amount of people who come out of the woodwork when someone dies? The people who haven't talked to them in years but suddenly, now that they're gone, it's like they were the best of friends? Yeah, they piss me the fuck off. I tried not to pay attention to it as we sat through the service, choosing to focus on honoring Monty instead, but that's over. All I can see now is the hundreds of people here that probably never knew him at all.

Let's be honest, half of them are probably only here to get closer to Monty's dad. You can tell who they are by the things they say.

"Montgomery was a fine young man."

"I met Montgomery during charity work last year."

"The loss of Montgomery is a tragic one. He had such a bright future ahead of him."

Yeah, if they knew him, they'd know he hated the name Montgomery. He said it sounded pompous. And other than enjoying the benefits of power, he had zero plans of going into politics like his father.

We step outside the church and start to head to our cars when a detective stops us. His badge sits on display on his hip, and he smiles kindly.

"Mind if I have a minute of your time?" he asks.

Mali's brows furrow. "Someone took our statements when he was reported missing."

He nods. "I know, and I have them. I'm just following up on a few things."

The four of us share a look, but it's Cam who shrugs. "Sure. I don't know what else we can tell you but ask away."

"Great." He pulls out a notepad. "So, you said you guys were at the docks that night. Around what time would you say you got there?"

Hayes hums. "Like six or six-thirty. Somewhere in there."

"Okay. And what was the plan for the night? Were you all just going to be drinking or did you intend to take the boat out?"

Mali goes to answer, all of them trying to make it so I don't have to say anything. They saw what a wreck I was after we were interrogated. But before a single word can come out of her mouth, Monty's mom comes over.

"Detective, I appreciate you doing your job," she says, "but it's not necessary. There's no way these girls were involved in my son's death. Please leave them be so they can grieve their friend."

He gives her a curt nod and turns to us. "I apologize. I'm deeply sorry for your loss."

"Thank you," Mali and I say in unison.

Hayes puts a hand on my lower back. "You want me to give you a minute?"

I love how he always knows exactly what I need. "Please."

He gives me a small smile and kisses the top of my head. "Cam and I will meet you guys at the truck."

With that, the two of them leave and I finally get to hug Monty's mom. Her and his dad were far too occupied when we got here, and I didn't want to be a bother. But my heart breaks for the woman standing in front of me.

"Mrs. Rollins," I say sadly, wrapping my arms around her. "I'm so sorry."

She takes a deep breath, and I can feel every ounce of the

pain she's experiencing. "Oh, Laiken. Thank you so much for coming."

"Of course. We wouldn't miss it."

As she releases me, she hugs Mali just as tightly. "Monty used to talk about you two so much. He would always say what great friends you were. I know he'd appreciate you being here. I just can't believe he's gone."

Tears are already building in my eyes as Mali rubs her arm. "None of us can. I don't think it's really set in for any of us."

She focuses all her attention on Mali. "I'm so sorry that your last interaction wasn't a good one. I hope you're not blaming yourself for any of this. That's not what I want for you, sweetheart."

Mali's head drops. "I'm working on it."

Mrs. Rollins nods in understanding. "Well, I'll let you girls go, but please don't be strangers. I'd love to have you over for lunch soon. Share some stories of Monty. But I understand if you're not comfortable with that."

I know I shouldn't. Hayes will have a conniption when he finds out. But Mali isn't the only one blaming herself, and if there is anything I can do to help ease some of her pain, I'm going to do it.

"That would be nice," Mali tells her. "I'll check my schedule and let you know."

She looks pleased with that answer and turns to me. "Should I expect you too, dear?"

I force a smile on my face. "How does Wednesday early afternoon sound?"

Mali's eyes widen as her head whips toward me, but she quickly masks her surprise as Mrs. Rollins beams.

"That would be fantastic. I'll have the chef prepare lunch for one o'clock."

"Perfect," I confirm.

We both give her another hug while we say goodbye, and the second she walks away, Mali looks at me like I've lost my mind.

"Uh, what do you think Hayes is going to have to say about that? Can you even handle that right now?"

I roll my eyes. "I have to, okay? I just do. And I don't know what Hayes is going to say, but that's for me to worry about."

She seems unsure, but she lets it go. "All right. I just hope you know what you're doing."

The truth is I don't. I don't have any idea what I'm doing, but that's nothing new lately. I haven't had a grip on things since Hayes's birthday a week and a half ago.

But I know I'm going to have lunch with Monty's mom regardless.

I owe her that much.

THE DAYS PASS AND NOTHING seems to be getting any better. As much as I try to let my life go back to normal, I can't. I don't even know what *normal* is anymore. But while I'm stuck in this never-ending nightmare, everyone else seems to go about their lives as if it's just another day. Even Mali has managed to pick herself back up and moved on.

So why am I still so broken?

Hayes is trying to stay patient and understanding, but I see him slowly getting irritated. He can't seem to make sense of why I won't just let it go like everyone else, while I can't wrap my head around how he can. I expected him to feel some kind of remorse. Regret for what happened because it being an accident doesn't make it completely guilt free. But there's nothing. Not a single tear has been shed for the life that was taken.

The arguments come more often, becoming part of our daily routine. He says that I'm nitpicking, and maybe I am. But I can't help it. My mind is a constant mess, and I'm trying to cling to the life I once had, but I'm not even sure that life exists anymore. Or even if it still can.

IT'S WEDNESDAY MORNING WHEN I finally bring myself to tell Hayes about the lunch I'm having with Monty's mom. Last minute, I know, but I figure if he's going to try talking me out of it, this way I don't have to hear it for long. He comes upstairs and sees me dressed, even though he knows I don't have work today.

"Are you coming with me to the bar, babe?"

Well, here goes nothing. "No. I have plans before I have to be at the rink."

He actually seems pleased with the fact that I'm getting out of the house when I don't have to, but I'm sure that won't last long. "Oh yeah? Going out with Mali?"

"No. Mali's working today." I pause. "I'm actually going to have lunch with Mrs. Rollins."

All of his motions halt. "Mrs. Rollins? As in *Monty's mom* Mrs. Rollins?"

"Mm-hm." I try to sound as nonchalant as possible.

He turns to face me and I'm not sure if he wants to scream, cry, or panic. Then again, it's probably all three. He's trying his best to maintain his composure as he breathes slowly.

"Are you sure that's a good idea?" He asks. "The pressure of that is a little much, no?"

I shrug. "Probably, but I already told her I was coming."

"So? Pretend you're sick."

"Oh, so she can be upset about yet another thing in her life right now? No thank you."

His fingers lace into his hair and he tugs. "What if you break down while you're there? You're hardly what I'd call stable lately. What if you slip up and say something that contradicts our story? How do you not see what a colossally bad idea this is?"

With each question he asks, the angrier I get. "Will you *stop* acting like I'm some fucking damsel in distress?"

He huffs. "Well, you haven't shown me anything different lately. Laiken, you don't owe this woman anything."

"Don't I?" I snap. "Her son is *dead*! The body of the boy she birthed and loved and raised is decomposing in the ocean right now! And that's if it's even still in one piece. The least I could do is have lunch with her and exchange some stories for her to remember him by."

He's pacing back and forth across the room. "Does Mali know about this?"

That question strikes a nerve. "Don't do that. Don't bring my best friend into this like I need permission from either of you to do something. It's just fucking lunch, H!"

"It's a fucking risk is what it is!" His shoulders sag as he stares at me. "Why are you torturing yourself for this?"

"Because one of us has to!" I shout.

He exhales heavily, shaking his head. "Laiken, I love you but I don't know what to do with you lately. I just keep trying and every morning I pray to God that you'll get a little better today. I'll do whatever it takes to bring back the girl you were before all this happened, but spending time with Monty's mom is *not* the answer here."

"No, it's probably not. I don't even think there is an answer for this."

"So, what then? You're just going to be miserable forever? Let his death hang over your head like a black cloud for the rest of your life? Can't you see how unhealthy that is? Do you really think that's what he would've wanted?"

I glare at him. "Oh, please. What do *you* know about what he would've wanted?"

He sits on our bed, holding his head in his hands. "I can't believe this. He's dead and he's still causing fucking problems for us. Is this what our future is going to be? Constantly fighting over this? Because if so, I can see why fifty percent of all marriages end in divorce."

Okay, ouch. Throwing the idea of divorce in my face while I'm grieving is *not* okay. But if he wants to use words as weapons, I can throw them right back. "Hey, you were the one who was all *let's get the government involved in our relationship.*"

"And I wouldn't trade it for a goddamn thing!"

Scoffing, I put a hand on my hip. "Let's not kid ourselves here. You and I got married for two totally different reasons. Me because I've been in love with you for years, and you because the sex is good. What did Cam call it? Pussy on demand?"

It's a low blow—one I know has no truth to it, but it hits

its target dead on. He stands up and stalks toward me, looking angry and pained all at once. I hold my head high as he stands in front of me.

"Let's get one thing straight," he growls. "There are a lot of things I will tolerate, but you questioning my feelings for you or the dire need to spend the rest of my life waking up beside you is *not* one of them."

The two of us stand there, both furious but also both so fucking scared. And when he finally grabs the back of my neck and pulls me in for a kiss that's just as desperate as it is rough, I'm thrown back into everything he is.

My hands grip at his shirt, trying to pull him as close as possible as his tongue tangles with my own. He walks me backward until I'm pinned against the wall, and he shoves his hand under my waistband. There's no teasing as his fingers immediately go for my clit.

I throw my head back as I moan. It's been too long since I've had him like this. Too long since we've let each other forget about the world around us and just existed in our own little bubble.

"That's it, baby," he says lowly. "You're my good girl, aren't you?"

"Yes," I breathe.

His lips press against my neck as his fingers work their magic. Maybe this is what we needed—to fuck our frustration out on each other and experience that spark we've always had.

"Stay here with me," he tells me. "Show me what a good girl you can be. Let's get in bed and stay there all day."

Just like that, it's like a bucket of ice water is poured over my head. I grab his wrist and pull his hand out from inside my jeans, shoving him away. He has *never* used sex as a tool against me, and I never thought he would, until now.

And judging by the look in his eyes, he knows he fucked up.

"Laiken," he tries.

But I point at him as he tries to step toward me. "Don't!"

My blood runs boiling hot as I glare at him, and he looks utterly defeated as he sighs. "I'm just trying to protect you."

I huff in disbelief. "Why? You said it yourself. Fifty percent of all marriages end in divorce."

THE BACK PATIO OF Monty's parents' house overlooks a large yard that's perfectly landscaped. The hill it sits on makes it so you can see the ocean out in the distance. I remember thinking how beautiful the view was the first time I saw it, but now, I can't manage to look at it for longer than a minute.

"It is so nice to see you," Mrs. Rollins tells me. "How have you been doing?"

I force a smile on my face, knowing there's no way I can tell her the truth. "I've been okay. Not great, but I'm just taking it day by day. How are *you*?"

She puts her tea down on the table in front of her. "It's hard. Parents aren't meant to outlive their children. But I'm working through it with a grief counselor. I just keep telling myself that Monty would want me to be happy."

"He would," I agree with her. "How is Mr. Rollins doing? Is he taking it hard?"

Her lips purse and she looks away. "They were never really close, those two. And the results of the investigation are causing some trouble for him at work. With the upcoming elections, his opponents are latching onto it, claiming he *let* our son drink underage and drive a boat while intoxicated."

Great. More guilt to add to the pile.

"That's horrible. None of this was his fault."

She smiles sadly. "I know that, dear. Everyone who matters knows that. It was a tragic accident and the result of bad choices on Monty's part. But you know how politics can be."

But that's the thing. It wasn't *solely* the result of his bad choices. A tragic accident, yes. And from Hayes's explanation of what happened, a little his own fault. But it doesn't lie entirely on him.

The pressure is intense as it pushes down on me, and I'm starting to realize why Hayes and Mali were so insistent on this being a bad idea.

It gets slightly easier as we pivot away from his death and onto happier stories—like how he snuck his mini horse into his bedroom when he was ten, only to freak out when it started to shit all over the place. I tell her about how we met because I accidentally tripped at a club and spilled my drink all down the front of him. I felt horrible, but he just laughed it off—and then proceeded to buy the shirt off the guy next to him for a hundred times what it was worth and buy me a new drink right after.

"Oh my goodness," she laughs. "That sounds just like him."

"He was very gentlemanly," I say, smiling at the memory.

"That doesn't surprise me. You were so special to him. Mali, too, but especially you."

My brows furrow as I take a sip of my water. "I'm not sure I know what you mean."

She gives me a small smile. "It's just a mother's intuition. He liked Mali. He was always smiling when he talked about her. But when he talked about you, I saw a look in his eyes that I'd never seen on him before. Like he was mesmerized by every little thing about you. He really loved you, Laiken."

My stomach twists, and there's a pain in my chest as her words set in. *Hayes was right.* All this time, he kept telling me that Monty wanted me, and I didn't believe him. And what Mali told me that night, about how he only hung out with her when I was around, it makes so much sense now.

A whole range of emotions flood through me at once. I'm livid for my best friend, because that means he *was* using her to have an excuse to stay around me. What better way to ensure seeing me than dating my best friend, right? But I'm also full of regret. I can't count the number of arguments Hayes and I had over this. How many times I called him delusional for thinking Monty looked at me as anything more than a friend. Meanwhile, he was spot on.

All this time he thought it was him that doesn't deserve me, but really, it's me who doesn't deserve him.

I GIVE MRS. ROLLINS a hug, promising that it won't be too long before I'm back, but that's a promise I'm not sure I can keep. Learning that Hayes was right about Monty all along, and that he *was* in fact using my best friend, it doesn't sit well with me. I'm seeing him in a whole new light, and it's not a good look on him.

I walk out to my car and as I get in, I send a text to Hayes.

> Hey. Leaving lunch. Just want you to know that I love you and I'm sorry about earlier. We'll talk tonight.

Putting my phone down, I start my car and go to pull out, when it vibrates. I smile to myself, thinking it's Hayes, but as I open it, I realize it's from a blocked number.

> How well do you really know the man you're married to, Mrs. Wilder?

There's an attachment with it—a voice recording—and when I press play, my entire body goes cold.

"You think I won't do my own dirty work? That I won't enjoy slamming your face repeatedly against the curb? You're not the only one with connections, Rollins. I'll strangle you and make it look like you fucked off to an island somewhere with a man named Ramon."

I can feel as my heart cracks in half. The Hayes that I know is *not* the same one in that recording, but it's his voice. There's no denying that. And the little voice in my head, reminding me of all the rage he felt toward Monty—it's louder than ever.

If I thought I was lost before, I don't even know what to call this. Hayes is my rock. The love of my existence. And now I don't know where to go from here. They don't give you a manual on what to do when there's a chance your husband could be a murderer. But when another text comes in, I realize all that might not be up to me.

> That's only a taste of the things I have.

Chapter 26

My thumbs fly across my phone as I type out my response.

> Who are you and what do you want?

I want him to pay for what he did. Check the envelope under your seat for further instructions.

Hayes
CHAPTER TWENTY SEVEN

Have you ever watched someone you love spiral out of control? Felt the desperation of wanting to save them but knowing there's nothing you can do? It's a special kind of hell to spend every day hoping and praying that they'll pull through this, but not knowing for sure that they will.

Laiken going to have lunch with Monty's mother is a move I never saw coming. I know she's been having a rough time, but it feels reckless—and not to mention self-mutilating. The guilt is already destroying her. Does she really need to make it worse by spending the day there?

But the message this morning was clear.

She was going, whether I liked it or not.

Thankfully, there's nothing like a little manual labor to work out your frustrations.

I grab a piece of drywall from the pile and stand it up, hauling it over to the wall it needs to go on. As I line it up and start to hammer the nail into it, I think about what Laiken is doing right now.

Is she okay?

Is she getting upset?

Is the ghost of Monty watching her in the bathroom like the sick pervert he was?

The sound of the sheetrock cracking echoes through the room and my eyes close as my head falls back. *Motherfucker*.

"Okay, that's the third piece you've damaged today," Cam

tells me. "At this rate, all the walls are going to be made of spackle."

I huff. "Well maybe if *someone* wasn't hogging the nail gun…"

He chuckles, coming over and finishing this piece for me. "Yeah, we're not doing this. That's not the issue and you know it. What's going on?"

"I don't know," I say as I run my hands over my face. "Laiken is just…a lot right now."

"Yeah, I've noticed," he replies sadly. "What's she doing now?"

A part of me considers not telling him at all. He's going to be just as pissed off as I was. Even Mali agreed it's a bad idea. But my anger has subsided now, and all that's left is worry.

I take a deep breath, letting it out slowly. "She's seeing Monty's mom for lunch today."

His jaw drops. "Has she lost her goddamn mind?"

"Yeah, I'm not answering that."

He looks around, shaking his head while he tries to figure her out. But good luck. I've been trying to do that for the last couple weeks. It's not going very well.

"I'm worried about her, H," he tells me.

I sit on the stepstool. "Yeah. Me too."

It's quiet for a moment, both of us thinking about the same thing. I had hoped that she would go back to how she was before this in the same timeframe that Mali did. And in a couple ways, she has. She finally went back to work after taking four days off and I don't have to force her to eat anymore. But in other ways, she seems dead inside.

It's like there's a piece of her that never left that island, and that scares the shit out of me.

"I don't know, man," Cam murmurs. "Maybe it's time to get her some help. *Professional* help."

My eyes narrow at him. "What?"

"There are a few places I found that we can bring her to for an evaluation." He pulls out his phone and starts messing with it. "They specialize in grief counseling, and if they admit her, she would only have to stay for a few weeks before they transition her into outpatient therapy."

I'm shaking my head before he's even finished. "No. Absolutely not."

His shoulders sag in defeat. "Hayes, she's crumbling."

"You think I don't know that?" I snap. "Fucking Christ, I have to see it every day. But the girl she was before this is in there somewhere. I know it. And I'm not going to abandon her by shipping her off to some loony bin."

"H," he tries, but I have no interest in whatever else he has to say.

"No. Okay? I said no. She's my wife, and I'll be the one to take care of her. End of fucking story."

Throwing his hands in the air, he looks frustrated, but he gives up—for now, at least.

I walk over to the table where I left my phone and check the time, but I see a text from Laiken waiting for me.

> Hey. Leaving lunch. Just want you to know that I love you and I'm sorry about earlier. We'll talk tonight.

My chest swells a bit. Moments like these are when I see the old her still managing to shine through. The message is from an hour ago, which means she's probably at work by now. Still, I type out a response and send it for when she gets done.

> I'm the one who's sorry. I'm just worried about you, Lai. But you're right. We'll talk tonight. I love you. 🩶

I don't want to get my hopes up, but this feels a lot like finding the light at the end of a long, dark tunnel.

FOR THE FIRST TIME in a couple weeks, I walk into the house with a smile on my face. I've been dying to get home. I thought about leaving early, but we had to get shit done if we want to meet certain deadlines and not fail any more inspections. I can't wait until the bar is done and I can be the boss who leaves for lunch dates in the middle of the day.

Or sex dates. Those are good, too.

Laiken is sitting at the small kitchen table—the one we have only used once since I moved in. She's not even doing anything, just staring off into space. I go up to her and press a kiss to her forehead. But something about the smile she forces onto her face feels off.

"How was work, babe?" I ask as I grab a beer from the fridge.

Her voice comes out lifeless. "I didn't go."

Fuck. So much for turning a corner. Now it feels like we've gone back three steps. Dread runs through me at full force. I know I shouldn't have gotten my hopes up. Not with how unstable she's been lately. But that text sounded so much like her, the *real* her, that I couldn't help it.

"Baby," I sigh, sitting across from her. "I know you're

hurting and I'm sorry you lost your friend, but you can't throw the rest of your life away because of it."

She scoffs. "That's easy for you to say. You never liked Monty."

"No, I didn't," I admit. "I couldn't. He wanted to take away the one person in my life that I can't live without."

Her eyes meet mine with a fire inside them, but while normally I'd be glad that she's feeling *something*, this seems to be directed at me. And the words that come out of her mouth make me feel like *I'm* the one who took a gunshot—but mine was straight to the chest.

"Is that why you shot him?"

Laiken
CHAPTER TWENTY EIGHT

I REMEMBER THE DAY WE STOOD IN THE PARKING lot of our beach; the day Hayes asked me to take him back. The look on his face when I told him no was heartbreaking. I'm not sure he prepared for the possibility that he wouldn't get his way, and it hurt more than he thought it would. But the expression on his face right now is one that will haunt me for the rest of my life.

"Wow," he says breathlessly, after a moment of letting my words sink in. "T-that's really what you think of me?"

My heart hurts. There's an actual stabbing pain that's shooting through it. "I don't know *what* to think. All I know is that I walked away and came back to find Monty bleeding out on the ground, and you saying you accidentally shot him."

"Yeah, emphasis on *accidentally*!" he yells.

"Well, for me, the emphasis is on *shot him*!" I shout back.

He sends the chair flying backward as he gets up from the table. "This is fucking great. My wife honestly believes I'm a murderer."

"I didn't say that!" I argue. "But think of how this would look to anyone else!"

"You're not *anyone else*! You're my wife!" he roars. "I just thought you would have a little more faith in me than this. You've known me for how long? If you truly think I'm capable of something like that, why are you even with me?"

"Because I love you! I'm not saying you killed him in cold

blood but you can't deny that something isn't adding up here. He just randomly took out a gun and started swinging it around? That doesn't make any sense!" I swipe open my phone. "And then there's this."

As I press play, the sound of his voice plays through the speaker. We both listen as he threatens to kill Monty in a way that sounds like he's talking about random Tuesday night plans, not someone's life.

"Of course, he recorded that," he mutters as it finishes. "Where did you get it?"

I huff in disbelief. "Why does that even matter?"

"Because I'm wondering if you managed to find anything else he recorded. Like the sex tape he illegally made of us, for example. Or maybe the video of Mali undressing he took with the cameras he hid all over her house."

My jaw drops, and there's a good chance I might throw up. "What are you talking about?"

"Your *good friend* Monty is what I'm talking about!" he roars. "Entitled rich prick by day, closet fucking pervert by night!"

I feel like my head is going to explode. There's so much going on. Too many pieces I'm trying to put together all at once. It's mental chaos and I'm dying in the center of it.

"What *sex tape*?"

He rolls his eyes. "The one he blackmailed me with. The one he took when he let us use his boat that day, right after he put a hidden camera on it."

Oh...my God. "T-that was fucking months ago! Why the hell are you telling me about it *now*? Why not then?"

"Because I didn't want to hurt you." He sighs in frustration. "Craig had already made you feel exploited, and this was so much worse than a few pictures. This was straight pornography. And I was taking care of it. I even paid a hacker five hundred dollars to get rid of any trace of it."

Fuck. "And the video of Mali?"

"He erased that, too—along with the hundreds of others. I think it's safe to say I'm not the only one he was blackmailing."

I rub my hands over my face. "This is all so fucked up."

He hums sarcastically. "Yeah, you're telling me."

I take a deep breath in an effort to compose myself, because we're never going to get anywhere if we're arguing. And besides, as much as I hate that he kept this from me, I can't exactly hold it against him while I'm keeping a secret, too.

One I *can't* tell him about.

My voice breaks through the heavy silence. "What *really* happened that night on the island, Hayes?"

"It was an accident."

"That's not what I asked."

He runs his fingers through his hair. "Cam and I were trying to get him to leave town. We used his own blackmail against him and told him that once we got back to the docks, we never want to see him again, or we would show you and Mali. At first, he acted like he was agreeing, but we should've known. Backing psychos into a corner turns them into rabid animals."

"So, you threatened him, and he went into the boat and grabbed a gun?"

"Yes."

"Then what?"

There's something in his eyes, something he isn't willing to explain, and I watch as he masks it over. "Exactly what I told you. I got it away from him and it went off."

More. Fucking. Lies. "Are you sure about that?"

"Yes!"

He's growing angrier by the second. The patience he once

383

had is quickly fading. But we're both too stubborn to stop before this goes too far.

"I'm calling bullshit," I say, feeling my rage build. "Fucking bullshit! Because I know you! You're not the kind of guy who could kill someone on accident and *not* beat yourself up over it!"

His arms fly in the air as he takes a few steps away then stops and turns around. "What the fuck do you want me to say? That I'm sorry he's dead? That I wish I could change what happened? What do you want to fucking hear, Laiken?"

I get up and move toward him. "The truth!"

"The truth?" he spits. "The truth is I'm *not* sorry! I'm *glad* he's dead! Throwing his body into the water and watching it sink beneath the surface was one of the most relieving moments of my fucking life! Because he's gone, and I don't ever have to worry about him being anywhere near you again!"

There it is. Everything I was terrified of hearing, thrown right into my face. It's deafeningly quiet as the two of us stare at each other, his confession lingering in the air. And there's only one question I can manage to choke out.

"Who *are* you?"

"I'm your fucking *husband!* And I will do whatever it takes to protect you, whether you like the methods or not!"

I tell myself not to say it. That I don't want to hear the answer. But as my eyes fall closed for a second, I realize I can't avoid it. I need to ask.

"Even kill someone?"

"Yes!"

The answer comes out so loud that it echoes around the room, and we both know there's no going back from this. There's no way to unhear the words that were just spoken. Everything we were trying to hide is poured out and spilled all over the floor, and there's no way to shove it all back in the box it came out of.

His jaw locks and his muscles flex as any chance of controlling his temper goes out the window. "Fuck!"

The door opens, and Cam walks in with Mali just as Hayes's fist flies through the wall. Both their eyes widen as they see what state we're in. H pulls his hand out of the freshly made hole in the sheetrock and there's blood on his knuckles. He must have caught a nail.

"Son of a bitch," he mutters.

I run my fingers through my hair, moving to help him clean it up, but Cam stops me.

"No. Just..." He pauses and takes a breath. "Go upstairs with Mali. You and Hayes both need a minute to cool off."

It's obvious he's just trying to protect us. Me more than him, probably. I lock eyes with my husband, and I'm waiting for him to say something. *Anything*. But when he looks away, I know it's because he agrees with him—and there's nothing more he has to say.

There I am—the same fifteen-year-old girl who fell in love with the boy that set my soul on fire with a single look. The girl who almost got her happily ever after. And I wanted that so bad for her. For *them*. But this isn't a fairy tale, where everyone lives happily ever after. This is real life, where it's dark, and cold, and brutal.

And no one makes it out alive.

Mali gently takes my arm, pulling me toward the stairs. And I don't look away from Hayes until I absolutely have to. Cam is trying to check his hand, but he doesn't want anything to do with it.

"I'm fucking fine!" he shouts, smacking a cup into the sink before storming toward the front door. "I need a goddamn cigarette."

I feel empty inside as I go up the stairs and into our

bedroom. Mali sits on the bed beside me and the moment I break, she pulls me toward her. My head rests on her lap while tears pour from my eyes, her fingers softly running through my hair.

I needed him to sound convincing. To explain what happened in a way that makes sense. A way in which anyone would believe that the recording of him threatening Monty and the tragedy that followed after was just a horribly timed coincidence. But whatever secret he's still keeping, it's only making it worse.

"What happened tonight, babes?" Mali asks. "What the hell did we walk into?"

Grabbing a tissue from the box, I wipe my eyes. "Karma from beyond the grave, I'm guessing."

"Yeah, I'm going to need you to elaborate a little more on that one."

There's no way to explain it. And even if there was, I'd never be able to get it out without breaking down again. So instead, I grab my phone and play the voice recording for her.

In case you were wondering, hearing it for the third time still isn't any easier.

"Well...that's fucking dark," Mali says as the recording ends. "But I mean, you don't honestly think Hayes killed Monty on purpose, do you?"

"No," I answer instinctively, then pause. "I don't know."

She gives me a knowing look. "Laiken. This is Hayes we're talking about."

"I know, and in any other circumstance, I'd never even consider the possibility." I look down at my lap. "But that proof of us sneaking around Monty threatened Hayes with? Turns out it was a sex tape. He rigged his boat with hidden cameras and let us borrow it for the day so he could record us."

"I was wondering when he was going to tell you about that."

My brows furrow as I look up at her. "You knew?"

She shakes her head. "Not for long. The night he died, Cam told me about the videos—of you and me. He figured it would make getting over the loss easier."

I don't know what's more surprising, that she knew and didn't tell me, or that Cam knew and didn't burn the whole damn world to the ground. And the betrayal of learning they all kept this from me cuts deep.

"And you didn't tell me?" I snap. "What the fuck, Mali?"

"You haven't been stable enough to hear it," she answers. "The mental capacity it takes to unpack something like that? Telling you now wouldn't have done any good."

My eyes roll. "I don't believe that. You just said that Cam figured it would make getting over the loss easier, and judging by how you look, I'm thinking he was right. You didn't think *I* could use something to make it easier?"

She purses her lips. "No, because what's going on with you isn't about Monty. It hasn't been. Not completely, anyway. You've been using his death as an excuse, but I know you better than that. This whole time, you've just been mind-numbingly terrified of what might happen next. The guilt that's eating at you isn't because Monty is gone. It's because you feel responsible for us being on the boat in the first place. And for leaving Hayes with Monty when you knew they didn't get along."

Tears blur my vision once more. I don't even think she realizes how right she is. More so now than ever. Three weeks ago, I was in post marital bliss, living my dream life. And now, it's in ruins.

"Let me ask you this," she murmurs. "Say Hayes *did* kill Monty intentionally...do you think he was in the wrong?"

There are a million ways I could answer that—could write

ten pages of an essay on the topic—but the first one that comes to mind is simple.

"No one deserves to die, especially the way he did," I tell her. "But I don't miss him anymore."

THE SHOWER RUNS AND steam fills the room while I sit on the floor, sobbing until I can't breathe. I can feel my heart tearing at the seams. Last night was a disaster. All I wanted was for him to convince me beyond a reasonable doubt that he didn't do this. That killing Monty was a freak accident and that's all there is to it. A good night gone terribly wrong. But he couldn't do that.

And if he can't convince me, someone who has been madly in love with him for years and hangs on his every word, he'd never stand a chance at convincing a jury.

I think about all the people who would lose him. My brother wouldn't have his best friend and be forced to open the bar, *Hayes's dream,* by himself. His sister would lose her big brother, leaving her with no one to walk her down the aisle on her wedding day. His mom would lose her son—the only man she's ever truly loved after her husband shattered her heart when he chose an addiction over her.

After thinking about it all night, if someone asked me right now if I honestly believe Hayes killed Monty in cold blood, I'd say no. I know the man that I fell in love with. He's kind and he's caring. He puts others before himself. And when he loves, he does it with absolutely everything he has. But a random group of twelve wouldn't know that about him. Not like I do. Or like the people that love him do.

So, it's time for someone to put him first for once—to keep him from spending the rest of his life in prison for a crime he didn't commit.

Grabbing my phone off the counter, I reply to the unknown number from yesterday.

> If I do this, you have to swear that he will be safe. Nothing can happen to him. That's my only condition.

It takes under a minute for the response to come through.

> Cross my heart and hope to die.

> No pun intended. 😉

That's nice. My life is falling apart, and this no-named asshole is making jokes. I let my phone fall to the floor. With my mind made up, I know there's no going back. My fate is sealed. But for now, I cry—letting the pain rip me apart and rock me to sleep, like the darkness is all I have left anymore.

CHAPTER TWENTY NINE

REGRET IS A FICKLE THING. THERE AREN'T MANY moments in my life that I wish I could change. I try not to dwell on the past or let things that already happened bother me. But even though the list is small, the argument we had last night is definitely at the top of it.

Hearing Laiken insinuate that I intentionally committed murder was a blow I never saw coming. She's the one person that knows me better than anyone—even Cam. And knowing that she thinks so little of me, I'm not sure there's a way to ever recover from that.

But that doesn't mean I'm not going to try.

I use the putty knife to smooth out the spackle that covers the hole I created last night. Sure, it could have waited, but I'd really rather not constantly be reminded of last night. Not when everything feels so unstable.

Losing Laiken is the last thing I want. I've never loved anyone the way I love her, and I know for a fact I never will. She's always going to be the one I'm meant to spend my life with, even if there comes a time when she's no longer in it. But there are no guarantees. And if I fucked this up beyond repair, I don't think anyone would be surprised.

As I finish patching the hole, I go upstairs to check on her. I'm half expecting her to still be sleeping, but when I walk into our room, I find the bed empty. Steam billows out from under the bathroom door, but the sound of the water hitting the tile tells me she's not actually in it.

I knock on the door twice out of respect, but when there's no answer, I push open the door. And the sight in front of me chips another piece off my heart and turns it to ash.

Laiken is lying on the bathroom floor, curled up in a ball. Her hair isn't wet, showing she never actually got in the shower. And freshly dried tears on her cheeks give away that she was crying.

She looks so broken.

Lifeless, even though she's breathing.

And as I lift her into my arms and carry her back to bed, I know that I have no choice anymore.

Cam was right. She needs help. And as much as I would love to be the one to give it to her, I can't be. I'm too involved in the reason she's gotten to this point in the first place. If I ever want the chance of her being okay again, I have to put her needs before my own, because a few weeks without her is better than a lifetime.

Once Laiken is safely and comfortably tucked in, I go back into the bathroom and turn off the shower. Then I quietly step out of the room, shutting the door behind me as I take out my phone. It takes everything in me to type out the text, and another five minutes to press send, but I finally force myself to do it.

> Okay, I'm on board. Meet me at the bar in twenty and we'll decide on a place.

There's a possibility that she might never forgive me for this. I know that. But if anything were to happen to her, I would never forgive myself. And there comes a time when you need to swallow the bitter pill and accept that you can't be someone's everything, no matter how much you may want to be.

I SIT IN MY truck, staring at the house Laiken fell in love with at first sight. She looked so damn happy as we stepped onto the porch, and I could've listened to her for hours as she talked about all the things I could do with it. Little does she know, the whole time, I was picturing our future inside those walls.

A couple kids.

A dog.

Family dinners in the dining room, and birthday parties in the backyard.

I saw it all happening with her. It was *right there*. I had it in my hands. And now it's so out of reach that I don't know if those dreams will ever come true for us. But what I do know is I have no interest in having any of that if it's not with her.

It takes ten minutes just to work up the courage to go inside. After talking with Cam for hours and going over all our choices, we found a place with a spot for her. It's forty minutes north of here, but they have a good reputation, and from the pictures, it looks nice. Neither Cam nor I were ever going to put her in some shithole.

Though, something tells me it could be paradise and she'll still be pissed about it.

The whole thing makes my chest hurt. I don't want her to

think I'm giving up on her or tossing her off on someone else. I hate this just as much as she's going to, if not more, but I know that she needs it. She's fighting demons right now, and we've all tried to help her, but we're just not enough. She needs professionals. People trained to deal with this level of trauma.

With my hand on the doorknob, I prepare myself for what's to come, but when I open the door and step inside, it's like I stepped into a time capsule and brought back to a month ago—before everything became such shit. The house is clean, music plays through the speaker, and the smell that wafts from the kitchen feels like home.

My brows furrow as I look around and find Laiken in the kitchen. She's cooking dinner and swaying to the beat. And when she turns around, her eyes meet mine, and she smiles in a way she hasn't in weeks.

"Hey," she says softly.

Putting down the spatula, she comes over to me and arches up on her tiptoes. Her lips meet mine, and she drapes her arms over my shoulders. It takes me a second to realize that this is happening—that it's not some sick dream meant to torture me—and when I do, I pull her closer.

"God, I missed that," she tells me.

I exhale as my grin widens. "Me, too."

"I'm making dinner. It should be done soon, and then I was thinking we could watch a movie together?"

Ugh, that's all I want. To hold her in my arms and breathe in the scent of her hair. But Cam is supposed to be coming here in an hour, after I have her packed and ready to leave.

"It smells delicious," I say, kissing her forehead. "I was hoping we could talk though."

She pulls her head back to look up at me. "I know, we need to, but do you think we could just enjoy tonight?

Things have been rough lately, and I really want to have tonight with you; being together like it was before everything went to such shit."

There's not a damn thing in this world that could get me to deny her right now. Not when I need this just as much as she does. Staring into her eyes, it feels like I'm finally looking at the Laiken I fell in love with, and I'm going to enjoy it while I can.

"Of course, baby," I reply. "Anything for you."

She smiles brightly, kissing me once more before going back to dinner. Meanwhile, I take out my phone to text Cam.

> I don't know what's going on, but I just came home to find Laiken cooking dinner and in a good mood. It's like all that shit never even happened.

I look over at her and admire the way her hips sway to the music as she stirs whatever is in the pot, until my phone dings.

> I don't know, H. I still think we should take her to be evaluated.

> I know, but can we take her tomorrow? I really just want to spend tonight enjoying her while she's like this.

> Okay. Keep me updated on how she is and I'll see you around nine.

> Thanks, Cam. I appreciate it.

Seeing him and Mali worry about Laiken as much as I have has been difficult. It's like we all would do anything to get her back to how she was before tragedy fucked our lives to hell, but we can't. The only thing we can do is sit around and be there in the moments when she needs us.

But as if the universe knew how much I needed this, I get her back for a night. It feels a lot like Noah and Allie in their final moments.

I walk up behind her and wrap my arms around her waist. "I love when you cook."

She hums, leaning back into me. "And I love when you hold me. It makes me feel like you love me."

"There will never be a day that I *don't* love you." I move my left hand and rest it on top of hers, showing our tattoos of each other's initials together. "You're my forever."

And as her head turns and our lips meet, the only thing I'm absolutely certain of is the truth in those words.

I USED TO TAKE simple times like these for granted. The nights we spent curled up together in bed like this while we watched whatever movie Laiken was wanting to see—I never appreciated them enough. I'd space out, thinking about things I had to do at the bar or get done around the house. It's so easy to get lost in life, but you don't realize how vital these little moments are until a bomb explodes in the middle of everything you care about.

Now, as some movie based on a romance novel plays in

the background, the only thing I'm lost in is her. The feeling of her body next to mine. The softness of her skin against my fingertips. They're things that I'm going to need to hold onto over the next few weeks, while she's rebuilding herself back to the badass spitfire that I've always loved.

She lifts her head from my chest and smiles at me, but her concern grows as she sees the single tear that escapes from one of my eyes. Gently wiping it away with her thumb, she comes closer and ghosts her lips against mine.

"I love you so much," she whispers.

God, if I could make the sound of her saying that my ringtone, I would. "I love *you*. I'm forever in love with you."

I feel her start to deepen the kiss, pressing her mouth on mine with more pressure. And I kiss her back with just as much fervor because she breathes the life into me. But when her hand starts to slide down my stomach, I grab her wrist.

Don't get me wrong, there's nothing I want more than to get wrapped up in her. Sex with us has always been different. More intense. More meaningful. It's not ideal, but it's the way we communicate all the feelings we can't manage to say. The emotions we pour into it are genuine and real. But right now, she's so mentally fragile that I'm terrified of being the catalyst that finally pushes her over the edge.

"Lai," I breathe.

She sighs, resting her forehead on mine. "Please."

The sound of her voice, so desperate and eager, it has my restraints ready to snap. We haven't had sex since the morning of my birthday, and that would be an adjustment in itself if I wasn't so worried about her. But it's no secret that I've never been able to keep myself from giving into everything she wants, and I don't think that'll ever change.

"Please," she repeats. "I need you, just for tonight."

She doesn't. Not in the way that she thinks she does. But

I'm not about to tell her no right now. And to be honest, I need this just as badly as she claims to.

Rolling her onto her back, I cover her mouth with my own and she sighs contently. My fingertips graze across her skin as I drag my hand up her thigh, until the only thing separating the two of us is the thin pair of panties she has on.

"I've got you," I promise.

I brush against her clit, reveling in the way she moans into my mouth and arches into my hand. I've missed having her like this—being able to control her entire body with a simple touch. I don't think she even realizes how much that turns me on.

She reaches down, frantically pushing the panties down her legs and kicking them off to rid herself of the barrier between us. I smirk against her mouth and bend my fingers just right as I slip them inside of her.

She's so fucking wet.

It's like she's been thinking about this for hours and finally got the courage to ask for it. To beg for what she wants.

"Fuck," she exhales. "Right there."

She doesn't need to tell me. I know her body better than my own. Every spot that makes her squirm. The spots that make her weak. How far I can tease her before it's just downright cruel. There isn't a thing about her body that I don't have committed to memory. Tucked away in its own little section of my mind.

"You're a goddess, Laiken Rose," I tell her honestly. "An absolute goddess."

Her eyes stare into mine, pupils blown from all of the arousal she's feeling. "*Your* goddess. Always going to be yours."

It's like she knows how badly I need to hear those words. The reassurance that regardless of what we're going through, she's still just as much mine as she's ever been. It feels like I might not drown after all.

"Love me," she pleads. "I need you to make love to me."

I drop a kiss onto her lips and pull my fingers out of her to get my boxers off, because who am I to not give her every damn thing she asks for right now?

Our sex life has always been colorful, with certain kinks and dirty talk, and there's never been a time where we're not completely worn out and sated by the end of it. But this isn't that.

This is two people in love, desperately clinging to each other and needing to be as close as possible while we hope we make it out in one piece.

I line myself up at her entrance, leaning over her and kissing her lips as I slide into her. Our moans mix together in the air as we're both overtaken by the feeling of being so connected. So completely intertwined.

"You are the best thing in my life," I say as I slowly pull in and out of her.

Her eyes water as she smiles, only half listening as she's lost in the feeling of us. "And you're the best thing in mine."

This is why we work so well. Why I was able to go from never wanting a relationship to all but begging her to marry me. Because she's my rule breaker. My game changer. The answer to all my choices.

She may have been the one to fall first, but it was me who ended up falling harder.

And I'm going to spend the rest of tonight doing everything I can to show her how true that is.

SHE LIES ON HER side while I spoon her from behind. My one arm is under her head while my other is draped over her, my fingers laced with hers. This morning, we couldn't have been further apart. But tonight, I've never felt closer to her.

"I love you, Laiken," I say, trying to put as much feeling into it as I can to make sure that's never a question in her mind.

Her hand squeezes mine. "I love you, too. I always will, no matter what."

As I hold her in my arms and let my eyes fall closed, I drift to sleep with ease for the first time in weeks.

THE SUN POURS IN through the blinds, and I wake up feeling so refreshed. Last night was exactly what we needed —something to remind each other why we fell in love in the first place. It confirmed for me that no matter how hard things may get, I'd rather go through it with her than have it easy with someone else. But as I roll over to pull her close, I find her side of the bed empty and cold.

My eyes peel open, thinking that maybe we're just on opposite sides of the king-sized bed, but she's not there. I reach over to my nightstand and grab my phone to check the time.

7:30 a.m.

Good. I still have some time to enjoy her before Cam shows up and we have to convince her that this place will be good for her.

I sit up and rub my hands over my face before I slip out of bed. Heading for the stairs, I glance into the bathroom, but it's empty. I tell myself that she's probably downstairs making coffee or eating some breakfast, but when I notice she's not there either, the panic starts to kick in.

"Laiken?" I call.

Nothing.

The whole house is quiet and her car isn't in the driveway.

My fingers fly across the keys as I dial her number, but as I put it to my ear and listen to it immediately go to voicemail, my gaze lands on the picture frame that's dismantled on the island. I feel like I can't breathe as I step closer, seeing her handwriting scrawled across the back of our wedding photo.

I'm so sorry.

Three words. Three simple words that manage to send my entire world crashing down around me. And sitting beside them, shining in the sunlight that comes through the window, is the ring I proposed to her with.

No.

This can't be happening.

She wouldn't fucking do this!

I rush out into the living room, expecting to see her shoes by the front door, but they're not there. Her purse isn't on the couch where she left it last night. And as I take the stairs two at a time, running into our bedroom, I open the closet and feel my heart shatter into a million pieces as I see everything she owns is gone.

The only sign she was here at all is the unmade side of the bed where she laid in my arms last night and told me she loves me.

But if she loves me, why the fuck did she leave?

Running back down the stairs in a panic, I try to call her again, but it still goes straight to voicemail. And that's when my entire body gives out and I crash to my knees.

Emotions flood through me in waves that threaten to pull me under, and honestly, I wish they would. Anything would be better than the pain I'm feeling. The way my chest feels like it's cracked wide the fuck open, spilling all my organs out onto my lap, it's excruciating.

She's my whole life, and I know they say you shouldn't do that—make one person everything to you. That a marriage should be equal, and you can't make your entire world revolve around one person. But I did anyway, and now I don't know how I'm supposed to go on without her.

I can't.

I don't want to.

Chapter 29

I SIT AT THE island, staring at the three words she wrote and spinning the ring around my finger—as if somehow that's going to bring her back. Like if I look at it long enough, I'll realize it's not actually there. That I hallucinated it, or this is all just a nightmare I haven't woken up from. But it hasn't happened yet.

I'm so lost in my thoughts I don't even hear as Cam walks in.

"What's up, dude?" he asks.

I open my mouth to say the words, but nothing comes out. It's as if I can't seem to admit it out loud, because then it'll be real. Then, I can't deny it anymore. But as Cam says my name, sounding concerned, I know I have no choice.

"She's gone," I choke out.

His head jolts slightly. "What?"

"Laiken," I specify, hating the way her name feels like poison on my tongue. "She's gone."

Cam snorts. "No, she's not. Don't be so dramatic."

He takes out his phone and goes to call her, and I don't even try to stop him, because when it goes straight to voicemail just like it did the twenty-seven times that I've tried to call her, he realizes it for himself.

"What the fuck?" He tries again but gets the same outcome.

I drop the ring onto the back of the picture and slide it across the island to him. "She left me this."

Cam's face looks like a mix between concerned and shocked as he realizes the note was written on the back of our wedding photo. "I don't get it. Why would she leave?"

I don't have the answer, not for certain anyway, but there's only one reason that comes to mind. Exhaling, I run my fingers through my hair and blink up at the ceiling.

"She thinks I shot Monty on purpose."

Okay, now we can add a little anger to the mix of his emotions. "She *what*? Why the hell wouldn't you just tell her the truth?"

"Don't," I tell him.

His eyes are getting wider by the second. "But you—"

"Stop!" I roar. "We're not talking about it! I know what I did! It's done! Just leave it alone!"

It's not like I haven't thought about it since the moment I realized she was gone. That she walked out and left me. But the truth is, the choice I made the moment tragedy struck that night is one I wouldn't change. Even if I could go back and know what I know now, that's one decision I would make over again.

And nothing he says is going to change that.

The front door opens, and both our heads whip toward it, hoping it's Laiken and she's changed her mind, but instead, Mali walks in. When she sees the look on our faces, she freezes.

"What's going on?"

Cam and I glance at each other, both thinking the same exact thing.

If she didn't tell Mali what she was planning, there can only be one reason for it.

She's fucking gone and has no intentions of coming back.

to be CONTINUED

A Shot of Pretty Poison
Available Now

CONTINUED

A SHOT OF PRETTY POISON

I can still taste her on my lips, lingering there like a shot of pretty poison.

I should hate her for what she did. No one would blame me for it—not even her brother. The pain I felt that day ripped me apart until all that remained was the shell of the man I used to be. And now I'm left to lie in the aftermath.

Devastating news has my life spiraling further out of control. If I don't get a handle on it, I could end up losing it all. But nothing cuts deeper than the shards of a broken heart, and the scars that won't fade make it hard for me to care.

Everything changed for us when tragedy struck. The events of that night still haunt all of our dreams. We think the darkest moments are behind us, leaving a black stain on our past, until we realize that this nightmare is far from over.

Someone is out there who knows our secrets and gets off on risking the lives of those I love most. You can't trust anyone, especially when your enemies crave the taste of revenge, but we're not going down without a fight.

I'll burn the world to the ground before I let anyone hurt her —even if she's responsible for hurting me.

A Shot of Pretty Poison
Available Now

THANK YOU FOR READING!

I hope you enjoyed the continuation of Hayes and Laiken's story. If you did, I would greatly appreciate it if you could leave a review. :)

Who is she?

THAT GIRL, KELSEY CLAYTON

Kelsey Clayton is a USA Today bestselling author of Contemporary Romance novels. She lives in a small town in Delaware with her husband, two kids, and two dogs.

She is an avid reader of fall hard romance. She believes that books are the best escape you can find, and that if you feel a range of emotions while reading her stories - she succeeded. She loves writing and is only getting started on this life long journey.

Kelsey likes to keep things in her life simple. Her ideal night is one with sweatpants, a fluffy blanket, cheese fries, and wine. She holds her friends and family close to her heart and would do just about anything to make them happy.

For inquires: management@kelseyclayton.com

For social media links, scan below:

KELSEY CLAYTON

The Pretty Poison Trilogy

A Dose of Pretty Poison

A Drop of Pretty Poison

A Shot of Pretty Poison

Malvagio Mafia Duet

Suffer in Silence

Screams in Symphony

Haven Grace Prep

The Sinner *(Savannah & Grayson)*

The Saint *(Delaney & Knox)*

The Rebel *(Tessa & Asher)*

The Enemy *(Lennon & Cade)*

North Haven University

Corrupt My Mind *(Zayn & Amelia)*

Change My Game *(Jace & Paige)*

Wreck My Plans *(Carter & Tye)*

Waste My Time *(Easton & Kennedy)*

The Sleepless November Saga

Sleepless November

SIGNED PAPERBACKS

Want a signed Kelsey Clayton book?
You can purchase them on her website.
Check it out.

Made in the USA
Middletown, DE
04 March 2025

72214816R00234